RETURN OF THE EXILED PRINCE

"So you'll take over Wave Six in command of the Prince's Men?" asked Shakov.

Victor drew in a tight breath. The Com Guard 244th Division had gone renegade for him, saving his life on Newtown Square. Their decision to support his drive to stop Katherine had cost them their positions, their top officers, and far too many lives to ever take their sacrifices lightly. They'd done so much for him already, he was nervous about telling Shakov his decision. But they also deserved the truth, and from his lips.

"I can't tell you how honored I have been to fight alongside the 244th, Rudolf." Victor glanced sidelong at some nearby infantry. "Though equal in all respects to the best the Federated Suns or Lyran Alliance have to offer, I can't drive on to New Avalon at their head. The Tenth Lyran Guard is en route, and I'll lead my Revenants forward from here." He paused, watched as Rudolf stroked his goatee, considering. "It has to be this way. This is your command now. These are your people. You will lead them."

Shakov might not have liked Victor's decision, but if so he never let one ounce of regret or disappointment show.

"I say welcome back to the war," he said with enthusiasm. "Highness."

ENDGAME

Loren L. Coleman

A ROC BOOK

ROC
Published by New American Library, a division of
Penguin Putnam Inc., 375 Hudson Street,
New York, New York 10014, U.S.A.
Penguin Books Ltd, 80 Strand,
London WC2R 0RL, England
Penguin Books Australia Ltd, Ringwood,
Victoria, Australia
Penguin Books Canada Ltd, 10 Alcorn Avenue,
Toronto, Ontario, Canada M4V 3B2
Penguin Books (N.Z.) Ltd, 182–190 Wairau Road,
Auckland 10, New Zealand

Penguin Books Ltd, Registered Offices:
Harmondsworth, Middlesex, England

First published by Roc, an imprint of New American Library,
a division of Penguin Putnam Inc.

First Printing, September 2002
10   9   8   7   6   5   4   3   2

Series Editor: Donna Ippolito
Cover art by Fred Gambino

 REGISTERED TRADEMARK—MARCA REGISTRADA

For Randall and Tara Bills.
Welcome to the neighborhood!

At the time of this writing, many BattleTech® fans (of which I am one) are breathing heavy sighs of relief to find out that the game universe will continue. FASA has closed its doors, but WizKids Games has stepped in at the fore. The exact details are still being worked out, but my confidence is very strong that we'll see more game products and novels. This novel, *Endgame*, would never have happened without contributions from the following people:

My thanks to Jordan and Dawne Weisman, Ross Babcock, Mort Weisman, Donna Ippolito, and Maya Smith for their support and hard work behind the scenes. Also to all the new people at WizKids Games (some of whom I am meeting again for the first time) Sharon and Mike Mulvihill, Pam, Mikey, Scott, and others who I hope to know well. Big welcomes for Janna Silverstein as well.

Special appreciation to the rest of the "Final Five," who all signed on to bring the Civil War to its end. Randall Bills, Blaine Pardoe, Thom Gressman, and Chris Hartford. And Mike Stackpole, a continued friend of the court.

Also a thanks to Yurie Hong, who helped me with the Latin, Tracy Yerian in chemistry, and Oystein for the very cool maps.

Love to my family: Heather, Talon, Conner, and Alexia.

Special mention for the cats—Rumor, Ranger, and Chaos—who all think they make great paperweights and lap-warmers. At least they are half right.

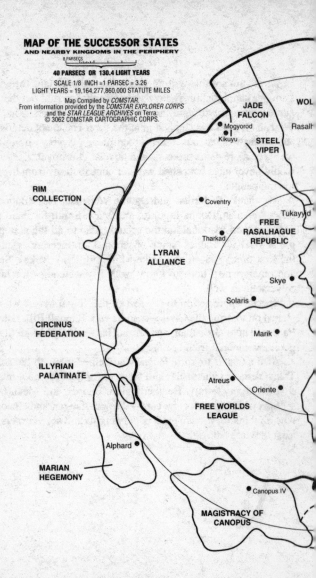

MAP OF THE SUCCESSOR STATES
AND NEARBY KINGDOMS IN THE PERIPHERY

8 PARSECS

40 PARSECS OR 130.4 LIGHT YEARS

SCALE 1/8 INCH = 1 PARSEC = 3.26
LIGHT YEARS = 19,164,277,860,000 STATUTE MILES

Map Compiled by *COMSTAR.*
From information provided by the *COMSTAR EXPLORER CORPS*
and the *STAR LEAGUE ARCHIVES* on Terra.
© 3062 COMSTAR CARTOGRAPHIC CORPS.

JADE
FALCON

WOL

• Mogyorod

Rasalh

Kikuyu

STEEL
VIPER

RIM
COLLECTION

• Coventry

Tukayyid

FREE
RASALHAGUE
REPUBLIC

• Tharkad

LYRAN
ALLIANCE

Skye •

• Solaris

CIRCINUS
FEDERATION

Marik •

ILLYRIAN
PALATINATE

Atreus •

• Oriente

FREE WORLDS
LEAGUE

• Alphard

MARIAN
HEGEMONY

• Canopus IV

MAGISTRACY OF
CANOPUS

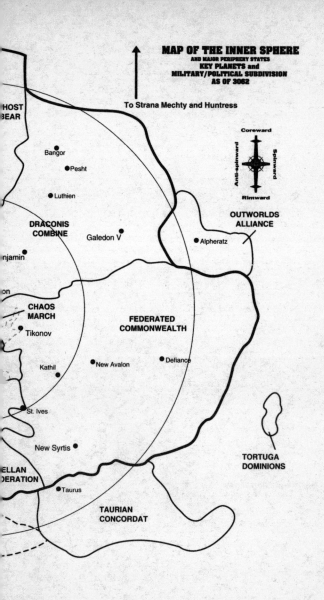

MAP OF THE INNER SPHERE
AND MAJOR PERIPHERY STATES
KEY PLANETS and
MILITARY/POLITICAL SUBDIVISION
AS OF 3062

To Strana Mechty and Huntress

Coreward

Anti-spinward

Spinward

Rimward

GHOST BEAR

● Bangor

● Pesht

● Luthien

DRACONIS COMBINE

● Galedon V

● Alpheratz

OUTWORLDS ALLIANCE

njamin

on

CHAOS MARCH

● Tikonov

FEDERATED COMMONWEALTH

● New Avalon

● Defiance

● Kathil

St. Ives

● New Syrtis

TORTUGA DOMINIONS

ELLAN DERATION

● Taurus

TAURIAN CONCORDAT

Castling

So many paths led to our civil war. So many wrong decisions and desperate acts, by both sides, as my sister and I played the game of appeasement and escalation. She seemed willing to embark on whatever course of action she thought would safeguard her power. I needed time, and I continued to hope for peace. I thought that with the evidence to link her to our mother's assassination, I might eventually topple her tyrannical rule without the call for war and bloodshed.

I no longer think that.

I no longer believe it was ever possible.

—From the journal of Prince Victor Ian Steiner-Davion, reprinted in *Cause and Effect*, Avalon Press, 3067

1

Christopher Pierce. I knew the man vaguely, which is to say that I remembered his name. His service jacket lists the failed defense at Salat as his last contribution to the civil war, but there was one other, later.

—*Cause and Effect*, Avalon Press, 3067

Salat, Tikonov
Capellan March
Federated Suns
26 June 3065

Sergeant Christoffer Pierce moved his seventy-ton *JagerMech* along Kowloon Avenue, the main street of downtown Salat, searching the dark city canyons. The heavy rain pounding like a thousand tiny mallets against the sculptured armor of his BattleMech enfolded the streetlamps, dimming their brilliance. Each city block was a black corridor broken up by small, glistening stretches where the subdued light shattered across the ferrocrete, winking at him in place of absent stars.

The drum of rainfall, the swaying gait of the *JagerMech*—any other time Pierce might have found them soothing. Not tonight. The constant background chatter bleeding over his communications systems spoiled that, a continual stream of new warnings mixed with fragments of orders and battle reports. The Fifteenth Deneb Light Cavalry had breached another sector of Salat.

". . . didn't see them. We're losing thermals in the down-pour."

"Two tracks, one hover, and a *Penetrator*. Southwest quarter, sighted from *Di-san* and *Huar*. That's Third and Flower."

"Calling for support at the industrial yards."

". . . being pressed back . . ."

"Hit that damn Typhoon with everything you got!"

And the battle for Tikonov continued.

Christoffer belonged to Sixth Company of the Third Crucis Lancers—Colonel Patricia Vineman's Tsamma Lancers—one regiment among several vying to control the world of Tikonov, be it in the name of Prince Victor Steiner-Davion or his sister, Katherine. Three months earlier, this had been *the* battle of the civil war, with Prince Victor on-planet and three times the number of troops rallied to either side. It was to be Victor's big push, designed to leapfrog over the embattled space of the Lyran Alliance and to win a strong base of operations in the Federated Suns for the allied forces. The beginning of the end, Colonel Vineman had promised. A welcome idea after two and a half years of hard, desperate fighting.

Then the prince had left, abandoning Tikonov and falling back into Lyran space. To regroup, according to the official word. To recuperate, said grapevine gossip. It was rumored that Victor Davion was so hard hit by the death of Omi Kurita that he had lost the will to fight. Pierce didn't believe that. He couldn't, and obviously neither could a number of like-minded warriors. They knew that Tikonov was an important world in its own right, but against the greater backdrop of the civil war, it was only one of several possible stepping stones on the path to New Avalon, capital of the Federated Suns and Katherine's seat of power. What would be the point of fighting on in Prince Victor's name if he were never coming back?

Salat was the latest battlefield testing their belief. The city sat astride an important travel corridor, one of several dominoes that had to fall before Katherine's loyalist ground forces mounted a serious assault to take back Arano Bay and its Battle-Mech production facilities. Sixth Company had been given only enough resources to postpone Salat's fall, but that would never be enough to hold the city indefinitely. They were a picket force, their job to delay the advance of Katherine's loyalists and give Victor's forces time to prepare a stronger defense farther along. A distraction.

Expendable.

Pierce shook his head, feeling the strain where his neuro-helmet sat heavily against the padded shoulders of his cooling vest. He held on to his control sticks with a desperate grip, his fingers aching as they rode the triggers at the edge of their pull. Searching for the enemy, his eyes darted from his heads-up tactical display to the monitor selected for thermal imaging to the rain-spattered ferroglass shields that surrounded the 'Mech's cockpit. They were out there, the Fifteenth Deneb, scattered through the city and pushing back the Tsamma Lancers. As if he needed further proof, neutral blue icons suddenly flashed over his display. They showed a Lancers medic company turning onto Kowloon Avenue behind him, retreating for the southern edge of the city with more of the wounded. As they came, he saw that it was a long column of rescue vehicles and transports. Pierce guessed that they might be pulling out the remnants of a shattered infantry company lost when the Fifteenth Deneb stormed Salat's eastern parkway. And the rest of the Fifteenth would not be far behind.

At the next corner, a blur against the dark backdrop of the streets caught his attention. Thermal imaging wasn't much help in this downpour, the drenching rain muting most temperature variations to only a few color-shades of difference, but it beat magnetic resonance in a city full of girders and rebar. It was good enough for him to ID the vehicle as a Hunter light support tank. He dropped his targeting crosshairs over the shadow, then yanked the reticle away as it flashed from dead-black to a warning-red. His HUD tagged the vehicle's icon as a Lancer tank, one of his own support units in Salat.

He made the identification in time to prevent a terrible mistake, but not in time to help the Hunter. An enemy gauss slug skipped up off the ferrocrete street and into the tank's right side, derailing one of its tracks and stranding it in the middle of the intersection. From back around the corner, twin lances of scarlet laserfire stabbed down and through the ruptured armor. They gutted the Hunter in less than a second, cremating the tank crew and rupturing ammunition bins. The top of the tank split open like a crushed pod, spilling a blossom of angry fire over the entire intersection.

Shards and shrapnel pinged off the *JagerMech*'s lower legs. Pierce rode back on the throttle, toggled both rotary autocannon into his primary trigger, and pulled his crosshairs over the hidden street just as an enemy *Cestus* stepped forward into the intersection. Like his *JagerMech*, the *Cestus* had a vaguely humanoid shape, with a thick torso and hunched shoulders. Kicking aside the ruined shell of the Hunter, it stalked forward through the intersection. The khaki-painted BattleMech was scarred along its right side from earlier damage. Careful of the buildings behind the *Cestus*, Pierce worked to lock his targeting computer over the wounded flank.

The targeting crosshairs burned a deep golden hue, and he pulled into the trigger. Both of his rotary cannon spat out several hundred rounds, the slugs tipped with depleted uranium for 'Mech-stopping power. The left-arm autocannon missed wide and chewed into the brick facing of a deserted hardware store, but the rotary AC in the *JagerMech*'s right arm pounded home with a long, destructive stream. Shards of armor rained over the streets to mix with glass splinters, stone chips, and puddles.

But the *Cestus* was not as seriously damaged as Pierce would have liked. It stood up under the savage assault, rocking back on its left leg. Then it straightened and threw back everything it had. Its main lasers drew molten weals down Pierce's left flank, and the gauss rifle spat out a nickel-ferrous slug to cave in the *JagerMech*'s centerline armor. Short-lived spears of ruby light from the *Cestus*'s secondary lasers splashed away more armor from his left arm, the hissing spatters dropping onto the wet-black streets. The *JagerMech* staggered to the right, its left foot swinging up too far for safety, and Pierce ducked left in an exaggerated, hunching motion. The bulky neurohelmet translated his equilibrium into a signal that was fed to the 'Mech's gyroscope. He heard a whining complaint as the gyro stressed itself to maintain the *JagerMech*'s balance. It rocked back onto both feet, and Pierce throttled down and reversed into a backward walk.

"Pierce, on Kowloon," he said. His voice-activated mike picked up his words, broadcasting them over the general frequency. "One Hunter down. Engaging *Cestus*." There was no direct answer, just the continued fragments of other battles.

The *JagerMech* shook again as the Cavalry *Cestus* worried it with lasers, slicing off all but a thin layer of armor on its left arm and leg. Pierce's targeting computer couldn't grab an angle on the *Cestus*'s already-damaged side, and his crosshairs flashed the alternating gold and black of partial lock. He pulled into extra-long bursts from his rotary autocannon, spending ammunition at wholesale rates, chewing armor from the *Cestus*'s left knee to its right shoulder and from its left hip up to its bulbous head.

Though Pierce doubted it was enough to take the *Cestus* out for good, the abuse he'd heaped onto the enemy 'Mech's plate proved too much for the moment. The *Cestus* pilot lost positive control of his sixty-five-ton machine. It rocked back, then overcompensated by diving forward, accidentally kicking a parked car as its right foot shot out from under it. Its shoulder knocked down the nearest streetlamp, which ended up buried under its armored bulk as the 'Mech sprawled out over the street. By now, a new threat wailed for Christoffer's attention.

Another BattleMech walked toward him from farther down Kowloon—a hulking shadow that filled the dark corridor. Whether it had been masked by the *Cestus*'s presence or had just now turned onto the avenue from a side street mattered very little. What did matter was the information tagged onto the HUD's threat icon. Pierce's mouth dried to the metallic taste of fear as he read the tag. *BNC-6S*.

A *Banshee*.

"Command 'Mech," he called out as he short-cycled his autocannon and jerked at the trigger. Pressed too hard, too fast, his right-arm cannon jammed. The other spat a long tongue of fire toward the advancing 'Mech, smashing eighty-millimeter slugs into its chest. "*Banshee*, 6S. On Kow—" It was all he had time for as the *Banshee*'s heavy gauss rifle flashed with coil discharge and accelerated 250 kilograms of nickel-ferrous material up toward hypersonic speeds straight into his *JagerMech*'s right side.

Even in pristine condition, the *Jag*'s armor couldn't take that kind of punishment. Plating shattered under the impact, raining down in thick shards and knife-edged splinters to the street. Supports of foamed titanium bent, twisted, and collapsed with the shriek of tortured metal. One broken support carved a gouge through his reactor shielding, bleeding waste heat into the 'Mech's interior. Another speared through his massive targeting computer, destroying the valuable piece of equipment. A shower of sparks flooded the wound and drifted out, to be quickly extinguished by the downpour.

"Pierce!" The voice of Captain Kremmins was nearly lost in a flood of static. From the poor quality of the transmission, Pierce guessed that the company commander had to be near the other side of the city, blocked in by taller buildings. "Pierce, fall back to . . . city's edge."

Except there was nowhere for Pierce to run. Behind him, the line of retreating infantry and medic vehicles continued to stagger from the cross street. Cutting out now would leave them vulnerable, and he held no illusions that the loyalists would honor the retreat. They wouldn't target medical units, not directly, but the rest of them would be fair game, and if the medics got in the way . . .

Waste heat bled up through the cockpit deck plates, drawing sweat from his exposed skin. Then, another slug smashed into his *JagerMech* from the *Banshee*'s heavy rail gun, taking his right arm off at the shoulder. With it went his rotary AC, which fell to the ground, a mangled length of steel. Fortunately, that was the jammed weapon and useless to him anyway. He pulled his crosshairs back over the *Banshee*'s silhouette, and drilled into it with several hundred rounds from his center-mounted pulse lasers. They stung out like emerald wasps, the fire from one splashing impotently off the rain-slick streets and the other doing little more than digging a small wound in the *Banshee*'s left leg.

The *Cestus* raised itself up onto its left arm and fired a gauss slug into the *JagerMech*'s right leg and a laser into its flank. The *Banshee* also opened up with its autocannon, the ten-centimeter bore suddenly alive with flame and lethal metal. Uranium-tipped slugs pounded Pierce's right leg, punching through the last of his armor and shattering the leg actuator hidden behind the *JagerMech*'s knee.

How Pierce kept the beleaguered 'Mech on its feet he never knew. The loss of the right arm pulled it in one direction, and the damage to its leg rocked it in another, the two actions roughly canceling each other out. Very roughly. Strapped into his command chair, shaken by the hard assault, Pierce felt like he was tumbling through the back of a cement mixer. He knew that he was all that protected the retreating column, but there was no conscious effort to cheat gravity this time. It was luck, and he was due a small piece.

"We're clear!" someone called from the column. It had turned off Kowloon and was out of immediate danger. "Get out of there, Sergeant."

"I'm not going anywhere," Pierce said softly, not sure if his mike picked it up or not. Triggering his pulse lasers, he carved armor off each leg. Then he tensed for the answering assault as the *Banshee*'s autocannon lit up with a determined fire. Tracers chewed through the downpour, bits of white-hot fire connecting the two combat avatars.

When the first tracer ricocheted off his ferroglass shield in a burst of white flame, Pierce almost laughed at the ineffective gesture. But then the full force of the ten-centimeter autocannon hammered in behind, starring the shield as the *Banshee* walked destruction across the *JagerMech*'s head. It was worse than before, and the cockpit shook under the murderous force while hammering echoes of the slugs mocked the earlier pounding of hard rain. Thrown against his restraining harness, Pierce nearly blacked out when a hard hammer-blow slammed into the side of his neurohelmet, but he was shocked back to consciousness by the jarring, painful fists that shook his entire body. He knew an instant of perfect clarity, staring at the holes in the ferroglass and watching as the rainwater leaking into his cockpit mixed with blood-spatter on the *inside* of his shield.

He felt the biting pain first in his right knee, then in his arm and shoulder. His hand had dropped from the control stick. Glancing down, he saw that it was partially severed at the wrist and had nearly fallen off his arm. Blood jetted out in warm spurts, splashing against his bare thigh, the chair, his smashed control panel. Pierce lifted his gaze to the ferroglass shield again, staring out through the rain at the *Banshee*'s hulking shadow as it continued to lumber forward. By the light of a streetlamp, he could just make out the Fifteenth Deneb's insignia of a chess knight. He frowned. "They aren't even a Steiner unit." In those last few seconds, he tried to remember why the Tsamma Lancers were fighting another command that was, nominally, also part of the Federated Suns.

Then the *Banshee*'s heavy gauss rifle cut his crippled leg out from under him, and he thought of nothing else but the fall and the jarring impact at its end.

2

When Katherine finally turned to the military to solve her problems, we thought it would be her greatest mistake. But she persisted. Perhaps it is more proof of the old saw that "everything, at its core, is politics."
—*Cause and Effect*, Avalon Press, 3067

AFFS Watchtower
Avalon City, New Avalon
Crucis March
Federated Suns
21 July 3065

A mix of several conversations leaked from the soundproof room, changing quickly to respectful silence as the cracked door was pushed wide open. Though preceded by her Champion and her Marshal of the Armies, Katrina Steiner-Davion noted that it wasn't until she entered the situation room that the twelve other members of the AFFS High Command stood to attention. So they had been briefed on the Archon-Princess joining them today. She spent a sharp glance on Jackson Davion, almost but not quite an accusation, but her Marshal of the Armies was far too satisfied with himself to be disturbed by such a lesser display of her displeasure. But for the fact that her cousin was so hidebound by his personal honor, Katrina might have considered him a threat to her rule of the Federated Suns.

Jackson stood just inside the door, then closed it and switched on the white-noise generator once she had entered the room. Katrina, meanwhile, gathered what information she could on the others as she moved toward her seat at the open-box arrangement of tables. The slender needle of the Watchtower was the military's corner of her Royal Court here on New Avalon, and she had called together the commanders of every major military department in the Armed Forces of the Federated Suns as well as representatives for her three March field marshals. Those who practically jumped to their feet she numbered as insincere. Most rose with casual respect and proud bearing, and that was safer. Then there were the last two or three, who stood slowly and with calculated defiance. One of these was a female general standing in for Duke James Sandoval, Field Marshal of the Draconis March, and Katrina immediately tagged her as a closet supporter of the duke's renegade son, Tancred. She would bear closer scrutiny in the future.

"Good afternoon," Katrina said, greeting them all impartially as she and her two seniormost officers found their seats at the center table.

This was one of the larger situation rooms in the Watchtower. An impressive flat-screen monitor covered one whole wall, while the other three were paneled in ash-blond wood. Flagpoles marched down two sides of the room, bearing world banners for every district capital in the Federated Suns and the Lyran Alliance. Near the door, a portrait of Katrina hung between the flags of New Avalon and Tharkad, the capital worlds of her two interstellar nations. The room smelled of cigars and cheap cologne, a scent Katrina identified as *male*, despite the presence of four women among the High Command. Yet another reason, among many, why Katrina rarely visited the Watchtower. There was far too much martial precision and calculated aggression for her to feel comfortable here. Besides, as the Archon-Princess, she had enough security advisors, intelligence aides, and generals who regularly attended her at the Davion Palace.

Katrina nodded, and everyone sat down quickly, with an economy of movement that suggested it was something they might have practiced. Knowing she would spend a good part of her day in the company of uniformed officers, Katrina had chosen a conservative suit styled after a paramilitary design. Ivory, with gold buttons and belt, the double-breasted jacket was similar to a fencing jerkin, while the knee-length skirt flattered her slender figure. She wore gloves to suggest at least some softness, but had pulled her golden hair back into a severe braid in a style similar to that favored by career-military women.

Strong, but not strident.

"Today," Katrina said, calling the room to business, "this very morning, in fact, the New Avalon *Daily* ran a headline certain to be picked up by other worlds. 'Where's Victor?' it asked. This is a question I myself have been asking for several months, ever since General McDonald forced my brother to abandon Tikonov and retreat back into the Lyran Alliance."

Halfway down the left-hand table, Field Marshal Stephanie Day, head of the Department of Military Intelligence, leaned forward in her seat. "Highness, the DMI has been working on that, but it is a low-priority concern at this time."

Katrina placed her hands flat on the table's smooth surface. Her ivory gloves seemed to float above the dark walnut grain. "Would you please elaborate?"

"We have battles taking place on over forty different worlds, and tensions that may erupt into open fighting on a hundred more. The DMI hasn't seen this kind of workload since the Fourth Succession War. Your Ministry of Intelligence is cooperating with us, as they did then. They have agreed to shoulder most of the investigation to find your brother, as he is currently . . . a noncombatant."

Day's pause spoke volumes to Katrina. The assassination of Omi Kurita had become common knowledge shortly after Katrina's enjoyable disclosure of that fact to Victor. No one doubted that her brother had been hit hard by the news that his "lotus blossom" had been clipped. All reports read fairly close to the same.

"Because he is not fighting in a BattleMech does not mean that he is not still an enemy of this nation."

Jackson Davion picked up the gauntlet, as Katrina had known he would. "Highness, this civil war is more than a personal struggle between you and your brother." He was one of very few she allowed to argue so openly, in front of witnesses. It was his way, and she needed him more than his contrariness upset her. Not only was he Marshal of her Armies, he was also a Davion and carried a certain *presence*. With his ruddy-white hair and deep blue eyes that always reminded Katrina and everyone else, no doubt, of her father, Jackson's support only added to her legitimacy. "It started without any aid from him at all, if you remember. A dozen worlds broke into open rebellion *before* Victor announced publicly that he would oppose you. He was still with ComStar at the time."

She nodded. "Serving as their Precentor Martial." Even in exile, Victor had been unable to give up the warrior's life. If only he had stayed away, Katrina believed those rebellions would have been short-lived, never developing into a full-fledged civil war. "Are you saying that my brother is not leading the opposition against me?"

Simon Gallagher, her Prince's Champion, tossed square-lensed glasses onto the table in front of him and then smoothed down the strands of hair he combed over his obvious baldness. "The easiest way to be perceived as a leader is to determine which way the mob will go and then jump out in front." Which adequately summed up his own rise to power in the AFFS. "Your brother may be seen as the leader, but even without him, there is still fighting on half a hundred worlds."

"But how many of those fights are truly important?" Katrina asked. She saw Jackson's frown, and knew his answer.

"Any opposition to your legitimate rule is important, Highness, but I take your point." He picked up a small stylus, tapped the corner of the table's glass inset. The touch-activated screen lit up with a menu of options, and Jackson quickly sorted through them to display a basic map of the Inner Sphere against the giant wallscreen. The realms of House Kurita, Marik, and Liao, as well as the occupied territories held by the Clans, remained blanked out in solid, primary colors, serving as a frame for the two halves of the Federated Commonwealth, the superstate conceived with the marriage of Katrina's parents. Like an hourglass tipped to one side, the Lyran Alliance formed the upper bulb and the Federated Suns the lower. Connecting them was a small stretch of unaffiliated systems known as the Terran Corridor.

While lacking the full definition of a holographic star map, it was still familiar enough to all present. Jackson uploaded the most recent data, and stars began to glow in a variety of colors, revealing at a glance the status of the civil war. Systems supporting Victor burned with a golden hue, those in favor of Katrina a calm blue. Red indicated fighting or, at the very least, severe political unrest.

Jackson Davion nodded to her. "The state of the civil war is that you, as the Archon-Princess, currently control more worlds than your brother. That said, there are still more contested worlds than either of you directly control, and many of these worlds have a profound bearing on the civil war. Kathil, with its shipyards, is one such planet, and so far, both you and Victor have spent several regiments each trying to hold it."

Katrina did not want to think about Kathil. It was a grinder, tearing to shreds any unit she or Victor sent in. The same with Tikonov so far, and Dalkeith, in the Lyran Alliance. "Still," she said, "there must be a hundred worlds with no direct effect on the civil war."

"Define 'direct effect,' Highness," Jackson said. "Political support, men, materials—every world has some stake in the civil war and something to offer." He used the stylus to draw a large arrow across the map display. It began at distant Mogyorod, on the far edge of the Lyran Alliance, jutted up to Newtwon Square and then across to Winter. "This was Victor's movement in the earliest wave of fighting. Starting out from Mogyorod, he picked up the Thirty-ninth Avalon Hussars on Newtown Square, then swung the Seventh Crucis Lancers on Winter to his side." Jackson continued drawing arrows as he talked, one of them shooting almost to the center of the Alliance. "From there, his force split into two drives. The Lancers secured factories on nearby Inarcs, while Victor eventually made his way to Coventry, where he rallied both men and materiel from that important production center."

From Coventry, he drew a new arrow, this one leading first to Alarion, then sweeping across the last of the Lyran Alliance to the Federated Suns world of Tikonov. "This was the Third Wave, where Victor picked up at least two more regiments that we know of from distant garrison duties. On Tikonov, we stopped his advance, and by the end of Wave Four, he had fled the Federated Suns to regroup. At the time, we presumed he was on Thorin." As he spoke, Jackson reversed the arrow back through the Terran Corridor, where it stopped between the two gold-tinged stars of Thorin and Muphrid.

"Why Thorin?" Field Marshall Angela Kouranth asked. As head of the Department of Military Education, she had a less solid grounding in strategic planning. "He could simply have moved laterally to Algol and remained in the Federated Suns."

Simon Gallagher took the question, always eager to stay on near-even footing with Jackson. "The populations of Thorin, and nearby Muphrid, are securely behind Victor. He also has his logistics network routed through those worlds." Gallagher's best claim to any glory came with his background in logistics. "And with the Skye Province at his back"—Gallagher glanced warily toward Katrina—"Victor had a shield against any large-scale offensive. Until recently, at least."

Katrina nodded at her Champion's veiled reference to the recent Free Skye rebellion. "Skye was a fight waiting to happen ever since the days of my mother's rule," she said. "We only narrowly averted a rebellion in '56." By *we*, she actually meant *Victor*, but she refused to acknowledge her brother as the one-time ruler of the superstate that was the Federated Commonwealth before it split back into the Lyran Alliance and the Federated Suns. "It took Ryan Steiner's mysterious death to quiet that trouble, but then his son, Robert, started up with his father's old tricks. Robert's games of brinksmanship have prevented us from moving large forces through Skye for *far* too long." Of course, the fall of rebellious Hesperus three days before meant that Katrina was almost in a position to cease worrying about such threats. And the cost . . .

She shook her head in wonder. "Who would have thought the Gray Death Legion would fold so quickly? At least they held the world and drained too much from Robert's force before they collapsed. Which leaves only one itch left to scratch."

"New Syrtis," Gallagher said, again jumping in ahead of Jackson Davion. "Do you still believe that Duke George Hasek will throw in with Victor?"

Katrina intertwined her fingers and set her clasped hands on the table in front of her. Her ice-blue eyes found those of General Franklin Harris, her analyst who currently supervised all actions taken by the Field Marshall of the Capellan March. He nodded in reply to her silent question. "No. But he will refuse to support *me*, which amounts to the same, Simon. Duke Hasek made it clear enough that he no longer views me as the sovereign ruler of *his* people." The memory of Hasek's outrageous defiance at last year's Star League conference still rankled. "He is second on my list, after Victor. Which brings me back to my earlier question.

"Where is Victor?"

"On Thorin, it would seem," Gallagher said.

"It would *seem* that way." Katrina speared her Champion with a glance, reining him in from too-quick answers. "But Jackson doesn't think so anymore." She nodded once, regally. "Bring him in," she commanded, and Jackson used a nearby intercom to buzz the adjacent room.

A side door concealed behind the flag of Woodbine opened, and an elderly man entered the situation room. He made his way unsupported but still with the determined care of the aged to the head of the table, where he stood next to Jackson Davion. His white hair had thinned since his previous time on New Avalon, but his gaze was as blue and diamond-hard as ever. He bowed respectfully to Katrina, and nodded to the few others around the room whose faces showed any recognition.

"For those who have never met him," Katrina said by way of introduction, "this is Quintus Allard. He was my father's Minister of Intelligence, and helped engineer some of our greatest victories in the Fourth Succession War before turning over the position to his son. I asked Quintus back from retirement almost specifically to handle this question." She smiled. "Welcome home, Quintus."

He smiled back in avuncular fashion. "Thank you, Katherine. Your invitation was hard to refuse."

She kept her emotions, and any immediate reply, in check. Quintus's comments could so often be taken two ways, which was only one of the irritations Katrina experienced in the presence of the old man. Even more cutting was his continued insistence on using her given name. In adopting Katrina, the form of the name used by her grandmother, one of the strongest Archons ever to rule the Lyran state, she had gone a long way to solidify her early power base. Quintus's refusal to call her Katrina could be chalked up to the set ways of an old family friend. She doubted that, but it could. Katrina had to balance on the edge of fond consideration for an old man and suspicion that he was subtly undermining her in whatever way he could.

"You have some input on the subject of my brother, I believe?"

Quintus nodded. "Victor Steiner-Davion is not on Thorin." Though his voice had a papery thinness, his tone was sure.

Field Marshal Day bridled. Despite Day's talk of working with the Ministry of Intelligence, Katrina knew of the rivalry between the two departments that went back several centuries. "How can you be certain?" she asked.

"Because I trust Morgan Kell to be smarter than this," he said. Archduke Kell of the Arc-Royal Defense Cordon was probably Victor's strongest support in the Lyran Alliance. "The Prince's Men, Tiaret, the Outland Legion all have been sighted on Thorin. Too many fingers point there."

"Perhaps that is just what Morgan wants you to think."

Quintus shrugged. "In which case, I would expect him to be even more blatant. Morgan Kell is a good commander and a fine leader, but he is *not* a trained intelligence agent. That level of subtlety is beyond him."

Katrina stopped the spiraling argument before it could get out of hand. Also, she didn't need Quintus extolling the virtues of Morgan Kell. "So where is Victor, then?" she demanded.

"I would hesitate to guess, Highness."

"Don't hesitate, Quintus. You were asked here to make such guesses."

He didn't even blink at the thinly veiled command. "The obvious worlds are Muphrid, Arc-Royal, and Alarion. Muphrid, as it is the sister world to Thorin. Arc-Royal, as it is the world Morgan Kell can protect with the most forces. Alarion, for the same reason with Victor's loyal forces. Because they are obvious, I'm not certain if anyone could make an educated guess as to which is more likely than another."

"And of all the nonobvious worlds," Katrina said, "we might as well take a blind stab at the star chart?"

"All but one," Quintus said then. His voice was low and speculative. "There is a world that is almost too easy to ignore as a candidate."

"New Avalon?" Stephanie Day asked, her overly serious tone mocking the old analyst.

Quintus shook his head, ignoring the offense. "Tikonov. Who's really to say whether Victor ever left?"

An interesting theory, Katrina decided. Given the deep frowns of half of her High Command, Quintus had just given them all the more to think about, which meant postponing a decision that much longer. She was starting to think that the old man would tell her enough to prove that he was no immediate danger, but not so much as to be truly useful.

She nodded. "Thank you, Quintus. We appreciate your analysis."

"My family has always been at the disposal of House Davion," he said, with another of his formal bows. Then he withdrew with the same studied care as in entering the room.

Katrina waited for the door to snick shut behind him. "So how much of what he says do we believe?" Her voice was careful not to display any paranoia, just the careful evaluation of untried information.

Jackson Davion tapped his stylus against the table's dark wood. "Your father trusted Quintus implicitly. Is there any reason we should not do the same?"

"Because the man was nursed on suspicion and can invent three lies in the time it takes anyone else to draw breath," Katrina snapped.

Field Marshal Kouranth frowned. "Then why ask him here at all?"

"Because I want Quintus Allard where I can watch him most carefully. His family could cause too many problems, but they'll think twice while Quintus is a guest on New Avalon."

Jackson Davion started in surprise at those words, but Katrina ignored it. She stood up, braced her arms against the table, and gazed around at her senior officers. By coincidence, *of course*, her cool gaze came to rest on General Tahmezed from the Draconis March. "It is time to start exerting control over those who might help my brother." She looked at General Harris. "Or those who will stand against me for their own gain."

"Back to New Syrtis again?" Jackson asked, edging out Gallagher this time with a touch of frustration in his voice.

"You spent the better part of last week explaining to me how Victor had been neutralized, Jackson. Do you still affirm that as the situation?" Katrina knew that everyone in this room had come here with their own agenda. She had several of them herself, in fact. By playing into Jackson's strengths for analysis and compromise, she had set him right where she needed him for this one. In reply, he nodded, though reluctantly.

"Then the time has come to turn more attention to other pressing problems. Yes, Quintus becomes a hostage against his family's good behavior, and you don't have to like that to know it is necessary. His family might throw support behind Victor *or* George Hasek. That would be unacceptable."

Jackson sat forward slightly. "So you intend to force the issue with both the Allards and the Haseks?"

"The Allards are *sidelined*," she explained, "and George Hasek forced the issue with *me*. Fortunately, we have a military plan in place to deal with the Capellan March. Is it ready?"

He nodded stiffly. "It was ready months ago. Although it was predicated on the idea that Hasek would use at least one of his New Syrtis regiments to strike first at you."

"Then we lure a command off-planet."

"Or turn one to our side," Gallagher said, stepping in on cue and instantly garnering the attention of every officer in the room. He smiled thinly. "The Vanguard Legion on New Syrtis is a mercenary regiment under the aegis of Duke Hasek but in AFFS employ. They have traditionally shown anti-Steiner tendencies, but they've got a new commander. I think the timing is perfect to sway his loyalty."

"So, we buy them off," said Field Master Carlos Post, Director of Mercenary Relations for the AFFS, nodding slowly. "We can hide very . . . favorable . . . terms in a new contract. If Colonel Dean will go for it."

Gallagher stood up alongside Katrina. "I can handle this, Highness. I've never met a mercenary who wouldn't sell his brother for spare BattleMech parts."

"I have." Katrina said, thinking specifically of Morgan Kell. Besides, there was no need to show herself *too* much in accord with Gallagher.

"Yes, we'll offer them new parts and supplies," he said. "And new 'Mechs, a favorable posting, triple combat pay—whatever it takes to buy us the key to New Syrtis. I will get this done, Highness."

Katrina looked from Jackson Davion, who clearly did not relish this particular strategy, to Simon Gallagher, who wanted it. That was precisely the reason she had promoted Simon as her Prince's Champion. To get around Jackson in a diplomatic way, as the need arose.

"Handle it, Simon. Bring me George Hasek. That leaves Jackson free to bring down my brother and finally put an end to this civil war." Katrina smiled to herself. Each to his own strength, just as she had planned from the beginning.

She sat down again, leaning back in her chair as she glanced around at her command staff.

"Any new business?"

3

I don't remember much about the battles fought on Muphrid or anywhere else during my time in seclusion. I read the reports, I remember sending off responses, through Morgan, but no details. I'm not certain whether to attribute that to shock, or to progress.

—*Cause and Effect,* Avalon Press, 3067

Hawkins Estates, Muphrid
Freedom Theater
Lyran Alliance
28 July 3065

With a cramp in his side and his leg muscles burning from exertion, Victor Steiner-Davion worked to maintain an even pace as the vineyard path turned up a gentle slope. He breathed in rhythm to his running step, sucking great lungfuls of sweet, morning air past the invisible steel bands wrapped around his chest. Stray vines slapped at his bare arms when he strayed off the path, but never too far. Like walls to a maze, tall, vine-covered trellises penned him in on either side.

A fairly simple maze, of course. The vineyards of Hawkins Estates—the largest on Muphrid—covered several dozen square kilometers, but the grapevines stretched over their steel frameworks in long, parallel rows. Victor could run up one path, then down another. Not a lot of variety, but then he wasn't looking for complications. He wasn't really looking for anything—wasn't trying to do anything but keep up with Kai.

Kai Allard-Liao, Victor's longtime friend and heir to the St. Ives Commonality, ran in the next row over, pacing Victor, giving him an encouraging nod at every break in the trellis system. Between breaks, Kai was little more than the flash of an ivory-and-gold running suit glimpsed through harvest-thinned arbors. It had been Kai's idea to start these morning runs and get Victor back into a light exercise regimen. The vineyard was the perfect site. With the harvest workers gone, there was little concern for security. The vine-covered trellises were tall enough to hide the two men, and a few security agents posted at the perimeter entrances guaranteed them privacy.

As Victor worked on lengthening his stride, working into a long, loping glide that ate up the ground, his body remembering. Keep your feet close to the ground and come down lightly on the heel to maintain a smooth momentum. Hold the arms loosely—no need to expend energy by excessive pumping or holding tight fists. Left foot, then right, just one foot after the other. No, he didn't need to think about running, but he did regardless. It beat the alternative: thinking about anything else.

Running was safer. Running was all technique and endurance. No political fallout if he didn't follow the correct path. No one's life hanging in the balance if he didn't finish on a critical timetable. No logistics concerns over ammunition and armor or where transport could be arranged for a regiment of infantry. If he started worrying about the civil war, he'd run into the problems of his troops stalemated on Thorin and a dozen other worlds of the Lyran Alliance and Federated Suns. He'd remember Tikonov, his forced departure and, worse, what had caused that retreat. He'd remember Katherine's oh-so-innocent expression as she sadly told him about Omi's death . . .

He stumbled and nearly pitched headlong onto the ground. Running top-heavy for a couple of seconds, he got his feet back under him.

"You all right . . . over there?" Kai spoke in cadence with his regular breathing.

"Fine." His form shattered, his side aching, Victor labored to regain a solid pace. *Omi* . . .

"Just perfect," he muttered, mostly to himself.

"Good," Kai said. A break in the trellis system allowed him to glance over to check on Victor. "Race you . . . the last leg."

Victor almost shook off the challenge. Kai would beat him easily. He was in better shape and had a longer stride to boot. But coasting along only invited more idle thought, more memories. Deciding to race, he drew on his reserves and focused toward the next break, where several paths opened up into a cleared area. It seemed very far away. Now Victor pumped his arms vigorously, driving himself, breathing shallow and rapid as he pounded up the slope. He didn't see Kai through the trellis gaps, and assumed his friend had pulled farther ahead. Victor didn't mind losing, but a small spark buried deep inside him flared to life at the possibility of losing a challenge without giving his best.

Victor ran faster.

The clearing was a small area that had served as a work hub during Muphrid's early harvest season. Here the workers brought their bushels of grapes to be stacked and loaded onto pallets for a small forklift to run back to the winery. There was also a wooden bench for resting, and a small station tied into the irrigation network that provided a faucet for fresh drinking water. Victor sprinted into the cleared area, then quickly stumbled down into a jog that carried him through the clearing and onto the start of the next path. He windmilled to a stop, and then walked back in time to see Kai enter the clearing at an easy jog.

"You . . . didn't . . . race," Victor panted, doubled over with his hands braced against his knees.

Kai smiled, his Asian features taking on a devilish cast. "I guess you win," he said, breathing much easier than his friend. He walked a few turns around the clearing to cool down his system.

Victor sat down hard on the bench. "Low, Kai. Very low."

He drew in deep breaths to fight the fire burning in his lungs and clamped one hand over the cramp in his side. The air here tasted of warm grape; fruit dropped and crushed under the feet of the harvest workers and left to cook in the sun. The hard-beaten ground was stained in a mottled pattern of reds and purples. A few late yellow jackets drifted through, searching for any remaining food.

Kai finished walking, shrugged, and settled into a routine of basic stretching exercises. "You held good form today, from what I *saw*." Though obviously not from what he'd *heard*. "I think we did about three kilometers."

"Not that hard," Victor said, finally regaining his breath. "Just putting one foot in front of the other."

His friend nodded. Kai's darker skin was still flushed from the run and stood out against his tracksuit. He had inherited his mother's gray, almond-shaped eyes, but his lanky frame and easy smile, those were definitely Kai's father looking out of him. Victor remembered Justin Allard as an intense but agreeable man, devoted to his nation and his family.

"Do you miss your father?" Victor asked suddenly.

Kai blinked. "What kind of question is that?" But he nodded. "Every day," he admitted. "Some days more than others." Victor would have let it go with that, but Kai decided to go further. "You're thinking about Omi, aren't you?" He spoke gently, tentatively. "I loved my father very much, but I think it's different between a man and a woman."

"Omi and I hardly spent any time together," Victor said, peeling off his light jacket, throwing it aside.

"Doesn't matter." Kai stripped down to the waist, doing a few last stretches to ready himself for some hand-to-hand sparring. "Omi Kurita was the best thing to ever happen to you, and don't tell me the two of you never discussed building a life together. You don't invest that kind of emotion in someone so easily."

All true. Victor winced as the wound tore open again and raw pain welled up. He and Omi had met on Outreach while the Inner Sphere was trying to come up with some defense against the Clan invasion. From the start, he'd felt an irresistible attraction, made extremely complicated by their birthrights. A Steiner-Davion and a member of House Kurita? With both families set against them from the start, friendship was rocky enough. That they had won through most of the opposition to kindle their friendship into something more had been proof enough for them that it would last. And it did, until an assassin's hand took Omi from him forever.

Katherine was behind it, of course, and it wasn't the first time she had relied on an assassin. The first—that Victor knew of—was when she'd paid to have their mother killed. She may even have used the same man to get their brother Arthur out of the way, though Victor had to admit that was only guesswork. Reasonable guesswork, though. Arthur had been gaining far too much popularity for Katherine to ignore him forever.

And Omi? Omi's death was nothing more than petty vengeance. A way to hurt Victor like nothing else could. Theodore Kurita, Omi's father and Coordinator of the Draconis Combine, had kept the news secret for half a year, but Katherine had known. She'd hoarded the information, no doubt savored it, until she could drop it on him for the most damaging effect. Victor knew this, but it didn't prevent Katherine's tactic from working. Omi's death hit him so hard that his officers had finally been forced to pull the plug on Tikonov and pack him away somewhere safe.

"Safe" meant divorcing Victor from the bulk of his personal escort force and installing him on Muphrid, the sister system to Thorin. A single battalion from the Twenty-third Arcturan Guard formed his security force, but they were busy luring off a full regiment of Katherine's loyalists in the wilderness region of the Great Tundra. A few security agents, and Kai, were all that was left to safeguard Victor. Hiding in plain sight, Morgan Kell had called it. So far, it was working. Life on Muphrid was barely touched by the civil war, and one could almost believe that the fighting was a fiction of the media.

Almost.

Kai finished stretching as Victor finally levered himself up from the bench. He stood opposite Victor and bowed, then took up a fighting stance. Victor mimicked him, never breaking eye contact. To the casual observer, the fight would have looked uneven, with Victor's mediocre height pitted against Kai's eight-centimeter advantage. He nodded his readiness, and Kai moved in to attack. With no mats and no safety gear, their sparring was limited to light contact only, and each man was on his honor for scoring. The first half-point was no debate. Kai came in low and fast, feinted a backfist to Victor's head, and then caught Victor in the midriff with a side kick.

"You aren't concentrating," Kai said, resetting himself on his invisible mark. "My mother could hold you off." They nodded at each other, and this time Victor pressed a halfhearted attack.

"Your mother is also a thirty-year master of tai chi chuan," Victor said, stumbling back as Kai threw a crescent kick right in front of his face. He gave his friend the point, then stepped back to ready himself again. "Just got a lot on my mind."

This time, Kai swept in with a roundhouse that Victor caught, throwing Kai to one side. They pushed each other back and forth across the clearing, Kai with an advantage on reach and Victor making short flurries meant to overwhelm his opponent.

"Isis will be here in a week," Kai reminded him. "Maybe she'll have some information for you."

Isis Marik had been Omi's guest on Luthien. The daughter of Thomas Marik, Captain-General of the Free Worlds League, she was a peer and a friend. Victor shook his head. "She shouldn't be coming here." He lunged in, pulling back his punch just as it touched Kai's ribs.

Kai stepped back. "Why? We can cover her security arrangements."

"That's not it." Victor drew in a deep breath and expelled it in a long sigh. "I'm certain she *does* have more information about Omi's death, Kai. I don't know if I'm ready for that yet."

"Which is why you sent Cranston—I mean, Cox!—to Luthien? Because you *didn't* want to know more?"

Victor smiled as Kai stumbled over the real name of Galen Cox, who had been forced to hide behind a new identity after *he* had run afoul of Katherine's plans. The deception had been exposed at the recent Star League conference. Victor also stumbled over the names from time to time, having known Galen far too long as Cranston.

"I sent Galen to Luthien to help with the investigation. At the time, I thought I had some insight about where the assassin might be hiding." Victor remembered how he'd suddenly felt so sure that the assassin had gone to ground on Luthien. "I think I was feeling guilty, and wanted to convince myself that I was doing something—anything—to help."

Kai had started to move in on an attack. Now he paused. "Guilty? Victor, why would you feel guilty?"

"It's the same assassin, Kai. The one my people *caught* on Solaris VII after my mother was killed. The same one we used to take out Ryan Steiner in retribution. He got away from us right after. We know he got involved in the resistance movement on Zurich, during the Offensive of '57. He's the same man who attempted the hit on Omi on Mogyorod. If I thought he could ever get close enough to Omi to harm her again, I would never have sent her first to Tukayyid and then home for safety."

"Tukayyid and Luthien are two of the safest worlds I could imagine for Omi, Victor. What more could you have done?"

"I could have killed the bastard when I had the chance!" Victor clenched his hands into impotent fists. "I should have. No one would have opposed me."

"Do you believe that would have truly stopped Katherine?" Kai asked quietly. "Do you really think he's the only gun-for-hire out there?"

Victor's anger fled as quickly as it came, leaving behind the same, gaping chasm at the core of his being. "I don't know, Kai." His voice sounded unsure, hollow, even to his own ears. "Maybe it wouldn't have changed a thing. But maybe Omi would be alive today, too. I don't know." Victor stepped away from the center of the clearing. He wouldn't be able to continue the match just now.

Kai picked up his shirt and warm-up jacket, slung them over one shoulder, and headed toward the path that would take them back to the mansion. "None of us knows much of anything, Victor. All we can do is deal with life as it happens. I can tell you this, though, from personal experience. The 'what-ifs' will kill you if you don't watch out. If you don't stay out in front, they can catch up and stomp you with the weight of an *Atlas*."

Victor nodded. That pretty well summed up his emotional state. Stepped-on. "I keep trying to get out in front of them, Kai. I really do." He found his jacket. "But I haven't figured out how. Not yet."

Kai was disappearing around the end of a vine-covered trellis, leaving Victor alone in the clearing. "There's no big secret, Victor," he called out, his voice just loud enough to carry back. "It's all about putting one foot in front of the other."

All the King's Men

The Divine Right of Kings was originally developed to strengthen the ancient Terran monarchies, which were then being threatened by religious extremists. Anointed by God, monarchs secured birthrights for their heirs and could demand the unquestioned obedience of their subjects. In this manner, rulers drew a mandate from the people without ever having to admit that they needed it.

They only got it half right, which is why all of these monarchies eventually failed. When one attempts to control the will of the people, the monarch ends up ruling by either the sufferance or ignorance of his subjects. This cannot last, and when the end comes it is often violent.

—From the journal of Prince Victor Ian Steiner-Davion, reprinted in *Cause and Effect*, Avalon Press, 3067

4

If Word of Blake was a distillation of all that was worst in the old ComStar organization, I have to believe that in the Prince's Men I have seen a distillation of what was best. Dedication, integrity, and the vision not to predict what should be done for the future, but to do what needs to be done—today—to serve the future.
—*Cause and Effect*, Avalon Press, 3067

Kalakos Pass
Olympus Range, Thorin
Freedom Theater
Lyran Alliance
12 August 3065

Demi-Precentor Rudolf Shakov would never forget this moment.

Strapped into the command couch of his sixty-five-ton *Exterminator*, racing up the scrub-covered side of Kalakos Pass at the head of a strike team, he dared any of the Eleventh Arcturan aerospace pilots to make another run at him. The one fightercraft that had already tried was now a smoking debris field scattered over several hundred meters of rocky mountainside, having encountered the withering firepower of Shakov's Partisan air-defense vehicles. He wouldn't mind force-feeding the pilots another lesson.

Two more *Lucifer*s dove down after but aborted when the Partisans filled the air with overlapping flak barrages. The pilots banked away, returning to the chaotic dogfight that raged over the pass and peaks of Thorin's Olympus Range, properly leaving this ground battle in the capable hands of BattleMechs. The metal-shod war machines stood defiantly at either end of the pass, a few of them making challenging runs across the open ground or fighting for height on the slopes. High-mountain air shimmered with gem-colored laserfire. Lightning arced out from the barrels of particle projection cannon, snaking downrange to smash armor into large, molten globs. Alarms wailed under the protest of missile-lock, and the antimissile system in the *Exterminator*'s right chest swallowed large belts of ammunition as it threw up a shield against the incoming warheads.

An unforgettable moment. Shakov would remember everything about it. Where he was and what he was doing when his commanding officer fell.

The Com Guard 244th Division was no stranger to the civil war. Also known as the Prince's Men for their early adoption of Victor Steiner-Davion as ComStar's Precentor Martial, they had joined in almost from the first shot fired. Leaving ComStar to follow Victor, they had saved the prince's life on Newtown Square and had rarely left his side thereafter. For security reasons handed down by Morgan Kell, the 244th had been permanently severed from Victor's escort force following their retreat from Tikonov. Precentor Irelon, commander of the Prince's Men, didn't like it, but he had no choice but to finally agree.

Shakov wasn't so sure about it himself, but he and the other officers would follow orders, at least with respect to Prince Victor's safety. Besides, they all knew there could be no going back to ComStar. Where Victor had been able to "set aside" his duties and appoint a martial *pro tem*, the Prince's Men had defied orders to chase after him. Lost 'Mechs could only be repaired with equipment salvaged from Lyran or Federation designs. Lost men could not be replaced at all. Slowly and painfully, attrition ate away at the Prince's Men, restricting the types of missions they could undertake. For the past several weeks, they had been assigned escort duty to supply convoys. The only reason they were defending Kalakos Pass today was because there was no one else to prevent a battalion of the Eleventh Arcturan Guard from overrunning an allied base camp.

Hoping to delay the inevitable, Shakov fought his *Exterminator* up the rubble-covered slope. A missile-support lance belonging to the Eleventh Arcturan already held the heights. Raining several hundred warheads over the entrenched Com Guard position, they were threatening to force them from the pass.

It was Shakov's job to silence the missile-equipped 'Mechs. The *Exterminator*'s long-range launcher spat out a flight of its own, drawing the attention of a *Cobra* while he worked into range for his lasers. The blue-white lightning arc of a lance-mate's PPC flashed up past him, carving into an Arcturan *Whitworth*, while a flurry of laserfire and the pounding lines of autocannon fire fell down the mountainside from the Lyran position. Emerald darts from a pulse laser chewed into Shakov's left knee, throwing a tremble through his 'Mech just as the call came in.

"'Mech down!" Adept Kevin Bills cried out. "It's—Blake's blood, it's—" From the timbre and sound of his voice, he might have been sitting right next to Shakov in the cockpit. His shock came through loud and clear over the Com Guard communication system, which was the best in the Inner Sphere.

"Irelon," said another voice. "The Precentor, he's—" Shakov expected to hear him say "down," reporting that Raymond Irelon's *Excalibur* had taken a crippling hit. A leg. Gyro burnout. Anything but: ". . . he's dead."

A numbing flash of denial swept over him, and he throttled back, flagging off from the assault. He looked at the upper-left corner of his neurohelmet to engage the new Optical Stimulation Technology, then blinked through a number of preset frequencies to access his private channel with the other officers. Recently developed by ComStar, OST allowed complete, hands-free communications. Activated by direct sight, it simply counted the blinks.

"Kevin, report! Confirm that Irelon is down and *out*."

"Affirmative, Demi Shakov." Bills sounded shaken and on the edge. "He took a gauss slug through the canopy."

Shakov's rear monitor was too small for good detail, and he wasn't about to turn his back on the nearby Lyran position to survey the battle below. Drawing in a steadying breath, he pulled his targeting crosshairs over the *Cobra*. The reticle burned the deep gold of target lock, and he triggered a new spread of missiles. "What is our status on the line?"

"DeLuca and I are holding the center," Bills said, naming his primary Level II commander. "Whoever's running things for the Guard, I don't think they realize who they . . . they killed."

That was only because General Linda McDonald was not heading this advance push. McDonald was the Eleventh Arcturan commander and had stood against the Prince's Men on Tikonov. She wouldn't forge the BattleMechs of the Com Guard officers.

"We're not giving them the chance to realize it," Shakov said, then blinked over to a command-wide frequency. "Brevet-Demi Bills," he went on, promoting the other man on the spot, investing him with enough authority to hopefully shake him out of his shock, "take charge of the lower battle. Form arrow-echelon-left and prepare to charge the Arcturan line. 'Mechs, concentrate center. Armor and battlesuits, break to the flanks and keep any encircling machines from coming in from the rear."

Shakov was next in line for command but too far out of place to regroup now. He hoped Bills's field promotion would give the rest of the Prince's Men enough faith to follow him. Kevin Bills was a young officer, coming up fast as the Prince's Men continued to lose top-rank warriors to the civil war. He also took orders as if they were the word of Jerome Blake himself, and right now, Shakov needed that more than anything.

"If we move forward, we'll have to run the gauntlet on those missile boats." Bills's voice took on the tight, tinny aspect of a private transmission. Shakov was glad to see he had enough sense to switch over to a private frequency. "It'll cost us."

Shoving his throttle forward, Shakov threw his *Exterminator* into its best uphill speed. The entrenched Lyrans slipped into range for his lasers, and he toggled them into his main trigger. "They're about to stop being a factor," he said coldly, just loud enough for his voice-activated mic to pick up for broadcast.

The *Cobra* shuffled down the slope a few meters, the Lyran MechWarrior putting himself between the rest of his lance and the onrushing Com Guard. Bad choice. Better the *Nightsky* with its death-threatening hatchet or even the *Catapult*, which still boated fifty percent again more armor than the *Cobra*. The *Cobra* was the newer design, though, and the lance commander probably thought it was therefore superior in all situations.

It wasn't. Shakov's extended-range lasers carved into the 'Mech with scarlet knives, puddling armor into the cracks and crevices of the rocky slope while a *Lancelot* tied its own lasers in with a PPC to scorch away more protective casing. The *Cobra* reeled under the assault, dropping to one knee in an effort to hold its place. Most of its return fire, offered as large missile spreads, flew wide at the close range. Those few warheads that came anywhere close were intercepted by the last firing of Shakov's antimissile system. Meanwhile, the Com Guard strike force split in two as a *Wyvern* and Adept Marrit's *Raijin* took to the air on jump jets. They sailed up and over the top of the Lyran position on long streamers of superheated plasma, then dropped down into ready crouches farther upslope.

Hatchet high for a decapitating slice, the *Nightsky* was faster to react, lighting off its own jets and sailing in toward Shakov's *Exterminator*. Adept Marrit in the *Raijin* was not about to leave her commander in such straights, however. Her PPC carved into the *Nightsky*'s back, slicing through engine shielding and splashing molten titanium down into the spinning gyro. Still, not quite so devastating until the *Lancelot* also turned its firepower against the *Nightsky*, which managed only a halfhearted chop at Shakov's shoulder. Then its entire hatchet-arm went tumbling down the hillside, severed at the shoulder by the *Lancelot*'s second volley.

The rest of the *Nightsky* followed a moment later as the *Lancelot* and the *Raijin* teamed together again to take a leg and burn out the Lyran's gyroscope.

For his part, Shakov continued to concentrate on the *Cobra*. The *Catapult* could certainly cause more trouble for the fight down in the pass with its Arrow IV artillery launcher, but it was being pressed by the *Wyvern* hard enough to forego any more barrages. And besides, the *Cobra* not doubt belonged to the Lyran lance commander. Shakov was not above looking for some payback.

It didn't take long for him to find it. With four lasers working the *Cobra* over at point-blank range, Shakov managed to knock the other 'Mech off its feet and to keep it down. An energy salvo blew out one of the *Cobra*'s upper-leg actuators. Another crisped its left arm down to blackened skeletal struts and a ruined missile launcher. The *Exterminator*'s fusion reactor spiked hard from the energy draw. Waste heat bled up into the cockpit, pulling a hard sweat that trickled through Shakov's dark goatee and down the sides of his neck. The sauna scent of too-warm sweat warned him that his heat levels were soaring too high, but he hung in and continued to trigger off his lasers as fast they could cycle.

His fourth set finally sliced deep into the *Cobra*'s chest, skewering its ammunition bin and dumping kilojoules of energy among the warheads. A bright orange blossom erupted from the *Cobra*'s heart, quickly bleeding into the golden fire of a catastrophic reactor failure. The *Cobra* simply ceased being, expanding outward in a ball of incandescent fire that picked up Shakov's *Exterminator*, carrying it back down the mountainside and laying it out on its back for a rough slide toward the bottom of the pass. Shakov surrendered his control sticks and clung to the arms of his chair with frenetic strength. Thrown against his restraining harness, he imagined being strapped into a steel drum being rolled downhill.

Then, for a moment, he didn't imagine much of anything.

". . . down and burning." Broadcasting battle results over the general frequency, Adept Marrit's voice kept Shakov just this side of consciousness. "So is the *Catapult*. The *Whitworth* is in flight for its own lines."

"Demi Shakov?" That was Kevin Bills, still looking for some

confirmation on Shakov's condition, though apparently expecting the worst if he was asking Marrit directly.

"Demi Shakov is still down," she said.

"Down," Shakov croaked out, his tongue thick and throbbing with pain from getting bitten more than once. "Down . . . but still here." Had he been knocked unconscious? It didn't seem so, though he might have been stunned from the long roll downhill. "I took a shortcurt." Almost the same one as Precentor Irelon, straight out of the war.

The thought sobered him up, dragging him back to the immediate battle. Rolling his *Exterminator* onto its front, Shakov levered his 'Mech back to its feet. "Report," he ordered, trying to make sense of his new view from the floor of the pass. Deep gouges carved into his canopy's ferroglass shield didn't help, but the only fighting seemed to be at the far end of the pass, with a few late vehicles—including his Partisan tanks—making for it with best speed.

"The Eleventh is pulling back," Bills informed him, sounding relieved. "We caved in their center just as they lost their missile umbrella. Wait one . . ." A pause as he took a private report. "Our Kanga squad just intercepted the *Whitworth* that you missed up on the mountainside. It won't be rejoining the fight. One of our vehicles is burning, though."

A three-man crew, likely dead, Shakov tallied. The Prince's Men could not afford many more trades like that. They would run out of men before the Lyran loyalists ran out of 'Mechs. "Are they pulling back to regroup or to retreat?" he asked, his tone sharp.

"Retreat. They've given up the pass completely, Demi Shakov."

"Pursue them to the Grand Ronde, and then fall back. We'll use recon flights to track them after they cross the river."

Bills acknowledged, and Shakov began his *Exterminator* on the long trek across the pass. Farther behind him, the *Wyvern* and the *Raijin* dropped down the mountainside on fiery jets. Safer, and in no hurry now, the *Lancelot* took a switchback path down the hill. Shakov hesitated, then turned back for the Com

Guard's original line. A half kilometer out toward the south head of the pass, he could make out a still, dark form that would be Precentor Irelon's *Excalibur*. A memory of the precentor's face rose to Shakov's mind, looking at him with that stern face, his iron-gray hair pulled back into a braid that hung over one shoulder.

"No matter what else," Irelon had said in his gravelly voice, "we see the Prince to New Avalon." That had been Raymond Irelon's aim. Now it had the weight of a dying wish.

So, they would see it through for him. No matter what, Shakov vowed, the Prince's Men would make planetfall on New Avalon to fight alongside their prince and precentor martial. Providing they found each other again.

"Victor," he breathed softly, careful of his voice-activated mic. "Victor, where are you?"

5

The following entry on Isis Marik appears in *Auburn's Peerage*: "Daughter of the current captain-general but passed over as heir to the Free Worlds League. Recently spurned by Sun-Tzu Liao after a nine-year engagement. After so many upsets, it is unlikely that Isis will have much influence on near-future political events." I have never known Misha Auburn to be one hundred percent wrong before.

—*Cause and Effect*, Avalon Press, 3067

Hawkins Estates, Muphrid
Freedom Theater
Lyran Alliance
23 August 3065

Isis Marik arrived at Hawkins Estates unannounced and near dinnertime. Shelley Hawkins personally showed her to the drawing room, never at a loss for idle talk. On the way, they passed a hologram gallery, where Isis glimpsed views of the Hawkinses rubbing elbows with holo-stars, barons, and a local duke. It wasn't the kind of company usually enjoyed by wine merchants, at least not in her native Free Worlds League. Apparently, social standing was one more commodity to be bought, sold, and traded in the Lyran Alliance.

Isis could only hope that the Hawkinses' loyalty to Victory could not be brought to the bargaining table as easily.

She found Kai in the drawing room, browsing a bookcase

filled with signed editions while waiting for dinner. He smiled and greeted her warmly, taking both her hands in his. Knowing Kai mostly by his reputation in fighting the Clan invasion and as champion of Solaris VII, Isis had always thought of Kai Allard-Liao as someone larger than life. Sun-Tzu had once dismissed most of those accomplishments with an airy wave, but Isis remembered seeing the worry behind her ex-fiancé's eyes. It didn't take much to see that Kai was a man whom even the chancellor of the Capellan Confederation feared. It wasn't until recently, however, that she'd really gotten the chance to know Kai. In him, she had found a friend just as concerned for Victor's welfare as she.

The two of them sat down on a leather sofa, whose overstuffed cushions creaked slightly as Isis settled back against them. She tugged nervously at the collar of her purple blouse, deciding that she could trust Kai with her concerns. "Why is Victor avoiding me?" she asked him softly.

Kai's eyes widened in surprise. "Isis, you've talked with Victor almost every day this week. I wouldn't exactly call that avoidance." But a knowing light behind his gray eyes hinted that he knew what she was getting at.

"He hasn't mentioned Omi to me even once." She caught his look of concern and shook her head in answer to his unspoken question. "I haven't brought up the subject either, waiting for him, as you suggested."

"Victor is healing, Isis. We have to give him the time he needs. Morgan and I believe he's on the right path if we just have the patience to see him through it."

"What good is being on the right path if you don't occasionally look to the horizon to see where you're going?" Isis drew one leg up under her, turning to face Kai. "He's staring at the ground, like he's worried he'll trip again."

With a sigh of frustration, Kai leaned back against the sofa. "I try to push him, when I can." He looked over at her and smiled, almost shyly. "When he lets me. Victor knows me far too well."

Which is about what Isis had figured, too, that Victor was too good at ducking Kai's concerns and convincing his friend to give him more room. "Well, he doesn't know me *that* well. Not yet." She uncoiled herself from the couch. "Excuse me, please."

Kai also stood up. "What are you going to do, Isis?"

He looked ready to follow, but she backed him off with a hard glance. "What I should have done before," she said. "I'm going to show Victor around."

Sitting at the desk in his suite, Victor reclined back in the swivel chair as far as he could without tipping it. He swung himself around in lazy circles, staring at the ceiling, counting each revolution as if it was an event worth his time. At ninety-nine, he reversed his direction, and began counting back.

Waiting for him on the desk were reports from Kathil—the latest body counts and estimates on destroyed military material already pulled up on the electronic reader. There was also a letter from his sister Yvonne, who was accompanying Tancred Sandoval back to Robinson. Things would come to a head once the pair arrived on the Draconis March capital, and Victor knew he should be doing certain things about that. He could recall the Tenth Lyran Guard, his personal unit, and send them back to Robinson to support any move Tancred made to oppose his father. He could also record a new entreaty to Duke James Sandoval, trying to win him back from Katherine.

Right now, it was much easier to spin and count lazy circles on the ceiling.

"Dinner," Isis called from the open door.

Victor stopped swinging around, looked over at her. "I'll be down shortly. They can start without me."

"No," Isis said firmly, stepping into the room. "I meant that you are taking me out to dinner." She looked around, nodded toward the open curtains, which were letting some natural light into the room. "Now, that's better. You've been shutting yourself away too much. And you are working?"

"Trying to. News from Kathil is mostly depressing. I've also been turning over the idea of whether to send the Davion Assault

Guard or my Revenants back to Robinson to support any move of Tancred's."

"How long have you been working on that?"

"About one hundred eighteen turns," Victor said cryptically. "Why am I taking you to dinner?"

"Because you owe it to me, Victor Steiner-Davion. I'm here to collect on the debt you owe me from Mogyorod."

A chill swept through Victor's body. Mogyorod. Isis had come there to visit him and Omi not long before the assassin made his first attempt on Omi's life. The assassin had crept through the halls and kicked in the door to the bedroom Omi and Victor had shared. Fortunately, Victor had sent Tiaret to see Omi safely home that night. Isis had run into the ensuing firefight, and ended up stabbing the assassin in the chest with a letter opener. That bravery had cost her a shattered cheekbone and several days in the hospital. Victor had promised her—

"Anything I want," she reminded him. "You said I only had to ask. So, I'm asking. I want dinner. Tonight."

Victor thought about begging off, at least for one more day. Whatever Isis's agenda, he wasn't prepared for it. But the hard set of her brown eyes told him she would brook no argument.

"Now," she said with a curt nod.

It was her only real demand. She didn't complain about how long it took him to get ready or make him promise to enjoy himself. She had a car waiting out front to take them to Anthony's Seaport, a restaurant in town, and Victor assumed she'd managed to clear the plan through the security detail Morgan Kell had left behind. When they arrived, there were more diners than he'd expected, and that was the last he thought about the other patrons, for a while.

Isis ordered plank-roasted salmon and coconut-battered shrimp. Victor was undecided, and so she ordered him a seafood fettuccini. He wasn't really hungry, but when the food arrived, the mussels were meaty and the shrimp delicate and delicious, not to mention the tender noodles smothered in pungent garlic cream sauce. Throughout dinner, he sipped a white wine, from Hawkins Estates, of course. Isis left him alone until dessert, then watched him pick at a crème brûlée. He was still trying to decide whether he liked the caramelized cream when she sprang her ambush.

"I was there, you know."

He stared at his plate, refusing to look at her. "Where?"

"At the Palace of Serene Sanctuary, the day of Omi's death."

The crème brûlée turned bitter in Victor's mouth, and the lump in his throat made it hard to swallow. "I know." The food suddenly sat like a lead weight in his stomach.

"They wouldn't let me near her at first. Then an O5P initiate pulled me past security. I held her hands during her last few minutes." Her voice was distant, far away on the world of Luthien. "Victor, why have you never asked me about Omi?"

He expelled a long breath. "It's not that I don't value your thoughts, Isis. I do." He paused, thinking for a moment. "I haven't asked for the same reason I sent Jerry to Luthien rather than charge off myself. I'm avoiding learning the details of Omi's final moments. I really don't want to know."

Isis nodded, accepting but not understanding. "May I ask why?"

Victor sat rooted to his seat, feeling not much more animated than a garden statue. Which reminded him that Omi had died in her gardens, and that suddenly called up a memory of her face. She looked so lost, staring out into space, whispering, "Oh, Victor . . ."

He winced at the image, probably dredged up from one of their last meetings. His involuntary action broke the spell. "I don't ask because of my mother," he explained. "After she died, I delved into her assassination. I watched the video over and over and pored over all the reports. I made a royal ass of myself, I'm sure, but I felt like it was something I had to do to help with the investigation. The problem was that, for several years after, whenever I thought of her, I saw her torn apart by the explosion rather than as the vibrant, loving woman she had been until that moment."

"You don't want to remember Omi that way," Isis said gently. "You want to hold on to those final memories from

Mogyorod." He nodded, and she took a sip of her wine, barely enough to wet her lips. "Victor, you still could have asked me about the time I spent with her before that day. Or we could have remembered those few weeks we shared on Mogyorod. But you haven't wanted to talk."

"We've talked," Victor said, but the words sounded defensive to his own ears.

"We've talked about the civil war, but more like it's something happening to someone else. I think it's time you stopped talking about it and got back to fighting it."

That touched something inside Victor that reminded him of anger, or shame. "You think that, do you?"

She nodded. "We all do, Victor. You're so wrapped up in your own grief or spending what little ambition you've got left on battle reports for worlds other than ones you should be aiming for. I'm surprised you have enough energy left to dress yourself."

"I think Omi would forgive me taking time to grieve for her," he said, the pain still fresh, "even if some others wouldn't."

"Truly? Then explain to me why she didn't stop you from running off to prosecute this civil war. And tell me why you didn't return with her to Tukayyid."

Isis's words, spoken oh-so casually, stabbed into Victor like cold blades. He rose slowly, standing over the table and looking down on her with a tight expression. "What gives you the right to use Omi against me like this?"

"Not *what*, Victor. Who." She glanced sidelong. "They do."

Victor followed her gaze to the couple at the next table, who were pretending to hold a conversation of their own. They couldn't have heard much of what he and Isis were saying, but it was just as obvious that they were hanging on every gesture and what few words they did pick up. The family two tables beyond that didn't even try to hide their fascination. The man nodded, and his wife smiled hesitantly. Their children stared at Victor with wide-eyed expressions approaching worship. In fact, the entire restaurant—at least that section within direct sight—seemed to be holding its collective breath to see what the prince would do next.

Victor wondered if this was how a drunkard felt when finally forced to admit he "has a problem." "Stop this, Isis."

"No." She shook her head. "You need it." Her smile peeked out from somewhere between concern and encouragement. "Talk to them, Victor. They're your people."

Caught out, recognizing the truth in what she said, Victor could only nod back at a few of the nearby adults. He smiled at the children, then slowly sat back down. "I wouldn't know what to say," he told her.

Isis smiled again. "That's understandable, but you had better start thinking hard on the idea. You can't keep your presence here a secret from Katherine's loyalists for too much longer. Especially," she added, with a touch of apology, "after our little outing." Meaning that she hadn't cleared it with Morgan, or security. "Sooner or later, Victor, your people are going to start demanding some hard answers." She looked around at the expectant interest surrounding them. "And I think it will be sooner."

"You're not giving me much of a choice, are you?"

"Victor, you haven't had a choice since declaring war back on Mogyorod. You know that. No matter what Katherine does to you, no matter who else is lost to the fighting, you can't walk away now."

No, he couldn't. Victor knew that, too, though he had resisted thinking about it for the past several months. He'd needed the time to recover his equilibrium, but now that he had it back, there was only that first, fearful step to take. Doubts still plagued him, worrying at his confidence about what might happen if he pushed himself again and wasn't ready. Yet, Isis had fanned a flame from the dying embers, and he was suddenly more worried about what might happen in his absence or if he failed to act in time. It was a cold burning, not unlike the feeling that had prompted him to foment a civil war against Katherine's tyranny in the first place.

It was time, again.

"If you will excuse me," he said, pushing his chair back and half turning in his seat. "I should say a few words to our audience."

Isis glanced around at some of the waiting, watchful faces. "What are you going to tell them?"

"I think I'll start with a simple good-bye." Victor kept his voice low and even. "We'll be leaving Muphrid now, after all." He glanced back at Isis. "More than that, though, I'll be leaving Omi behind. Again." He closed his eyes and asked forgiveness of her memory. "As much as I am able to, at least. As before, I can't afford to take her with me."

"She would understand, Victor." Isis looked down at her hands. "She loved you that much."

"I know," Victor said, more to himself than to Isis. "And that's just what makes it so hard."

6

We put him to some of our very best people, using
the latest and most effective techniques, and still there
were some things we never learned. Like who he was,
and from where he'd originally come. Either he didn't
know himself, or he had long since devoured whatever
core of humanity he'd been born with.

—*Cause and Effect*, Avalon Press, 3067

Imperial City, Luthien
Pesht Military District
Draconis Combine
8 September 3065

After eight hours on his feet, walking the streets of Luthien's
Imperial City, the one who had stolen Naga Orano's life welcomed the sight of his modest home. A duplex, really, shared
with a man who likely worked for the Yakuza. Naga was careful never to know for sure, looking the other way and appreci-
ating the occasional gift left on his stoop or passed to him with
a handshake and a friendly smile. And if that handshake felt a
trifle odd for missing two joints on the right little finger, Naga
was careful not to notice. He was a simple officer for the civil
patrol. It wasn't his job to investigate the affairs of organized
crime. In Combine society, with its ancient Japanese philosophy of respectful courtesy, what you did not know for certain,
you did not know at all. A very helpful philosophy, all things
considered.

What Naga knew right then was that he was foot-weary and ready to call it a day. His brown uniform stuck to his skin in the late-summer humidity, and his knee hurt where a shoplifter had kicked him that morning. The taste of road dust coated his tongue and scratched at the back of his throat. He needed a hot shower and a cool drink. That would be enough, for now.

A small garden ran along the front of the duplex, and as Naga turned down the walk, he saw that his neighbor had been working in it again. A new white-pebble path curved around the jasmine bush and actually poked over onto his side, making one final turn around a fist-sized rock. A very familiar-looking rock. Veins of reddish-blue quartz winked in the sunlight, drawing his attention. The top of the rock looked stained with a greenish cast. If Naga were to pick it up, he'd expect to find an interesting trail of crystalline flakes embedded into the back side like a path of tiny glass flagstones. That rock could have come from anywhere. It could have meant anything.

What it meant right now was that he was no longer Naga Orano. He was the assassin who had killed Omi Kurita.

A key let him in the front door. He tossed his cap onto a nearby chair and moved directly for a shoji screen that rested near a wall. The painted screen displayed a dragon cowering under an outcropping of red rock as a yellow bird flew overhead. The assassin had thought it an amusing coincidence that the real Naga Orano had owned such an item. According to Combine folklore, the yellow bird was the only enemy of the dragon.

Behind the screen was a connecting door to his neighbor's half of the home. In the year and a half he had lived here, the assassin had never had cause to open it. There hadn't even been a key, though he'd made one soon enough. Now he pulled that key from his pocket and used it to leave behind his latest assumed identity. Once through the door, he locked it behind him, then moved to his neighbor's bedroom to strip out of his uniform and to dress out of the new closet. He kept only Naga's civil patrol shield, shoved deep into one pocket. A stop in the bathroom— he peeled away the fake burn scars that turned one side of his face into a plastic ruin and added a touch of iron gray to the dark hair at each temple.

It wasn't his best disguise, but speed counted for more than perfection right now. The assassin left by the front door, pausing to sneak another glance at the offending stone while pretending to retie his bootlace. From this angle, it looked mostly innocent. Then he strolled quickly up the walk and turned to follow the street toward the local commercial district.

It was too much of a coincidence that such a stone would be planted in front of his Luthien home. The assassin's plan to kill Omi Kurita had hinged on that stone—or a very similar one. A plan that was two years in the making. He had discovered a means to infiltrate her Palace of Serene Sanctuary, slipping past the Order of the Five Pillars, who were its caretakers and who ran their own offices from the palace. The O5P had forever maintained tight security, until Theodore Kurita's reforms demanded a better working relationship between O5P agents and his Internal Security Force. ISF agents took several dozen billets at the palace. The instant rivalry caused no end of friction, and it is a known concept of physics that friction leads to wear. In this case, security suffered. The ISF routinely disrupted the tranquility of the order, and O5P agents most often pretended that the ISF was either absent or incompetent. If the ISF stationed a guard, O5P placed a second one. They shared the palace dojo, but opposing agents never worked out at the same time. This level of disregard carried over to new agents as well, allowing the assassin access to the palace in one of his most daring roles ever.

Once inside, observation of Omi Kurita's routine had yielded several avenues of possible termination, but only one with close to a hundred percent guarantee of reaching the target. A simple stone, planted in her gardens. The story was well known among the palace residents, whispered from one to another so as never to embarrass the lady Omi. She had given that stone to Victor Davion, who had properly named it. He later asked her to plant it in her palace gardens, among the roses and nasturtiums he himself had tended during a former stay on Luthien. No one was to disturb the Warrior's Path stone. Omi visited it often.

By lightly upsetting the stone, the assassin had guaranteed to draw Omi Kurita's attention. When she stepped among the flowers to adjust it, her touch triggered the device he had carefully concealed, and poisoned darts stung outward. Only one had to find flesh; Omi had actually been struck by two. Paralysis set in at once, quickly leading to heart arrythmia and then death.

In any other assassination, he would already have been off-world and halfway to safety by the time Omi Kurita stopped breathing. In the Draconis Combine, there was no such avenue of escape. He had predicted, accurately, that Theodore Kurita would close the borders and all but paralyze his own nation in an attempt to secrete the news *and* to find his daughter's killer. The assassin had had two advantages, though. First was the immediate shadow war that sprang up between the O5P and ISF, hampering the intelligence gathering of both organizations. Second was the old axiom that prey always distinguishes itself through movement, and he was not going anywhere. His next identity—taking the place of a civil patrolman laid up in hospital after being caught in a house fire—had already been selected.

For the extravagant sum Katrina Steiner-Davion had promised and paid for this assassination, for the successful conclusion of such a difficult and crowning achievement, the assassin had resigned himself to two years of quiet living on Luthien, right under the eyes of those who were hunting him. He sat in on meetings where pictures of his old face were handed around, and three weeks ago had even shaken hands with the visiting *gaijin* Victor Davion sent to Luthien to assist in the investigation. The man had stared right through him, despite previous statements that he was sure the assassin had never left Luthien. This Galen Cox wasn't looking very hard. In fact, by all appearances, Coordinator Kurita kept him busy with lectures and paperwork investigation, never allowing him to actually *hunt*.

This series of mistakes helped the assassin now. Following his carefully rehearsed escape plan, he turned in to a noodle shop, one of the first places to present itself. It smelled of old grease and hot spices, and he ordered bento with extra sauce. While they dished it into a paper bowl, he used the payphone to call a cab, giving a street address on the next block over. He dug Naga's badge out from his pocket, flashed it to the woman at the counter, and, bowl in hand, exited through the kitchen and out the back door.

It opened onto a protected alley, where the assassin dumped the meal into a nearby trash bin while checking the area for any surveillance. Nothing he could see. He crossed the alley and entered another restaurant by the back door, again using the badge to send kitchen help back to work. From the front door of this restaurant, he saw the cab waiting for him, two buildings down on his left, in front of a small hostel. The assassin turned right and flagged down a passing rickshaw. A veteran, the driver slowed his scooter just enough for his passenger to mount without the need to coast his cart to a complete stop.

"Museum of Industrial Art," the assassin told the driver. The man nodded and gunned the throttle as he slipped into traffic.

So close. Another six months and Naga Orano would have saved enough from his salary to afford an offworld vacation. The assassin could have easily disappeared anywhere in the course of that trip. He hadn't been given a choice, though. Coincidence or cause, he'd been set running earlier than planned. Now his route would pass from the museum to the park and a new disguise, then to another restaurant and finally to the spaceport. From there, it was a short hop between Imperial City and the cities of either Shunari or Hokado. Only then, if it looked right and *felt* right, would he change faces and lives again and make his attempt to flee Luthien on an outbound DropShip.

Running was always a problem. Running now was dangerous, but then, he was a most dangerous man. The assassin settled back into the rickshaw seat, carefully watching the passing crowds.

Anyone who got too close would find that out.

7

There is no "best" kind of warfare, unless it is the kind of war where no one is hurt and disputes are settled without violence. Some people call that peace. Civil war, however, is actually the worst kind of war—a destructive conflagration that consumes the state, pitching brother against sister and father against son.
—*Cause and Effect*, Avalon Press, 3067

Castle Sandoval
Granite Falls, Robinson
Draconis March
Federated Suns
7 October 3065

The stretch sedan followed a long road up to Castle Sandoval, approaching the gray stone edifice in a roundabout manner meant to show off the extensive grounds. Robinson's early autumn had nearly finished with the tree-lined drive, and the sedan's passing swept dead leaves into its wake, making them dance with haunted life. Ignoring the approach to the castle, Tancred Sandoval stared out through the rear window for a time, watching the rust-colored leaves chase each other back to rest. This wasn't going to be easy.

As if reading his mind, Yvonne Steiner-Davion touched his knee and squeezed with just enough pressure to remind him that he would not face this alone. He laid a hand over hers, shifting in his seat to face forward again. His younger cousin, Dorann

Sandoval, sat in one of the sedan's rear-facing seats and looked up through the sunroof.

"That would be Mai," Dorann said, nodding at the VTOL that raced by overhead.

A *Kestrel,* Tancred guessed, though he couldn't be sure. The VTOL was a dark blur through the skeletal canopy of tree limbs, and so many of the rotor-propelled craft looked the same from below. He let his gaze wander back out the side window just as the sedan turned the last corner, bringing into full view the magnificent castle that had been the Sandovals' estate on Robinson for fifteen generations. It seemed darkened, somehow. Forbidding. Tancred shifted uneasily. He had rehearsed this in his mind a hundred times since receiving his aunt's summons, but now that he was here, it was all happening too fast.

There had been no parade inspections to greet Tancred's return home this trip. No social event to show him off as heir to Robinson and the Draconis March. His DropShip grounded without fanfare, and his cousin met him and Yvonne with a chauffeured stretch sedan. There was a definite family resemblance between Tancred and Dorann Sandoval. They shared the same china-pale skin and oil-dark hair, though Dorann's was long and plaited where Tancred's was shaved into the topknot that was the custom on Robinson. Both stood tall and slender, and they might have been taken for brother and sister by anyone not familiar with the extensive Sandoval dynasty.

Dorann had kissed Tancred on the cheek and embraced him, but she seemed to lack for energy. Her greeting to Yvonne was formal and solemn. "Grandmother is expecting you at the castle," was her only immediate comment.

Dorann was referring, of course, to Countess Jessica Sandoval-Groell, her grandmother and Tancred's aunt. It was significant that *she,* and not his father, the Duke Robinson, was expecting him.

"The rest of the family?" he'd asked.

"Most of them will be there," Dorann promised with a shallow nod. "Enough." A slight pause, pregnant with caution. "Mai

Fortuna is also on Robinson. She's in residence at the Rangers' command post and has promised to meet with you tomorrow."

"Not good enough," Tancred said, then nodded at the sedan's visphone. "Call ahead to the castle and make certain Mai is there *before* I arrive. Tell them to make it happen."

Apparently, they did. The VTOL made the rooftop landing pad before the sedan rolled to a stop in the middle of a large courtyard. When the chauffeur opened the door, Tancred stepped out with a glance into the gray overcast sky, which hung like a dark omen over his ancestral home. He brushed his uniform straight, then extended a hand to assist first Yvonne and then Dorann from the back of the sedan. As they ascended the marble steps of the castle, Yvonne's hand rode lightly on Tancred's right arm while his cousin followed behind. Except for her red hair, Yvonne so resembled her mother that she might have been Melissa Steiner's double. More so even than Katherine, who played up the similarities at every opportunity, while Yvonne was content to be herself. It was a quality Tancred had always found endearing.

"Here we go," he said in a stage whisper as they crossed the vestibule. Already he felt the eyes of servants and aides boring into him from any number of hidden vantage points.

His relations waited in the drawing room. They were knights and ladies of the realm, a baron and baroness, and the countess. Eight nobles, which constituted a quorum in the Sandoval dynasty. There were no joyous welcome wishes or congratulatory hails. All of them were treating the occasion with the solemnity it deserved.

Jessica Sandoval-Groell was the only one to approach. She clasped Tancred by both hands, and he gave her a dutiful kiss on the cheek.

"Where is he?" he asked quietly.

The countess's flint-gray eyes were lively despite her years. She glanced toward the closed doors of the nearby library. "You have obligations before you talk to your father," she reminded him.

Tancred shook his head. "He is still Duke Robinson. I won't do this to him until I see for myself."

Letting Yvonne fall a step behind, Tancred transferred one of his aunt's hands to his arm and led her across the drawing room. The others trailed after, drawn along in his wake like the leaves he'd seen dancing on the road.

The library sat deserted, but beyond it, the doors stood open into his father's study, now converted into his newest war room. General Mai Fortuna, a distaff cousin and commander of the Robinson Rangers, stood respectfully to one side of the door. Tancred ignored her for the man in the wheelchair, his father, Duke James Dassert Sandoval. The Duke of the Draconis March had pulled himself half out of his seat to get a better look at a star chart he was examining. Iron-gray hair ringed his balding pate; that, and the amber eyes both men shared was about all that Tancred truly recognized in his father. Gone were his formidable presence and strong voice, and the convictions he had let shine through his strong features even in the worst of times. James Sandoval looked old and spent, his body a dying shadow of its former strength. When Tancred came in, it took the duke a moment to focus on his only son, and when recognition finally bloomed, it was tinged with anxiety.

"Tancred. You've brought word from Ashio? We have driven back the Combine?"

So, it was worse than Tancred had feared, despite his aunt's letter of warning. "The First Robinson Rangers gave up Ashio last year, Father." Tancred's voice was soft but not pitying. "Mai led them back to Mallory's World. Proserpina is all we have left."

The duke shook his head. "A trick," he said adamantly, a touch of his former strength coloring his cheeks. "All a Drac trick."

Not a trick, Tancred knew, but a reprisal. He stood next to his father and looked down at the chart, saw the force lines being drawn from Combine space back into the Federated Suns' Draconis March. He remembered the day, almost three years ago now, when Arthur Steiner-Davion had been killed shortly after graduating from the military academy on Robinson. It was Arthur's death that finally convinced Victor to launch his civil war against Katherine, though Tancred's father had immediately blamed House Kurita. Whether he truly believed that or not, he had used it as an excuse to launch several hard probes across the border. Soon, the March forces controlled or contested seven important Kurita worlds. Those initial successes were heady wine for the Sandovals, longtime stewards of the Draconis March. But as the Dragon turned its head toward them, several reversals sent their forces reeling. Now only the Combine world of Proserpina was in Sandoval hands while the Combine's counterassault had claimed at least four worlds in the Federated Suns: Cassias, Addicks, Breed, and Kessai IV.

It was this failure to prosecute his private war against House Kurita that eventually broke James Sandoval, though Tancred had to wonder how much his own desertion had contributed to his father's condition. If he'd remained to help shoulder some of the responsibility rather than adding to his father's burdens . . .

He gave himself a mental shake, knowing he couldn't afford such thoughts. Besides, he would make the same choices even if he had to do it all over again.

And now? "I'm home, Father. As I promised." There was no forgiveness in Tancred's voice, especially as he recalled that last meeting where his father had all but challenged his son, and he had pushed back.

"That's good, boy. Very good. I should bring you up to date on where we are in the fighting and our plans to continue."

Tancred shook his head firmly. "I can handle that for now. Mai will help me." He reminded his father of the general's presence, still waiting at attention by the door. "You should rest now."

Looking beyond Tancred and Mai, James Sandoval gazed at the assembly crowded into the rear of his study. Doubt clouded his once-strong features, but he nodded. "Yes. Yes, I will rest now." He eased back into the wheelchair. "It is good to have you home, Tancred. There is much to do, much to do."

Dorann moved forward without being asked. "Uncle, let me

help you." She took the wheelchair handles, but mostly for steering. James Sandoval propelled himself well enough.

He had strength, but not direction, Tancred thought. His aunt Jessica nodded slowly. "For the greater good of the Draconis March, Tancred."

Tancred returned the nod, then gave Yvonne his arm as he led her on a tour of the room. She had offered to remain on the DropShip, but Tancred wanted no illusions regarding his return. Yvonne's presence would confirm to the rest of the Sandoval family where his ultimate loyalties lay, and they would not follow his father's previous endorsement of Katherine. So, when each of his eight relatives nodded to Tancred as he passed, supporting him, investing in him the power of the Draconis March, they also, through Yvonne, promised their support to Victor. It was the first thing today that sat perfectly at ease with the new Duke Robinson. Victor had lost the Federated Suns when Katherine stole it from Yvonne, who was serving as his regent at the time.

Justice demanded that she help restore it to her brother.

His last moment was with Mai Fortuna, who stood her ground proudly. Tancred expected no apologies for her actions, and he knew she expected no leniency. "Dorann told me you arrived with the Second Robinson Rangers," she said.

Now that he had recognized her, Mai wasted no time in reporting. "The First Rangers are in no shape to move off Mallory's World. The Robinson Academy Battalion never made it off Ashio." The loss of so many good soldiers hurt them both, Tancred knew. Mai was a consummate officer, and had been following the orders of her duke, but Tancred had predicted the bad ending to such an invasion and had warned her of the consequences. "I stand under your judgment, Duke Sandoval."

Hearing his father's title attached to him, Tancred smiled wanly. This was not the way he had expected to come to power. It was never what he wanted, only what was necessary. And that included how he would handle Mai Fortuna.

"I am promoting you," he said, though his tone belied any illusion that this was a reward. "I may be Duke Robinson now, but you are still the better general, Mai. The March needs its best right now, and perhaps for years to come. As a marshal of the Draconis March, you are answerable only to me. You will head my strategy and logistics center."

"Strategy and . . ." Words failed her as the implications rolled over Mai Fortuna.

Tancred nodded. "Planning and support. For what you did to the Rangers, I can never again allow you to lead troops into battle. You are removed from the chain of command, Mai. Not exactly disgraced, but you are dispossessed."

The word snapped her head back like a violent slap. To lose the privilege of piloting a BattleMech was the greatest fear of most MechWarriors. Mai had no doubt expected forced retirement. To keep her active in the military, but remove her from direct command, was perhaps the more cruel punishment. Tancred watched as she debated a resignation. Then, as he'd expected, his citing the needs of the March drew her back to his side. She nodded, then half bowed to Yvonne as well. "I will do what I can, for as long as I can." She paused, glancing from Yvonne to Tancred. "Victor may demand my head to hand over to Theodore."

"He can't have you," Tancred said.

"You told me once that whoever won the civil war—whether it was Katherine or Victor—would require someone to answer for the unsanctioned attacks against House Kurita. Who will you give him?"

"No one. I'll make peace with Theodore Kurita however I must." Tancred reached out to lay a hand on Mai's arm. "If Victor has demands, they will have to be for something other than family."

"What else will you give him?"

Tancred picked up a stylus and turned back to the star charts his father had been working over. With slow precision, he traced a line from Robinson down through New Valencia and then on to New Avalon. He glanced up at his cousin and senior general, and saw on her face that she understood exactly what he meant to do.

"Everything else he needs," he promised.

8

I never doubted that we would someday lay claim to all the evidence necessary to bring Katherine to justice. I had good people pursuing it at a risk beyond our normal standing. All we required was opportunity and time. We manufactured the former. We ran out of the latter.

—*Cause and Effect,* Avalon Press, 3067

Davion Palace
Avalon City, New Avalon
Crucis March
Federated Suns
20 November 3065

Katrina met with her intelligence liaison in the Office of the First Princess, leaving him standing on the other side of her desk while she scanned through economic reports on the monetary costs of the civil war. A gas-fed flame burned ceramic logs in the fireplace, warming the room. Outside, a heavy wind battered sleet against the office's ferroglass window, a reminder that winter was not quite finished with New Avalon's southern hemisphere. Spring would come late. Though still a few months in advance of a Terran-standard year, it wouldn't happen soon enough for Katrina.

As she finished each electronic file, she used a stylus to check the item off her noteputer. "The fighting on Tikonov alone has cost over two billion kroner in damages and lost production," she said aloud, trying to convince herself of the number.

The comment was not intended to start conversation, but Richard Dehaver took it as such. "Certainly that is not the worst in damages."

She found the worst entry, shook her head. "It will be hard for another world to top Kathil. Three regiments and one full RCT destroyed so far. Lost production at the 'Mech factories. Civilian damages." She stabbed the stylus against the touch-sensitive screen, deleting the item. "And one *Avalon*-class cruiser—a WarShip!—destroyed." The *Robert Davion* was not the only WarShip destroyed in fighting, but it was the newest and most expensive to date.

Katrina sat back, massaged her temples for a moment with the heels of her palms. Giving it up as futile, she dropped her hands back to the desktop and toyed with the gold bracelet she wore around her right wrist, thinking. "You brought news of New Syrtis?" she asked, finally looking up at her intelligence aide.

Richard Dehaver stood easily, his casual suit tailored perfectly to his wide shoulders. Red hair and a freckled nose lent his face a boyish cast until you looked into his eyes. Brackish green, they were flat and lifeless, like staring into a dark pond. Eyes that had seen much in their time with the Ministry of Intelligence and how held back many secrets. "I do have news concerning New Syrtis," Dehaver admitted carefully, "but I was going to let Simon Gallagher bring it to you."

Which meant that Katrina would not like it, no matter who brought it to her. "How bad?" she asked.

"Fighting on New Syrtis is hard-pitched but favoring George Hasek. Gallagher's plan to buy the Vanguard Legion's loyalty away from Hasek has also proven overly optimistic. They . . . refused."

In colorful terms, no doubt. She brushed away her anger and pride, writing the mercenaries off as unimportant in the larger scheme. "Anything else?"

Dehaver nodded. "Your operative from the Rabid Fox covert teams failed. He rushed the duke's office and met with more armed resistance than he could handle."

Katrina raised a dangerous eyebrow. She had not told Dehaver about her order to the Rabid Foxes, hoping to remove George Hasek quickly and quietly, but then Dehaver often had a way of finding out things she didn't want him to know. If only he had discovered Victor on Muphrid, before her brother had come out of hiding and left the world of his own volition, *then* they might have had something to talk about. "For a man who came here on other business, you are remarkably well-informed."

Dehaver's expression was impassive. "That is all part of my job, Highness."

She leaned forward, hands clasped on the desktop. "Why are you here, Richard?"

"Reg Starling."

Katrina stared back at him. Dehaver was one of very few people to actually know that Starling was an assumed identity for Sven Newmark, an old business associate of hers who had also been in the employ of her cousin Ryan Steiner. Victor had ordered Ryan's death after learning of his connection to their mother's assassination, but if there had been any hard evidence of the contract itself, it had disappeared with Newmark. Sven Newmark later adopted a new life as Reg Starling, making a name for himself as one of the Alliance's most controversial artists. This was all before Katrina came to power, of course, and she had never bothered much about Newmark, aka Starling. When a report landed on her desk telling her that Starling had been "removed" for subversive efforts, she thought of him even less.

Until his resurrection.

In May of the previous year, Dehaver had brought her news that the artist had come out with a new and ongoing series of paintings. Entitled the *Bloody Princess* series, they targeted Katrina directly as the subject of many controversial compositions. Which was a pleasant way of saying that Starling portrayed her as a bloodthirsty tyrant. Then, just six months ago, he had sent a copy of his final painting to her with a blackmail note painted on the back of the canvas, demanding ten million kroner for his silence and permanent disappearance. Katrina had the copy locked away here in her office. She didn't need to look at it to see it. The painting was impressed perfectly into memory.

It showed her as a withered crone trying to wear two gaudy crowns and with blackened stumps in place of her perfect, white teeth. In one clawlike hand, she squeezed blood from a dying world, in the other she worked the puppeteer rods of a marionette. The marionette could only be Reg Starling himself, wielding a red-crusted painter's knife and using a second blade to saw at the strings that bound him to his evil mistress. And he was not being hauled out of a box, but from a coffin at graveside. The tombstone in the background was actually a blank spot of canvas, inked in with gray and lettered very carefully to read SVEN NEWMARK, 12 MARCH '36 TO ???

Katrina forced herself to speak normally. "You told me before that you were convinced Reg Starling was still alive. If you are bringing this to me again, can I assume that you have proven yourself in error or that Reg Starling has been apprehended?"

"Neither, Highness. Though not for lack of trying. As you may remember, this man has a gift for disappearing when he doesn't want to be found."

"Why should I remember anything about Starling or Newmark?" Katrina asked, furious with her intelligence chief. "I would prefer to forget they ever existed at all. So what *have* you done to aid me in this?"

Dehaver was unflappable. "I've been looking into the events surrounding your mother's assassination," he said easily.

Katrina contemplated him coldly. "Why would you do that, Richard?"

"If Reg Starling *is* Sven Newmark, he most certainly was involved. Now he's trying to implicate you. It would be useful to know what corroborating evidence exists. If any."

Katrina noted that Dehaver was not asking for the truth, but for any evidence. "So?" she asked calmly. "What did you find?"

"I found a land-sale scam that put twenty million kroner in someone's pocket around the same time as Melissa Steiner's death."

Katrina felt like someone had just knocked the wind out of her. "You . . . what?"

"The year of your mother's death, the Federated Commonwealth issued a tax credit to a corporation in the amount of twenty million kroner. That's how much Reg Starling claims was paid for the assassin. The details of the tax break are a matter of public record. The corporation paid the twenty million for near-worthless wetlands, bought from an 'unspecified source.' The property was then donated to the Commonwealth for reclamation as a nature preserve, and a tax credit issued for the full amount."

Katrina nodded. "You make a good case against the corporation, Richard. Not me."

"Except that the CEO was later ennobled and given a land grant, at your recommendation. That could satisfy a quid pro quo argument."

Katrina remembered that. She waved off her agent's implication. "That was a public relations decision."

"It is suspicious, Highness."

"But it is not evidence. Not unless this 'unspecified source' is somehow tied to my mother's assassination."

"Those records have been lost, Highness. Very deliberately and carefully lost."

"You're worried that Reg Starling has those records and will support your theory? Whatever Reg Starlings has, I'm certain they're faked. We'll prove that, *if* they ever turn up."

"Of course, Highness." Dehaver waited, watching Katrina most carefully, expecting an order.

Instead, Katrina asked, "What progress have you made in locating this Reg Starling?"

"He's on New Avalon. We know this from the artist he paid to make a copy of his last work."

"Perhaps that is a ruse designed to throw you off the scent."

"No," Dehaver said quickly. "I believe he wants us to know he's here. Watching." He paused. "It's been so long since he contacted us that I'm beginning to wonder if his blackmail scam isn't a cover for a more deadly game. I'm increasing your security, Highness. No exposed events until he's captured."

Katrina worked around the edges of her nerves, deciding how far she should go to approach this blackmailer who *claimed* to have solid evidence implicating her. But maybe he did have something fabricated. Sven Newmark had been a most resourceful man.

"Starling might have something that is useful to us. As misguided and dangerous as he is, I can't overlook the fact that he might be able to shed more light on my mother's assassination." She came to a decision. "Gather the ten million he is asking for, Richard. If we have to, we'll use it to lure him into our hands. Bring him into the open. Let's see just what he thinks he knows."

Half a world away from the Davion Palace, Francesca Jenkins walked around the Provost Gallery with her silent companion, showing interest in the works of any neoclassic artist. They had waited a full hour to talk of anything significant, until certain they had not been followed. It was a routine similar to one they had observed every day since making planetfall on New Avalon. At times, Francesca wondered if she could ever go back to a seminormal life where she didn't have to wonder if a man's quick glance of interest wasn't the prelude to his pulling out a weapon and trying to kill her.

"I'm worried about this," she said finally, cuddling back into the encircling arms of Agent Curaitis as they pretended to enjoy a tortured representation of Sun-Tzu Liao's Celestial Palace. With twenty centimeters on her, Curaitis stood with his chin resting on the back of her head, the image of an affectionate boyfriend, husband, or lover, while getting a good look around. Only the lack of any real comfort in his arms, the awkward way in which he held her, denied that there was anything between them but a few years of sexual tension from living in close quarters and more than one adrenaline-laced evening.

"It will work," he promised.

"You've done this just as many times as I have," she reminded him.

In fact, it was on this mission that the two of them had been introduced and became a team, both of them working for Victor Davion to gather evidence against his sister. Francesca had been assigned to Reg Starling, trying to get him to reveal his secrets. And he did, though only after his death at the hands of Katherine's agents. The package Starling had left for Francesca gave Victor his first hard evidence against Katherine. If it could be proven. They needed to establish a provenance, which Newmark alias Starling could no longer do. Not directly, anyway.

Resurrecting Reg Starling was a complex mission, but with the help of a master forger and Curaitis's bag of tricks, they had pulled it off. For two years they worked the charade, careful not to arouse suspicion by moving too quickly. Now they were finally playing directly to Katherine's paranoia with their blackmail scam. The more direct evidence they compiled on her attempts to cover up Starling's evidence, or if she ever tried to simply pay him off, the more legal weight they stockpiled. Katherine herself would end up validating the evidence to be used against her.

Francesca pulled Curaitis along to another display. "We've never released sketches before. It's not in character. Reg always destroyed his sketches."

"Symons sold some from Upano last year. That establishes a precedent."

"But not a very good one," she said, frowning at the memory. Valerius Symons was the forger they had paid to create the *Bloody Princess* series, and who was now "vacationing" under the watchful care of Heimdall. "The man was greedy, and it could have cost us the entire sting."

"And you can be certain that the odd occurrence has been noted by Katherine's people." Curaitis squeezed her hand, offering some limited comfort. "By doing so again, we gain two things. First, it tells them that the last time was no mistake, but a careful move to draw extra attention to the *Bloody Princess* series. Which it did."

"Thank the fates that the *great* Valerius does good work," she agreed.

"Second, it puts more pressure on Katherine here and now.

Once it gets out that there may be a connection between her, Starling, and Newmark, scandal vids and gossip will do the rest."

Francesca stopped in front of the next display, a new piece by S. Lewis, and seized the chance to stare up at Curaitis. His dark eyes remained fixed on the artwork, an atrocious rendering of a JumpShip against a twisted, warped spacescape. His eyes never once sought her out. "If we do this now, when do we make our final move?" she asked.

"Six months," he said. "Maybe longer. The speed is set by Katherine's agents."

Francesca wrinkled her face in distaste, thinking about all the time ticking past. Another gallery patron, just passing by, looked over and nodded support for what he assumed was Francesca's critique. The painting was *that* bad. They moved on to the piece they had both wanted to see on the wall: a copy of Reg Starling's *Bloody Princess VIII*. If the last painting made her almost physically ill, this one might have tempted Francesca with mental unbalance. It showed a twisted caricature of Katherine clawing her own eyes out and squeezing them to water a pot of flowers with the blood and pulp. The flowers were *mycosia pseudoflora*, favorites of Melissa Steiner-Davion that had been used to camouflage the bomb that had killed her. It helped harden Francesca's heart to occasionally view her target, even by proxy, and be reminded that the sacrifices were worth their goal.

"I suppose," she said softly, laying her head back against Curaitis's chest as if fawning over her man, "if there is at least *some* public attention, that makes it harder for her to ever say she was not aware of the situation, *or* the implications."

"Potential legal weight," Curaitis said, and his eyes flickered just briefly to find hers. Troubled, they looked away again. "That's a third reason. Are we go?"

They did nothing without being in agreement, one of the reasons their partnership had worked so well. She nodded, still leaning against him. "We're go," she said. "Let's start the countdown, and hope that next year is Katherine's last one in power."

9

Loyalty, despite the popular saying, cannot be won
or lost. It gives back in equal measure whatever you put
into it. And if it sometimes turns a blind eye to our
human failings, well, often that is when it is needed
most.

—*Cause and Effect*, Avalon Press, 3067

Sandstain Plateau, Thorin
Freedom Theater
Lyran Alliance
24 January 3066

After running for half a day before the determined sweep of
the First Alarion Jaegers, Brevet-Precentor Shakov saw no reason for Morgan Kell to order the Prince's Men to hold fast on
the Sandstain Plateau. A poorer chunk of Thorin real estate he
had yet to see. It was large and it was flat, which gave almost
all the advantages to the larger force. The Jaegers claimed that
honor, with nearly two full battalions of 'Mechs deployed. The
244th countered with speed and superior coordination and not
a little bluff as Shakov's men managed time and again to
bloody the loyalists' noses before dodging away. It made the
Lyran force a touch overcautious, which was the only reason
this skirmish had lasted as long as it had. Neither side wanted
to expose itself, knowing that one mistake could turn the entire
battle.

Shakov was not about to make that mistake. From fighting

the Jaegers on York and again on Tikonov, he knew their best strategy relied on bogging an opponent down with their rapid deployment of armor and mechanized infantry. Once that happened, they slipped heavy 'Mech assets onto the flank or into the rear, and it was all over. Today, Shakov was teaching the Jaegers' CO, Colonel Hoffman, the value of a highly mobile screening force. With good flatland to work with, he kept a fast armor company out on his distant flanks to harass and pin down any attempt to get around his line.

"New contact, eastern line," one of his armor commanders reported. "Four heavy 'Mechs, angling west-sou'west."

Shakov traded some long-range fire with a Lyran *Penetrator*, coming out on the worse end of the deal as the *Penetrator*'s large lasers worked him over. One slashed a bright scarlet beam past his cockpit canopy, stabbing into his left shoulder and missing his ferroglass shield by half a meter. He let fly a new set of missiles, the dirty gray exhaust cloud rolling off to his left side. Then he angled away from the *Penetrator* while ordering up a pair of Burke tanks to threaten it with better firepower.

"Kevin, stop-gap that *Penetrator* if those Burkes don't push him back. Mind the line for me." Shakov pivoted his *Exterminator* and chased his battle partner into the backfield. Watching Tiaret's graceful leaps, her Elemental battlesuit covering dozens of meters with each determined bound, he wondered how other MechWarriors had ever taken to calling Clan Elementals "toads."

Demi Bills ran his rebuilt *Raijin* up into the gap. "Don't take too long, Precentor Shakov. The Jaegers are massing for a new push."

Or they wanted the Prince's Men to think so. Blinking through his preset frequencies, Shakov found Demi-Precentor Dutchell, who commanded Shakov's eastern armor assets. "Dutchell, I want you to swing wide from that lance and let them past. Find someone else to busy yourselves with for a few minutes. Let their plan work this time!"

Dutchell copied the order and danced his hovercraft in to engage a mixed company of Jaeger infantry and heavy armor.

Shakov would let them be delayed just long enough to allow those 'Mechs into a killing zone. Then, he would call back the armor to hammer in from behind while his own team and a few others acted as the anvil. A quick, sound plan, except for the trio of *Fenrir* battlesuits that leapt into the fray against Demi Dutchell and his tank column. For a moment, the loyalist strategy came within a shaved coin of actually working, stalling the faster armor while another lance of 'Mechs drove onto the Com Guard flank.

"Blake's blood," Shakov cursed, "what are we doing out here?" He turned his lance in at the Jaegers, pressing them back on the eastern flank before the Lyrans did the same to him. "Buy them some time," he called out on a general channel.

A pair of new *Stiletto*s ran in too close, and Shakov tied both lasers and missiles into his main trigger. The barrage worked through the left-flank armor on one of the lighter 'Mechs, and then one of his rare jumping Kanga tanks bounced in to core through the *Stiletto*'s missile-storage casing. Destructive energy tore through the machine's entire right side, erupting in a large fireball out the back as cellular construction materials channeled the explosion away from the fusion reactor. Still, that kind of raw force was never easy to walk away from. The MechWarrior lost control of his machine, which spun around in a quick pirouette before slamming facedown into the hard-packed earth. A pair of Com Guard Zephyrs skated in with lasers and short-range missiles, making a run right past the downed *Stiletto*. It didn't get back up.

"We're free," Dutchell called out. "Eight machines ready to kick you in the side, Precentor."

Shakov nodded. "Too many for us to turn against *and* keep up the line," he said. "Prepare to fall back to new coordinates following." He swore again, under his breath this time. "Morgan Kell wanted us out here for some reason. Anyone else have an idea?" Silence greeted him for a long set of heartbeats.

Then a new voice said, "I might."

Shakov hadn't expected an answer. Especially not in *that* voice. He could tell by the strength of the call, powerful enough to cause a crackle of squelched static, that the transmission did not come direct 'Mech-to-'Mech—not by anyone using Com-Star equipment anyway. It had to be a signal bounced off a satellite. Or a DropShip.

"Heads up," he called out with a sudden burst of enthusiasm, running his *Exterminator* forward at its best speed of nearly one hundred kph. "We're about to have company."

Tiaret had already fastened herself to the shoulder of the second *Stiletto*, digging into its armor like a black tick biting onto a large gray dog. Shakov chased after them, trailing the *Stiletto* back toward its own lines, leading forward a full Level I unit of 'Mechs and armor. No one fired on the light 'Mech, leaving it to Tiaret. A flurry of brilliant energy pocked and sliced at the *Exterminator*, which Shakov returned with savage accuracy. Two of his medium lasers stabbed into the head of a nearby *Falconer*, staggering the seventy-five-ton machine. It turned on its left foot and stumbled away, the pilot obviously shaken.

Morgan's choice of the plateau made more sense now. It would be an easy feature to recognize from orbit and a natural landing site. Shakov glanced up through his ferroglass shield, found twin hard points of light falling down right over the top of the Alarion Jaegers. At what had to be a three-gravity braking burn, it took only a few seconds for that first falling star to transform into the bright drive flare underneath an *Overlord*-class DropShip. "From here, it looks like you're falling a bit off course," Shakov said then, reminded of a similar situation from the very start of the civil war. Only then he'd been one of those in the DropShip. "That's the Jaegers' side of this battle."

Victor Davion apparently remembered that day as well. "Sorry. We assumed you would be on the winning side of the fight."

Nearly the same words Shakov had spoken to Victor as the Prince's Men dropped onto Newtown Square at the start of the war. One set of the DropShip's massive hangar doors slid apart, and before they fully opened, a *Centurion* had already jumped free of the descending vessel to sail down on its own jump jets. Another trio of BattleMechs, all painted the same ivory and gold, bounded out behind it, one after another. The *Overlord*'s massive array of weaponry stabbed down from the sky after them, raining destruction over the Alarion position. "We'll stick with what we have, though," Victor said. "You're the hammer, and we're the anvil."

Forgetting the optical-selection technology at his disposal, Shakov simply slapped at the toggle that cut his communications system over to the 244th's all-hands frequency. The news was too good not to share.

"In case you aren't paying attention," he said, commanding the ear of the entire division, "Prince Victor just arrived. Clear this landing field—and, people, I mean now."

With a pair of *Overlord*s dropping behind them and the Prince's Men pushing from the fore, the Alarion Jaegers were not about to entrench and get caught in such a crossfire. Victor watched from a bridge monitor as Kai Allard-Liao dropped his 'Mech into the loyalists' backfield, leading a full lance of his St. Ives Cavalry. They didn't do much more than play herald to his arrival, though, trading a few long-distance lasers and some light autocannon fire before the Jaegers surrendered the field and pulled off to the northwest.

Kai decided to remain on patrol, heading up the security perimeter being drawn around Victor's temporary base of operations. Trusting his friend's "all clear," Victor took a lift down to the *Overlord*'s main hangar. Prometheus, Victor's Clan-designed *Daishi*, was the only 'Mech left to the cavernous bay by then, racked into its maintenance alcove. The hundred-ton assault machine was as ready for combat as only a six-month overhaul could make it. Fully armed and armored. The newest communication equipment installed. Freshly painted in blue and white and trimmed in silver, the OmniMech once again bore the colors of Victor's Tenth Lyran Guards, the "Revenants." His crest, a skeletal warrior highlighted against a lightning strike, was an insignia the machine hadn't known since Victor's acceptance of the post of the Com Guard's Precentor Martial.

"Soon," Victor murmured to himself as well as to his 'Mech.

He knew that Prometheus was unlikely to set foot on Thorin, not if all went as planned, but there would be other fights. Victor was here to rejoin the war effort, for better or worse.

If the war effort would have him.

As he gained the head of the lowered ramp, that concern was put to rest. Tiaret waited there in full armor, her Elemental battlesuit towering over him at nearly twice his height. Despite Kai's best assurances, Victor's former bodyguard was obviously not about to take additional risks with his safety. Her bulk hid the ramp from Victor's eyes for a few steps, and then she stood aside to let him see the procession hastily formed up by the Prince's Men. Infantry lined the ramp on both sides all the way to the ground, weapons held at inspection. At the foot of the ramp, Rudolf Shakov's *Exterminator* stood opposite a pair of Challenger X battle tanks. Both lines then alternated between one of the surviving Com Guard MechWarriors and a pair of vehicles, stretching half a kilometer out onto the plateau.

"Time to review your troops," Isis Marik said quietly, appearing at his side. Dressed in the purple and gold of House Marik's Free Worlds League, she wore a single-piece jumpsuit. Her chestnut hair was pulled back into a simple, functional ponytail.

"Did you arrange this?" Victor asked her, spotting Shakov waiting at the bottom of the ramp.

"No. I take it as a good sign, though."

Victor nodded. "We'll see." Isis was not a MechWarrior or otherwise trained for the hardships of thirty-first-century warfare. She did not know that this kind of review was more fitting for the parade ground, for the visiting brass, not for a battle commander. Shakov no doubt intended it as a gesture of respect, but also one of caution.

Victor and Isis made the short descent down the ramp, then waited just off the nonskid for Shakov to approach. He was still in MechWarrior togs, the shorts and coolant vest more appropriate to the cockpit than the mountain's chill. Gooseflesh stood out on his arms and legs as he saluted.

"Brevet-Precentor Rudolf Shakov, welcoming the prince to Thorin."

Prince. Not "martial" or even "general," Victor noted. He returned the salute, then clasped Shakov's hand warmly and held on to it for a moment. "I'm very sorry about Precenter Irelon," he said first. "Raymond was a good man, and a friend."

"And he never doubted that you would return," Shakov said in a low voice. His dark eyes warmed to Victor. He stepped back, stood stiffly to attention. "I stand ready to be relieved," he said formally.

"Relieved?" Victor was confused, the word slipping out even before he realized what Shakov was saying. This was not a review; it was a change of command ceremony! Without questions or doubts, Shakov had formed up the Prince's Men to return them to Victor's direct authority. Warmth flooded him, warding off the chill, buoying Victor's spirits. How had he ever earned the allegiance of such men?

Smiling for the first time since Isis's challenge that he must return to the war, Victor gave Shakov a quick, negative shake of the head. "You're not off the hook so easily, *Precentor*." He said it loud enough for those nearby to hear, confirming Shakov's adopted rank. "You've done a fine job here, and you still have some work to do. And you are still under the command of Morgan Kell. I haven't relieved him on Thorin. Not yet."

Shakov frowned. "You won't command the end of the Fifth Wave?"

"No," Victor said, "but only because the Fifth Wave terminates early. Next month, in fact. The fighting is about to take on a whole new direction, and a great deal more importance. I'm back to bill Katherine for the costs of her brinksmanship games."

That brought a smile to Shakov's face. "Sounds like the commander I came to know. So you'll take over Wave Six in command of the Prince's Men?"

The silence stretched out as Victor drew in a tight breath for what he had to say. The Com Guard 244th Division had gone renegade for him, saving his life on Newton Square. Their decision to support his drive to stop Katherine had cost them their positions, their top officers, and far too many lives to ever take their sacrifices lightly. They'd done so much for him already that he was nervous about telling Shakov his decision. But they also deserved the truth, and from his lips.

"I can't tell you how honored I have been to fight alongside the 244th, Rudolf." Victor glanced sidelong at some nearby infantry. "Though equal to best the Federated Suns or Lyran Alliance have to offer, I can't drive on to New Avalon at their head. The Tenth Lyran Guard is en route, and I'll lead my Revenants forward from here." He paused, watched as Shakov stroked his goatee, considering. "It has to be this way. This is your command now. These are your people. You will lead them."

Silence reigned for several long heartbeats, and Victor shifted his weight uneasily. "If you have anything to say to me, now's the time," he added.

Shakov gave no sign of regret or disappointment, though Victor was sure he felt them. He stepped forward to extend his hand and accepted another handshake as easily as he had accepted Victor's decision.

"I say welcome back to the war," he said with enthusiasm, "Highness."

══ 10 ══

Most people, when they set the board for chess, play from the point of view of the king. That is who they are. In the civil war, Katherine's supporters certainly considered her to be one king, which made me the other. That was one way to look at it . . .
    —*Cause and Effect*, Avalon Press, 3067

Fortress Laiacona
Ecol City, Thorin
Freedom Theater
Lyran Alliance
22 March 3066

Through eight months of hard fighting, Victor's people had managed to hold Ecol City and with it, Fortress Laiacona. The granite edifice, rising out of the southern suburbs, was a source of pride for all citizens of Thorin. Erected over three hundred years before, it was a true relic of the original Star League. Though demolished during the First Succession War, it had later been rebuilt as a monument and then, with the Star League's rebirth, pressed back into service as a garrison post. Though small—by Star League standards—the fortress housed a full battalion and provided a stronghold close to Thorin's largest spaceport and the world capital of Ecol City.

A banner displaying the Star League crest of a white Cameron star against a black field hung down the conference room wall opposite large double doors. Victor hadn't the heart to order the League colors struck, and left them as a reminder for his people to hold themselves to the highest standard, no matter what Katherine did. He also ordered banners for the Lyran Alliance and Federated Suns brought into the room and hung across from each other. The sword-and-sunburst of the Suns stared across a dark cherrywood table at the Alliance's mailed fist.

Equal, yet forever separated.

Victor remembered the last planning council he'd held in Fortress Laiacona. Standing room only, with the commanding officers and execs of four different commands and a handful of local nobility all packed around the long table. He'd been a different person then, with more optimism to share and looking specifically to build some synergy. Today's session gave everyone a great deal more table space as Victor had only invited Morgan Kell, Kai, and Rudolf Shakov as military advisors. They were the people who would lend him strength as his own waned. Also present was his sister Yvonne, newly arrived from the Draconis March, who was here on her own behalf and as Tancred Sandoval's representative.

The five clustered at one end of the table, nearest the double doors, waiting as technicians made a final sweep for listening devices and then cleared the room. Tiaret closed the doors after them, taking her place just inside the threshold, filling the frame with two hundred well-muscled kilos. The dark-skinned Elemental had arrived unannounced, again assuming her duties as Victor's personal bodyguard. The prince was careful not to make any extra show of his appreciation. He knew that to Tiaret's way of thinking, his time "away" did not exist. He would shame her now by welcoming her back at his side, though he certainly had missed her impressive, steadfast presence.

"We're calling this our Sixth Wave," Victor said, shifting in his seat as all eyes turned expectantly toward him, "though not for any new worlds we've planned to take. In fact, there is little more we can do to reinforce worlds we're losing to Katherine's loyalists." He looked to Morgan Kell. "Unless you've come up with something in the last few days?"

Morgan tugged at his gray beard with his left hand and shook his head. "Most of the fighting has boiled down to its essentials. Our next moves have to be carefully considered." He borrowed Shakov's noteputer, performed some rapid, left-handed input over the tiny keyboard. Morgan's right sleeve was pinned up to the shoulder, a result of the same blast that had taken the lives of Victor's mother and Morgan's wife. His reasons for opposing Katherine ran as deeply as Victor's, and he had stepped in just in time after news of Omi Kurita's death had crippled Victor's ability to command. In fact, he was still nominally in command here on Thorin. Victor had refused to relieve him, feeling like he still needed time to get back in the swing.

"We're going to lose the double system of Wernke and Talon," Morgan said. "Marlette as well, unless we find some way to reach it in time. Cavanaugh II, Dalkeith, Tikonov, Kathil—those could still go either way." Morgan passed his noteputer to Shakov. "There are battles being fought on another thirty or so worlds, but nothing of consequence to the larger picture of ending this civil war. *That* comes down to two worlds, and two worlds only: Tharkad and New Avalon."

"What about New Syrtis?" Shakov asked. "You don't think it significant that Katherine might destroy George Hasek?"

Kai fielded that question for the table. The Allard-Liaos still had strong ties to the Capellan March and New Syrtis, despite their forced return to the Capellan Confederation. "George Hasek won't abandon the Capellan March while there is fighting on any of his worlds. He blames Victor for ceding New Avalon and the Federated Suns to Katherine in the first place." He looked over at Victor. "Never mind that you would have had to mobilize the Star League against your own nation to prevent it." Then he turned back to Shakov. "I doubt we will see Hasek or any of his loyal forces on New Avalon."

Victor nodded agreement. "Ardan Sortek is on New Syrtis, but apparently he hasn't been able to win George over to our side." He paused, giving the matter some thought. "Is there anyone else we can send to New Syrtis to try to win Hasek back to our cause?"

"The Second Ceti Hussars are on Taygeta," Morgan said slowly. "They've been holding out for neutrality, but we might swing them. Katherine's preferences on how to deal with 'neutral' units is a matter of record."

"I'll work them," Victor promised, feeling a flash of his old optimism. "Maybe we can do some good there."

"Whatever we decide to do," Morgan reminded all present, "we don't have a lot of time. The Skye rebellion has so far protected us from feeling Katherine's full wrath here on Thorin, especially with General Esteban's defection to Free Skye. Lately, she has abandoned Freedom to make a second push at Hesperus, but even without the Gray Death Legion to oppose her, I doubt she can take and *hold* the planet. If Katherine's loyal forces secure Skye, it opens us up to a devastating counterattack."

"So if I understand this correctly," Yvonne said, "we have to move quickly but with precision, which means the Sixth Wave will concentrate forces on important worlds where fighting is already under way. Worlds we'll need to bring this civil war to an end. Yes?"

Victor reached over and trapped Yvonne's left hand under his right arm. It felt warm, especially against the table's slick wood surface. He hazarded a smile, which his sister returned. Yvonne had come a long way from the shy, uncertain ruler he had left as regent to the Federated Suns while he was away fighting in the Clan homeworlds. She was no longer the distraught sister breaking the news that she'd lost the realm in his absence. The hardships of the civil war had brought out the worst in many people, but the very best in others. "That sums it up nicely, Yvonne. And with Tancred on New Valencia routing Katherine's First Chisholm Raiders, he's in the perfect position to support any drive toward New Avalon."

"Better than that," Yvonne reminded him. "Don't forget that Tancred began to push out from the Woodbine Operations Area. The task force helped subdue Tsamma and moved through Meinrad a few months back. If they hold to schedule, and the plan, they should arrive at Galax in the next few weeks." The triumph in her voice was plain for all to hear as she talked up Tancred Sandoval.

Kai looked a question at Victor. "Galax?"

Victor smiled, and noticed how good it felt. "Right before civil war broke out, Katherine moved the Davion Heavy Guards to Galax, ostensibly to protect the shipyards. She stranded them without transport as a means of sidelining them for the duration. They took all ground facilities and the world capital two years ago, but we've been unable to free up enough transport to rescue them."

Yvonne was nodding excitedly. "The task force has enough extra transport for the Heavy Guard 'Mechs and aerospace for certain. They might also be able to bring out some armor and infantry battalions. They can strike from Galax while Tancred moves in from New Valencia."

"Unless Tancred Sandoval is forced to turn back for his March," Tiaret said from her post by the door, drawing the attention of the others. Until now she had stood her quiet guard over the room, silent and still as a mountain. Now that mountain shook itself from dormancy, her deep voice rumbling. "There are battles being fought behind him, are there not?"

Morgan nodded. "She has a good point. The Draconis Combine left Addicks under threat by the Davion Assault Guards, but Theodore's forces still hold Cassais, Breed, and Kesai IV. If fighting escalates while Tancred's back is turned, the entire Draconis March is open to invasion."

"The fighting won't escalate," Victor promised quietly. "It's over." He saw the surprised looks from Morgan and Shakov, but not Kai. Victor had told his friend this morning of the price Tancred had paid on the prince's behalf.

His sister confirmed it. "The Eighth Crucis Lancers were destroyed on Proserpina ten days ago," she said, naming the final Combine world that had been held by rogue forces from the Draconis March. "We're keeping it quiet so that Katherine can't use this against us, but Tancred struck a deal with Theodore Kurita. A deal that might put the March into revolt if Katherine learns of it too early. Under the arrangements, survivors from any Davion unit on *any* world will be repatriated back into the Federated Suns. In exchange, Tancred agreed to a cessation of all hostilities"—she drew in a steadying breath—"and relinquishes claim to the worlds of Kesai IV and Breed."

Shakov looked thunderstruck, but Morgan accepted the news with a determined nod. "Sate the Dragon and put him back to sleep."

Victor looked to Tiaret, whose Clan idea of honor might regard the move as unworthy of her commander. "We've bid away two worlds for our chance at New Avalon," he explained, using terms more understandable to a Clan warrior. He felt small under her hard gaze, a self-conscious twinge that worked at his confidence.

"It is not the only trade you are making," Tiaret said. "Is it?"

He shook his head. "No, there is another." He looked at Shakov, and a sudden cloud of suspicion stormed up on the other man's face. "I'm sorry, Rudolf. I know what you've done—what it's cost the Prince's Men—to hang on to this world, but we're giving it up. Thorin and Muphrid are necessary worlds only so long as we're here. Let Katherine's loyalists garrison them. We're moving back into the Federated Suns, and we'll burn our bridges behind us. There will be no falling back this time."

Victor had never doubted the Com Guard warrior's ultimate loyalty. It had been proven too many times over the course of the civil war. The depth of it still amazed him as Shakov wrote off the world his previous commander had died for, turning immediately to practical concerns. "What about our logistics network?" he asked.

"We're terminating that as well. It's stretched too thin as it is. We need to establish a solid base of operations inside the Federated Suns, complete with new logistics sources and infrastructure."

"Tikonov," Shakov said, with quick understanding. "We're going back for Tikonov."

"And Kathil," Victor told him. "We need both if we want to strike at New Avalon, and we'll have them. I intend to leave off everything else and hit them with enough to subdue both worlds quickly. Those are our Wave Six objectives."

"Except that you're forgetting one thing," Shakov said, frowning his concern. "When we abandon Thorin for the Federated Suns, the loyalists will have the equivalent of three Regimental Combat Teams to throw after us. What's to stop them from following close on our heels?"

Morgan Kell rose to stand over the table, his left arm braced against the table's top. "Leave that to me," he said. "I'll rally the ARDC and cause enough trouble for the Lyran Alliance that Katherine will look back fondly on the Skye rebellion and wish that had been her only worry." He caught Victor's surprise. "If we're looking at the end, Victor, we have to consider Tharkad. You leave Nondi Steiner sitting there as regent when you bring Katherine down, and you'll move this from a civil war to the level of a Fifth Succession War, I promise you."

Victor nodded dubiously. "Weren't you the one who cautioned Phelan about the difference between a risk and a gamble?"

Morgan smiled, thin and hard. "I don't tell my son everything, Victor. Nor you, either. I have what it takes to turn that gamble back into a risk, and a good risk at that. Trust me, Victor."

"With my life, Morgan." Victor nodded. "With my life." Then he looked around the table, polling his family and friends. Everyone gave him a decisive nod. Even Tairet, who usually held back from such votes of confidence.

Still, Victor couldn't help feel a thrill of uncertainty that Morgan was so ready to abandon him. Victor had stumbled once already, and drastically. The civil war might have been lost then, all those lives spent for naught. He would fight such a repetition of history with every fiber of his being, but the worry was there nonetheless. It had happened before . . .

And if it happened again, who would be there to pick up the pieces?

* * *

And that was the other way to view the board, Victor later wrote in his journal. His kings would be Tharkad and New Avalon. From the middle of the game, he was trying to capture both.

11

At times, it seems ironic that I ended up with ComStar, serving as Precentor Martial for their Guard. ComStar acolytes, adepts, and precentors hand-delivered so many disheartening—even terrible—missives to me and my family over the years that for a time I saw their approach as the crowing of a raven. An ill omen.

—*Cause and Effect*, Avalon Press, 3067

ComStar Station VII-Rho
Hoodsport, Braunton
Benjamin Military District
Draconis Combine
4 April 3066

The assassin entered ComStar's Hoodsport facility with a smile and some extra spring in his step, knowing that David Lo would be excited about starting his new adventure. Even the stark, utilitarian feel of ComStar's messaging station did little to dampen his enthusiasm. As an accountant on Braunton, managing the books for one of the hundreds of small agricultural concerns with interests on this agrarian Combine world, his supposed life to date would have centered around adding up long columns of numbers and researching the depreciation on agricultural equipment. Not an exciting life, even by local standards.

"Four weeks' stay on Solaris VII," he said to the uninterested, robed ComStar acolyte. "Just what I need." Traveling to the Game World to watch the 'Mech gladiatorial games was the kind of vacation people looked forward to their entire lives. Then, with the inspired confidence of a man who spends his entire life with numbers, he added, "I've got their betting system beat like a sorry Davion."

A new planet and three new identities later, the assassin was finally beginning to feel . . . secure. Not safe—that would come with crossing the border into Lyran space—but there was a new confidence that he had made it away from Luthien unobserved and was again in control of his life. David Lo was one of the dozen solid identities he'd seeded throughout the Draconis Combine before ever making his first attempt at Omi. They had existed only on paper or in the glowing phosphorous of a computer screen until he needed them.

After planetfall on Braunton, it had taken him only two weeks to establish himself in the role and begin the slow process of booking an interstellar vacation through local travel agencies, shopping the best deals and finding a kennel for his dog, purchased yesterday in another city. He would travel third class, saving as much of his savings as possible to enjoy Solaris VII. He had accommodations and tickets to several BattleMech matches, including the summer team-event tournament. The irony was that it was only under the reforms of Theodore Kurita that the ever-paranoid Draconis Combine had relaxed its borders enough to allow such unrestricted travel. Without that, gaining access to Luthien to begin with—much less escaping after the death of the Coordinator's own daughter—would have been nearly impossible. But that was what they called *progress*.

The white-robed acolyte showed little interest in Lo beyond the transaction of filling out the message forms and collecting ComStar's payment. Customer service wasn't high on the list when your organization had a virtual monopoly on interstellar communications. For centuries, the HPG network had been the backbone of ComStar's strength, and even the Word of Blake schism hadn't sapped that within the Combine. The acolyte would likely be born, grow up in service to ComStar, and die without ever seeing any change in that status quo. After a few minutes, the assassin stopped trying to engage the other man in conversation, and let his enthusiasm ebb a bit further when presented with the bill. Interstellar communication was not cheap, and the accountant would probably be thinking of the dozen different ways ComStar gouged its customers for this necessary service.

Still, his smile returned when the acolyte promised that David Lo's message would be batched into the queue and sent out with the afternoon transmissions, and there was no need to fake that. The text was a simple communiqué to Lo's friends living on Solaris, informing them of his visit. Actually, it would hit a mail dump for agents in the assassin's employ who would put new plans into motion to help secure his border crossing.

And all was well within the assassin's world, until the acolyte punched David Lo's name into the computer and told him that he had a message waiting.

The assassin's eyes narrowed dangerously as his mask slipped for the briefest instant. "That's not possible," he said.

Fortunately for his life, the acolyte had eyes only for his computer screen. "David Lo," he read out loud, "general delivery, Hoodsport. Apparently, you have a friend on Avon wishing you good journey."

Avon, the system he had traveled through between Luthien and Braunton. The assassin slipped back into his role with a new caution. "Avon, eh?" He laughed. "Who is it?"

The acolyte printed a quick hard copy of the short message, folding it into thirds with practiced ease and sealing it with an official ComStar hologram stamp. "From Noble Thayer," he said, sliding it over the counter.

It was all the assassin could do not to throw David Lo aside and snap the acolyte's neck. All of his internal alarms were ringing at full alert, tightening his muscles and following him out with a gut-wrenching pull. The only thing saving the other man's life was his obvious lack of guile. No need to kill the messenger.

"Thank you," he said, accepting the missive with the deliberate care of a bomb-disposal expert being handed an unknown package. He heard the wooden tone in his own ears and decided against further attempts to carry on as David Lo. He turned abruptly from the counter, searching the face of every customer waiting in line behind him as he made his way back to the street and Braunton's humid growing season.

Any passing eyes that found him were potential agents. Nearby parked cars—those over there with the reflective windows—could be observation blinds. He started to cross the street, then recalled that the only time he had been captured was when Victor Davion's people clipped him and shattered his leg in a wonderfully staged traffic accident. The assassin turned down the walk instead, hurrying past the ComStar compound and several other commercial buildings.

Humid . . . hunted . . . one man against a world. The assassin couldn't help remembering Zurich and his time on that tropical planet during the Marik-Liao Offensive of '57. There he had met a wonderful woman, Cathy Hanney, but he rudely thrust the memory of her face from his mind. He had let her die at the hands of a torturer. He had also helped form an underground movement and toppled the occupation force sent in by House Liao. In effect, he had traded Cathy off in order to kill the provisional planetary government.

His name, at that time, had been Noble Thayer—better known as the Dancing Joker.

Someone was playing games. Dangerous games. The assassin couldn't be certain who it was, though House Kurita certainly figured prominently in his speculation. It was someone with the resources to penetrate this identity and who knew how many others there had been. Did they know for certain where he was, or had similar messages been sent to other blind drops? Were they trying to force him to ground, or to run? Too many questions—the assassin could only go on instinct, and his instinct warned him to get as far away from David Lo's life as he could.

He was also not about to carry this letter on his person. Radioactive tracers in the ink? A microtransmitter in the foil hologram? But he had to know what the letter said, in case it clued him to his opponent. Slowing his walk only slightly, he broke the seal and read the quick two lines of text.

> *David,*
> *Here is looking toward the end of your journey.*
> *It will pass quickly.*
>
> *—Noble Thayer*

It had to be someone with access to Victor Davion—or one of Victor's people; they were the ones who had the most complete history on him. It was someone who wanted the assassin to know he was being hunted, and was promising him a quick end. Well, both of those points would now work against his opponent. The assassin was on his guard again, his senses finely tuned to his surroundings and with some idea of the resources set against him. His tormentor had let him know that he could follow a slow and carefully plotted trail.

Now the assassin would see how his enemy fared on a fast hunt.

New Valencia
Crucis March, Federated Suns

Tancred Sandoval had cleared the DropShip hangar of everyone but himself and Mai Fortuna when the ComStar precentor finally found him. It might have been easier, he thought a moment later, to have simply retired to one of the *March Hare*'s many briefing rooms. Then he decided it truly didn't matter. The fighting for New Valencia was over, and he had not interrupted any truly important work. There were only a few techs welding armor onto the leg of his *Nightstar* and others doing an inventory on the hangar's munitions stores.

And, to be honest, he had felt that flutter of trepidation that it was a red-robed precentor and not some third-year acolyte come to find him with the latest message batch. Tancred also knew how to read rank insignia. The clasp at the precentor's throat identified him as an Alpha XXI. In ComStar terms, that placed him in their HPG Operations branch, with twenty-one years of service as a precentor. If this wasn't the senior ComStar official on New Valencia, then some member of the First Circuit had to be on-planet as well. ComStar did not send their senior staff without reason, and rarely was that reason good news.

So, with the acrid taste of hot metal still burning the hangar air and to the sound of slamming bulkhead doors, Tancred and Mai waited nervously for the ComStar agent to come to business.

"Precentor Joren Thelps," the elderly man said, introducing himself. "Forgive any disruption my arrival may have caused. Let me assure you that your family, to my knowledge, is fine, and that no major setback in the civil war has occurred." He smiled thinly. "At least, not for the allied camp." It looked like even ComStar personnel understood their own sometimes-doomful! image.

Tancred couldn't help the measure of relief that loosened the tension in his shoulders. "Never crossed our minds, Precentor Thelps."

Nodding politely, the precentor accepted the lie for the courtesy it was.

"What brings you out here?" Tancred asked.

Thelps drew a noteputer from inside of his robes. The kind with a verifax reader, the best security you could place on a ComStar transmission. "When we see several verifaxed messages coming in under the names of Yvonne and Victor Steiner-Davion, bound for the new Duke Robinson, ComStar prefers to make certain the transaction is handled with all due alacrity." He handed over the electronic reader. "With the compliments of Precentor Martial Gavin Dow," he said, then bowed formally and withdrew.

"All right . . ." Mai drew out the last word into a long question. "What was that about?"

Tancred stared after the retreating precentor. "I'd guess that

Dow has moved from hanging over Katherine's side of the fence to a more comfortable straddle. Looking to build a few bridges in case Victor wins the war."

"If that's true, then something *has* happened." Mai pulled at a lock of her curly, red-gray hair. "Think Victor has struck out for Tikonov?"

"We'll see."

Tancred already had his thumb pressed against the verifax reader, allowing it to sample his DNA for a check against the encryption key. With the sample taken, the noteputer would unlock any messages coded for his DNA as a recipient. Mai could probably have opened some of them, in case Tancred was indisposed or dead. It took the tiny computer less than a minute to unlock them all.

"Two personal messages from Yvonne. An official missive from Victor." His eyes widened as he read. "Precentor Thelps was also politic enough *not* to mention that there is another order here from Katherine as well." He opened that file first, scanned it. "She commands me back to Robinson, though more politely this time. Katherine would 'hate to invoke her powers to strip me of title and land, and place the Draconis March under a new regent.' "

Mai scoffed. "Can she do that?"

"If she could, believe me, she already would have done so." He paused, then decided to hedge his evaluation. "Well, she *could* strip me of my title and my responsibilities to the march, and she will if she wins this war. But to do so now would alienate whatever friends she has left in the march, and we both know she hasn't the forces to place the entire march under martial law."

"Wouldn't have to be the entire march," Mai reminded him. "Robinson would do well enough, and it's virtually undefended."

Tancred dismissed the idea with a determined nod. "Let her try. My guess is that Jackson Davion would override her anyway. This is a one-way trip for us, and he'll know that, even if she doesn't. We only go home if we win." He deleted Katherine's file, opened Victor's, and spent the next few minutes reading carefully through the text. There was an audio and video component as well, but the transcript was enough for now. "He's done it, Mai. Victor's escort force has abandoned Thorin, and he's moving toward his next targets."

"Which are?"

"Hidden within the text of Yvonne's personal messages," he said with a fond smile. "Maybe you can't keep secrets from ComStar, but Victor's certainly going to try." He thumbed the reader off. "But I already know the basics, and so will Katherine's advisors. It will be Tikonov or Kathil. He'll need at least one of those worlds in order to jump for New Avalon. The question becomes, what can we do to help him?"

Mai clasped her hands behind her back in a parade-rest manner, then proceeded to walk the hangar in a long, slow circuit as she mentally chewed on both planets. She stopped at one point to stare up at Tancred's *Nightstar*, no doubt remembering where hasty judgement had brought her once before. By the time she returned, the fire burning behind her brown eyes told him that she'd made up her own mind.

"We know what Katherine has on New Avalon. She's doubled her garrison in the last half year by adding the Fifth Donegal and Nineteenth Arcturan Guards, and there are other regiments on the move as well. As I see it, she can gather them on New Avalon to bolster her own defense, *or* throw them at Victor wherever he makes planetfall. Removing her strategic options would be our best attack."

Tancred nodded. "So we force her to commit in one direction or the other, which means that she is reacting to us." And following that chain of logic to its end, the last link was filled with the reddish-gold brilliance of a sunburst. "Tikonov or Kathil are stepping stones. Victor won't want to bog down. This war isn't over until he lands on and takes New Avalon.

"And that's where we'll go," he vowed. "To prepare the way."

═══ 12 ═══

Backroom deals are a necessary evil of politics. I
have made my share of them, it's true, but always with
the feeling that they were better avoided when possible.
Katherine—so help me, I think she enjoys them.
                                    —*Cause and Effect,* Avalon Press, 3067

Davion Palace
Avalon City, New Avalon
Crucis March
Federated Suns
19 April 3066

The holographic clock read 2210 hours when Katrina Steiner-
Davion arrived at the palace communications center. The red-
burning numbers hung in the air at the center of the room,
visible from every station. More than a simple clock, this was
the official time stamp that would be appended to any outgoing
or incoming transmission. Its accuracy to New Avalon's planetary clock was recalculated every quarter-minute and guaranteed to one ten-thousandth of a second. ComStar was just *that*
anal, and this highest-quality equipment was only part of their
demands for allowing a remote station to take control of their
local hyperpulse generator station.

A ComStar precentor continued to work with Katrina's two
on-duty communication officers, building the real-time network. He paused in his operations just long enough to bow re-

spectfully to the Archon-Princess and to update her on the status.

"We nearly have it, Highness. The HPG centers on Freedom were locked down due to nearby fighting. They should be realigning dishes now."

Katrina nodded curtly. Being reminded of the ongoing fighting in Skye Province was no way to improve her mood, and she needed a clear head for the virtual meeting about to take place. She wondered for a moment if Gavin Dow had arranged for the reminder as a way of disrupting her concentration, then decided against it. Freedom was the world where ComStar had tapped a spur off the HPG command circuit she had financed to run between Tharkad and New Avalon. She wrote it off as coincidence, nothing Machiavellian.

An opportune coincidence, she reminded herself, careful never to give Gavin Dow or any of ComStar too much in the way of unselfish motives. Shortly after accepting the throne from Yvonne, Katrina had faced the logistical nightmare of running two interstellar nations from one capital. Her solution had been to invest billions of kroner, through ComStar, to build the command circuit. Hyperpulse generators pierced the veil of space and time, allowing instant communication between worlds up to fifty light-years apart. Both worlds needed HPG stations to send and receive, of course, and they rotated their dishes into alignment to do so. In order to transmit the message across the next vast distance, one station then swung its dish to relay all batched messages further along. That created delays that could add up to several days, even for highest-priority messages. By building a second HPG station on worlds between New Avalon and Tharkad, a real-time circuit could run from one capital world to the other. The delay was measured in microseconds—the time it took for a receiving station to pass its signal on to the transmitter.

"We have it," one of her officers announced. "Signal strength is good. Encryption in place. Live video is holding on alpha band." He toggled over to the feed, and a large wall screen winked to life with the image of a man in Com Guard uniform.

"Clear the room," Katrina ordered, and watched until all three men had left before turning back to the monitor.

The waiting officer had silver hair, trimmed close at the sides, and yellow-green eyes that reminded Katrina of a hunting cat. He wore a powder-blue smock and trousers with gold trim along the legs and arms and broad gold cuffs. He also wore his cape, though with the hood thrown back over his shoulders and eschewing the flat cap. His only visible rank device was the clasp that held his cape, a solid gold ComStar insignia that only Com Guard's precentor martial was allowed.

"Archon-Princess," he said, greeting her formally and nodding a slight bow at the camera on his end.

"Precentor Martial." Her answering tone was much colder, and her nod barely perceptible. The right-side corner of Dow's mouth was turned up ever so slightly in a mocking grin that Katrina wanted to smash with a very large rock.

When he ran off from ComStar to prosecute this war, Victor had named Gavin Dow as precentor martial *pro tem*. As much as she hated to admit it, it was actually a good political move on her brother's part. Dow was also Precentor Tharkad, the official ultimately responsible for all ComStar activity in her Lyran Alliance. The fact that he was no strong supporter of Victor's meant that no one could claim that ComStar was playing favorites in the civil war. If anything, Dow had already helped Katrina more than might be considered judicious.

"I will come straight to the point, Gavin." Katrina crossed her arms over her chest, defiant and commanding. "My sources indicate that Victor's forces have abandoned Thorin, and that Victor may be reentering the war. I'm expecting him to again cross through the Terran Corridor for a strike into the Federated Suns."

Gavin Dow's lean face betrayed none of his thoughts. "My sources say the same," he allowed, "though I believe you are only half right concerning Victor's aims."

Which was so very *ComStar*. Too long the guardians of communication and higher technologies, many of ComStar's people still enjoyed the hoarding of secrets. "If you know something, then out with it," she said. "I have no time for guessing games."

"Archon Katrina," he said, dropping the "Princess" in an effort to play up their stronger Lyran associations, "I have always maintained that we are better allies than antagonists. I would have thought the case proven, with what I brought to your table on Marik last year."

She didn't really need the reminder. She couldn't forget that it was Dow who had penetrated the Combine's veil of silence, delivering to Katrina the news that Omi Kurita had been killed by an assassin's hand. *Her* assassin's hand, in fact, though that was a detail no one would ever know. "You brought me useful information, and I paid you in political coin, Gavin. ComStar will have voting rights at the next Star League conference. If you have something for me now, you might find me generous again in the future."

Dow nodded, clasped his hands behind his back in a position of military rest. "I can tell you that Morgan Kell has sent encrypted messages to his son, Phelan, and to Dan Allard." Phelan, Khan of the exiled warriors of Clan Wolf, and Allard, commander of the elite Kell Hounds, were the core of Morgan's defense in the Arc-Royal Defense Cordon. "I have seen evidence that a half-dozen units are mobilizing in the ARDC, including a regiment of the Kell Hounds and Phelan's Alpha Galaxy."

"Tharkad!" The name escaped Katrina in an excited burst. She forced herself to be calm. "Would he dare? Morgan has been very careful not to alienate himself from the Lyran people, always claiming that the ARDC was in the best interests of the Alliance, necessary to safeguard the Clan border. To turn against Tharkad, even in Victor's name, would ruin that image." She shook her head. "Either we are missing a vital piece of that puzzle, or Morgan is rallying troops to aid Victor in Suns' territory."

"As you decide, Archon. I can only tell you that Morgan Kell is not headed for the ARDC at this time. From Thorin, he took transport to Milton and is apparently bound for Zaniah."

"Zaniah?" The monastery? Morgan had spent a number of years in seclusion at the MechWarrior's retreat there, returning to the Inner Sphere only in time for the Fourth Succession War. Was he seeking spiritual guidance? Katrina hardened her thoughts, returned to her original agenda. "If he wants to pray, we should give him something to pray about. My loyal forces on and around Thorin cannot mobilize in time to intercept Victor, but you have four divisions in the Terran Corridor who could stop him, now and for all time."

Dow shook his head. "We have discussed this, Katrina." His familiar use of her name spoke the rebuke for him. "The First Circuit will not authorize any *direct* interference in your civil war."

Hidden beneath her arms, Katrina's hands clenched into fists so tight her nails dug into her palms. If she'd had something to throw at the wall screen, she might have done so. "Your excuses are wearying, Gavin, and I'm tired of your circumspect manner. Tell me straight what you are *able* to do."

He paused, considering his words. Katrina watched him for any sign of relenting, and knew by the hard gleam in his eyes that Dow was not willing to go nearly as far as she wished. "I can only apply a stricter definition to earlier agreements between ComStar and your nations. More specifically, the mutual defense contracts. If Victor's forces threaten any world where the Com Guard are stationed, you are authorized to commandeer those troops for your own needs." He smiled slightly. "If nothing else, this will bolster any necessary defense of Tharkad or New Avalon."

Katrina did not bother to hide her frown. "That is not much."

He shrugged, a casual gesture that did not match the calculating light behind his cat's eyes. "It will have to do, Archon. I have gone as far as I am willing, at this time." He gestured to one side, and the video feed winked over to the ComStar insignia for all of three seconds. Then, static reclaimed the screen as the HPG network fell apart, the various stations reclaimed by local control and returning to their regular business.

Scheming, self-righteous bastard, Katrina thought. She uncoiled her arms with deliberate slowness, staring at the static-filled screen while she contemplated her next move.

Winning Dow's assistance had been a long shot, she knew. That didn't mean she shouldn't have it, just that she wanted it without paying the heavy price that Dow would demand on behalf of ComStar and himself. Consort? Perhaps that was his game, if he were looking to leave ComStar behind at the end. Primus of all ComStar? She didn't see how he expected her to give him that. Whatever his endgame, there was no mistaking that his sights were set at the highest levels.

But then, so were hers. Katrina had risen to power from nothing, trained from birth to rule and yet denied that by the birthright of her older brother. Such an antiquarian method of rule. She had learned so much from both her father and mother on the gaining and keeping of power—much more than Victor ever had, always so busy with his martial toys, his games of honor and glory. Did he often wonder how she had managed to win power without ever needing to use a BattleMech company or an infantry regiment? But she required them now, with her brother up in arms, and more than she had available. If she could not find them from one source, then another?

Katrina drew the data crystal from her pocket, weighed it in the palm of her right hand. The golden bangle on her wrist winked back a soft light. She had already watched this message once, weeks before, but she had waited on any decision. After checking the door to make certain it was still securely shut, she slipped the crystal into a playback unit. Katrina didn't know the intricate details of such an elaborate communications system as this, but she knew enough to play back a recording and to make certain all security recorders were turned off. They would be anyway, for her talk with Dow, but she checked them again, to be certain.

The wall screen immediately darkened to black, then faded into a close-up of another man who had stood hundreds of light-years away from her when making the recording. Like Dow, his looks were striking. A sharp widow's peak of dark hair stabbed down toward strong features. His brown eyes held a predator's hunger, and the scar that traced a crescent from over his left eye down to his jawline hinted at his warrior pedigree. Unlike the precentor martial of ComStar, however, the rough visage of this man claimed some of her *personal* interest.

Vladimir Ward, Khan of Clan Wolf, was only the second man in her life to own that distinction.

"Katrina Steiner-Davion." His image saluted her with a hard-won smile. There were no titles or formalities. Vlad had already accorded her the highest honor, using her full surname. In the Clans, warriors alone won surnames, and they came from long, honor-bound heritages.

"I must tell you that I find this unending struggle between you and your brother distasteful and further proof that your resurrected Star League is nothing more than a political maneuver to be used against the Clans. Victor would have done better to learn more from our ways. Our wars are never so lacking in direction—so *wasteful*. While I acknowledge that it was he who set the terms of this trial and not you, that would not have stopped me from immediately declaring the Star League a farce and leaping forward to seize Terra by the throat." He paused. "I have not done so for two reasons.

"First and foremost, Clan Wolf is still bound by the original Truce of Tukayyid. This is no small consideration, though it may be outside the understanding of the Inner Sphere. We may not strike forward without loss of honor until our agreement with ComStar expires. Even so, I believe I would have waited out this difficult time for you. Ever since our first meeting in the Kiamba system, where you had gone seeking the Jaguars and found my Wolves instead, I have looked for the opportunity to see you *tested*." He held up a placating hand. "Do not misunderstand me. I know you for a leader and as a woman I would call my equal in all things but for battle. What we shared during your brief stay with us, I had never thought to find anywhere."

She paused the recording. Vlad's rough intensity had softened, just enough that Katrina knew she was glimpsing a possible vulnerability. It thrilled her, raising a light flush on her cheeks. She toyed with the gold bracelet Vlad had given her to symbolize a Clan bond cord, and remembered that time, first as his prisoner and then as his *guest*. Her knees actually felt weak, a condition she had always thought confined to the pages of lurid romance novels. Katrina had gone looking for a secret alliance with a Clan. She had found it, and much more. For the second time in her life, she looked beyond alliances and empires to find a man worthy of standing at her side. And this one was much stronger. A leader she could never hope to control. A singularly unique distinction, that admission.

Katrina's fingers danced over the controls as she forwarded the video past the next section, where Vlad's message turned slightly more personal. This was not the time for reminiscence, but for action. She found the next mark, and started the message again.

"I have carefully followed your progress in dealing with your brother," Vlad said. "Your forces have repeatedly dealt him strong and worthy blows. If not for that, I could not make this offer."

The video image pulled back, found Vlad standing next to a holographic star map of the Lyran Alliance and surrounding space. Worlds of the Clan Occupation Zones stood out in bright colors—green for Clan Jade Falcon, reddish-brown for the Wolves, and blue for Clan Ghost Bear. Lyran stars burned a simple white but for a small triangular stretch of space of red stars that dug into the Alliance like a cancer. Those red stars formed the Arc-Royal Defense Cordon, the territory under the control of Morgan Kell.

"I am proposing to attack through Jade Falcon territory into the so-called Defense Cordon. My ultimate target will be the abjured Clan warriors living in exile under *Khan* Phelan." He colored Phelan Kell's title with so much scorn and loathing that Katrina found herself envious. "I expect the Kell Hounds to bid themselves into Phelan's defense, and despite their mercenary standing, they have proven themselves an enemy worthy of Clan Wolf, so this, too, I would welcome."

He waited while the video image focused back in on his close-up. Katrina carefully checked the door again. Taking this message skated dangerously close to conspiring with the enemy. It amused her to think that Victor's campaign to stop the invasion might actually open the door for an public alliance between her realm and Clan Wolf someday.

"I would welcome the Trial," Vlad continued, "but I will not seek it without your permission. This *civil war* is your battle to be won or lost." He emphasized the two words with more distaste than he'd used even for Phelan's title. "And in the Clans we do not interfere in another's battle. If you decide that the defense cordon is *not* a direct party to the struggle between you and your brother, I may attack as I see fit. If you claim them for an opponent, however, I will be honor-bound not to interfere unless attacked." He nodded once, decisively. "Such is the way of the Clans."

The message simply winked out of existence. No splash screens or heraldic score. No emblems of vaulted ego.

Katrina retrieved her data crystal from the reader. Would she accept Vlad's offer? That was the question burning in her at the moment. Vlad accorded her the status of an equal, an honor she felt certain was not common among many Clan Khans and *never* given to one who was not a warrior. He offered to help, and in such a way that he would not rob her of honor or glory, as if such mattered to her.

She wished for the counsel of Richard Dehaver or even that of Simon Gallagher, her Champion, but that could not be. Her relationship with Vlad would not bear close scrutiny at this time, and to let it leak out now could ruin her standing among the other lords of the Inner Sphere. That would not do. Silently, she damned her brother. If Victor had not thwarted—again!—her rise to control the Star League, the appearance of impropriety would no longer be an issue. In fact, she could have parlayed it into a wonderful new alliance to promote peace in the Inner Sphere.

So, what did *she* want? That was what it finally came down to, and what Katrina wanted was Vlad, as an equal and an ally, and more.

"If I take his help," she reasoned aloud, softly, to the empty room, "then we are no longer equals. It implies that I require his help and cannot defeat my enemies alone."

Her knowledge of Clan society was not perfect, but this argument felt right to her at least. It was different than demanding assistance from Gavin Dow, whom she would never consider an equal or a full ally. Vlad's offer was likely another test, probing her worth. Katrina was not about to falter. She would win her victories alone. Then Vlad would see that just as she would not rule him, neither would Katrina ever allow Vlad to rule her.

She found a blank data crystal, slipped it into the recording unit, and began to mentally compose her reply.

= 13 =

Ask people to name the ten most important worlds of the civil war. Though every answer is likely to contain some differences, almost all lists would certainly mention Tharkad and New Avalon. Fortunately, there is at least one list out there that would also mention the world of Zaniah III.

—*Cause and Effect*, Avalon Press, 3067

St. Marinus House, Zaniah III
Freedom Theater
Lyran Alliance
13 May 3066

The elevator from St. Marinus House opened onto a small landing a half level below the mesa's weathered, sun-baked surface. Morgan Kell embraced the waves of heat that washed into the car. His pores opened, and sweat immediately dampened his brow as his body fought Zaniah III's desert temperatures. Struggling for breath as the baked air thickened in his lungs, Morgan forced his breathing to a slow, even pace until his body remembered and adjusted. It had been so long.

He stepped onto the landing, then glanced back with a nod when Brother Phillipe made no move to follow him out of the elevator. The robed monk half bowed and stepped forward enough to block the doors from closing. "Peter is at the Gessetti Shrine, Duke Kell. You remember where that is?"

Morgan nodded. "I do. I spent many of my own hours there, praying for understanding."

"And did you find it?" Brother Phillipe looked at once hopeful and worried. No doubt he had spent his own time there, and to little avail.

"I did not," Morgan admitted. "I simply knocked on its door long enough that when I was ready, understanding found me."

Brother Phillipe's smile faltered almost as soon as it had formed. "Duke Kell, you realize that Peter has been told of your arrival?" He waited for the answering nod. "He did not wish to meet with you, but as he is not an actual member of our order, we cannot sequester him from the outside world. I thought you would want to know this."

Morgan rubbed at the sweat itching its way through his beard as he considered the import of that. If Peter Steiner-Davion were not ready to face him, would he be ready to face larger, more demanding challenges? "Peter has been here ten years, correct?"

"Almost. He came to us in May of 3056. Since then, he has diligently applied himself to all manner of meditation and prayer. We knew he would never formally join the order, but he sought seclusion at a time he most needed it, and we do not deny any what they desire."

Morgan thanked the brother for his help, then began to climb the wide ramp that led up and around to the brilliantly lit, reddish-yellow mesa. The actual monastery was located underground, though most areas for meditation and prayer existed out among the elements. Being at the mercy of the sun and cutting winds, left alone to one's own thoughts, had a way of focusing the mind. It all seemed so foreign to Morgan now, though he knew that the only real changes were in himself. St. Marinus House was still a sanctuary for MechWarriors who had renounced their violent past or were seeking a greater perspective on their lives. Named for the Roman martyr who had chosen not to renounce God in order to win a promotion to centurion, it was a place where the warrior was left with only himself to contemplate and with which to come to terms. All other outside concerns would be stripped away. At least, for a time.

Morgan's time here had been cut short by the death of his brother and the return of a threat only he could answer. He would have been content to remain forever, though by then, he had been ready to see through his destiny. Peter Steiner-Davion had apparently not yet reached that plateau. The surviving brother of Victor and Katherine, Peter had quietly entered the monastery after his rash and selfish actions had nearly brought two nations to war. No one had heard from him since, and the Inner Sphere had all but forgotten him.

Except Morgan, who was here to bring him back.

It was a short hike to the Gessetti Shrine. Sweat drenched Morgan's uniform and matted his gray beard before he found the correct bluff face. His eyes burned with the dazzling sunlight. His mouth thirsted for water. He ignored these physical discomforts as best he could, though he began to wish he had brought along a water bottle for safety's sake.

The shrine was hewn directly into the rock, wind-weathered but retaining enough detail to see how Manrett Gessetti had spent the last twenty years of his life carving it. Sitting back on his calves, Peter knelt on the ground before the shrine, wearing nothing more than the simple loincloth most monks wore above ground. His skin was tanned to a dark, freckled bronze, and the sun had lightened his reddish hair to a red-blond. He was thin but not starved, well-muscled from the physical labor necessary to keep the monastery self-supporting.

"I am not leaving, Morgan Kell," Peter said without turning around.

Morgan knew he had made no noise. Not one kicked stone or the crunch of gravel. His shadow fell only a few steps to his left. Peter must have picked up some difference in the sound of the wind or had read his approach in the more mystical manner that came to those deeply attuned to their surroundings.

"I will not try to force you, Peter. I am only here to ask. You are needed."

Peter shook his head, keeping his back to Morgan. His long

hair was tied back with a leather thong, and a few light wisps blew free alongside his deeply tanned face. "No one is needed in the way you mean. Thinking that is what nearly brought me to disaster, and what finally brought me here." He rose in one fluid motion, but still did not turn around. "Who gave me up?" he asked.

"Gave you up?"

"I wrote Yvonne and Arthur to tell them I was withdrawing of my own free will, but never told them to where. Only Kai and Omi knew I was bound for Zaniah." Peter seemed to think that one of them had broken a promise of silence.

"They may have been the only ones to know you were bound here, but others knew you had arrived. Not every man remains in St. Marinus House forever. I heard, Peter, and I kept your secret. Kai likely would have told me," Morgan admitted, "and only me, if I had thought to ask him about you." He paused, then said, "Omi took your secret to the grave."

That pricked his armor, and Peter winced as if stuck. "I heard about her death and how it affected my brother." He said nothing for a long while, and Morgan waited with him, sensing that Peter was not finished.

"Victor and I were never close," he said, but it was more a statement of fact than a confidence. "We weren't exactly rivals, but we weren't exactly brothers either. I wouldn't allow it." Another long pause, as both men listened to the hot winds scouring the mesa. "But I never—not once—envied Victor anything he possessed until I got to know Kai and Omi. Their dedication to Victor, and their respect for him, helped me see that I really didn't know my own brother."

Morgan nodded, understanding at least some of what Peter was telling him. "Your brother could use your help, Peter." He paused, thinking about what he wanted to say. He counted the trails of sweat that ran down his back. "I believe you're wrong that people aren't needed. They are. The problem is when people believe they are needed because it is important to *them*, not to others."

If Morgan's words struck home, Peter gave no sign. Finally,

he said, "I once made a promise to Omi. She asked that I intro-
duce her to Peter Steiner-Davion as a friend when I discovered
who he really was. How do I do that now, Morgan?"

"You do it by being her friend still, Peter."

Peter turned around to face Morgan. His dark face had
crow's feet at the corners of his eyes from ten years of squinting into the sun and wind. He looked a very well-preserved
forty, not the young thirty-one he really was. "You think Omi
would have asked me to come back for Victor's sake?" he
asked.

"I think she would have counseled you to stay here, at St.
Marinus House, until *you* were ready to leave. The same as I
do." Morgan let that admission sit with Peter a moment. "The
difference lies between whether you are ready to leave and
whether you *want* to leave."

Peter rocked back on his heels, staring up into the sky,
breathing through his mouth as he tasted the warm, sand-
blasted air. Finally, he whispered, "Damn you, Morgan Kell."
His gray eyes sought out the elder man's, held them. "If Kai or
Omi had come for me, I always accepted that I would go with
them. When I heard it was you, I told myself there was nothing
you could say to make me want to go back. I was right. You
were right. I don't want to go back, but that's not the issue." He
glanced around the mesa with a look of sadness. "Will I be able
to return here?"

"I don't know, Peter. Probably not." Morgan breathed the
hot, cleansing air, thought about his own life since leaving Zaniah. "No," he said finally, certain. "Once you give yourself
back to the Inner Sphere, you are caught up until and unless the
Inner Sphere finally releases you again."

Peter took that with the same stoic acceptance. "I don't want
to go back, Morgan, but I will. You knew that. That's why you
came here to ask me to support Victor."

"That is not quite the reason I am here," Morgan said.

Peter frowned, his first show of confusion since Morgan's
arrival. "Then why are you here?"

Like Morgan before the Fourth Succession War, Peter had

come up with his own scenario, which was not *quite* accurate. That was the problem with incomplete data. Morgan had no doubt that what he was to say next would be as much of a shock as his own brother's death had been. "I came to pledge my support to you," he said, "Archon Peter Steiner-Davion."

14

I remember a time when I couldn't wait to jump into the cockpit of a 'Mech. And, later, when I wanted more than anything to lead men in battle. I think it's a common enthusiasm among those of us who are born to the legacy of a MechWarrior before we truly appreciate how many men and machines we end up leaving strewn over the battlefields of our years.

—*Cause and Effect,* Avalon Press, 3067

Coland Heights, Tikonov
Capellan March
Federated Suns
5 June 3066

Victor Steiner-Davion led the command lance of his Tenth Lyran Guard through Tikonov's Coland Heights Granite Quarry, herding ahead of them twice their number in medium and heavy 'Mechs from the First Republican. A handful of warheads slammed into his *Daishi*'s left hip, shaking the hundred-ton machine and jostling the main control stick. Victor flexed his grip around the handle, fighting for better purchase, then dialed down the coolant flow of his life-support system. After a moment, he dialed it back up again, shaking his head at his own duplicity. His cold sweat and clammy grip had little to do with the cooling vest he wore.

It had everything to do with being back in the command seat of a 'Mech.

Spread out over several kilometers in a long north-south line, Victor's Revenants pushed eastward, fighting uphill toward Coland Heights' spiny ridge. Aerospace fighters and scout VTOLs swept forward in the first wave, establishing air superiority and spotting for the ground troops that came after. Battle-Mechs ate up the ground in huge strides, pressing back the loyalist defenders, breaking trail for tanks and infantry carriers. There were no reversals and very few determined counter-attacks. Assault VTOLs busied themselves by swarming from one hard-fought resistance to the next, like hornets deviling a pack of scrapping dogs.

They were only three days into the coordinated assault to take Tikonov away from Katherine's loyalists—a two-month strategy—and this was Victor's first heavy firefight in over a year. As it turned out, the First Republican Guard couldn't stand against the Tenth's unbridled force, not after the Revenants had been held out of battle for so long. Just to be sure, Victor had added Rudolf Shakov and the 244th Division into the fight. The Prince's Men ranged ahead to pick at the Republican flanks, worrying them, buying some occasional relief for the Tenth Lyran.

Victor needed that relief. With little time for planning and less for practice simulations, he felt his lack of preparation in slowness at the controls and a general concern for his readiness. Any delays measured in fractions of a second, but even those were potentially deadly in a firefight. So now, alternating between extended-range lasers and pulse technology depending on range, Victor remained careful of his heat curve, not trying anything too fancy as he worked himself back into the familiarity of combat. He felt the restrained power of Prometheus urging to be loosed, like a war dog on a leash. Slow and easy, he reminded himself. There was plenty of fighting between here and New Avalon.

His caution saved him from the Republican trap. A *Falconer* twisted back to flail at him with the azure whip of a particle projection cannon, but the PPC missed wide and cut a blackened scar into the nearby cliff facing instead. Victor ducked aside regardless. Flinching away from the arcing blast, he turned in closer to the dark cliff as a Typhoon urban assault vehicle rolled out from behind a nearby pyramid of quarried granite. His tactical display flashed warning icons, giving him a second's notice before the UAV's autocannon chewed hot metal into the *Daishi*'s leg and two *Falconer*s paired up to bracket Victor's OmniMech with gauss rifles and particle cannon. Both PPCs cut at his left arm and shoulder, turning pristine armor into blackened ruin.

The five-point harness held Victor to his seat as Prometheus lurched sideways into the cliff facing, digging its right shoulder into the blue-speckled rock. Armor tore away in long strips, peeled back cleanly to expose the upper arm actuator, and rubble shifted dangerously underfoot. The hundred-ton *Daishi* pulverized most of the rocks to dust and gravel, but a few pieces rolled with his weight, twisting the OmniMech on its ankle joint in a stomach-tightening wobble.

"Hang in, Victor." Leftenant General Reinhart Steiner's voice was clear and precise, an advantage of ComStar technology, whose improved battlefield communications systems were decades ahead of the rest of the Inner Sphere. "Help is on the way."

Help came in the form of Reinhart's captured Clan *Masakari*. A deadly design, the eighty-five-ton OmniMech was easily as lethal as Victor's larger *Daishi*. What was more, Reinhart fought it like a Clan MechWarrior. Planting both feet in a wide stance, he struck at one of the *Falconer*s with four PPCs tied through his targeting computer. The destructive energy washed down the side of the *Falconer*'s long torso, burning away armor and splashing it to the rocky ground in impotent pools. Several megajoules of energy cored through to shave away physical shielding from around the *Falconer*'s fusion reactor, forcing it to shut down or risk a catastrophic containment failure.

The cost of such destructive power made itself felt when the *Masakari* overheated, its fusion reactor spiking heavily to meet the power draw. The core of the OmniMech glowed a blurred-white on Victor's thermal imaging. Gray smoke from scorched myomer and actuator fluids seeped from rents in the *Masakari*'s armor. The heat-addled machine would be going nowhere fast, having turned itself into a static weapons emplacement.

Victor was not about to leave his cousin hanging out for a target. He wrestled his controls to keep Prometheus on its feet, then swiveled his upper torso on a turret-style waist to bring his crosshairs over the offending Typhoon. His own assault-class autocannon spat out a long tongue of fire as it hammered slugs tipped with depleted uranium into the side of the UAV. Following up with pulse lasers, emerald darts ate up the rest of the vehicle's protective armor. The brute force of his attack shoved the vehicle sideways over the quarry floor, but was not quite enough to stop it cold. He cursed under his breath, careful not to let the voice-activated mic pick it up as he braced himself for a second assault.

An attack that never came as a *Victor*, the prince's namesake 'Mech, smashed a gauss slug through what was left of the Typhoon's right side. The hypersonic mass spent most of its kinetic energy in the crew compartment, leaving the UAV a gutted shell. Late, a trio of Cyrano heavy VTOLs marked with Com Guard colors fell over the cliff edge and dropped down to hover over the center of the large quarry. Their long rotors beat the air so close together that Victor could hardly believe they weren't clipping each other. Then he was calling out warnings as the Cyranos' beagle probes uncovered two more machines hidden in ambush, sharing that telemetry with the Tenth Lyran Guard.

The Cyranos left another hidden UAV to the BattleMechs while their three lasers, one mounted at the nose of each craft, concentrated on a Republican *Nightsky* and cut through its hatchet-wielding arm. The *Victor* and a brand-new *Templar* combined firepower to tear apart the second Typhoon.

Reinhart Steiner locked into a 9-0 *Firestarter* OmniMech, cycling only a pair of his weapons at a time, bleeding off accumulated waste heat for two volleys before stabbing out again with all four cerulean beams. He gimped the *Firestarter* by slicing away armor and coring a PPC through the lower-leg actuator. As the other 'Mech limped from the far side of the quarry,

he was forced to let it go, his heat building up again to the point
that his *Masakari* refused to obey the throttles.

His balance regained, Victor had squared off against the second *Falconer*. Whether the Republican MechWarrior had taken
heart from the *Daishi*'s earlier stumble or was simply ignoring
the differences between his seventy-five-tonner and the assault
'Mech, he met Victor head-on with weapons blazing. Tying all
five lasers and his autocannon into a single trigger left the *Falconer* minus both legs, an arm, and its stabilizing gyro.

It also left Victor as immobile as his cousin, gasping for air
as each breath pulled hot coals down into his lungs. The back-
wash of waste heat smashed through his cockpit with almost
physical force, wringing a cleansing sweat from every pore in
his body. He sat there staring through the ferroglass shield as the
First Republican Guard, lighter now by almost three hundred
tons of equipment, pulled back to the eastern side of the quarry,
and put a thin stand of ponderosa pine between themselves and
the pursuing assault lance.

The Cyranos spun on their axes to sweep for any remaining
surprises, finding none. In perfect formation, the VTOLs shifted
track to angle northeast and sped from the quarry, chasing a fleeing, fast-of-foot *Battle Hawk*. They cleared the quarry just as a
pair of Yellow Jacket VTOLs, these painted in the blue and
white of the Revenants, took their place over the prince's position.

"Precentor Shakov sends his regards, Highness," one Cyrano
pilot transmitted on the allies' general frequency.

Of course he did. Victor determined that he would review
with Shakov the necessity of keeping to one's own flight corridor. Later. First, they had to finish pushing the First Republicans
off the heights and into the plains, where they could be surrounded and corralled.

Victor worked the controls, slowly coaxing Prometheus out
of its heat-induced stupor. "Enough of this standing around,
Rein." He left his communications open to the lance frequency,
enjoining them all to form up on his position. "Up and over the
top. We lost some ground on this shortcut." A half kilometer, by

the looks of his tactical display. Nothing too far out of line. Not yet.

"Understood, Victor." Reinhart was also moving slowly, his *Masakari* swinging around to come in at Prometheus's side. "Though if it wasn't for that hundred-ton monster you love so much, we'd be able to keep up with our line much easier."

Victor winced as a mental twinge brought Omi's face to the front of his mind. He could certainly remember saying in the past that he loved piloting Prometheus, but only in that much-overused and casual manner people adopted. He carefully set aside the memory, doubting he would ever again use that word so casually.

"We'll see what we can do," he said, shoving his throttle to the forward limit. Prometheus kicked up into a hard run, breaking over fifty kilometers per hour by the time Victor hit the far side of the quarry and bulldozed his way through the trees.

"You in a hurry to get somewhere?" Reinhart asked.

Victor nodded to himself in his cockpit. "New Avalon," he whispered fiercely.

15

Tancred Sandoval once recited an old family axiom
to me, that "the foundation of any military victory is
preparation." He explained that this included more than
logistical concerns, but referred as well to a state of
mind in which your enemy is clearly defined. By this
argument, a civil war is a structure built on quicksand.
—*Cause and Effect*, Avalon Press, 3067

Gaveston's Gorge, New Avalon
Crucis March
Federated Suns
10 July 3066

Gaveston River wound its way through the magnificent gorge,
its waters wide and shallow and muddy. High cliff faces formed
two sides of a long arena, with laserfire scorching the air overhead and missiles arcing across the three-kilometer divide.
Fighting the river's grip, Tancred Sandoval slogged his *Night-*
star up onto a spit of orange clay. He drove a gauss slug down-
river, a silver fist that punched into the gut of a *Watchman*
belonging to the retreating Third Robinson Rangers. Shattered
armor dropped into the river, yet the forty-ton *Watchman* remained in better overall condition than Tancred's battle-weary
'Mech.

On his damage display, wire-frame schematics blackened
more than sixty percent of the *Nightstar*'s outline due to armor
loss, and red telltale lights warned of problems ranging from

ruptured heat sinks to an impending gyro failure. Alarms wailed
for attention, spiking in volume as the Watchman's laser ex-
ploited earlier damage and pierced an arm actuator. Around him,
warriors of the Second Rangers fought and fell, and Tancred
began to seriously rethink this precipitous assault on New
Avalon.

Though the Third Robinson Rangers had never shown close
allegiance to the Draconis March or the Sandoval family, Tancred had still never thought to fight against them. Nominally,
they were under his command as Duke Robinson, except that
Katherine had co-opted the Third Rangers early in the civil war,
naming them as one of her defenders on New Avalon. She now
threw them against their brother unit in this challenge for the
continent of Rostock. Their loyalty to the tyrant-princess was
obviously stronger than to their new duke. Maybe if he hadn't
opposed his father, or if he'd solidified his position as new
march lord before running to Victor's aid . . .

He thrust that thought aside. There were already too many
"maybes" in this battle, and it was about time for some new
ones.

As if summoned by his thoughts, a young voice called out,
"Incoming!" A new series of eruptions slammed across the river
and a half-kilometer stretch on either bank, sending up geysers
of brown water and blackened earth. One of Tancred's *Centurion*s lost its left arm to the artillery barrage, the BattleMech
thrown aside roughly but quickly regaining its feet. A lone Pegasus hovercraft dipped down into a new crater, too fast. The
opposite edge caught its armored skirting, tearing away the rim
and spilling its cushion of air. The hovercraft grounded, jumped
back up, and then rolled end over end along the river bank, tearing into the wet-dark clay until it finally flipped out into the river
and was lost to deeper water.

Tancred blinked sweat from his eyes, adjusted his grip and
tied in his particle cannon with his remaining gauss rifle to
hammer again at the retreating *Watchman*. A *Lynx* had moved up
to support his comrade, bringing fresh armor and a particle cannon. "Three Battalion," Tancred called out over the general

channel, too busy to toggle for Major Hershen direct. "Dig that damned artillery out of the far canyon."

"It will open us up on our eastern flank," Hershen said. He was a good officer, but had grown cautious with the travails that had plagued the Second Rangers in the civil war. "The Third might press us back."

"Let 'em come." Tancred worked his controls as the arcing whip of a PPC dug into the armor on his right leg and undercut the titanium femur. The support held, but not by much. "Ardan Sortek's running too far behind schedule. I need that artillery silenced."

Hershen still wasn't sure. "Colonel?" he called to his CO.

Colonel Theodor Mikul jumped in just fast enough to keep Tancred from relieving Major Hershen of his command. "The duke gave you an order, Jon! The next time you question him on the field, I'll personally bust you back to leftenant and assign you to Field Marshal Fortuna's field camp!"

It was no coincidence that every MechWarrior assigned to Mai Fortuna's planning staff was also relieved of BattleMech operations, and Major Hershen took the threat as seriously as Mikul intended. He personally led his battalion command company on a wide flanking maneuver toward the high wall of the gorge, where his jumpers might work up the half-kilometer face to silence the offending artillery.

Tancred waited out a new artillery barrage, the shells ripping over the battlefield, then said, "Mikul, pull back our fighter cover. Have them hit the Third Rangers from behind in two minutes."

The colonel complied before voicing any disagreement, and when he did, it was over a private channel to his duke. "That's going to cost us," he finally said.

Tancred knew that. Air superiority over the continent of Rostock was a day-by-day challenge, and it was a dangerous gamble to distract your pilots before they had safe skies. "It'll hurt more if we lose Three Batt. We need to buy ourselves more time."

"Do you really think Sortek will make it?" Mikul asked.

The ninety-five-ton *Nightstar* had sunk down into the soft clay, anchoring it into place. Tancred rocked the great machine back and forth to break the suction, then waded the last stretch of turbid water to a gravel bank. "Ardan was Hanse Davion's Champion," Tancred reminded the regimental commander. "He doesn't know how to fail."

"Yes, sir," the colonel said dutifully, then broke off under a hammering rattle.

Tancred recognized the sound of light autocannon scraping armor off Mikul's cockpit. He checked through his left-hand ferroglass shield and saw the colonel's red and black *Gunslinger* stumble but keep its feet. The assault machine staggered to the river's edge, kicking up more of the dark mud that now stained the lower half of every Second Ranger 'Mech.

"I hope he shows up with a miracle in his pocket," Mikul said, voice haggard. A *Bushwacker* and a *Nightsky* moved up to shield them both from the Third Rangers for a moment.

"I think we can settle for the battalion he promised."

Mikul was still shaking off the violent storm of autocannon fire. "That would depend on which unit, wouldn't it?"

All too true, Tancred thought. Ardan Sortek had gone to New Syrtis, where he'd gathered up the Second Ceti Hussars and what was left of the Davion Light Guard to make a thrust straight for New Avalon. He'd slipped through the aerospace cordon three days before, a week behind Tancred's combined task force, and in a brief, jumbled transmission, this morning had promised a battalion's support at the gorge. But if the Light Guard were as badly damaged as reports claimed, Tancred couldn't see them as much help.

Moving out from the shadow of Mikul's security 'Mechs, he traded long-range weapons fire with two *Maelstrom*s. They cost him more armor and a ruined pulse laser, though he managed to drive a gauss slug into the elbow joint of one *Maelstrom*, turning it into a mangled twist of metal struts and myomer. The *Watchman* from earlier had pulled back behind a rock column for protection, though a pair of daring Fulcrum hovercraft quickly chased it back out again. Mikul hammered at the *Watch-*

man with his own rail guns, chasing it farther downrange and providing some cover for the exposed Fulcrums. One of them failed to make it back to the safety of the Second Ranger lines, trading itself for a crippled Manticore. Tancred watched as the *Maelstrom*s and the *Lynx* fell back together, tensing for the expected call.

"Incoming."

Time again. Artillery rained over the Second Rangers, raising another storm of gravel and shrapnel with deadly force. Some of the razored metal cut into the *Nightstar*'s weakened leg, bursting the knee actuator and locking the limb in a permanent cast. "They're going to nickel and dime me to death," Tancred complained. "Pull up our reserves in case I need to fall back." Or in case he went down under the guns of the Third.

"Can't do that," Mikul said, falling back to escape the destructive umbrella thrown out by an LRM carrier. "Hershen's flank is crumbling, and I committed the reserves behind him."

Tancred looked to his HUD, counted icons, and read taglines to double-check Mikul's assessment. Right on the money. Major Hershen had been cautious but correct. The Third Rangers pressed forward, trying to stall Tancred's advance as they pulled all hover-capable craft back to the southern side of the river and used them to support a 'Mech counterassault.

Tancred cursed fluently but softly, careful of his voice-activated mic. Most of his vehicles were tracked, unable to redeploy as quickly as those of the Third. He himself was trapped on the wrong side of the sluggish Gaveston. He twisted his *Nightstar*'s path back toward the turgid waters, sloshing up to the ankles and maintaining some forward momentum to ward off the pull of the clay and muck. Halfway across, he slowed as a freshly armored *Devastator* worked its way upstream, threatening his arrival on the opposite bank. "General McBride," he whispered to the Third commander, "you finally decided to come out and play."

As if in answer, the *Devastator* struck out from extreme range with extended-range PPCs. One azure bolt skipped off the water, breaking into a dozen smaller arcs that danced and skittered like grease on a hot plate before fully grounding. Tancred punched a gauss slug into the *Devastator*'s chest, blooding the other 'Mech for what looked like the first time. Waiting for his remaining rail gun to cycle, he felt the desperate loss of his left-arm gauss rifle more than ever. He kept his thumb pressed down on the firing stud, so hard that the lower knuckle pained him.

A new gauss slug loaded through the breech, and capacitors discharged through acceleration coils, pulling the nickel-ferrous mass up to hypersonic velocity. The silver blur flashed out from the end of the rifle, and Tancred quickly toggled for his particle cannon as well, which chased after the slug with an arc of man-made lightning. Both slammed into the other assault 'Mech with stunning force, smashing armor into shards and splinters and cutting a deep, angry furrow up one side.

A hard blow, but the *Devastator*'s return fire proved more than the battered *Nightstar* could take. Particle streams washed over Tancred's left side, burning away a few kilograms of remaining armor and crisping myomer into half-melted ropes. The *Nightstar*'s right arm fell useless at its side, swinging free from the shoulder joint. Then a gauss slug punched through his ruined kneecap, snapping the leg in two like a dry twig. The other caught him low in the center, impacting over the already-damaged gyro housing and turning the stabilizer into a ruined mass of metal.

There was nowhere to go but down. Tancred surrendered the controls and gripped either side of his command chair. The *Nightstar* fell first onto the ruined stump of its right leg, which helped ease it toward the river before it rolled onto its right side, the cockpit half buried in the brown waters. Tancred's restraining harness kept him in his seat.

"The duke!" someone called over the main channel. "The duke is down!"

On the HUD, several icons broke from their engagements, moving to Tancred's aid, then sparks shot out of a nearby panel, and he lost all external sensors. He sprayed down the electrical fire with a nearby extinguisher. He heard the heavy trickle of running water, knew that his cockpit was flooding, and quickly found the rising level against the lower right wall. But that was still not as bad as the approaching *Devastator*. Tancred watched General McBride pound toward him, stalking the riverbank, watching for any sign of life from the *Nightstar*. The Third Rangers' CO waited with gauss rifles levered in Tancred's direction. Were they giving him a chance or calling in a directed artillery strike?

"Mikul," he said evenly, jaw set, "keep your people in line. Don't make it easy to roll up our flank."

Inexplicably, the Third Rangers suddenly fell off from their assault. The *Devastator* backpedaled, then turned back for its own line. Tancred frowned. Was the pilot worried by the Second's center pulling in to concentrate its forces? Or was it clearing the way before the next artillery strike, which was certainly overdue. The answer to his questions followed a few seconds later.

"'Mechs on the ridge," came a new warning, the voice of Hershen. "Two lances . . . a company . . . Davion Light Guard!" The major's voice had never sounded so good. "They're ours. Here they come."

Though lacking his tactical display, Tancred didn't bother asking for verification. Through the portion of his canopy's shield not underwater, he could see the light- and medium-class 'Mechs of the Light Guard storming up to the nearer edge of the gorge wall, leaping forward on plasma jets. At least two companies, taking to the air and then dropping in freefall for nearly half a kilometer, lighting jump jets off again in time to catch themselves from the lethal drop.

"About time," Mikul said.

"That's just the way it works," Tancred replied, relaxing into the awkward, side-sitting arrangement. "The cavalry always makes it, but only in the nick of time."

"If that's true, what does it say about Prince Victor making a timely arrival?"

Tancred frowned, unease creeping back to take doubtful root in his mind. He could have done without that question. He could have done without it just fine.

"Wait and see," he said, dialing for a strong voice. "And let's hope Ardan Sortek has some answers."

Tancred met with Ardan Sortek in the shadow of the gorge wall, protected from the worst of the afternoon heat by shade and the beginning of the evening winds. He exchanged his sweat-drenched cooling vest and shorts for a dry field uniform while Colonel Mikul set a bivouac perimeter and organized longer-reaching patrols to be coordinated with the Davion Light Guard. The Light Guard still had a company on top of the gorge wall, but they were 'Mechs without jump jets and no safe way down. They spread out along the upper plateau as lookouts.

Ardan Sortek waited inside a hastily erected tent, toweling himself dry after peeling himself out of his own MechWarrior togs. A thermal cooler packed with water, sports drinks, and various juices lay unzipped on a foldout table. "They're warm," he said as Tancred stepped under the open tent flap, "but at least they're wet."

"Thank you." Tancred retrieved a container of apple juice, which he figured would be the least vile drink when warmed to Rostock temperatures. Also, his body needed something with more substance to it than water. "And thank *you,* Ardan." This last was all he would get in about the timely rescue, Tancred knew, and so he kept it simple and direct.

Though pushing seventy-three, Sortek had lost none of his strength or the smooth features that used to make Hanse Davion rib his best friend about looking so young. The only betrayal of his age was a thick shock of snow-white hair, worn short and unruly. Tancred only hoped he would age half as gracefully.

"Have you heard anything from Victor?" Sortek asked.

Tancred shook his head, collapsed onto a camp stool. "Not since leaving New Valencia. ComStar is working with Katherine here on New Avalon, denying us access to HPG messaging."

"More than that," Ardan told him. "We were late because we ran into a Com Guard unit. The local 299th Division is supporting her as well." The elder warrior looked at him with a thin smile that never touched his hard brown eyes. "Can you use a salvaged *Excalibur* and a *Hussar* missing one arm?"

"We could." Tancred took a swig of warm juice. "Can't you?"

"The *Excalibur*'s too big for the Light Guard. As for the *Hussar*, well, we are in the unenviable situation of having more machines than manpower just now."

Reading between the lines, Tancred knew that the Light Guard had suffered heavily in the fighting on New Syrtis and were down a good number of MechWarriors. "We'll put them to good use. In fact, I might need the *Excalibur* myself after losing my *Nightstar*."

Ardan shook his head. "Hold that thought. We have some more extras, including my backup ride. George Hasek didn't send us on *quite* empty-handed." No doubt there was a story behind that touch of bitterness. "I redesigned a new variant on the *Templar* and brought two of them with me. I think you might like it."

Tancred nodded, trying to recall the specs on the Federated Suns' newest OmniMech. "Eighty-five tons?"

"That walks and fights like it carries an extra fifteen."

"We can certainly use some extra weight around here. Quite frankly, Ardan, if you hadn't brought in the Light Guard and the Second Ceti, we'd be in bad shape." He breathed out heavily. "The First Crucis managed to rescue the Davion Heavy Guard off Galax, and they're hitting the continent of Brunswick hard and furious, but even with your two regiments added in, we're short by half of what Katherine's mustered."

Ardan glanced toward the wall. "My one regiment," he said softly, correcting Tancred. "That's all I've got. Minimum support."

That halted the conversation for a handful of seconds. "But the Second Ceti Hussars," Tancred sputtered. "Your last message said you were bringing in—"

"They're here. But we lost a third of their BattleMech strength and most of their armor support on our burn into the system. The FCS *Lucien Davion* caught us just short of the planet's atmosphere and safety. Burned down four DropShips, all hands lost."

Simple math told the rest of the story. "And the Davion Light Guards?"

"What you've seen is what we have left. One battalion. Limited armor and infantry support, but good aerospace reserves. I also have some elements from the Vanguard Legion, a mercenary outfit that fought for New Syrtis. Good people, Tancred. Wish I'd had room for more of them."

It was getting so that a person needed a scorecard to keep the players straight. Tancred, leading the bloodied Second Robinson Rangers, the First Crucis Lancers, and the Davion Heavy Guards. Ardan Sortek, with remnants of the Light Guard, a mercenary troop, and two battalions of the Second Ceti Hussars. Not quite a force to stand up to Katherine's six strong commands.

And the challenge for New Avalon would only get bigger.

"If that's what we have, we'll make do with it," Tancred said suddenly, decisively. "We can hold out indefinitely in the wilder areas of Rostock, especially once we get a supply corridor set up from Brunswick. Katherine has left us that opening, concentrating her own forces on Albion."

"Of course. She'll stack everything she can right on top of Avalon Island until we pull the palace down around her ears." Ardan sounded as disgusted with the idea of storming Avalon Island and tearing down the Davion legacy as Tancred felt. "We'll make it work, Tancred, for as long as we can. But you know there is only one thing that's going to swing this our way."

Tancred did know that. It was the reason he had hit New Avalon early, without guarantee of any support.

Ardan smiled sadly. "Have you heard anything from Victor?" he asked, echoing Tancred's own question.

16

It's an old military superstition: Never hold formal ceremonies in the middle of a war. They give the common soldier a false sense of superiority too easily lost in their next defeat. Such ceremonies are usually the desire of generals or politicians who feel the need to show themselves a leader, and they are generally regarded as superfluous. Except when they're not.
—*Cause and Effect*, Avalon Press, 3067

Rockland, Tikonov
Capellan March
Federated Suns
23 July 3066

The Thirty-fifth Tharkan Attack Wing thundered over Rockland's parade field low and fast, just this side of supersonic flight, shaking the stage. Victor waited and watched with the rest of the large assembly, all eyes turned toward the six aerospace fighters overhead. They broke from their diamond formation into a chaotic knot of tangled vectors before bursting free into a "federation crown"—each fighter pulling into an escape rector that radiated straight up and out from a single point.

It was Victor's cue to take the podium for his brief address to the four thousand MechWarriors, tank crewmen, infantry, technicians, and support personnel drawn up into orderly ranks fifty rows deep. They were a sea of faces, raised trustingly toward the man who had brought them to civil war. Victor hesitated, gauging their resolve as he thought about all he'd asked of them already, and of how much more remained.

Standing next to him, Reinhart Steiner nudged Victor with an elbow. "Victor," he murmured.

It was enough to get him moving, breaking from the middle of the line of senior officers to approach the speaking platform. He stepped up onto a ten-centimeter-high riser, a concession to the holocamera crews who were recording this event. The riser added some height to Victor's one hundred sixty centimeters, and it was either that or cut down the podium so that his uniform could be clearly seen. He wore an old dress uniform of the Federated Suns military: dark green trousers and jacket, with rowless spurs on the trouser cuffs. His single epaulet, worn on the right shoulder, displayed the silver sunburst of a field marshal. Extending down from his left shoulder was the Sunburst vest, a semi-breastplate that radiated golden spokes across his chest. He wore no field cap, and the light breeze moving across the open grounds ruffled his sandy-blond hair.

"This morning," he began, "forces working in opposition to my sister's unlawful rule launched an assault near the Earthwerks production facilities on Tikonov. We had hopes of depriving our opposition of any further logistics support, making their position on this world untenable. We have succeeded beyond all initial expectations, having accepted the unconditional surrender of the Third Tikonov Republican Guard. Since that surrender, our forces have monitored the withdrawal of the First Republican and Fifteenth Deneb Light Cavalry and the subsequent liftoff of seventeen DropShips. I think it is finally safe to say that Katherine's loyalists have abandoned Tikonov."

He waited as applause swept the grounds, well-meant but weary. This had been no easy battle. Some commands had been fighting on-planet for better than three years. Even with Victor landing such a large relief force, the cost had still amounted to two months of hard resistance.

"This victory would not have been possible without the bravery and sacrifices made by thousands of strong men and women, military and civilian. I wish I could identify them all for you and bestow the countless citations and awards they are due. To men like General Jonathan Sanchez, of the First NAIS Cadre"—Victor gestured back to the line of senior officers—"who remained behind when we were first pushed off Tikonov, then held Katherine's forces in check for as long as it took us to return. To women such as Margot Hoi, CEO for the local Ceres Metals division, who defied the Free Tikonov Movement and helped turn over their Asano Bay facilities to the allied forces. They are due much, and I hope to see them receive it.

"In their place, and in the stead of hundreds of others I could personally name, I will make a single award today. To a man who is forced to remain behind, and so will be asked to carry the honor of every Tikonov veteran." Victor picked up the award, which had been placed for him on the podium, and read from the citation. "For courage in the face of overwhelming opposition, for duty to his comrades in arms, and for the sacrifices he made to safeguard lives, it is my honor to present the Golden Sunburst to Sergeant Christoffer Pierce of the Third Crucis Lancers."

Pierce waited at the end of the line of officers, the only enlisted man on the stage. He limped forward, escorted by Isis Marik. He favored his right knee, which Victor knew had been fused immobile. In fact, the list of his injuries read like a surgeon's nightmare. Isis had selected Pierce from hundreds of potentials, and she was the one who had brought Victor the report. Kneecap and shoulder destroyed. Right hand severed at the wrist. Apparently, his command chair had broken loose from its mounts during a fall. His arm was pinned between it and a console edge, preventing him from bleeding out before medical help arrived. This miracle must have been the reason Isis had selected him.

"Highness," Pierce said, drawing himself into stiff attention and rendering a salute.

Victor returned it, noticing that Pierce had been fitted with a state-of-the-art prosthetic hand that looked like flesh and could function in most ways like the hand the sergeant had lost. Still, he wasn't surprised when Pierce offered his left hand to shake. There were a few things a prosthetic could not give back, and one was a true sense of touch. The hand might function perfectly well, but it would feel like a cold, numb weight at the end of his arm. Morgan Kell had once explained to Victor that the loss of human warmth was a major reason why he rarely wore his own prosthetic.

The medal was a black disk bordered in red enamel, with a starburst insignia raised in silver, gold, or a diamond finish, depending on the importance of the award. Isis had demanded gold, and Victor hadn't argued, though the battle's significance was hardly in keeping with the exploits of other recipients. Pierce's brown eyes filled with pride and reverence at the honor.

"I have a question for you," Victor said as he showed the man his citation and the medal. He kept his voice low, so it wouldn't carry further than Pierce and Isis.

"Highness?"

"How did you face up to that moment?" Victor sensed that there was more to this story than he had been told.

There was no need to explain to which moment Victor referred. "I believe I was in shock, Highness. I remember thinking that the Deneb Cavalry, well, that they were supposed to be on our side. A Davion unit. I think the pain of that betrayal was stronger in me, at that moment, than the loss of my hand."

Victor nodded, glanced appreciatively at Isis. She had chosen well. "More than the loss of your life as well?"

"I knew I wasn't going to die." Pierce spoke with such assurance that Victor believed him.

The prince smiled tightly. "You were in shock."

"No, sir. I mean, yes, sir." If it bothered Pierce to correct Victor, the need to answer his prince to the best of his ability was greater. "What I meant to say was that I knew I couldn't die. I wouldn't allow it."

Victor held the medal up to the right side of Pierce's chest, pinched the fabric of the sergeant's uniform with practiced efficiency, and adjusted the clasp on the back of the medal to free the pin. "Why wouldn't you allow it?"

"Because my prince had ordered that we continue to fight for Tikonov, no matter the cost."

His words slapped at Victor, shocking him into a long pause. He remembered those words, spoken offhandedly at his command center, right before the forced retreat. He had never thought they might have spread outside the room, much less that they might filter so far down through the ranks. In effect, Pierce was saying that Victor—or his belief in Victor—had kept him alive. Victor avoided the gaze of Isis Marik as he finished pinning the medal in place.

"Somehow this doesn't seem enough," Victor said.

"The medal is fine, Highness." Pierce glanced out at the assemblage. "That you came back for us—that's what is enough." He stepped back, saluted, and let Isis escort him back to his place.

Which should have been the end of the short ceremony. Reinhart Steiner, General Sanchez, and Margot Hoi would take over at the arranged press conferences scheduled for immediately after. Victor would be free to rest, and later to plan. Instead, he turned and moved back to the podium in determined strides.

"There was a time," he said, "when I wasn't sure if I'd make it back to Tikonov. A time when I faltered and almost let you down. Almost abandoned the trust placed in me by men like Christoffer Pierce." He tried not to think about the best way to phrase what he had to say. He knew he must just speak plainly. "It's been a long war. I think we've all had those moments— those crises of faith—as we weighed the personal cost against the greater goal."

A silence had fallen over the assembly, and Victor sensed each man and woman looking within, remembering their own such moments. He could not see the faces of his officers, but he didn't need to turn and look to know that they also would be reflecting. They, more than anyone, would have known such times in the civil war, likely weighed with each life lost, taken, or simply abandoned. Omi came first to Victor's mind, as she always did, but this time there were others as well. Raymond Irelon, with his solid trust in Victor. Galen Cox, buried so that Jerrard Cranston could continue. His brothers, Arthur and Peter. His father. His mother. He swept his gaze over the ranks, picking out each hopeful face and trying to instill in his warriors the sense that each and every one of them was important, appreciated, and vital to the war effort.

"That we are here, now, speaks for the best in all of us. Perhaps we have stumbled along the way. Perhaps we have fallen. But we have also picked ourselves back up, reminded of why we are here. Why we are fighting. Why it is worth the cost, no matter how painful, to tear away the veils and expose tyranny where it has dressed itself in self-righteous garments. We began this journey knowing the costs would run high. We continue it now, if for no other reason than that the cost has run so high, and we owe it to those who have paid the price so far. Whatever can be done must be done, and *will* be done, to see this through."

Applause and shouts of approval roared over the parade grounds as the assembled thousand defied their weariness and rallied to Victor's call to set themselves on the final road. It was not the response Victor had expected, but it lifted his own spirits, and he let himself soak in the reviving support. They weren't applauding him, he knew. They were acknowledging that their own sacrifices were worthy of the approaching end. They were applauding themselves, and they deserved it.

Victor waited until the tail end of the uproar, turning to face the holocameras to be certain that there would be no mistake about whom he was now addressing. "And to Katherine," he said directly, "my sister. Murderess. Usurper. Tyrant." He nodded once, short and final. "Your end is near."

17

It's a sad thing to admit that you do not know your own brother, but my relations with Peter were strained even before he disappeared. I knew him then as a hotheaded, self-involved young man with a tendency to leap first, leap again, and only later look back to see where he had landed. Who he was after ten years on Zaniah I couldn't begin to guess.

—*Cause and Effect*, Avalon Press, 3067

The Triad, Tharkad
Donegal Province
Lyran Alliance
18 August 3066

Nondi Steiner waited respectfully behind her desk, staring at the large screen, where the cold eyes of her niece and Archon gazed back from six hundred light-years' distance. Katrina stood within a war room—perhaps in the AFFS Watchtower, perhaps in the Davion Palace itself—backed by a large video map on which force markers for two armies maneuvered and clashed. Aides and officers swarmed around her, all dressed in the dark green uniforms of the Federated Suns. Not one of them wore Lyran blue. Only Katrina.

Nondi tried not to notice, shifting her gaze away as Katrina considered Nondi's report that Peter Steiner-Davion had landed on Tharkad, where he'd set up residence in one of the family's older lodges. The screen dominated the room, however, and Katrina's image called her back. There wasn't much else in her office in the Triad, Tharkad's Royal Court. A large, square desk and a few chairs. The flags for Tharkad and the four province capitals lining one wall. A large portrait of Katrina on one side of the door and a hologram of Nondi's first BattleMech on the other.

"And you say that Peter has shown no interest in visiting our mother's grave?" Katrina asked.

"None. His DropShip strayed from its approved flight path, heading straight for Resaurius. Perhaps Peter guessed that we would detain him if he grounded in Tharkad City."

Katrina glanced around her, apparently looking at people who were off-camera. "Or someone warned him. I don't like this, General. Not at all. Peter comes home now? Just as Morgan Kell disappears and Victor readies a move against New Avalon? If this is the beginning of a two-pronged push toward *both* capital worlds, it places us in a difficult position."

As General of the Armies as well as Katrina's regent, Nondi had been preparing for just such an event for two years now. "I have four solid regiments on Tharkad, including both Royal Guard units and the promised ComStar forces. In your name, I pulled the Eleventh Arcturan Guards and the Alarion Jaegers from Skye. They will arrive within the month." Nondi crossed her thick arms over her broad chest. "If Morgan Kell comes to Tharkad, he will not be leaving."

"Which is precisely my worry," Katrina said, a tightening around her eyes the only sign of her displeasure. "I had always assumed that, when the time came and I needed it, the strength of the Lyran Alliance would come to my aid here on New Avalon. I did *not* expect that there would ever be a need to bring AFFS troops to your aid on Tharkad. Find out what Peter is up to, and report back to me at once."

Nondi nodded decisively, then her face fell. "How?" she asked.

Katrina gave her an encouraging smile, full of icy calm. "Pay him a visit," she said, "and ask him."

*   *   *

A frosted mist had visibility down to a hundred meters, but it was light enough that Peter Steiner-Davion could observe his aunt's arrival at Resaurius Keep. Watching from an open third-floor window, he breathed deep the cold air. It burned his nose but left a hint of last night's snowfall on the back of his tongue. The taste of Tharkad. His years in Zaniah's desert clime hadn't burned it from his memory. He exhaled a stream of cold-fogged breath, stared through it as the wrought-iron gates rolled open and Nondi Steiner's hoverlimo pulled into the courtyard.

Two Strikers flanked the dark sedan, their wide, heavy wheels throwing out icy sprays of gray slush. The light urban tanks peeled off to take up positions covering the front of the main keep and the gates. Their readiness belied the hoverlimo's casual speed and the unhurried way Nondi exited the sedan and stood for a moment in the courtyard. Exposed. Defiant. The solidly built woman was further bulked up by a warm parka, and her frozen breath collected about her head in a thin wreath, obscuring her face even though her hood was down. She kicked her way through an area of undisturbed snow, knowing better than to trust the often-icy paths already cut through the courtyard, then stomped her way up the steps.

Probably to dislodge any clumped snow from her boots, was Peter's first thought. Except that she pounded every step hard enough to carry the sound up to him. He quickly corrected himself. Nondi Steiner was assaulting his keep, bulldozing forward as if she had a regiment of BattleMechs at her back. He stared off into the veil of mist, knowing that she very well might and that he wouldn't know it until a *Zeus* kicked down the fortress walls.

"She comes ready to fight, certain in her posture of strength," Peter told himself, "but at least she comes." His voice was a familiar comfort to him and, on Zaniah, often his best company. He turned from the window with a last glance at the two armored vehicles, nodded to the man who waited further back in the room's shadows, then walked to the door leading to the hallway.

His aunt could not be kept waiting for long.

In the perhaps three minutes it took for him to reach the first-floor drawing room, Nondi Steiner had already given her parka to a servant, finished half a cup of orange tea, and was in a belligerent mood. Peter read it in the determined set of her jaw and her drill-boring gaze. She stood near the blazing fire and looked Peter over critically as he entered the room.

"Desert robes, Peter? On Tharkad? I would think you'd be wanting something more after living so long in the heat of Zaniah III."

So, Katherine's intelligence circuit was operating at full force. But not perfect, he knew, or Nondi would have arrived with a regiment of the Royal Guard. Peter looked down at his attire, the light robes similar to the ones he had worn at St. Marinus. "One of the first lessons learned on Zaniah is that one cannot fight the desert. You learn to accept and get along with it. I have found this to work equally as well with the frigid clutches of Tharkad." He accepted a glass of ice water from a uniformed corporal and took a drink. "Besides"—he felt a touch of his old brashness suddenly reemerging even after all his years of solitude—"I was told to expect a warmer welcome."

Nondi set her tea on the fireplace mantle. "Told by Morgan Kell?" she asked, staring after the corporal who had left the room by a side door.

"Morgan isn't here, Aunt Nondi. I accepted a few squads from the Twentieth Arcturan Guards only because I knew Resaurius Keep would be lacking a full staff. And I did want to come back here."

She nodded. "Yes, I remember how this was always your favorite place. Comfortable enough for a child to run around in, impressive enough that the man in you could appreciate it." She glanced around the large room, with its stone walls and vaulted ceilings braced by rough-hewn timbers. "I never liked it. It pretends to be a stronghold, but a determined lance could tear it down in a few minutes." She looked at him again, her gaze level. "It won't keep me out, Peter."

"You were invited."

"That's not what I mean, and you know it. Katrina isn't certain about you yet, which is why I allowed myself this *friendly* visit. We want to know what you have in mind."

"What I have in mind is to prevent the civil war from touching Tharkad, and I'm hoping you will help." He saw his aunt's frown before she could hide it away. Nondi wasn't meant for subterfuge. "You don't believe me?"

Nondi's wide shoulders rose and fell once in a hard shrug. "You travel in suspicious company with Morgan Kell. Had his Defense Cordon not been so critical in repelling the Jade Falcons last year, he would have found himself on the list of traitors for having helped Victor on Tikonov and Thorin. Now we're waiting to see where he goes next."

Peter had thought himself inured to most hardships, but his aunt's blind arrogance was wearing at him already. "Morgan follows where I lead, and I have come back to Tharkad. I do not wish to be here, but this is where I am needed." He sipped from his sweating glass, enjoying the water's purity and wishing it could cleanse his mind of doubts. "Katherine cannot be allowed to rule, Aunt Nondi. I hope you've realized that by now. I am here for Tharkad, and I'm asking you to endorse my claim."

"Your claim?" Nondi clenched her hands into fists, held them rigidly at her sides. "You want me to endorse you?"

Peter set aside his glass, pressed his palms together in a praying manner before him. "With you will come the armies. After Tharkad is secure, I will win popular support when Morgan Kell disbands the ARDC and returns those worlds wholly to the Alliance. Any unit currently fighting under Victor's banner in the Alliance will surrender to your mercy, and we will have peace. You will be looked upon as a savior rather than as Katherine's puppet."

"I will not betray the trust handed to me for personal gain." She threw the offer back at Peter with angry vehemence. "Katrina is the true Archon."

"Yet she is not here on Tharkad, and I am." It was his last offer. "What kind of Archon has Katherine been, abandoning her nation in a bid for greater power? You look at her, Aunt Nondi, and you see House Steiner reborn. But Katherine is a Steiner-

Davion, the same as I or Victor. You see what she wishes you to see. She tells you what you want to hear. Has she poisoned your mind so completely against the rest of us that you will cling to the illusion of her while the entire Lyran Alliance burns around us?"

Nondi crossed her arms over her chest again. Peter could almost hear her mind closing to him, swinging shut like a vault door. "Tharkad does not burn, Peter. Here we will maintain order and honor until the chaos ends."

"Anything burns, given a hot enough spark."

She gazed at him with fresh anger. "Is that a threat, Peter *Davion*?"

"It is a challenge, General Steiner, one you have forced me to make." Peter's demeanor had turned as cold as the weather outside, and he shivered involuntarily. He had held out some hope for talk and compromise, but as Morgan had warned him, Nondi was lost to Katherine's thrall.

A new officer entered the room, the man who had shared the upstairs window with Peter. He nodded once, and Peter indicated him with a gesture to Nondi. "You might remember Richard de Gambier, former commander of Tharkad's Second Royal Guards. He will show you back to your car. I'm sorry that we cannot allow you to return with your Striker escort, but we felt it best that you be unable to make any rash decisions. Your tank crews are waiting in the sedan if you would care to give them a ride. Otherwise, we will see that they make it back to Tharkad City, one way or another."

Nondi walked over to him, staring at him with calm fury. "You've stepped over the line, Peter. You give me no choice but to bury you."

Peter nodded sadly. "Alongside my mother? And my brother?" He caught his aunt's wince of pain at the reference to Melissa's untimely death, though she evidenced no real reaction to mention of Arthur. "You may find that harder than you think." He gave her his back, pausing for a heartbeat or two before moving toward the door. "One cannot fight the desert, Nondi Steiner. Not even with the snows of Tharkad."

18

For years, the ARDC waited, like a hammer poised to strike at Tharkad. The handle would eventually be placed into Peter's hands, though it was Khan Phelan Kell who truly struck the first blow. Morgan Kell promised aid, and he delivered.

— *Cause and Effect*, Avalon Press, 3067

Werewolf
Tharkad System
Donegal Province, Lyran Alliance
24 August 3066

Khan Phelan Kell stood with his feet planted wide against the *Werewolf*'s tiled decking, sensing the shift in gravity as aft thrusters fired to slowly swing the *McKenna*-class battleship around while massive attitude jets rolled her over twenty degrees. Holding on to the back of his father's chair, Phelan allowed himself to lean with the turn. He grinned, enjoying the strain on his arms. Though only a spectator, his was flushed with the excitement of combat as he watched his Wolf-in-exile warriors fight this battle of dueling titans.

The *Werewolf* shuddered, but lightly, as two Killer Whale missiles slammed into her broadside, tearing large craters in the WarShip's starboard armor. Phelan knew that oxygen would be bleeding out from these new wounds in streamers of frozen, glittering crystals like blood trails to attract more of Nondi Steiner's aerospace fighters. The small fightercraft swarmed thick and heavy around the Wolf-in-exile flagship, deviling the mammoth vessel but slowly being thinned by Phelan's own fighters and the point-defense weaponry of his escorting DropShips. They could cause appreciable damage—Phelan had firsthand experience of what a single fighter could do to a WarShip—but were hardly the crew's main concern.

That was the Lyran battlecruiser framed within the large, forward monitor. It was now falling into the *Werewolf*'s wake, but far from forgotten. A new *Mjolnir*-class battlecruiser, heavily armored and bristling with weapons, the Alliance ship *Yggdrasil* continued its own hard burn toward the flotilla.

Glancing between the monitor and the massive holographic tank that dominated the WarShip's central control area, Phelan's father leaned forward intently. Such accurate displays allowed even the uninitiated to follow complex space battles. In the tank, colored points of light and tiny models represented the fighters, DropShips, and WarShips currently spread out over several thousand cubic kilometers high above Tharkad's solar system. The First Kell Hounds, both regiments of the elite Blue Star Irregulars, and the Twentieth Arcturan Guards RCT—the assault forced Morgan Kell had summoned up in support of Peter Steiner-Davion—swam almost lazily through space. Of course, Phelan's WarShips transported his own forces, but still a fleet of half a hundred DropShips burned from the zenith jump point toward Tharkad itself.

And now the *Yggdrasil* arrowed in at them while the *Werewolf* circled around much slower.

Morgan swiveled in his chair to face his son, concern drawing a long expression over his face. "We don't pursue?" he asked.

Phelan shook his head lightly. "Neg. Not immediately. Star Admiral Shaw will give our damage-control people a few minutes to work their magic. With harjel, we can actually rearmor our more critically damaged sections." Phelan relaxed his tense grip as the *Werewolf* trimmed her flight. "Besides," he conceded, "the *Mjolnir*s gave up DropShip-carrying capacity for a larger fusion drive system. They can outrun us regardless."

"The *Yggdrasil* is burning for our fleet."

"They can't do as much damage to our DropShips as they think they can," Phelan assured him. Then he smiled tightly as his father caught his use of a contraction and raised a heavy eyebrow. Seventeen years with the Clans, and Phelan still spoke with the lazy syntax of one born to the Inner Sphere. He would forever be a part of both worlds. "They will turn away," he said. "Watch."

Like two parents protecting their young, a *Cameron*-class and a *Black Lion*–class battlecruiser swung out from their guard over the invasion fleet. Both WarShips belonged to Phelan's Wolves, together massing almost two million metric tons. As they took up a protective station in between the *Yggdrasil* and the allied forces, Phelan could well imagine the challenges being issued by the captains of both battlecruisers, each one spoiling to get into the fight. They would never interfere with Wolfgang Shaw's personal duel without an invite or being fired upon first, and so Clan rules of engagement worked as a deterrent. The *Yggdrasil* would turn away or risk odds of three WarShips against its one.

Of course, that was before the *Werewolf* got distracted in a rescue attempt.

"Central, Bridge," the rough voice of Phelan's star admiral called out over the private announcing circuit that tied the two critical spaces together. "Khan Kell, the mercenaries are in trouble." From his tone of voice, there was no mistaking Wolfgang Shaw's personal distaste for mercenaries. That he even mentioned them was a measure of his concern for losing the fourth and last WarShip that safeguarded the allied feet. "Orders?" he asked.

It took Phelan's technicians only a few seconds to find the *Fredasa*-class raider that the Blue Star Irregulars had captured from Clan Jade Flacon. Renamed *Kerensky's Blues*, they had offered it without reservation as part of the assault force, early on matching it against a Lyran *Fox*-class corvette. neither crew had any idea how to fight such a vessel, though, and finally they matched speed and course to stand off from each other and pound away with their weapons.

Apparently, the Lyrans were faster learners. Since the last time Phelan had checked their status, the *Fox* had slashed in front of and beneath the *Fredasa* to gouge at its poorly armored underbelly. "Roll," a nearby helm-trained officer called out beneath his breath. "Roll from them."

Either the *Fredasa*'s attitude jets had suffered damage or the mercenary crew had yet to break themselves of two-dimensional thinking. They turned the *Fredasa* onto an escape route, pitching up and maneuvering on her thrusters. It gave the Lyrans that extra moment, and their naval-class weapons dug deep into the raider's bowels. The drive flare from the raider's fusion engine dimmed for several long seconds and then abruptly went out, leaving the vessel in the middle of its turn, in a continuous flat spin. The corvette hammered at them again.

"Wolfgang, swing us wide and run off that corvette," Phelan called.

"We will lose momentum to do so."

Phelan glared at the nearby comm panel. "We'll lose the *Fredasa* if we don't. Render aid to *Kerensky*'s *Blues*."

Shaw's immediate turn was sharper than the last, pulling Phelan hard to his left. The new burn shed some of the *Werewolf*'s forward velocity and angled them out further from the fleet, but Wolfgang Shaw had planned ahead for his return to the main battle. Even before the *Werewolf* came within weapons range, he'd already used maneuvering thrusters to spin his battleship around and slide into the fight aft-backward, burning at a three-gravity deceleration. Phelan flexed his legs deeply to absorb his extra weight, watched the main screen as the star admiral masterfully parked the battleship ahead of and above the two smaller vessels. The *Fox*-class corvette began an escape run far too late.

The broadside firepower of a *McKenna*-class battleship was designed to carve through even the best WarShip armor. The *Fox* could hardly stand up to a single brace of naval-grade weapons, and that was without the damage it had previously taken from the *Fredasa*. Two heavy particle projection cannon carved long, blackened scars across the corvette's nose and down its port side, burning away whatever armor the smaller vessel had left. Molten globs spread out into space, quickly dimming to cold, dark cinders. Then the *Werewolf*'s main guns hammered into and through the softened metal, chewing into the *Fox*'s flesh and gutting its bridge, forward weapons bays, and likely most of its centerline spaces as well. But engines and thrusters kept burning brightly as the *Fox* powered into a spiral path, running deeper into the system, recklessly and so obviously out of control.

Even under three gravities of weight, Phelan felt the side-lurching bump of a detaching DropShip. "Damage control ship away," Shaw informed his khan as the *Werewolf* donated its *Elephant*-class tug and repair vessel to *Kerensky's Blues*. "Rejoining the fleet," he said. Having decelerated to a near-stationary position relative to the inward fall of the fleet, the *Werewolf* now powered into a forward-driving burn that would put it back on the chase for the *Mjolnir*.

"Not soon enough," Morgan said, his one good hand gripping the arm of his chair. "They're going through."

True enough. While Phelan was watching the corvette's death on the monitor, his father's attention had rarely wandered from the battle tank. Phelan looked back in time to see a holographic model of the *Yggdrasil* finishing its broadside slash down the length of his *Black Lion*, still intent on reaching the DropShip fleet. Weapons fire did not show on the model, but Phelan could well imagine the raw destructive force each vessel had unleashed. It made him angry to think of the Wolves he would lose to such a reckless charge and the danger presented to the allied fleet of DropShips.

Ordering the fleet to disperse, Star Admiral Shaw was far ahead of him on that last worry. Like a school of silver fish scattering before a predator, the DropShips all turned away from their direct Tharkad burn to power into escape vectors. With each critical second, they sought safety by the power of πr^3, creating an expanding sphere where the *Yggdrasil* would be lucky to chase down one or two of them. The maneuver put solitary

DropShips at risk from fighters, and dozens peeled away from the *Werewolf* in order to pursue easier prey. The assault force stood a better chance with them than against the battlecruiser.

The roaring power of the *Werewolf*'s fusion drive trembled through the battleship's deck plates as Shaw ordered up the War-Ship's maximum thrust. Like burdened Atlas, Phelan bent under his own weight, but slowly. Dropping hard to the deck under five gravities of acceleration promised broken bones and wrenched joints. Better to ease into it, no matter the initial strain on his muscles. Other crewmen, also caught out of their seats, did the same. Many stretched full length over the tilted deck, distributing their new weight evenly. Phelan managed to remain on his knees, still able to watch the battle tank and monitor despite his hunched back. As the acceleration dropped back to three gravities, and then two, Phelan was the first to struggle back to his feet, once more standing proudly as a Wolf Khan should.

The *Yggdrasil* had claimed its first victim, reaching out with its gauss cannons to disable an ancient *Triumph*-class troop carrier. As the WarShip coasted past a moment later, weapon bays filled with autocannon smashed the *Triumph* into five thousand tons of scrap metal. The DropShip sat dead in space for the span of a single heartbeat, and then erupted into a silent ball of incandescent light as its fusion drive exploded in a catastrophic failure. The temporary sun lit up the *Yggdrasil*'s outline, sliding along the lines of its wasp-bodied design, illuminating the battlecruiser's crest of a gauntleted fist. Four platoons of infantry, maybe four armor companies and a crew of fifteen, all hammered into oblivion.

"Whose was that?" Phelan asked coldly, watching the dying flare.

"Twentieth Arcturan Guard," one of the technicians called out, studying the data that flooded his console screen. "One lifeboat launched. One . . . two escape pods."

If the Lyran aerospace fighters allowed them to be picked up. Phelan's hands were clenched into tight fists, and he relaxed them only with supreme effort. His dark gaze swept from monitor to battle tank, and he nodded at his father. "That is the only one they will get," he promised formally.

The *Black Lion* was having difficulty maintaining a level course, but was still under power and in no immediate danger except from a new wave of aerospace fighters. Phelan watched closer the maneuvering of his *Cameron*-class battlecruiser, which knifed into the path of the *Yggdrasil*. The Lyran WarShip made its own end-for-end turn and decelerated in an attempt to avoid another point-blank pass with a Wolf battlecruiser, but Star Admiral Shaw had left them with little choice but to face the vengeance of his small fleet. As the *Cameron* stabbed at them from extreme range, backed by a half-dozen assault-class DropShips, the *Werewolf* rolled up from her other side with weapons reaching out at their farthest range.

Return fire bloodied the nose of the *Werewolf* as the *Yggdrasil* powered back at them. The *Mjolnir*'s naval gauss slammed a rail-driven mass through one of the weapon bays, silencing the battleship's forward lasers. The Lyran captain was not avoiding the *Cameron* so much as taking his second stab at the Wolf-in-exile flagship. Even with the earlier damage and the weapons fire the *Mjolnir* had soaked up from the *Black Lion*, Phelan knew there was no ignoring a ship of its class. It had twice the *Werewolf*'s weight in armor and even held a slight edge in firepower at close range.

But that was at close range, and nose to nose. A *McKenna*-class battleship like the *Werewolf* could be so much more dangerous.

Phelan heard Shaw's order to silence the main drives and prepare for a forward broadside. The thrumming power that had coursed through the decks fell into a calm silence as the drive flare was extinguished, and he felt the swing of the *Werewolf* as it rotated on its centerline axis to present a full side-on target to the *Yggdrasil*. The Lyran WarShip's gauss and particle cannon worked over the *Werewolf*'s port side with vicious, terrier teeth, but they were fighting with a Wolf and about to learn what that meant. As the *Yggdrasil* coasted from extreme range into a more comfortable distance, the *Werewolf* opened up with a half-dozen naval-grade particle projection cannon.

Silver-blue streams of twisting, splitting energy tendrils lanced out from the *Werewolf*, four of them grabbing onto the *Yggdrasil* with powerful jaws. The coruscating lances carved through armor with the kind of brute force even a Lyran would appreciate if not on the receiving end. Large streamers of molten armor rained into the vacuum, some freezing into thin sheets or cold spears, most separating into rounded nodules before the cold touch of space finally trapped them in a black crust. A second energy volley chewed past ruined armor and deeper into the nose of the Lyran battlecruiser, silencing the naval gauss and turning the once-majestic bow into a twisted, half-melted ruin.

The main bridge was opened to space, but the *Yggdrasil* still had someone in command. It began its own turn as a way of putting fresher armor toward the *Werewolf* and bringing into range its own broadside weaponry. Phelan grinned savagely. He knew that the *Yggdrasil* had little in the way of decent armor left to either side, not after close-in passes with his flagship and the *Black Lion*, while the *Werewolf* damage-control teams had no doubt done their work. Before the Lyran WarShip could smash the battleship's keel, Star Admiral Shaw rolled his vessel over to put the *Yggdrasil* right above them. A *McKenna* was designed such that its broadside weaponry could all fire into the killing zone right above the vessel, overlapping an incredible amount of firepower. As distance shrank, the *Werewolf* added autocannon to its barrage, exposing the *Yggdrasil*'s throat and clamping down with feral strength as it hammered into the other ship again, and again.

"Cease fire," Phelan ordered, using the nearby comm panel to flash an alarm at his star admiral, guaranteeing attention. "That's enough, Wolfgang!"

Weapons fire from the *Werewolf* ceased as if a single switch had been thrown. "We are letting them go?" Shaw asked. The star admiral was just this side of respectful, questioning his khan but wary of challenging him outright.

Phelan watched for a few more seconds as his flagship completed its roll, then braked to slide over the *Mjolnir* with a new broadside held ready. Not a single laser or missile spread came from the *Yggdrasil*. The vessel was not under any maneuvering burn. A sensor technician monitoring outputs from the other WarShip looked over at Phelan and shook her head.

"The *Yggdrasil* is not going anywhere, Wolfgang," he said. "They are dead in space." Phelan stood with a hand on either side of his father's chair, willing away the bloodlust that had almost caught him up as well. "We are Wolves," he said. "We hunt only what is necessary to live. We do not slaughter for sport. *Quiaff?*"

The star admiral kept any arguments to himself. "*Aff*, my khan." His tone was both subdued and subordinate. As it should be. "We are reading a general withdrawal of all loyalist Drop-Ships and fightercraft. Our way is opened."

"We should recall all DropShips," Morgan reminded his son, craning back to check that Phelan had not forgotten. "And *Kerensky's Blues* might need further assistance."

"The mercenaries are back under power, though weak," Shaw said, overhearing Morgan through Phelan's comm system. "I have already sent word for the fleet to reform."

Phelan nodded. "Excellent work, Star Admiral Shaw. Also, extend *hegira* to the retreating loyalist forces." The Clan term allowed for an honorable withdrawal by the defeated side. "Any fightercraft or DropShip moving to aid the *Yggdrasil* or that *Fox*, or that retreats to the zenith recharge station, will be considered a noncombatant."

The admiral acknowledged the order. "What of those who refuse our offer?" he asked.

"The offer stands for all, and is sundered for all as soon as one loyalist craft approaches within fifty thousand kilometers of Tharkad's orbit. We leave our Snapping Jaws aerospace cluster behind us with the *Cameron*. They can intercept any foolish enough to follow."

Morgan released himself from his harness, unlocked the seat, and spun it around to face Phelan. "It may not be a matter of foolishness," he said. "Nondi Steiner will order loyalist forces to run any blockade you set."

"That is her decision to make," Phelan said, crossing his arms over his chest, "but I will not handicap my warriors in order to compensate for Nondi's poor judgment. Those aerospace forces may have my best offer."

Nodding agreement, Morgan still cautioned, "Peter may order you to relax that offer."

Phelan watched as the monitor swung from the ruined *Yggdrasil* to a calmer spacescape, a bright star glowing off-center that would be Tharkad's sun. He lowered his voice, taking private audience with his father. "You asked me to safeguard the assault force into Tharkad, and that I will do. But you should also have a talk with Peter, to caution him on what he *orders* of my Wolves, and what he *asks*. There are certain conditions I will not compromise." He sought out his father's gaze, a mirror to his own concern for his exiled Wolves. "Where we can," he promised, "we will obey."

"As a favor to your cousin?" Morgan asked.

Phelan shook his head. "For the man who would be our Archon."

19

Find a way to always turn failure into a new
opportunity, and you can conquer the galaxy. It sounds
simple enough, until you realize that there are others
out there with the same potential.
— *Cause and Effect*, Avalon Press, 3067

Rockland, Tikonov
Capellan March
Federated Suns
7 September 3066

No ordinary conference room could have held the congress of
officers and tactical staff that Victor Steiner-Davion had assembled to plan the final assault on New Avalon. To accommo-
date them, he ended up commandeering the Rockland Base
sports complex. His aides set out eight long tables in one of the
gymnasiums, seven to seat a delegation from each allied command plus one more for Victor's personal staff. Plenty of room
was left between each table for some measure of privacy, but
the excited buzz of conversation echoed in the cavernous space
and made the assembly feel much closer.

Victor stood over his table, arms braced against the star chart
spread across its surface but staring out over the gathering.
These people were drawn together and united behind him, be-
hind the single purpose of removing Katherine from power.
Even the latecomers, Colonel Warner Doles and his Blackwind
Lancers, had found instant acceptance among a majority of the

allied commands. Of course, it didn't hurt that Kai Allard-Liao publicly vouched for them despite the official censure handed down from Sian. Kai had even requested that his reserved "chair" be placed at the Lancers' table, though he spent most of his time standing around the maps with Victor and Yvonne and a cadre of senior officers.

"Drifting off?" Kai asked, pulling Victor back to the local planning session.

Victor shook his head. "Just remembering the last time we pulled together such an assortment of forces. You and I, Hohiro, Anastasius Focht . . ."

"On Wolcott," Kai said. "When we were planning who would go after the retreating Jaguars to the aid of Task Force Serpent."

"A lot of good men didn't come back from that campaign." Victor remembered saying farewell to Omi Kurita, wondering if he would be coming back to her, never thinking how much harder it would be on the person left behind.

Tiaret also leaned over the table, bracing her arms across from Victor's. "Victor Steiner-Davion," she said, awarding him all three names, "I think you should remind yourself how many fewer warriors would be alive today if the Smoke Jaguars had succeeded in breaking the Tukayyid truce."

"Or had simply waited for it to expire in '67," Kai said. "In fact, we're still looking at that problem from Clan Wolf."

Victor knew the arguments. They were the same ones that had convinced him to oppose Katherine in the first place. "Leaving my sister in power is no longer an option," he agreed, then tapped a knuckle on a golden star at the center of the chart. "New Avalon in the New Year."

It was their newest rallying cry, coined recently by Yvonne in a public statement concerning Peter's organized assault against Tharkad. She had walked a fine line, endorsing their brother's actions on Victor's behalf but never conceding the possibility that Peter might give up the throne after. "New Avalon in the New Year," had been Yvonne's way to turn attention back to the

Federated Suns, promising an end to the civil war. The phrase was quickly adopted by every allied command.

"We can make it happen," Leftenant General Jonathan Sanchez promised, taking charge of this current meeting. Commander of the smallest coherent force in the First NAIS cadet cadre, he was still the allies' most-studied general, with two doctorates in military history and the authorship of more papers on strategic and tactical topics than most officers knew existed. "I doubted it before," he admitted, "but the stunning success of the Davion Assault Guards on Kathil has opened the door a bit wider."

Precentor Shakov walked up in time to catch the general's last comment as he dropped three new readers filled with analyses and the latest batched communications onto the table. "The Eighth Donegal hammered the final nail into the coffin of the Fifth Davion Guards last year," he said. "The Assault Guards rolled over them with the momentum of . . . well . . . of the Assault Guards." Not for the first time Victor wondered about Rudolf Shakov's caustic wit. It had been a while since Shakov had felt comfortable enough to actually make any jest, and Victor took it as a good sign here.

Yvonne raised her hand tentatively, interrupting before General Sanchez could resume. "I thought the studies made by General Killson's team"—she nodded at the commander of the Twenty-third Arcturan Guard—"concluded that we would receive very little logistics support from Kathil."

Nadine Killson stood with arms wrapped around herself, still disturbed from studying the destructive arena that had been Kathil. "Some, but not much," she admitted.

Reinhart Steiner buoyed her with a steady look. "Some is better than none at all."

She thanked him with calmer eyes. "True. But we had hoped to call several WarShips out of Kathil. The Second Chrisholm Raiders managed to subvert the crews of at least two *Avalon*-class cruisers, that we know of, and they have since disappeared. We'll be lucky to rally a couple of *Fox*-class corvettes to our side. In fact, I should check to see if my team has any further news on that." She excused herself with a nod to the others.

"It's not the material support," Victor explained to Yvonne, returning to her original question, "or the WarShips, though we certainly could have used both. Kathil was one of two worlds this side of New Avalon from which Katherine could launch a serious counterassault against Tikonov." He pointed out a small flag with the Federated Suns crest on it that rested over the Tikonov system on the star chart. "We have to keep Tikonov open to us. At least until we've established a solid base on New Avalon."

"Which means controlling the continent of Brunswick," Sanchez stated with unequivocal certainty. "Albion may hold a larger variety of industries, and of course it has the NAIS and Avalon City, but Brunswick holds the keys to Albion. There are more military industries on Brunswick, including Achernar BattleMechs, and two of the world's four main spaceports."

Reinhart Steiner frowned his confusion. "If that's true, why has Tancred spent so much effort on the continent of Rostock?"

This one Yvonne fielded, having followed Tancred's plans and his limited victories with more attention than anyone else. "Though it's slightly smaller than Brunswick, Rostock has more open, uninhabited terrain." Her voice rang out clear and proud. "Tancred's forces are causing less civilian damage and disruption there, while tying down several of Katherine's regiments."

"Duke Sandoval never had a chance of securing New Avalon with the forces at his disposal," Sanchez agreed. "But his attempt to divert Katherine from Tikonov, giving us time to prepare, worked admirably."

"Now it's our turn to pull out of the fire," Victor said.

He was about to work up more on the New Avalon assault but was preempted when Colonel Patricia Vineman, commander of the Sixth Crucis Lancers, rapped on the table for attention. She held one of the electronic readers Shakov had brought over from the Com Guard table. "Reports from the Third and Fifth Crucis Lancers on Marlette," she explained, mentioning the second world from which Katherine could stage an effective counterassault against Tikonov. "They've confirmed that Katherine retreated the Fifteenth Deneb and the First Tikonov Republicans to Marlette."

"A backfire." Warner Doles had drifted over with Shakov, holding reports generated by his own staff. Now his outburst drew immediate attention. "Sorry," he said, apologizing for the interruption but continuing on. "It's an old Capellan trick. Katherine's using a backfire strategy against your advance. It'll be that much harder to jump from Tikonov straight for New Avalon, and if it slows us down at all, she can hope to bring in more defenders."

"Or take that time to deal with Tancred," Yvonne said, worrying. "Victor, Katherine will land two more regiments on New Avalon in the next month. We have to get to Tancred's aid."

He nodded. "Colonel Doles, how would you deal with this backfire?"

"You either ignore it and hope it doesn't undercut your advance, or you smother it quickly."

Victor looked around at his officers, trying to decide which command was best suited to such a task, mindful that for every warrior he pulled off his main assault, he gave Katherine that much more of an advantage on New Avalon. "Rudolf," he finally said, nodding at the 244th's new precentor. "I need you to redeploy at once on Marlette. It's a lot to ask from your people—"

"The Prince's Men will be off-planet in twenty-four hours, Highness," Shakov said without hesitation. "Who else can you give me?"

"I can split away one regiment from our assault force."

Shakov paused to consider. "That's not enough to take Marlette," he said finally. "Even with two regiments of the Crucis Lancers already there."

"I know, but it's enough to pin Katherine's forces in place. And not to put too fine a point on it, Rudolf, but the Prince's Men have atrophied so much that I would have had to fold you into the Outland Legion if you accompanied us to New Avalon."

Shakov nodded at the blunt assessment, knowing the truth of it. "Who are you sending in with us?"

Victor waited a moment for volunteers, but no one wanted to split away from the New Avalon assault. Not that he blamed them. So many had sacrificed so much to make it this far. They wanted to be there for the endgame. Whoever he selected would obey, but not wholeheartedly. Except, that is, for the one logical choice.

"My Blackwind Lancers would be honored to assist Precentor Shakov on Marlette," Warner Doles said. He offered Shakov his hand on it. "If you'll have us."

A messenger jogged up to Victor's table, having been passed through by Tiaret as Victor watched Shakov take Doles's hand. The messenger's urgent whisper warmed Victor's ear.

"It would seem we have some planning to attend to," Shakov was saying to Doles. "Bring your people over to our table. Let's get them introduced and working over maps for Marlette."

"Pass the orders to your people," Victor told them both. "Then I need to borrow Colonel Doles for a moment. Meet us in the outer hall," he said to Doles, then nodded for a few others at the table to join him. "Kai, Yvonne."

He looked around for help. "Someone also send for Captain Harsch." Harsch led the on-planet contingent of the Valexa militia, currently tied into Sanchez's cadre and under his direct command. If Yvonne was counted in as Victor's sister, the other three men held only one possible tie in common and that was if one made the leap in remembering Valexa's close position to the border.

Reinhart Steiner caught on first, and asked, "Everything all right?"

"I'm not sure yet," Victor said. "That's what we're going to find out."

A few more faces lit up with sudden awareness and interest. General Sanchez merely grumbled at the interruption as Victor led his small group away. "What the hell is the Capellan Confederation up to now?" he asked no one in particular.

*   *   *

Apparently, according to the messenger, the Capellans were up to sneaking a JumpShip into the Tikonov system and then sending down a single squadron of fighters under a broadcast message requesting a parley. The *Melissa Davion* was already running a search pattern, the WarShip working to ferret out the Capellans. Victor didn't put much faith in that. Tikonov had been a Capellan system before Hanse Davion won it in the Fourth Succession War, and the Capellan military probably knew more intrasystem pirate points than his people could calculate in a month.

The lead pilot had demanded immediate access to Victor and, given Tikonov's volatile state, the spaceport commander had decided there was no harm in putting her on the same base with the prince. Now she waited in the outer hall, calm and compact, her brown eyes never resting long in any one place. She held Victor's gaze for only a few heartbeats as the prince came through the doors, then she glanced first at Yvonne and then at Kai. Her expression widened only slightly as Tiaret followed, the Elemental accompanying Victor without being asked. She placed herself between Victor and the Capellan, allowing them just enough room to look past her.

Warner Doles and Captain Harsch came through the doors together only a few seconds later.

"You asked to see me," Victor said. "I hope you don't mind a few extra witnesses." His tone suggested that it didn't matter whether the pilot minded or not.

She shrugged. "Fah Li Shei, Prince Victor," she said, introducing herself. "I come on behalf of his Celestial Wisdom, the Greatness of the Confederation, Chancellor Sun-Tzu Liao." She waited a moment with grave respect for her master's position before continuing. "He would offer you his support in this time of need. I have brought supplies, men, and a battalion of 'Mechs, at his command, to help oppose your sister's minions."

Warner Doles snorted a half-laugh. "Some help. What can one battalion hope to accomplish?"

She turned a dark-eyed stare on the former St. Ives officer.

"That would depend on the battalion," her voice was low and dangerous, "wouldn't it, Colonel Doles?"

It was no coincidence that she recognized the commander of the Blackwind Lancers without introduction. Doles's uniform was simply that of Treyhang Liao's Free Capella Movement, the ex-patriots who had refused to submit again to Confederation rule. His regimental patch was on his jacket, left behind in the other room.

"Fah Li Shei," Victor asked cautiously, "what is your current duty assignment?"

"Ying-zhang. First Battalion Leader." She smiled. "Of the Warrior House Dai Da Chi."

Victor was stunned, and he saw Tiaret tense for an attack. "Sun-Tzu sent a Warrior House to support my drive against Katherine?" The Confederation's Warrior Houses were second only to the Capellan Death Commandos in their fanatic devotion and incredible skill, and House Dai Da Chi ranked at their fore. No doubt Fah Li Shei was an accomplished assassin, terrorist, and MechWarrior as well as a pilot.

"He has."

Doles scoffed. "Despite his use of the local Free Tikonov Movement against Victor Davion in the last two years?"

"Free Tikonov is only remotely associated with his Celestial Wisdom and, in this case, acted directly against orders." She apparently caught the skepticism. "It has always been the Chancellor's position that the Tikonov Reaches belong to the Confederation. Why should he support their bid for complete independence?"

Victor looked to Kai and Doles. Both gave grudging nods, conceding the point. Kai hid any further feelings behind an impassive mask, though Victor would never doubt his friend's ultimate loyalty. Warner Doles looked as if he had bit into something spoiled and bitter.

"Sun-Tzu's offer is . . . *appreciated*," Victor said, forcing the politeness out, "if a bit late in the war. I can hardly work your people into my plans on the very eve of our departure."

"You made room for the Blackwind Lancers."

"True, but there is a difference. I *trust* them. I do not trust any offers from Sun-Tzu Liao." His politeness had definite limits.

"The Great One has spent five years avoiding any overt assistance to your sister, including efforts to prevent her accession as First Lord of the Star League. You are being very close-minded, Victor Davion."

Victor recalled Sun-Tzu's efforts on Marik in '64 and knew that they had been more for his own purposes than any late hand of friendship. Still, any offer of support had to be considered. "Can you pledge complete support to my cause, Fah Li Shei? If I were to place you on the line next to Colonel Doles's people, could you work together?"

She seemed to seriously consider this. "*Wo bu neng*," she finally admitted quietly. "I cannot. In fact, it would be hard to control my warriors from exacting their own justice against the *bing le feng* Lancers."

Victor wasn't certain of the translation, but by Colonel Doles's face, it was not complimentary. "I appreciate your candor, *ying-zhang*. You see my situation, then."

"We could be stationed far apart . . ."

"I have to know that any member of the assault force can work alongside any other at a moment's notice. I can't be juggling your rivalries into my plans. I'm sorry," he lied. Then inspiration struck. "The best I can offer is to include your forces in our garrison of Tikonov. Katherine may try to take this world back once we have moved on to New Avalon." His offer was just beyond the level of insult. The idea of a prideful Warrior House accepting a garrison assignment from him seemed so unlikely that Victor felt easy in the offer.

He felt less so a moment later, when Fah Li Shei accepted with a curt nod. "If that is all you can find for us, we will submit. The Sum of Wisdom has commanded that we serve."

Victor had been ready to leave the House Dai Da Chi pilot for Tiaret to escort from the building. Now he paused, actually considering her offer. There had never been a chance that he would land on New Avalon with Capellan troops backing him, *especially* those of a Warrior House. His people wouldn't have been more insulted unless he rode in with the Death Commandos in tow. Likewise, he had recognized right away that he couldn't trust them with Doles to help stop Katherine's loyalists on Marlette. But here on Tikonov?

"That would free up more of my Valexa militia to accompany General Sanchez's cadre," Harsch said, obviously thinking along the same lines as Victor.

And the Outland Legions' second 'Mech battalion, and perhaps the Revenants' infantry, which Victor had thought to leave behind. Yvonne looked at a loss, and Colonel Doles's reaction was plain enough for all to see. Kai gazed back steadily, and then nodded once. "New Avalon in the New Year," he said, a concession of defeat.

Victor nodded. "Welcome to the team, *ying-zhang*." Not a greeting he had ever thought to make. Victor turned back for the door. "Somebody get the Capellans a table."

20

We are defined by our flaws. Our failures show us
the limit of our abilities.

—*Cause and Effect*, Avalon Press, 3067

Tomoe Sakade Memorial Spaceport
Nagoshima, Buckminster
Benjamin Military District
Draconis Combine
27 September 3066

When the assassin first noticed the long, colored pennants
snapping in the breeze all around Nagoshima's spaceport, he
thought little of them. He figured them for propaganda, spuri-
ous gaiety meant to convince Buckminster's population that the
Draconis Combine was not so oppressive as antigovernment
pamphlets claimed. Before he walked past the baggage claim,
though, he saw one semiviolent protest, an arrest, and had identified at least three agents who either worked for the Combine's
Internal Security Force or were part of some local authority's
undercover operation.

Buckminster was not exactly a tourist's paradise.

Of course, that was the exact reason he'd chosen the world
as a stepping-off point to the Lyran Alliance, selecting from depleted stock his newest identity as Customs Inspector Ji Hendal.
As Buckminster was a prefecture capital and a frontline world,
House Kurita had assigned heavy military forces to safeguard
the planet. That their security concerns would come to logger-

heads with the local agricultural community did not factor into their plans. But after a decade of crops trampled under the latest military exercise or false alarm, of the soldiery treating local businesses, their sons and daughters, and the people's needs with thinly veiled contempt, was it any surprise that Buckminster had become home to many overt and covert antigovernment groups? Buckminster's average citizens "cooperated" with authority when necessary, but avoided it when they could. As a lower-level bureaucrat without much actual power, the assassin figured to slide through the planet's society quickly and unnoticed. That idea lasted less than an hour.

The cab ride into Nagoshima allowed him to slip fully into his new role, so that by the time the cab turned in to the White Crane district, Ji Hendal was fully prepared to suffer the locals' polite avoidance. The cab drove him through a business neighborhood of small stores and smaller, curbside restaurants, and the scent of barbecued pork set his stomach rumbling. He debated whether or not Hendal would stop the cab and leave the meter running in order to pick up a bento meal of noodles and pork. Then he saw the new set of pennants fluttering from street corner posts and the awnings of nearby stores. Not bright, solid colors like the ones at the spaceport, but shades of green, then gold and pink.

Green. Gold and pink.

The memory was still there, suffused with the adrenaline-imprinted detail of the assassin's escape from Silesia, the Steiner sector in Solaris City, only minutes behind the death of Ryan Steiner. Steiner had been talking to another man in his private office, separated from the assassin by half a kilometer and a window of so-called bulletproof glass. One perfect shot from a Loftgren 150, drilling a sabot-loaded, armor-piercing round through the window and into a point just above Ryan Steiner's left ear, was the end of that troublesome man. The assassin had then killed his "minder" as well as a dupe meant to take the blame in his place, and then escaped right under the nose of Victor Davion's men.

The assassin's agents had draped banners over half of Silesia in a false code of colors meant to distract Victor's Intelligence Secretariat. Blue and white along one neighborhood, orange and white in an entirely different direction. Red, silver, and scarlet right past the home of his latest victim. Black. Green. Gold and pink. Now it was the assassin who spotted those colors all along his path of supposed retreat, trying to divine some meaning from them.

Coincidence? He couldn't afford to believe that, though it certainly could be the case. There were more pennants strung up around the White Crane district that meant absolutely nothing to him; odd color combinations in which the other banners disappeared as background noise. But gold and pink together? And there, an entire side street of blue and white? His mouth dried, tasting coppery and raw, and the assassin quickly swept the nearby walks for any surveillance. He assumed that the cab driver was nothing more than he presumed to be, if only because if the ISF had him in a vehicle of their choosing, he was finished.

Still, he cast nervous glances at the door locks as the back of the cab suddenly seemed a great deal smaller, a paranoia the assassin was not used to feeling. He clenched one fist so tightly that his fingernails cut into his palm, and he centered on the pain. Paranoia was for others, and he banished it through force of will. Then the cab turned down the proper street to reach the boarding home address for Ji Hendal.

Silver, red, scarlet . . . the colors that had been in front of Ryan Steiner's address.

"Keep driving!" the assassin ordered, dropping all pretense of Ji Hendal's identity. His words tumbled over each other in a mad rush. "Don't slow. Just keep going!"

The driver frowned. "That was the place. You want to go somewhere else now?"

"Out of the city," the assassin directed, then fell back against the cloth seat as he thought it out. This man would have to die now, he knew. Quietly, on some back road and left for some nosy dog to find later. He was not the real problem, though. One hundred and fifty light-years since Braunton, stops on seven different worlds, and burning through more identities than he had ever used before in the space of six months, and still it had not been enough. His enemy was always one step ahead of him, pacing his effort to flee the Draconis Combine.

Except that the enemy had left him too long. One jump, and he would be back in the Lyran Alliance, with three times the resources at his disposal. Port Moseby would be his best chance if he could make it. *When* he made it! It would take time, and a great deal of money, but he doubted that whoever was dogging him could match his wit and desperation with the kind of finely tuned operation it would take to draw a final net around him.

He would escape. He would find a way through the noose being tightened around his neck, and whoever was trying to hound him into a corner would be left with nothing but the realization of failure. And if that enemy got too close, the assassin would prove to him that one did not stalk death.

That death always stalked you.

Brunswick City, New Avalon
Crucis March
Federated Suns

Staring through one of the sedan's mirror-tinted windows, Francesca Jenkins watched the streets of Brunswick City blur past in a haze of rain and darkness. She pounded one fist against her thigh, finding it increasingly harder to concentrate so close to the payoff for this five-year operation. The pain helped her focus, keeping her on track when an eager giddiness threatened to distract her. A small receiver tucked into her right ear felt strangely warm as Curaitis's thick whisper vibrated against her eardrum.

"Bring it in, Reg," he said.

She thumbed a button on the intercom. "Third and Jeffers," she told the driver, "just like we talked about."

Francesca had, by her way of thinking, the safer job in their final operation. She rode in the back of the armored sedan, separated even from the driver, an old agent-friend of Curaitis's, by a thick sheet of tinted, bullet-resistant ferroglass. No one outside the car could see her except as the vaguest shadow. Infrared might pick up a hazy outline, though with her hair tucked up into a ball cap and a heavy trench coat protecting her profile, there would be no way to say that Reg Starling was not the vehicle's sole passenger. Riding hunched down in the seat, Francesca held on with one hand to the unframed canvas that was Reg Starling's final study of Katherine. It was the original, as painted by Valerius Symons, of *Bloody Princess IX*. So much effort to recover what was, in the final standing, nothing more than a brilliant forgery. This had to paint Katherine into a corner.

She smiled tightly at her own pun, then punched her thigh again. There were few scenarios in intelligence work more dangerous than an actual "payoff." Emotion ran high on both sides, and if the blackmailed party wanted some measure of vengeance or thought to take some other risk, here was where that would happen. Given the furious undercover efforts spent against them in the last ten months, ever since Katherine's agent began to negotiate Reg Starling's payoff, neither she nor Curaitis believed this would go as easily as they hoped.

Curaitis, in fact, was incredibly exposed, acting as Starling's agent in the artistic sense of the word in collecting the payment, ostensibly for a minor commission. He made contact with the mark, led Katherine's man on a short hike while he watched for covert surveillance, and then called her as Reg Starling to make the final trade. His message to her, "Bring it in," was their code phrase warning Francesca that he had spotted light surveillance, but was cueing the sting regardless. No risk, no reward.

Curaitis and the mark stood waiting together, surrounded by a crowd of weather-daring revelers. Third and Jeffers placed the meeting right in the center of Brunswick City's nightclub district, but the Davion Heavy Guards had taken control of the place two months before, despite the battle still raging for control of the continent of Brunswick. It made for the perfect drop site, harder for Dehaver to smuggle in and set up a support team than it had been for the two agents to arrange their sting. As the sedan pulled up near the predetermined corner, Francesca got her first and only look through the darkened window at the agent who had sheltered Katherine so well.

Richard Dehaver.

The intelligence man was taller than Curaitis by a few centimeters. His pale face looked drawn, and his eyes were two dark pits in what might otherwise have been a handsome face. His hair was wet-dark and slicked back under the drizzling rain. He wore a peacoat for warmth, and his hands were in his pockets, with a gun in one of them, no doubt. At his feet on the rain-blackened walk sat a large duffel like any military man might carry, presumably filled with ten million kroner. "It's all about perceived value," Francesca whispered to herself, but then saw Curaitis nod as the mic sewed into her trench's collar transmitted to his earpiece.

He had left his system permanently latched open as well. "I was instructed to take possession of the original," Dehaver said, his voice distant but intelligible through Curaitis's transmitter.

They had expected that. Still, Curaitis held up under his supposed instructions. "The painting was never offered."

"I think a ten million kroner price allows the customer some rights in this transaction." Dehaver nodded toward the waiting sedan. A nearby pedestrian staggered into him, and he shoved the stranger away. "Call it a good-will gesture. After all, he can always paint another one. This simply proves to us that there is no mischief planned before Mr. Starling leaves New Avalon. I'll take it as is."

"In this weather?" Francesca asked, thinking of Reg's eccentric manners. "Absolutely not." She waited while Curaitis relayed the stubborn message.

"The painting can be placed inside the duffel." Dehaver nodded down at the bag. "I doubted that you would want to take any container provided by me very far anyway."

Curaitis didn't wait for her acquiesce. "Any other requests?"

"He could sign it."

Francesca felt a hopeful grin prick at the edge of her mouth and knew it wasn't her smile. It was Reg Starling's. "He wants *that* much more proof that Reg is really in the car. Agree, but watch him."

She picked up the canvas and fished a pen from her jacket. With a flourish, she forged Reg Starling's name on the back of the canvas. At her signal, Curaitis picked up the duffel, carried it to the vehicle, and passed it through a partially opened door while Francesca huddled in safety against the far side of the sedan. While he waited outside, she tore away the green plastic hood that had protected the duffel's opening from the weather, then dumped the money over the floor and unused seat. Her chest tightened and a wave of dizziness hit her as she performed a quick eyeball of the piled bundles—ten million kroner!—making certain everything looked on the up and up. Then Francesca quickly pulled the bag over the canvas and allowed Curaitis to retrieve it. After the door was securely closed and locked once more, she did a rough count of the bundles. Fifty bundles, at two hundred thousand kroner each. She rifled through two of them, checking for false bills inserted in the middle, and then waved a small detector over them to check for bugs, tracers, or other sundry and unpleasant surprises.

"It all looks clean," she said, then hit the intercom button. "Drive," she told the man up front. She leaned back against the supple leather seat. As the sedan pulled away from the corner, Francesca glanced back through the window, suddenly worried for Curaitis. But he was resourceful and decently protected, so she calmed herself by thinking about what they had finally accomplished. "We did it," she whispered to him.

Except that the money was far from clean, and Francesca wasn't more than twenty meters away when the chemical dead man's switch cut out.

The plastic hood had done more than keep out the night's drizzle. It had been a barrier to prevent oxygen and water vapor in the air from mixing into the nitrogen-filled duffel. Once Francesca dumped the bundles of hard currency onto the seat, about the same time as her brain swam from breathing the now nitrogen-rich air, oxygen began attacking the ultrathin coating of sodium that an NAIS scientist had painstakingly applied to several of the money-bundling straps in a layer only a few molecules thick. It corrupted the alkali metal, the exothermic reaction eventually forming a layer of sodium hydroxide while giving off hydrogen gas and heat.

As the first layer deteriorated, oxygen finally worked its way through to the second layer underneath. It consisted of potassium, also a Group I metal but even more reactive—so much more that oxygen finally struck a spark against the potassium, and the metal burned in a brilliant, yellow-white light. Like a match lighting the fuse of a bomb, this tiny bit of fire caught in the chemically treated currency. At better than four thousand meters per second, the chemical bomb erupted, flashing the other bundles in sympathetic detonation.

Francesca might have noticed early had she been touching one of the three deadly warm bands or watching their glossy surfaces suddenly cloud over pale white. She didn't. A little less water vapor in the air this night might have bought her an extra thirty seconds. A different plan, where she wasn't so worried over the exposed position of Agent Curaitis, might also have made a difference.

No matter how else things might have gone, Francesca Jenkins wasn't more than ten seconds toward safety before the rear of the sedan filled with fire.

Curaitis had waited for some overt play, knowing that Dehaver would have something ready. They had their backup plans ready. If necessary, "Reg Starling" would abandon the sedan and the money, dive into a nearby club, and make a quick sex-change operation. It didn't really matter that they keep the blackmail payment, just that it had been made and Curaitis could *prove* that it had been made through his remaining contacts in the Secretariat. All he had to do was keep Francesca and himself alive for another ten minutes.

He accomplished half of that.

The fireball erupted, and long streamers of fire smashed out the sedan's rear windows, bursting through in reddish-orange gouts of twisting flame. Then the top of the armored sedan cracked along the rear line, peeling the roof back like a giant's tin-opener. Curaitis watched the sedan squash down on its suspension, pressed to the street by a fiery hand, then leap five meters into the air before falling back to rest on burning tires.

Luckily, Dehaver was as caught by surprise at the early detonation of his bomb. Recovering quickly, he pulled a snubnosed gyrojet pistol from his coat pocket. But Curaitis was already moving with determined speed as he ducked and spun beneath the single shot, feeling it tug at the collar of his jacket. The roar of the gyrojet in his ear, the burn of the muzzle flash against the side of his neck were all that he would remember afterward. A lifetime of training, with help from the Davion Heavy Guard, saved his life. He knocked Dehaver down, landing on top of him as several nearby pedestrians suddenly pulled pistols and crowded around, shielding the scuffle from any Secretariat snipers or other nearby agents. One unknown man pulled a gun and aimed it in the wrong direction, into the mass of Guard infantry, and earned a pair of forty-five-caliber slugs to the chest.

Curaitis disarmed the other agent with a violent twist, fracturing Dehaver's wrist and sending the gyrojet clattering to the wet pavement. Dehaver yelled in pain, but quickly bore down on it as he clenched his jaw so tight that the muscles stood out on the side of his neck.

"You won't kill me," he said through bared teeth. "Whomever you work for, you'll want me alive."

Burning with rage and helpless frustration, unable to close his ears to the crackling flames that continued to consume the sedan, Curaitis couldn't help the extra pressure he suddenly applied to Dehaver's wrist. "Unless we work for *her*," he said savagely, wanting to scare the man.

It worked, for a moment. Dehaver's soulless eyes glanced around in pain and in a panic, no doubt wondering how Katherine had managed such a skillful operation without his knowing. Then he decided for himself that it wasn't possible. "Victor," he said. No loathing. Just a total absence of emotion.

Curaitis crabbed around to kneel on Dehaver's back. He

freed his laser pistol from its holster at the small of his back, placing the barrel in the killing position at the base of Dehaver's skull. "That's right," he said. "Victor."

He glanced through the legs of his guard detail, unable to keep from looking at the burning vehicle. Two people worked to smother flames from the clothes of one body that had to be the driver. The back-passenger section continued to burn so hot that pieces of the sedan's body glowed orange. There would be no rescuing anybody from there. Curaitis would be lucky to recover some charred bone and ash, though he would. His partner deserved at least that from him, and so much more if he could only decide how to pay it.

"Francesca," he whispered sadly.

Damn.

"I can give her to you," Dehaver said. It took Curaitis a moment to realize that the man wasn't offering Francesca back to him. Dehaver had already weighed his ability to resist any determined interrogation and understood the only choice left to him. "Katrina." He spoke the name in a venomous whisper. "I can be very convincing in front of the right people."

Curaitis hauled him to his feet, never easing off the pistol. "You'll talk," he promised. "You'll tell me everything I want to know. But if you think you are ever going to be set down in front of someone with the power to commute your sentence, you are sorely mistaken. There's going to be no law involved with this. Just me." He spun Dehaver around, fastened onto him with a gaze of blue ice.

"I'm the only person you'll ever talk to," he promised, voice flat and cold, "for the rest of your life."

21

When I heard that Phelan Kell was lost on a mission, I refused to believe it, not even when the supposed pirates turned out to be Clan invaders. I have always thought my cousin to be a discipline case, that's true, but as a MechWarrior, I considered him to have few peers. I don't think I've ever told him this. Perhaps I never trusted him enough to look past his self-doubts and accept it as a compliment rather than as a way to bestow on him my validation.

—*Cause and Effect*, Avalon Press, 3067

Methow Valley, Tharkad
Donegal Province
Lyran Alliance
13 October 3066

Running his *Timber Wolf* in a sharp, sawtooth path over snow-dusted ground, Phelan Kell avoided the brunt of heavy strafing runs. He dropped his targeting crosshairs over a blue-and-gold-painted *Banshee*, his weapons voicing the Wolf khan's displeasure. The upper half of his 'Mech shook as enemy launchers released a score of long-range missiles, the warheads streaking out with deep-throated roars on fiery trails. His extended-range lasers stabbed bloody lances after, ripping at the enemy, clawing for the throat.

Despite the freezing temperatures of Tharkad's winter, sweat rolled freely off Phelan's brow. The *Timber Wolf* was not a cool-running OmniMech, designed with firepower in mind and depending heavily on the life-support system. His reactor spiked hard under the lower draw. Waste heat leeched up through cockpit deck plating as a new slug of charged coolant raced through the coils built into his full-body cooling suit. Phelan shivered with appreciation, then again as a silver blur flashed past the nose of the *Timber Wolf*'s forward-thrust head. He twisted the seventy-five-ton OmniMech back to the right, giving way as a Royal Guard *Hauptmann* moved up to support the *Banshee*, for now avoiding its heavy gauss rifle. It also pulled him out of line from the pair of *Eisensturm* OmniFighters, whose particle cannon scoured the ground where he had been a moment before.

It was a reminder—as if he needed it—that there were actually two battles being fought by his Clan warriors, one in and one above the snow-carpeted Methow Valley. He gave up his tactical screen for an eyes-on study of the dogfight. Royal Guard aerospace fighters swarmed under Tharkad's leaden skies thick as migrating swallows, overwhelming his few Clan Wolf pilots by dint of numbers. Those not boiling around the Wolves formed into pair after pair to make attack runs down the wide valley. Here, they scoured armor off Ranna Kerensky's *Executioner*. There, a pair of *Lucifer*s scattered Elementals by raining LRMs into their midst. Tossed aside like misshapen dolls, the armored bodies instantly regained their feet and bounded toward the nearest enemy machine, claws already grasping for purchase against its armored hide.

He had already selected his private frequency to Ranna Kerensky, star colonel to the Fourth Wolf Guards. "What do you think, Ranna?"

"I think I would call down the rest of the Snapping Jaws cluster," she said, naming the Wolf aerospace forces left to safeguard their WarShips, "and damn Peter Steiner if he objects."

From her tone, Phelan could imagine the fierce set to her bright blue eyes—that go-to-the-devil look that came with her more spirited opinions. It was a trait inherited from one of her genetic ancestors, and there was no doubting which one.

Ranna was a sibko-born descendent of Natasha Kerensky, the Black Widow herself.

Phelan didn't wholly disagree with her view, but he knew he had to see beyond his role as khan. He was also a part of Peter's Lyran coalition, representing the Wolves-in-exile, just as the Kell Hounds stood for the ARDC and the Twentieth Arcturan Guards stood for the regular Lyran military. No matter how much the warrior—the Wolf—in him chafed against those restraints, he understood the need to work within the system this time. His father had made a serious and convincing argument for it after backing Phelan's stand on an uncompromising aerospace cordon of Tharkad.

Still, there was no denying that his Wolves were in an exposed position. The Methow Valley was an open cut running between the nearby foothills and the impressive trees of Stahlwurzel Forest. His people were caught between a full regiment of the Royal Guard armor brigade camped in the shadow of the forest's mighty trees and the assault battalion of Battle-Mechs pressing them from the foothills. His gut said to turn and *bite*, a wolf's natural reaction. His head warned him of the price his warriors would pay against the loyalists' veteran aerospace brigade and how it would damage Peter's authority to have the Wolves playing their own private game within the coalition.

Phelan spent some of his anger against his communications panel, slapping at the contact that toggled up his lead aerospace pilot. "Wolf One to Sky Lead. Carew! You've spent enough time as a flying target today. I want you to extend and escape. Take your flyers home."

"Are you certain?" Carew asked, speaking in the rushed, clipped words that told Phelan he was hanging into this fight by the slimmest margin. "Home" was currently the satellite-production facility of local TharHes industries, seized by the Kell Hounds to provide on-planet access to fresh armor and munitions. It was far enough that fightercraft could not be easily recalled to support any ground action. "You do not need air cover?"

"I'm looking at another type of cover for now," Phelan

promised, then switched over to the general combat frequency. "This is Wolf One. Prepare an echelon-left shift due west. Command Trinary, blaze the trail on my mark. Wolf Guards, follow up on Ranna's order." He turned out of his sawtooth pattern early, angling the *Timber Wolf* for the nearest point of the Stahlwurzel. "We are taking the forest. Go!"

Two stars of OmniMechs and twenty men and women of Phelan's finest Elemental infantry suddenly shifted track and threw themselves at the entrenched armor, covering the ground in long strides and bouncing hops, respectively. 'Mechs kicked through a few light snowdrifts, hammering the loyalist line early, thanks to the better reach of Clan weapons. Elementals leapt onto the backs and sides of several Omnis, hitching a ride. Phelan slowed his own machine just enough so that a full point of five Elementals could clamber up and latch on to their carrying holds. Next to him, Ranna's *Executioner* carried an equal number of the armored infantry. She was exercising a commander's prerogative to join in the first push.

"The armor line is crouching down," Ranna said, indicating the steadfast hold of the enemy armor. They didn't break in the face of the Clan push, even when she committed her Wolf Guards behind it. Now it became a race, with the Lyran assault battalion falling behind as the Wolves pushed for the forest.

Phelan nodded. "They just don't want us going in there."

The *Timber Wolf* shrugged off fire from two particle cannon as Phelan reached out with his missiles, bracketing an old Schrek PPC-carrier and pounding its armor with nearly half a hundred warheads. The tracked machine began a slow withdrawal along the edge of the forest, too unwieldy to maneuver around the giant trees. Stray warheads also flushed out a pair of *Fenrir* battlesuit troops that had been hiding in ambush. A large laser devoted to each cut them down before they could bring their weapons against him.

More of the four-legged battlesuit troops ran from hiding now, pacing the Lyran vehicles that finally pulled back from the path of Phelan's trinary assault. He gained the edge of the dark forest with little trouble, stepping under a tall cover of steel root oaks and redwood cedar. With each heavy footfall, clumps of snow rained down through the branches from the white canopy high overhead. The trees were massive. They dwarfed his Omni, forcing him to step around them rather than take a 'Mech's usual path of simply shouldering through.

They would also provide protection from the pursuing Royal Guard if they were foolish enough to follow his Wolves. Phelan blew out a satisfied breath, which turned into a warning shout to his trinary as his sensors painted a new threat onto his HUD as a heavy gauss slug punched into his chest.

A *Barghest* waited farther into the forest, its four legs braced against the recoil of its heavy gauss cannon. As Phelan fought for control of his *Timber Wolf*, he also spotted icon tags for a *Stiletto* and a *Hatchetman*. New heat flooded his cockpit from damaged reactor shielding, and his sweaty grip slipped on the throttle. His Omni rocked up against a tall cedar, scraping away its leathery bark, and then paced deeper into the gloom and the waiting *Barghest*. Which was the best thing he could have done, as it turned out. Heavy gauss rifles did not operate well at point-blank range, and the next rail-accelerated mass smashed into the thick bole of a nearby cedar instead. The tree toppled with a cracking groan, falling between Phelan and the new enemy machines, buying him a brief moment of respite.

"All right," he said, fighting to keep any tremor out of his voice, "so they *really* did not want us coming in here." It was a solid plan. Use an armor line to hold the Clan force in the valley, then pound them with aerospace fighters until additional 'Mech forces worked through the forest to reinforce the western flank. Then they'd have Phelan's people in a pincer. "Some Royal Guard officer must have trained in a Davion academy."

But nothing rocked the Wolves back on their heels for long, and this time the reaction of turn and bite played just fine. Elementals jumped free of the *Timber Wolf* and Ranna's *Executioner*, working their way over and through the branches of the fallen redwood, swarming the enemy 'Mechs as Phelan worked his way around several large trees. Some of his other warriors reported enemy contact inside the forest, but that it was no more than a company or two. Not enough to stop them.

Not one Elemental had touched the *Barghest*, leaving it for their khan. Phelan appreciated the show of confidence, though he would also have appreciated a point or two of armored infantry tearing that heavy gauss rifle off the back of the four-legged BattleMech. His own missiles were no match and difficult to fire through trees, so he shunted them off his main trigger and tied in his medium lasers instead. Drawing his crosshairs over the loyalist, he settled them on the kicking-donkey insignia of the Second Royal Guards. "Always ready to make an ass of themselves," Phelan whispered, remembering the old insult from his cadet days at the Nagelring, before being captured and adopted into Clan Wolf.

An insult that the other warrior proved in the next heartbeat when he chose to fire on the *Executioner* moving up behind Phelan. Clan honor normally demanded that warriors involved in single combat respect that engagement. If one fired on an outside target, he also drew that warrior into the fight. Obeying that tradition in the valley's running battle had not been possible. Here, though, in the forest cloak, Ranna would have waited for Phelan to deal with the *Barghest* himself. But not now. She unleashed everything she had at the offending 'Mech, joining her firepower to Phelan's. Between the two of them, the *Barghest* lost both right-side legs and suffered a cracked gyroscope housing. It toppled over, landing on the fallen *Stiletto*. Elementals leapt out of the way just in time as the two 'Mechs piled into a tangle of helpless metal.

The *Hatchetman* attempted to disengage, staggering back into the protection of the deep forest with three armored infantrymen still clinging to its back. Its autocannon chipped armor from the shoulder of Phelan's OmniMech, and that gave him all he needed to take the *Hatchetman* as his next prey. "Press them," he called out to his warriors. "Drive them into the forest. Pull them down." Careful of his Elementals, Phelan fired his lasers into one of the *Hatchetman*'s legs, blowing through its lower-leg actuator.

It fell over a moment later as an Elemental warrior dug through and used her laser to cut out the hip joint.

Leaving the hapless 'Mech to his infantry, Phelan pulled his *Timber Wolf* around to rejoin Ranna as she set the Wolf Guards in a defensive line. Should any of the pursuing assault battalion decide to chance the forest, they would find the same reception that had been planned for his Wolves.

"Let them come," Phelan growled, though he doubted they would. The skies and the valley might belong to the loyalists. For now. But the forests . . .

Those belonged to the Wolves.

22

When the *Robert Davion* was lost over Kathil, the entire AFFS felt the blow. WarShips are an appreciable part of the military budget. What no one counted on was the kind of losses we'd see with more than one WarShip fighting the same battle. The GNP of entire worlds was thrown away into the vacuum of space. It was a mistake. And we paid for it.

— *Cause and Effect,* Avalon Press, 3067

FCS **Melissa Davion**
New Avalon System, Crucis March
Federated Suns
15 November 3066

Victor Steiner-Davion's first battle for New Avalon did not take place on the ground or in a 'Mech. It happened five hundred kilometers outside of the planet's orbit as his *Avalon*-class WarShip, the FCS *Melissa Davion,* and three remaining *Fox* corvettes tangled with Katherine's own space-defense force. The dual-hulled cruiser rocked violently with each terrifying hit. Alarms clamored for attention, and Victor imagined damage-control parties yelling for each other down lonely, outboard corridors. At times, he knew, those crewmen were silenced by the whistling hiss of escaping atmosphere. It was his fervent hope that more often a hastily applied patch or the slamming of an airtight door fought back against the deadly vacuum of space.

The *Melissa*'s bridge was spared most of these deadly distractions, though not all. Two young petty officers spot-welded their patch into place, securing the screaming pinhole breach that had touched every crewman on the bridge—for just an instant—with the cold threat lurking beyond the ship's armored hull. Victor's ears popped as atmospheric stabilizers built pressure back up toward normal. He breathed deep of recycled air, tasting the dry, ozone scent left behind by carbon-dioxide scrubbers.

"You should be down in central," said Vice Admiral Kristoffer Hartford. Glancing up from his holographic display, he added, "Highness."

Victor wasn't sure. The cruiser's executive officer had taken over central control, the hub for all damage-control activity and backup for the bridge, and Victor had commandeered her empty seat. Anchored into the chair by a five-point restraint not unlike a BattleMech safety harness, he clutched at the armrests with new strength as he considered the idea. Was he jeopardizing everything by remaining on the cruiser's bridge and risking his life? "I've been protected long enough, Kris. I'm here until you park this thing over New Avalon and our assault force arrives."

If it arrived. And if Victor's WarShips could clear New Avalon's defense force out of the fleet's way.

Seventy-nine JumpShips held station back at the zenith pole, an armada scraped together from every world within Victor's immediate reach. They had ferried one hundred eighty-three DropShips to New Avalon in one of the biggest single troop movements ever made. Those troop carriers were only eight hours behind Victor and catching up fast, hoping for a clear run at the planet. If they didn't get it, his assault would become little more than a shooting gallery, with Katherine's four WarShips bursting open 'Mech-laden DropShips like overripe fruit, spilling flesh and seeds into space. Only nothing would ever grow from them. All any vacuum-frozen body could expect was a fiery cremation as it fell into New Avalon's atmosphere.

Without the hoped-for WarShip reinforcements from Kathil, that might be Victor's fate as well. Katherine, meanwhile, had kept control of the FCS *Lucien Davion* and the *Alexander Davion*, both *Avalon*-class cruisers, as well as the corvettes *Antrim* and *Murmansk*. Naval-grade lasers lit up the space between the capital ships for brief flashes as each side jockeyed for a superior position against the enemy. Missile launchers disgorged their remote killers, and rail guns accelerated massive payloads of silent death through the endless night. At times, there seemed to be more fightercraft flashing across the view monitors than there were stars, though the *Melissa*'s two escorting squadrons of assault DropShips prevented them from straying in too close to the dual-hulled cruiser.

Unfortunately, the same could not be said for the *Intrepid*, Victor's fourth *Fox*-class corvette. The *Intrepid* had lost first its own escorting vessels and then most of its avionics and control systems to the massed-wave attacks of aerospace fighters. It rolled out of control on the far side of New Avalon now, slowly spiraling around the backside of the planet. Whether it would plunge into the atmosphere or orbit around and be finished off by the patrolling cruisers was still anybody's guess.

"Helm, bring us around," Hartford ordered, then speared his fleet comm officer through the back with a hard gaze. The man shifted uncomfortably, as if aware of the admiral's attention. "Fleet, pull back the *Kentares* and the *Donnings*. Order the *Robinson* to take the crown, and slow their approach."

Victor tried to follow his admiral's maneuvers on the main screens, watching the three remaining *Fox*es pull away from Katherine's twin *Davion* cruisers. The FCS *Robinson* limped onto a slightly different course, pitching up and away from the other two, but neither the *Alexander* or the *Lucien* bit on the lure.

Hartford scratched at his salt-and-pepper beard, shaking his head. "They're not going to play our game."

Both the *Alexander* and the *Lucien Davion* kept to the loyalists' side, never straying far from New Avalon, no matter what advantage the allies offered them. They knew their priority, which was to stand between New Avalon and the incoming assault force. In their defensive position *and* with heavier firepower in the two cruisers, their position was very solid. Admiral Hartford ran Victor's fleet in at them repeatedly, first trying to push the loyalists toward atmosphere and then making several attempts to pull apart their battle group to isolate and destroy one of the cruisers.

And each time, the allies' WarShips came away with the worst of the bargain.

Hartford sniffed loudly and sneered at the main display, as if testing the air and finding it wanting. "Helm, pick a point in between those two cruisers and take us after them. Guns, call it out and fire at will as soon as we slip back into range. This is going to get ugly."

Then he turned to stare at Victor again, testing his resolve. Victor glanced at the sealed door. "I'll leave this bridge one step behind you, Kris."

"Highness, if we're ever going to push them out of New Avalon's shadow, I have to take us in closer this time."

"Don't let me stop you."

"Fleet!" Hartford shouted, spending some of his frustration on the air. "I want the *Robinson* running slightly ahead and high. Tell the *Kentares* and the *Donnings* to angle wide to our port, like they plan to get between those loyalists and dirtside."

Holding that formation, the allied WarShips dove back at New Avalon. Their own aerospace fighters swarmed forward, forming a new arrowhead that bulldozed through the Lyran screen and began harassing the loyalist WarShips. Enemy fighters and several combat-escort DropShips returned the favor, striking at their flank and running, usually preferring one of the *Fox*es to tangling with a cruisers. They had learned on previous passes to avoid the interior of any pyramidal formation, where all five ships—four now—overlapped enough raw firepower that anything straying in did not fly out under its own power. At least, most of them had learned. An assault-class *Overlord* tried it again, thinking to slip up behind the *Robinson*. The allies left it holed and savaged and bleeding its final oxygen reserves into space.

Central control updated the bridge in the brief lull, reporting light structural damage to the WarShip and the serious loss of both starboard broadside naval gauss cannon. Hartford accepted this with barely a grunt, then ordered Katherine's fleet displayed on the main viewscreen. Her two *Avalon*-class cruisers held the center of their formation. The split hulls of the catamaran designs reached out port and starboard, inviting the allies into the loyalists' strong embrace. The *Antrim* and the *Murmansk* flanked the *Alexander* and the *Lucien* at a good distance, running slightly ahead and ready to blunt any radical maneuver made by Victor's admiral.

"It's like staring down the barrel of a long gun," Victor said quietly.

Hartford shook his head. "That shows two-dimensional thinking, Highness." His voice remained just this side of hostile, though Victor knew it wasn't anything personal. It was simply the manner of the man he had selected as fleet admiral. Hartford was a short man, thick across the chest. A third-generation naval officer, he showed the same rugged independence that Victor expected from almost any veteran spacer. They often seemed bred for the job, almost enough to convince Victor that the Clans had the right of it with their genetic breeding programs.

The *Melissa* trembled as a fighter squadron hammered against her underbelly. On an auxiliary screen, Victor watched them dart away like striking piranha. "How do you see it, then?" he asked.

The answer didn't come for several long seconds, as if the admiral was deciding whether or not to bother. His weapons officer called out range on one of the *Melissa*'s remaining gauss cannon, ordering a continuous fire pattern. Hartford watched carefully. Finally, he held up his hands as if grabbing a large invisible ball. "It's a sphere, sire. We're in the middle, and wherever you have a *hard* threat"—he pointed at the main screens and then at an invisible point on his sphere—"that sets the radius." He cupped his hand back around the space. "The threat spreads out until it envelops the sphere. The greatest danger centers around the threat location—call that the pole—and it fades almost to nothing after you cross the equator."

"There are four loyalist WarShips out there," Victor said. "Once they break up, that gives you five overlapping spheres of varying size."

Hartford nodded once, curt and final. "Welcome to my world." He checked the screens, the holographic display, and ordered new reports from his bridge officers.

He made it through most of them before the first hard-hitting shocks slammed into the *Melissa Davion*'s nose, blunting the sharp point on her port hull and tearing gaping rents down the inside of the starboard. On the screen, the *Lucien Davion* swung into a broadside. Flashes of sharp blue light strobed along the cruiser's hull where naval gauss ports discharged their acceleration coils and railed heavy masses in the *Melissa*'s direction. The *Alexander* drove forward and swung out to threaten the allies' two flanking *Fox*es.

"Helm, turn us more to port. Bring our fore-starboard weapons to bear."

Victor glanced over at his admiral. "Haven't we lost all heavy weapons behind that?"

"So there's less damage they can actually do to us on the starboard side," Hartford said, his eyes never leaving the screen. "Helm, dampen main engines. Prepare for a hard starboard turn and acceleration on my mark."

With momentum in the driver's seat, the *Melissa* coasted forward into the budding chaos. Her forward autocannon and capital-class lasers began to probe outward as the *Lucien* slipped into their range, evening out the disparate weapon exchanges. Central called out damage reports as if marking time in the battle—avionics, one of the KF drive's superconductor rings, the starboard grav deck. Victor heard the deaths of fine crewman in each report. Hartford seemed to catalog the damage as nothing more than ruined systems. Losing the last starboard-side gauss cannon, he gave his helmsman the signal for a starboard turn, which would run away from New Avalon and swing the task force wide of the loyalist fleet.

"Now we swing around and kick the *Lucien* right in the ass," he shouted to his bridge.

Except that two of the allies' corvettes would never make the turn.

The *Alexander Davion* had thrust forward out of the loyalist formation farther than ever before, angling in to cut off the *Donnings* and the trailing *Kentares*. A full wing of allied aerospace fighters jumped on the *Alexander*, trying to force it away. The cruiser swam out of the clustering craft, leaving them to a trio of escorting DropShips that made short work of the stinging assault. Broken fighters littered the *Alexander*'s wake. A few fires flashed along the cruiser's starboard side, quickly extinguished as atmosphere in those areas vacated to space. They would never be enough damage to slow the hunting leviathan.

There was no swinging turn, the *Alexander*'s captain content with his forward run and no doubt planning to trade broadsides as he passed each *Fox*. The cruiser rolled its starboard side down fifteen degrees, compensating for the slightly higher plane it had pitched onto during its forward thrust. At medium range, the *Alexander Davion* outgunned each corvette by better than three hundred percent. Admiral Hartford yelled for Fleet-Comms, ordering the corvettes to disengage on immediate escape vectors.

Victor waited with white-knuckled grips on the arms of his seat while the corvettes began their turns too late to evade the loyalist cruiser. The FCS *Admiral Corinne Donnings* slid past the *Alexander Davion* first, spitting out a half-dozen ship-hunting barracuda missiles and slapping at the larger vessel with naval-grade lasers and autocannon. Its point-defense weaponry worked some defense against the enemy fightercraft, but the armor it had left was too thin to hold back the cruiser's main assault.

For every barracuda sent its way, the *Alexander* responded with a killer whale from its AR10 launchers. Capital lasers softened the *Donnings*'s armor, cutting gaps that the cruisers filled with streamers of hot metal and the cold, wrenching punches of gauss packages. Battered, crippled, and broadcasting distress messages, the *Donnings* pushed past the cruisers on a sputtering drive flare, pushed onto a direct course with New Avalon. Lifeboats and escape pods began to separate from the smaller

WarShip even as the *Alexander Davion* turned its full attention to the *Kentares*.

Surprisingly, the *Kentares* was already dropping escape pods into the black void, as if accepting its doomed fate. It turned in and pitched up, preparing to slash across the *Alexander*'s bow in an attempt to avoid the terrifying broadside slavo awaiting it. Except that the *Alexander* turned with the *Kentares*, not about to let it go so easily. The loyalists' preoccupation with the tactical maneuver might have blinded them to the *Kentares*'s other preparations. More likely, the crew of the *Alexander Davion* simply couldn't believe them.

One of Admiral Hartford's officers was quick to respond to the warning alarms, calling out the problem before he'd even finished a check of all sensors. "Admiral! We have a building EM source nearby! No . . . no IR." An electromagnetic pulse was the telltale of an arriving JumpShip or WarShip, although any attempt to jump in-system this deep into New Avalon's gravity would be suicidal. The lack of an infrared signature meant that wasn't the situation, however.

The sensors officer double-checked. "Detecting weak gravitational disruptions . . . and a building EM field. Sir, it's the *Kentares*! She's jumping out!"

Kristoffer Hartford went pale, his face blanching as if all the blood had drained from his body. Slapping his harness release, he leapt for the Fleet-Comms station and toggled for open communication. All Victor could do was lean forward against his restraints, eyes glued to the main screens. "No! *Kentares*, no!" he prayed.

Of course, an attempt to charge the Kearny-Fuchida drive and jump out of the New Avalon system from *any* position close to the planet was just as deadly as jumping in-system. More so, in this case, as the presence of any nearby KF drive coils would form a gravitational anchor, distorting the forming field and—at best!—aborting the jump. The *Kentares* was driving into point-blank with the *Alexander Davion*, and it was a close call as to whether the loyalist *Antrim* or the *Melissa* herself might be too close to the deadly attempt.

Admiral Hartford managed a single order to abort their jump before the *Kentares*'s final transmission bled through the static and whispered out over the open bridge communications. "God save the prince."

The *Kentares* swam through a distorted field of energy. Stars faded to small red coals. The corvette shimmered, much like the wavering illusion created by heat rising over a desert highway, then twisted into a grotesque parody of its former strength. The wide aft end of the vessel froze in space, or at least slowed to a crawl, while the bow lanced forward in a blurred fist. The thick middle now stretched out like taffy as the hull melted and ran like wax. Then the back end snapped forward as the corvette began to jump, dragging across the bow of the *Alexander*.

Victor would never be certain of the actual circumstances because the electromagnetic field of the jumping corvette distorted all cameras during that moment, but it looked to him as if the *Alexander Davion*'s KF drive was suddenly wrenched *through* the cruiser's hull like a fish being deboned. It shredded the War-Ship's metallic flesh, destroying weapons bays, control spaces, and the main fusion drive in its attempt to follow the *Kentares* through hyperspace. In the end, it just couldn't make it. The field shattered, and cloaked stars jumped back into focus. Rocked hard by the final gravitational pulse, the *Melissa* slammed sideways as if struck amidships by another vessel. Victor saw what might have been the aft drive section of the *Kentares* or possibly some twisted wreckage torn free from the FCS *Alexander Davion*. A few stunned fightercraft tumbled through the scene. Then the screen brightened into a wash of hard, white light as the decimated *Alexander* finally exploded under extreme duress.

Thrown onto the deck by the *Kentares*'s shock wave, Admiral Hartford was holding a broken arm protectively against his side. He paid less attention to the ruin his corvette had made of the space-born battlefield and more to his original maneuver. "Fire!" he shouted, his voice laced with pain. "Forget the *Kentares*, she's lost. Fire on that damned cruiser! The *Lucien*!"

Victor blinked his way back to some semblance of coherent

thought, alternating his gaze between the auxiliary screens and the holographic display. Not only were the *Kentares* and the *Alexander Davion* missing from the earlier battle model, the *Antrim* had tumbled out of control, and the *Lucien* had allowed Victor's flagship to slip into its aft quarter. Both the *Melissa* and the *Robinson*—Victor's only remaining corvette—opened up on the remaining loyalist cruiser at the same time.

The WarShips' destructive power hammered into the *Lucien*'s rear thrusters, mangling them with feral dedication. Victor saw the brief blossoms of missile impacts punching into the cruiser close to its aft weapons bays. The *Lucien* began to turn, maneuvering on forward thrusters only, but too slow. The *Melissa* trimmed into a full port broadside, and as the *Lucien* turned, Admiral Hartford walked his deadly fire down the length of the other cruiser, battering it into submission before any matching firepower responded.

A naval gauss slammed through the *Melissa's* weapons bay, which held her capital-class autocannon. Another burst bulkheads so close to the bridge that the floor bucked again, tossing Hartford onto his broken arm and opening a new whistling breach along one seam. Artificial wind tugged at Victor's hair, and his ears popped, but the damage-control petty officers had a patch vacuum-sealed over the hole within seconds.

"Sir," a communications officer shouted, "the *Lucien* surrenders. She surrenders!" Validating the announcement, the *Melissa* calmed and shook under no more weapons fire.

"Cease fire," Hartford ordered through clenched teeth. "Tell the *Lucien* to stand down all maneuvering and quiet her engines. Helm, put us behind them. If they so much as fire a maneuvering thruster before we've got a prize crew on her, open fire." He drew in a shaky breath. "Have any rescue tugs render immediate aid to the *Donnings*, the *Intrepid*, and the *Antrim*."

"I have the *Intrepid*," Fleet Comms answered quickly. "She's in a stable orbit over New Avalon. The *Donnings* is lost, sir. She hit the atmosphere thirty seconds ago."

There was no need to describe the results. WarShips did not enter atmosphere on purpose, or more than once. The bridge observed a moment of silence, whether called or not, as each crew-man wished their comrades in space a quick end. "Someone should say something," the weapons officer said softly. "For the *Donnings* and the *Kentares*."

"We will," Victor promised, releasing his harness in order to help Hartford back to his own seat. "After. We'll say something for them all, I hope." He nodded at communications. "For now, contact the assault force. Tell them they have a clear approach to New Avalon."

And they did. The *Lucien* surrendered, and the *Murmansk* ran for the nadir jump point. Most of the enemy fightercraft and assault DropShips turned for succor from New Avalon itself, and so there was nothing left to stand in the allies' way. One of the bridge technicians pulled up a camera angle for the planet on the main screen. Turning slowly under the WarShip's watchful eye, the upper half of the world filled the monitor, the peaceful blue-green marred only by the angry drive flare of a retreating loyalist *Excalibur*.

"Katherine," Victor whispered to himself, careful even of his admiral. "Katherine, I am here."

23

So many people supported my sister's rise to power. She played a masterful game of intrigue and politics, I admit. But the ones who amaze me are those who stuck by her for so long, never seeing, or allowing themselves to see, what she was. At what point did they stop caring for the truth?

—*Cause and Effect,* Avalon Press, 3067

Davion Peace Gardens
Avalon City, New Avalon
Crucis March
Federated Suns
20 November 3066

Katrina had chosen the Davion Peace Gardens for this morning's public address. Also known as Peace Park, the lush grounds bordered Mount Davion and reached around the main NAIS campus for Avalon City. It was a popular retreat in these first weeks of spring when green shoots brought skeletal trees back to life and color unfolded from wintered bulbs. A brisk wind ruffled the park's thick grasses, carrying the chill touch of last night's rain as well as scents from early-blooming crocus and daffodil. The breeze picked up a strand of Katrina's golden hair, wrapping it over her face. She plucked it away with practiced grace, her gaze never straying far from the small assembly of reporters and holocam crews who waited on their Archon-Princess.

She walked slowly, unhurried and maybe a touch sorrowful. The cobblestone path was one of many that trailed under the outspread branches of a small, tight forest of trees, each course leading to various gardens or memorial statues that commemorated actions of heroism and sacrifice. Her backdrop for today's short speech was a monument of dark stone and steel sitting in the bowl of a grassy amphitheater. A memorial flame burned and guttered above the trio of figures. A wolfhound, torn and bloodied, sprang to a young girl's rescue while a dark panther, sculpted after an oriental style, stared hungrily at the child with its obsidian eyes. A wonderful, moving piece, she had chosen it most carefully but not without reservations, as the statue commemorated the Kell Hounds' rescue of Katrina's mother, Melissa, during the Fourth Succession War. It also stood as testament to the loss of Patrick Kell, Morgan Kell's brother. If played correctly to the media, though, it would show how far the Kell Hounds had fallen from her good graces.

Taking her place in front of the memorial, Katrina paused to study it. Not that she expected to find new meaning in the tableau, except to confirm her choice of wardrobe. Her white pantsuit and vest trimmed in silver and blue stood out nicely against the dark stone and blue-polished steel. But then she had judged that the day before, leaving nothing to chance.

She took a moment now to give everyone watching a moment to remember the memorial's genesis. It was a wonderfully tragic story of personal sacrifice, something that Katrina wanted the people of New Avalon to consider in what she had to ask of them. With Victor already in control of the continent of Brunswick and beginning serious drives onto the continents of Rostock and Albion, she needed her people's strength now more than ever.

A difficult admission, but true nonetheless.

"People of New Avalon," she began, clasping her hands in front of her, holding them at her slim waist. "There is no easing the pain we all feel as the brutalities of my brother's civil war strike home with a vengeance. This disruption to our lives, the threat to our safety and security, and the uncertainty of what tomorrow may bring weigh on us all. Our only consolation is in knowing that what we suffer now is nothing that hundreds of worlds have not felt over the course of this long and desperate struggle."

She held the camera's gaze for a moment. "We suffer Victor's rage at being unable to match the martial glories of our father," she said finally. "We suffer his inadequacy of true leadership, always cloaked by the need to wage war against the enemy. Any enemy. Even one he creates within his own family. So many times we have reached out a hand in friendship and peace, only to have it knocked aside by Victor's paranoia. We suffer"—Katrina paused for effect again—"we suffer Victor's impotence to avenge himself upon the assassin of Omi Kurita." She glanced down in shame to admit, "His love."

Rage, inadequacy, paranoia, and impotence—traits that people abhorred in any leader, especially in a son of Hanse Davion. And Katrina had all but declared that Victor and Omi had been lovers. Katrina knew—she *knew*—that it must be true, but where proof was lacking, accusation served just as well. Hadn't Victor reminded her of that only recently? People would draw the necessary conclusions for themselves.

"Victor totally controls our continent of Brunswick," she said, admitting to what the news media had reported days before. "With our forces spread out in response to earlier assaults led by the renegade Tancred Sandoval, there was little we could do to stop this. It was necessary, in fact, to protect Albion and therefore safeguard Avalon City, the seat of power for all of the Federated Suns and one of the strongest guiding lights in the Inner Sphere."

Careful never to slight her Lyran Alliance, Katrina was forced to walk a fine edge in declaring New Avalon the more important capital. It was, of course, with *her* here. But she couldn't admit that directly.

"It is necessary that we all resist this assault on our home by every means available. So it now falls to you, my *First Citizens* of the Federated Suns, to assist in this struggle—to help prevent Victor from bringing to New Avalon the same darkness that Stefan Amaris once brought to Terra. Like the Great Usurper, Victor's power rests in those who collaborate." She piled all her loathing onto that last word, weighing it down with contempt, as for something unclean.

"Resist him, my citizens, if in no other way than through civil disobedience. Protect yourselves from Victor's wrath, certainly, but unless you fall under the sights of his weapons, refuse to support his campaign of bloody violence. Walk off your jobs and return home. Help your neighbors in their time of need, but deny relief to the soldiers of the enemy." She softened her gaze, letting the weight of her responsibilities peek through to the average citizen of New Avalon. "I know that I am calling for the isolation and the collapse of industry on Brunswick. I know that I am calling on you to endure great hardships. But the power rests in your hands, as it has forever. Without *your* help," she promised them, "Victor's rebellion cannot succeed.

"It is up to you."

As if Katrina planned to let her fate, and the fate of her two hard-won nations, rest in the hands of common citizens. Not while she still had her armies . . . and her alliances.

The soft strains of a light, calming symphony filled her private chambers in the Davion Palace, warring against her current mood and losing the battle as she rudely switched off her hidden sound system. She crossed the sitting room with determined strides, ignoring the French doors that opened onto her boudoir and storming her living area instead. Crossing the room, she went to a white oak armoire facing a couch of ivory silk. She rolled back the cabinet doors to reveal a small tri-v holographic set, then shoved a data crystal into its reader slot.

It had been delivered to her by a merchant courier, and Katrina knew the identity of the sender. The opening screen confirmed it, showing a frozen storm of gray static. She looked at the inside of her gold bangle, the bracelet Vlad had fashioned for her, and used its "registration" markings to calculate today's security code. She tapped the final numbers into a small datapad. Her code permanently unlocked the contents, and Katrina made a note to secure the crystal in her personal vault or destroy it immediately after viewing it.

"He has launched against Arc-Royal," Katrina whispered to herself, somewhere in between anticipation and need. "The Wolves will force Phelan and Morgan Kell to retreat from Tharkad."

It was all part of the latest plan, conceived in secret with her Champion, Simon Gallagher, shortly after Richard Dehaver's mysterious disappearance. In effect, it was little more than a return to her original scheme. Free the Lyran Alliance, after which Nondi would rally all available troops to storm the Federated Suns like a Tharkad avalanche. Roll over Tikonov and Kathil, secure the outer system jump points, and Victor would be trapped here to *her* justice.

Of course, if the cavalry arrived too late, Katrina could simply meet them in Federated Suns space, and they would escort the Archon back to her Alliance capital. With New Avalon so heavily threatened, Katrina was not above looking for a fallback position. All she needed was to take Vlad up on his earlier offer, releasing her personal claim to settling with the renegade Wolves on Arc-Royal. Katrina had messaged him several months ago with the change in her position. It galled her, being forced to any admission of weakness, even a small one, but she would find a way to reimburse Vlad's efforts on her behalf. She would not remain beholden to any man, and especially not to a potential partner.

But Vlad Ward's visage was not one to warm her heart this time as his holographic image filled the small display. He stared out at her with grim anger. "Katrina," he said, his voice curt and chill, awarding her neither titles nor surnames. "Your *request* is flatly refused."

This was *not* what she had expected.

"When you claimed the entire Defense Cordon as a party to your war, my opportunity to attack the abjured Wolves was denied. I accepted this as an equal, as was my promise. You . . ." He glared even harder. "You would now give up that enemy simply because you bid poorly during the batchall? If you underbid, call up reserves. If you have no reserves, it is a poor leader who commits everything when she knows it still is not enough. Did you truly believe that my Wolves were yours to whistle for as you needed them? Am I a stravag mercenary, to be bought with political or personal coin and told where and when I may do battle?"

Katrina dropped back onto the sofa, her knees giving way before Vlad's onslaught. What he was saying had not been her intent at all. In fact, Katrina could hardly follow Vlad's reasoning. Because she did not admit earlier that she needed him, he could not now interfere? She was supposed to cement their place as equals by giving him evidence of her inferior position? What kind of logic was that?

Clan logic, apparently.

Vlad's face had flushed in anger, his scar a pale slash running down the side of his face. He calmed himself now with visible effort. "Apparently you still have much to learn of our ways. If you are truly my equal, Katrina, this we will learn in short order. My Wolves will not interfere. Your enemies are yours to defeat, or not. I leave this up to you."

Although Katrina saw the irony in Vlad's farewell statement, so close to the finish of her own address, she did not find it the least bit amusing. Rising slowly from her seat, commanding her knees to rigid attention and holding her back straight, she crossed to the reader slot and ordered it to blank the data crystal. That done, she took the crystal carefully from the port and then flung it across the room with savage calm.

Retaking her seat on the couch, Katrina pulled her legs up under her and stared across the empty room. Not much had really changed except that her on-planet armies would have to shoulder a slightly larger burden. They would win New Avalon for her and then be pressed to retake Tharkad, or Tharkad would rise in her name and eventually lend aid to her in the Federated Suns. With just a bit of luck, she would win both planets, and once she had them firmly in hand, no one would ever threaten them again. As for Vlad . . .

If he was not willing to help her, she would get on without

him. Later, when he wanted to accord her the status of equals once more, she would make him pay for this abandonment. It would happen eventually, she knew. They were drawn to each other in a way neither could resist forever, and Katrina could be patient.

When she needed to be.

24

November and December 3066 were the winnowing months as Katherine's call for resistance bogged us down into several desperate, defensive battles. No RCT or regiment went untouched, and we lost two commands, though admittedly the Davion Light Guard had actually been all but destroyed back on New Syrtis.

It was not a merry Christmas.

—*Cause and Effect*, Avalon Press, 3067

Daring Flood Plains, New Avalon
Crucis March
Federated Suns
28 December 3066

Stalking across the dry basin, Victor's *Daishi* left dusty footprints in the orange clay, tracks that were quickly pounded into a well-worn path by a dozen BattleMechs after him. The long, deadly summers known to Rostock's interior had finally baked the Daring Flood Plains dry, drinking up every shallow lake created by spring run-off and summer floods. Hard, cracked flatlands stretched out over several hundred kilometers, from horizon to pale horizon, making it hard to believe in native life on New Avalon. Victor knew the lie, knew most of New Avalon as green and inviting, but lifeless was how it looked just now through his canopy. An alien planet. Bleak. Inhospitable.

And still possibly the most important world in the Inner Sphere.

The Tenth Lyran Guards marched abreast in short columns, each company-sized 'Mech unit supported by two lances of armored vehicles. The independent columns swung out to either side of Victor's position in rough arcs stretching north and south as the prince worked to bend his flanks forward, encircling the retreating Seventeenth Avalon Hussars. Reinhart Steiner commanded the northern arm of the maneuver. Kai Allard-Liao augmented the Guards' shortened southern reach with what was left of the Outland Legion. Shortened because Victor had left two companies under the command of Reinhart's exec, Cale Eidt, as a security unit for Yvonne, who traveled a half-day behind them with one of the Revenants' mobile infantry regiments.

Wide-spaced flankers saw little in the way of combat, waiting for their opportunity to collapse inward against the loyalists' main body. So far, the Hussars had proven adept at avoiding the ready jaws of Victor's trap. Victor would push forward, and then one of his columns would be struck with stinging, light autocannon fire or a concerted salvo of PPCs from behind a jumble of flood-piled boulders, littering the trail with armor shards or pools of dull-orange splatter that quickly cooled to a crisp and smoking black. When that happened, Victor turned after his tormentors, driving them again into full flight but giving up precious time.

The Hussars' rearguard force knew their business, mounting a strong and mobile opposition. It was enough to delay Victor and his Revenants, slowing them so much that they were now six hours behind schedule to link up with Tancred Sandoval. It was not enough to stop them completely, though. Dust clouds wafting up on the eastern horizon told Victor that the Hussars' main body was close, and he almost had his people in position. He grimaced, reminding himself that this wasn't the first time.

In the last sixteen hours, the Hussars' mixed regiment had retreated from one defensive line to another, looking for some escape and finding only dry dunes and columns of standing rock behind which to grab perhaps thirty minutes respite. What was left of their VTOL squadron warned them when Victor approached on a flanking maneuver, giving them time to prepare one last stand before flight. Infantry had been sacrificed early, abandoned at Borge Ridge, where the Outland Legion had taken charge of some six hundred prisoners. Next spent were remnants of Katherine's Fifth Donegal Guards, and then the slower machines of the Hussars themselves. Armored vehicles and 'Mechs littered the Hussars' path of retreat like garbage strewn along a highway, as the loyalist regiments were whittled down into two reinforced battalions. Still they kept together, fighting a determined resistance and coming all-too-slowly to the final conclusion: That there was nowhere left to run.

"Victor, we have them." Kai's voice was clear and strong, touched with an eagerness Victor knew as his friend's only concession to excitement. In battle, Kai was normally as somber as he was deadly.

"We've nearly had them for half a day," Victor said, stretching his neck muscles to work some relief into them. Sixteen hours in the cockpit was beginning to wear on his stamina. A determined dryness persisted in his throat, and he swallowed painfully. "This time I want them finished."

"No, I mean we have Ardan Sortek and some of the Ceti Hussars. Their flanking force just made contact on the far southern reach."

Victor's muscle aches and concerns over dehydration were forgotten as he checked the monitor displaying his strategic map. There was no sign of Tancred's or Ardan Sortek's transponders, but then Kai's didn't register either at this range and through the small rise of petrified dunes separating Victor from his friend. Still, he took the report for the good news it was. Terrific, in fact. As of yesterday, Tancred was being pinched between the Third Rangers and the balance of the Seventeenth Hussars. That Victor was this close meant that he had made it in time to bring relief to his beleaguered friends.

Reinhart Steiner had been monitoring the command frequency and jumped in ahead of Victor. "What's Tancred waiting for?" he asked. "Have him bring in his people."

"The Third Rangers are still between us and them, and they broke the Second's secure frequencies two weeks ago." Kai's voice lost some of its enthusiasm. "Tancred has Sortek here to help us coordinate a combined effort to catch the Third unaware, and smash them."

Victor winced. He knew how hard setting up the destruction of the Third Robinson Rangers must be on Tancred. Though they were Katherine's unit through and through, they still claimed some heritage from the Draconis March. Tancred's Draconis March. "What does Ardan say about time? How far off is the Third?"

"Fifty kilometers. Maybe less by now. Call it forty minutes."

Victor checked Reinhart's location and saw that his cousin was about in position to close the door on the Seventeenth. "In forty minutes, we'll be involved in some heavy fighting of our own," Victor estimated. "We don't want Tancred chasing the Third into us then."

"Then, we let the Hussars go," Reinhart Steiner said easily, though Victor knew he had to be swearing beneath his breath. "Have Kai start the push, and my arm will fall back under pressure and open the door. They'll take it, Victor. They'll run like they've run each time so far, and by the time they figure out we're not in pursuit, it will be too late for them to help the Third Rangers."

"All right," Victor said. "We let them go, but first we give them a sting that will stay with them when they retreat to Albion. Reinhart, you slam the door on them a second time before falling away in full retreat. Kai, just do what you do best. And put Ardan's Ceti regulars at the front of your line. I want the Hussars to think that Tancred has already rejoined us."

His two subordinate commanders acknowledged their orders with no further discussion. The instant acceptance surprised Victor, who had expected at least some argument or refinement. That left him to worry over his impromptu plans another moment longer before he banished any remaining doubt. There were many things one simply did not have time for in the cockpit of a 'Mech.

Second-guessing oneself headed that list.

*   *   *

Victor had long since shucked his neurohelmet and sweat-drenched MechWarrior togs, changing them for a mostly fresh field uniform. An energy bar and an electrolyte-packed sports drink that tasted of stale orange was his nod toward nourishment, despite the polite argument given him by a Revenants' field medic and then again by Kai and his own sister.

He was just coming off an inspection of the bivouac perimeter being set by his 345th Mobile Infantry when the final company of the Second Robinson Rangers straggled in off the Daring Flood Plains. Tancred's *Templar* brought up the rear. The new 'Mech was last to lumber to a halt inside a makeshift staging area, which was really nothing more than a large triangular plot of ground sketched out between a rock bluff and two lines of parked armored vehicles. It didn't surprise Victor at all that Tancred had opted to bring his company in last. In a similar situation, after asking so much of his men in a long, desperate campaign, Victor would have done the same.

He caught Tancred as he scaled the chain-link ladder down from his cockpit. He pulled him off several rungs short of the bottom, and wrestled him into a back-slapping hug. It was the first chance he'd had since the Star League conference two years before to personally thank his friend for all the aid he'd given so selflessly. Kai and Yvonne waited patiently, though Yvonne shifted from one foot to the other with pent-up energy.

"You're a mess," Victor said, holding Tancred at arm's length and studying him.

Tancred looked a few pounds light, to be certain, though his pale skin was typical of all the Sandovals. He was also coming off twenty-eight hours with little sleep and was coated in the whitish scale of dried sweat. The residue stained his cooling vest and shorts, and Tancred dug more grit from the corners of his eyes.

"Well, you're looking great, Victor. Damn good, in fact, compared to reports we were getting last year." From almost anyone else, the words might have been offensive, but Tancred's amber eyes held nothing but respect for his friend and former sovereign.

"I am. I'm better." Victor nodded at Kai. "He slapped me around a bit, and so did Isis."

"Isis Marik is here?" Tancred looked around. It was obviously difficult for him to drag his eyes away from Yvonne once he found her. But other than a few Second Ranger Mech-Warriors watching the nobles from a fair distance, there was only Ardan Sortek clambering down from his own *Templar*, a bit slower than the more youthful duke.

Kai shook his head. "She's on Brunswick," he told Tancred even as Yvonne finally threw herself into the other man's arms.

If Yvonne cared about Tancred's disheveled state, it didn't show. She clung to him with a desperate relief that Victor remembered from his reunions with Omi. His earlier smile faltered a moment, but it was impossible to disapprove of his sister's choice, and he certainly wouldn't begrudge either of them a moment's happiness. He traded a sad smile with Kai, who also had to be missing his wife and family.

"Isle de Mograyn," said Kai, picking up where Victor had left off. "At the 'Mech production facilities there. She's trying to undo some of the damage Katherine caused with her call for civil disobedience."

"We would have been here a month ago if it hadn't worked so well. Only twenty percent of Brunswick's population actually answered her request to defy our occupation of the continent, but twenty percent of the labor force suddenly walking off from critical jobs was enough. We stumbled badly. It cost us the Twenty-third Arcturan Guards before we managed to get back on our feet."

"How bad was the Twenty-third damaged?" Tancred asked over Yvonne's shoulder.

An awkward silence answered him. There were no Twenty-third Arcturan Guards anymore. "They weren't our only losses," Victor said after a moment, "but they were the heaviest hit. And the Assault Guards, who soaked up a two-week counterassault that might have pushed us off Brunswick." He shook his head. "I can only imagine the damage if Katherine had gotten anything closer to fifty percent response with her call for resistance."

"I don't think she's ever had that kind of support here on New Avalon," Tancred said. He released Yvonne, then scrubbed at his oil-black hair, digging at his scalp. He normally shaved his head into a long topknot, traditional for Robinson males. The longer hair was matted from hours under a neurohelmet, and short areas were no doubt itching under several days of dark stubble.

"I hear her plan may have backfired on Albion," Ardan Sortek said, joining the conversation. A contemporary of Victor's father, Ardan boasted a healthy trimness that had not faded with age. His snow-white hair was a sign of his years, but his eyes showed the same bright strength as from his time as Secretary of Defense. "Without meaning to, she inspired a good percentage of Avalon City to simply walk off in protest of her usurping the throne from Yvonne's regency."

"Only took them six years to make their intentions felt," Tancred said dryly.

Victor nodded slowly, then waved the small group toward a hastily erected mess tent. "I think we've all learned hard lessons lately. Katherine was due a few."

"If there's a quota, I think you've all filled yours up." Yvonne sounded more hopeful than certain.

Victor wasn't even hopeful. In fact, he had learned another lesson today, waiting for something to go wrong in the battle and waiting for—expecting—his friends to correct him. It was a plan born from haste and need, but it didn't make his decisions any worse than they would have been two years ago, or ten. If anything, he was drawing on the additional years of experience. Victor knew it was time to come to grips with the fact that the only person left doubting him anymore was *him*. But understanding that and *knowing* it—accepting it without reservation and second-guessing—were two very different states. He had to work on that.

He would have to let go of his doubts before he got any closer to Katherine's final defense of Avalon City.

25

New Avalon in the New Year. That was our rallying cry. In truth, 3067 brought to many worlds the beginning of the end.

—*Cause and Effect*, Avalon Press, 3067

The Nagelring, Tharkad
Donegal Province
Lyran Alliance
19 January 3067

The Nagelring Academy boasted some of the best equipment Lyran kroner could buy, thanks to noble patronage as well as a healthy military budget. Gaining access to the facilities hadn't been at issue when Peter Steiner-Davion targeted the Nagelring early in the assault on Tharkad, but it served him well enough now as he convened a meeting of his senior officers and advisors in the main battle-review room. Also called the academy's "war room," the facility was infamous for its ability to dissect a training battle and show in glaring detail—slowed or frozen in holographic playback for all to see—the mistakes of a Mech-Warrior cadet. Students referred to the room less affectionately as the blunder-*bust*, for all the cadet-corps demotions that happened after such reviews.

The holographic tableau swarmed with miniature life, displaying for those gathered a battle that had recently taken place half a world away. Armored tanks were fast insects scurrying over a wind-swept spaceport tarmac, drawing the eye away from slow, small infantry that displayed hardly bigger than an ant. BattleMechs stood no more than six centimeters tall in this production, barely large enough to discern the hound's head crest of the Kell Hounds. Even so, the war avatars might still be thought of as masters of this battlefield until one considered that the blurry gray walls seen now and then were the indistinct outlines of twenty-story-tall DropShips.

There was no sound of autocannon fire or the hard crackle of a PPC blast. No tremors shook the table as several thousand tons of upright, walking metal stormed the field in giant strides. Still, resolution was impressive, pieced together from gun-cam footage where possible and extrapolated from sensor logs where not. Peter watched as a *Dragon Fire* belonging to the First Alarion Jaegers silently disintegrated under an intense laser barrage and then a fusion-reactor overload. The *Dragon Fire* expanded into a ball of burning plasma and smoke, one shattered leg smashing into the side of a nearby *Axman*. The image slowed and froze in place, making the *Axman* look like it had grown a new limb from its ruined shoulder.

"Colonel Julie Hoffman," Morgan Kell said, waving his hand over the fireball that had been a functioning 'Mech not seconds before. "Intel was spotty on this before, but the way the Alarion Jaegers folded after the *Dragon Fire*'s loss confirms it in my mind."

Phelan Kell leaned back into his chair, rocking it onto two legs and studiously ignoring the frowns sent him by the regular line generals who stood to either side. "That's the problem with personality cults in your military organization," he said. "You lose your prima donna, you lose your heart to fight."

"That sounds a bit strange coming from a Clan Khan," Peter said cautiously, setting aside his glass of ice water. Phelan still made him a bit uneasy. The fact that he was Morgan's son weighed a lot less to Peter than that Phelan actually preferred most Clan ways to those of the Inner Sphere. "I thought you excelled in promoting the individual over the unit."

"Only to the point of personal honor and our bloodname heritage." Phelan crossed his arms over his chest, his well-worn leathers like a second skin. "Any warrior beneath the commander is ready—in fact, eager—to step in and turn tragedy into triumph. What could be more glorious?"

Peter shook his head. His years at St. Marinus had prepared him to accept many things, but Clan philosophy was not on that long list. Not yet. It would have to be added, he knew, if he succeeded on Tharkad. Unless he convinced Victor to retake the Archonship once it was won.

In the meantime, Lieutenant-General William Harrison von Frisch represented another challenge waiting in the wings. The commander of the Fourth Skye Rangers RCT had come in only a few days before, ready to pledge his allegiance to Peter's cause and ladle another helping of political trouble onto the young noble's plate.

"Do we know how much of the Jaegers' operational strength survived that battle?" he asked, turning the topic back to their review.

"Operational strength?" Major General Bella Bragg, the last of the five, shook her head decisively. "If reports are correct, that unit no longer exists. Armor losses are at ninety-two percent. Infantry losses estimated at seventy percent. BattleMechs, eighty-nine."

Morgan jumped in on the end of that last statistic. "Colonel Hoffman's aide, Lieutenant-Colonel Helen Johannes, rallied two lances and led them out of there. They'll cause us some trouble, I'm sure, but for all intents and purposes, we control the spaceport, and the Jaegers can be considered a defunct command."

"What about the Eleventh Arcturan Guard?" Peter asked, naming the larger and more dangerous loyalist command that had come in with the Jaegers. "The Golden Lions?"

Morgan changed the holographic projection. Colors swirled together and faded. Shapes bent into a new landscape as Drop-Ships and painted tarmac bulged upward into a virtual diorama of glaciers and caves looking with dark eyes over a snowy battlefield. Peter could almost smell the old snow of Tharkad's mountains as he watched holographic 'Mechs slog through knee-deep drifts.

Data was less complete this time, as evidenced by the stuttering playback of the northern battle. The Golden Lion RCT swarmed down from caves to smash into the side of a long column belonging to the veteran Twenty-first Rim Worlds, a regiment of the Blue Star Irregulars. The mercenary line cut in two, a battalion of the Eleventh Guards' heavy armor held the narrow cut while the bulk of the command savaged the rear element. Holographic imaging grew spottier thereafter as dying machines fed less and less data back to one of the few surviving command 'Mechs.

"After they destroyed the Rim Worlds' command battalion, the RCT bloodied the trailing units in a chaotic free-for-all that worked against the mercenaries' normal ability to bring heavy strength to bear in close quarters." Morgan's face was a neutral mask, though he was obviously giving a eulogy. "The remaining forces are trying to reorganize under Major Hank McCoy, but I don't give them great chances. McCoy is far too self-centered."

Bragg picked up her noteputer, paged down through the reports. "The Eleventh Arcturan Guard has pulled back to Tharkad City. They're not likely to leave again while we're so close."

Which upped Tharkad City's current garrison to four regiments, including both of the Royal Guards. Everyone chewed on that bone for a moment, taking the time to warm their hands around mugs of steaming chocolate or strong coffee. Except for Peter, who sipped from his water and used its crisp, clean bite to clear his mind. "Close" was a relative term. Only a short, fifty-minute maglev ride separated the Nagelring grounds from Tharkad City, although that still covered over one hundred kilometers of frozen wasteland.

Morgan seemed to know what Peter was thinking, and nodded. "Plenty of maneuvering room to make hidden stabs at the capital."

"Which will eventually require the Fourth Skye Rangers," Peter said, letting his resignation come through. General von Frisch stiffened to attention. "I'm not exactly happy with this situation, General. I want you to know that. Personally, I think this is Robert Steiner's attempt to cover his back after Skye's attempt to secede."

"Duke Robert was arrested before the secession declaration and held in military prison," the Ranger general said woodenly, cautiously.

"Yet here you are." Bragg was not above scoring points off her forced ally. She was a formidable woman with a deep, gravelly voice, and her candor could be refreshing or disturbing, depending on which end of it one fell. "Come on behalf of Robert Steiner to seek some insurance."

Von Frisch glared daggers at Bragg. "On his release, the duke ordered us to stand down. How could he possibly have orchestrated Skye's secession while in prison?"

Peter was almost willing to bet the general that if a way existed, Robert had found it. An impressive feat of deniability, to get yourself arrested and claim after the fact that, if free, such an event would never have happened. He didn't say a thing, though, sipping at his water and coming again to the conclusion that he needed the Skye Rangers, just as the Lyran Alliance also needed the Isle of Skye. Accepting Robert's pledge, and his help, would bind him to the Alliance. For a time.

"Even if Robert did not order the deed, he did help foment the secession, knowingly or otherwise." Which was as forgiving as Peter was willing to be at this time. "However, if he has come to help reunite the Alliance now, I can hardly refuse."

"And my Hussars?" Bella Bragg asked. Her regiment was also waiting in the wings, having come over from Alarion, where Victor had left the Thirty-ninth Avalon Hussars in garrison over a year before. She was here on her own authority, though nominally representing Victor.

Peter shook his head as he spoke in apology. "I can't accept them at this time, General. Your aid and advice are still welcome for as long as you wish to remain with us, but your troops stay off-world." He held up a hand, quietly forestalling her outburst. "Please understand that what Morgan has helped me build here is a coalition representing every faction within the Lyran Alliance. The Skye Rangers help complete that picture. If I am to win Tharkad, I must do it through commands such as these. Though we all know the reality, Katherine has so tied the truth in knots on Tharkad that *any* traditional Davion unit firing on a Tharkad garrison would incite the people and raise them against me."

Bragg nodded slowly, reluctantly conceding the point. Phelan came to her aid. "That sounds good on paper, Peter. Still, I can't see how we will take Tharkad City without the Hussars. Not if you intend to move quickly."

Leave it to the Wolf to boil down his choices with ruthless efficiency. Peter shook his head. "I don't."

The Nagelring, for all its honor as the Lyran Alliance's prestige military academy, had originally been assigned very little in the way of defending forces. Peter had considered that a strange oversight until Morgan Kell pointed out that, except for some top-of-the-line simulators and a small warehouse of parts and supplies, the academy boasted little in the way of hard military resources. It only became important with his presence and the garrison of most of his assault force.

"Taking control of the Nagelring was a political maneuver," he explained, "designed to make some of the hard-liners on Tharkad question my aunt Nondi's regency and Katherine's long absence." And for all of Nondi Steiner's reputed tactical brilliance, Peter trusted Morgan's assessment of her strategic blinders. "Now that we're here, she will have no choice but to jump at us like a greyhound chasing its rabbit. I expect that at least one Royal Guard regiment is already on maneuvers, working to strike at us from behind."

"Or ComStar's Sixty-sixth Division," Morgan reminded him. "Don't sell short Precentor Kesselring's ambition."

Dag Kesselring came from a noble Lyran family. He had pledged support to Katherine even before Martial Gavin Dow reaffirmed the Com Guard's mutual-defense pledge with House Steiner. "Or the Com Guard," Peter agreed. "Or the Eleventh Arcturan or Twenty-fourth Lyran. Nondi has someone out there, and when they fall back, she'll send others. In the meantime, I'm recalling the Kell Hounds and the Blue Star Irregulars to give her an even bigger target.

"We draw our line here," Peter said, "at least for the next month. And we let my aunt spend effort coming to us for a change."

DropShip Jú-zi Tian-kong
Marlette

Rudolf Shakov's Nightshade dropped down at the foot of the DropShip's ramp. Not that his VTOL pilot was left with a great deal of choice. The *Jú-zi Tian-kong* was a *Seeker*-class DropShip, 3,700 tons, and had left very little room between its black-painted, spheroid hull and the steep cliff face that framed in the narrow valley. The DropShip's landing lights carved back enough of the night to show Shakov the danger, and the last few meters of descent were made with his heart hammering in his throat. It was hard to tell whether the pounding thumps in his ears were the echo of the VTOL's engine off the cliff or his own heartbeat.

Te Mun Chen, the Blackwind Lancers' new executive officer, came forward with an outstretched hand as Shakov jumped from the Nightshade's passenger compartment. "So sorry about tight quarters," Chen yelled over the VTOL's chattering blades, then joined Shakov in jogging toward the quiet of the hangar. "We see valley, make good hide place. First Republicans still upset about raid two days ago. Other DropShips hide deeper in Norrets."

From Chen's broken English, Shakov gleaned that the Blackwind Lancers' first battalion had caught a Republican DropShip offloading ammunition stores on the far side of the Norret Mountain Range. Besides a downed patrol lance, the explosion had cost the loyalists two loader 'Mechs and damage to one of the DropShip's armored landing struts. Now, while the entire First Republican burned time and resources in scouring the eastern ridges, the Lancers dropped themselves quite literally into a hole to rest up and make contact with the various allied commands on Marlette. Including the Prince's Men.

Chen led Shakov along the various bays to one space that held a large, half-disassembled, broad-shouldered assault 'Mech. Painted the tan and ivory of Free Capella, the ninety-ton *Emperor* wore a blue mask painted under its cockpit area that stared down with yellow serpent's eyes. Chen picked up a nearby wrench and slammed it roughly against the *Emperor*'s foot. The dull clanging rang out like a wounded bell.

In defiance of his size, Colonel Warner Doles had somehow worked himself halfway into the knee actuator. Now he crawled out and slid down along the curve of the *Emperor*'s leg. He was coated along one side of his body with thick red grease, the kind in which myomer bundles came packaged. He smelled of grease and 'Mech coolant, but somehow found a clean spot on his dungarees to wipe his hand before offering it to Shakov.

"Working on your own 'Mech?" Shakov asked. Many Mech-Warriors thought such work beneath them. Shakov simply knew that he wasn't qualified except for the most basic maintenance.

Doles glanced up at his machine. "It was a gift." The large man shrugged. "One gift among many, actually. Learning to take care of it was the least I could do, and I try to keep my debts covered. Chen tell you our news?" The Lancers' XO smiled and turned to the man. "*Ni zhao yi-xie ka-fei*," he said, falling into *Hanyu*, the Confederation's primary language.

Chen nodded and tossed Shakov a casual salute. "Luck, Precentor Shakov."

"Same to you," Shakov said, then looked back at Doles as Chen went off. "What did you tell him?"

"Nothing important. I just thought it would be easier if he wasn't here for this conversation."

Shakov felt the smile slide off his face. "The last time I had a conversation like that, I was looking over my shoulder for months. You aren't about to wish me the peace of Blake, I hope."

"Nothing like that," Doles assured him. "I just haven't told him yet that I've been speaking to the CO of the Third Crucis Lancers about joining forces to give Katherine's loyalists a good kick in the head."

"You haven't mentioned that to me, either."

"I know. I'd like you to cut us loose from your oversight, as easy as it's been, and let us slide in under General Macon. Not that I mind working with your people. They're good soldiers, but I'm hoping to convince you of a plan I've worked up, and that would mean you're going to be busy elsewhere." The muscles along Doles's jaw bunched up in frustration. "You've heard the word from Tikonov and the mess we apparently left behind there?"

"I have," Shakov said. Victor was not going to be pleased when the news found him on New Avalon.

"I have some ideas. I'd like to put them in front of Victor Davion."

Shakov saw no harm in that. "As soon as this civil war is over, I'm sure Prince Victor will be very interested."

"I'd rather he see them sooner," Doles said. "Look. We can all see where the fighting on Marlette is going, and that's nowhere. We'll sting the loyalist force, make them think twice about jumping for New Avalon, but that's about all we'll accomplish. That's fine; it's all we were meant to accomplish. But not to put too fine a point on it, Precentor, one mixed battalion is not going to make a difference either way."

A warm flush worked its way up Shakov's neck, spreading over his scalp in a slow crawl toward understanding. "What are you saying, Colonel?"

"I'm saying you should clear Marlette and go find your prince. I've given you two good reasons to go, and I have half a dozen more lined up if you really want to argue it. Like the fact that General Macon also thinks we should send whatever we can to Victor's aid in case the New Avalon fighting is as fierce as we're hearing, and—"

"All right." Shakov held up a placating hand. "You're storming a friendly beachhead, Colonel. Blake knows I've been thinking many of the same things for the last week." He offered out his hand, met the Lancer colonel's firm grip, and held it long enough to mean good-bye, luck to them both, and a few other understood thoughts. "Colonel . . . Warner . . . our thanks."

Doles shrugged. "You've done all right by the Lancers, Precentor Shakov. And as I said, I like to keep my debts covered." He nodded toward the hangar door. "Now get to New Avalon, and take care of your own."

26

There are no absolutes, and eternity is simply created from overlapping lives. Even hope must "spring eternal," because it simply cannot last. We can always hope that a thing will endure forever, even while we know it cannot.

Sometimes, that is a good thing . . .

—*Cause and Effect,* Avalon Press, 3067

Feintuch, Port Moseby
Freedom Theater
Lyran Alliance
17 February 3067

High winds pushed the sleet nearly horizontal down the streets and avenues of Feintuch. Sitting in the back of a cab, the assassin watched the frozen rain batter his side window with the sharp drum of icy fingernails. Not one house he passed showed a light to the storm, and the streetlamps all stood darkened. Power outage. He shook his head slowly, because that was what David Maass would do as he prepared to step out into the tempest, if only for the short dash into his house. He paid the driver, zipped his parka up tight, and wrapped his scarf over the lower half of his face. Opening the door, he kept one gloved hand squashed down on his papakha, the furred hat threatening to fly off with the howling winds. Then he ducked out of the vehicle.

He kept his head bent into the onslaught, squinting against

the stinging ice. He dredged chill air through the scarf, the taste
of wool flavoring each breath. He glanced around out of habit.
The walks were deserted. Only city employees and travelers,
such as David Maass, had the terrible luck to be outside in such
terrible weather. He jogged in stuttering half-steps for better
footing, then kicked the sleet from his boots as he stomped up
the porch and fumbled for keys to a door he had never before
opened. Once inside, he slammed the door against the wind's
determined grasp, relishing the pain-filled howl, which he
locked outside. He turned around and leaned back against the
wall, dark eyes searching the nearby living room.

Home.

For now.

He tugged the scarf down beneath his chin, shaking his head
to free the heavier water from his papakha. He checked the
lights for power, found none, then quietly roamed through the
rooms, getting to know this temporary home. He would stay for
a month at least, which sounded good. It had taken long enough
to get here.

From Buckminster to Port Moseby in five crawling months.
Possibly a new record, even for him. He had taken his time, hiding out in various safe houses before backtracking along a previous route. He'd spent a week in a hospital on Camiann as John
Doe, an amnesia victim. He'd buried himself deep in new identities and thrown out dozens of false trails. All to distract whatever enemy—whatever inexplicable force—continued to dog
his flight. The more he thought about it, the more certain he was
that his pursuer was no common investigator or military officer.
This was something else. Something different. There were
strange forces that occasionally embodied themselves among
mortals. A rare occurrence certainly—he had never met another
before—but the assassin knew it was so. Knew this, because he
thought himself one of them.

No common man could have lived his life or accomplished
half his achievements. The assassination of Omi Kurita—in the
stronghold of her own palace, no less—was a feat to be savored
as beyond the ken of others. His crowning triumph to date,

though he never forgot a single life taken in his long career. He had even studied, after the fact, every death attributed to Noble Thayer from his time on Zurich. Before that, the events surrounding Ryan Steiner's death had tested his skills . . .

The assassin stopped halfway down a long hallway, clamping down on his thoughts. Omi . . . Thayer . . . Steiner . . . these were all memories from past lives, recently turned over by his stalker's spade. There was no profit in such reflection except to discover whatever purpose his enemy intended.

He suddenly felt eyes on the back of his neck and turned rapidly to glance behind him. The hallway stood dim and empty. The house was dead but for his presence. Satisfied, the assassin moved down to his master bedroom, swept the darkened room once with his cold gaze, and then froze at the sight of the ghost in the mirror. Enough gray morning spilled through a window to grant the assassin a dark reflection, and it was not David Maass who stared back.

It was Karl Kole.

His wool scarf and Russian-style cap triggered the memory, affectations in costume that he had studiously avoided for over ten years. Karl had lived his short life on Tharkad, where winter never truly ended. It was one of his deeper identities, planned against the death of Archon-Princess Melissa Steiner-Davion. Melissa's failure had been her love for *mycosia pseudoflora*, flowers identical to the rare *mycosia* blossoms that Prince Hanse Davion had selected for their wedding. Wherever Melissa went, bouquets were brought to her side. The assassin had formed flowerpots from a ceramic explosive. Having planted the *mycosia* blossoms in those deadly containers, Karl Kole was able to smuggle them in to where Melissa was making a charity appearance. Fiery explosions ended her life in a very public manner.

The assassin could hardly forget that contract; the spotlight that had shined more attention on him and his career than any before or—with the exception of Omi Kurita—since. That he had allowed even one of Karl's affectations to slip into his current role was a troublesome sign. He walked forward slowly, his dark eyes never leaving the mirror, not even daring to blink, as he unwound his scarf and dropped the sleet-damp papakha onto the bed. Even without the clothes, it was Karl who stared back at him, but only until his eyes dried painfully, and he finally blinked. Then there was only himself, the assassin, staring back. The illusion had persisted in his mind only so long as he held Karl Kole's gaze. Glancing away brought him back to himself. It also hammered into his forebrain an uncomfortable truth, one that had been lurking in the background, held off by the illusion, and now screaming into his thoughts. That he was not alone.

The realization stole over him with ironclad certainty even as his own awareness of the intruder radiated back out into the room. Discovered, the shadow unwound itself from a dark corner, a blur of dark robes and flashing steel. The assassin barely had time to turn, seeking out his tormentor and recognizing the Asian features even if he did not recognize the man. House Kurita. And just as he had thought, no ISF or military agent. This was a small, bookish-looking man, with deep reserves and a hand guided by strong forces. Forces that were a match for his own.

But even as the katana's blade bit cleanly through his neck, with barely a whisper of pain before darkness claimed him, the assassin managed a true smile. Not one belonging to Karl Kole, David Maass, or the host of identities he had ever assumed, but his own. A firm belief in his own superiority, armored by the knowledge that no one—no other force—could ever take away what he had already accomplished.

That would live forever.

27

Peter once said to me that politics is a business unfit for warriors. Peter was a warrior. No matter what else he became later, it was good for the Alliance that he never forgot his early lessons.

—*Cause and Effect,* Avalon Press, 3067

The Nagelring, Tharkad
Donegal Province
Lyran Alliance
23 March 3067

An early morning breeze drifted in through the open hangar doors, tasting of snow and 'Mech coolant. The shouts and cheers of warriors preparing for battle echoed through the cavernous space, many of these for Peter as he crossed the hangar's stained ferrocrete. He stepped up onto the diamond-deck lift platform a Nagelring technician had lowered near the feet of a *Fafnir,* the 'Mech that was soon to be his. Staring up past its square-trunk legs and a centerline vault that housed the Battle-Mech's ECM suite, Peter rose toward the cockpit. Tucked back between linebacker shoulders, it was protected on either side by massive acceleration chambers for his heavy gauss rifles. The hundred-ton machine was painted Steiner blue with thick gold accents, the one 'Mech in Peter's entire assault force that laid claim to the colors of the Royal Guard, the Archon's traditional unit.

The only insignia he would carry into battle was that of the

Lyran Alliance, a gauntlet set against a diamond-shaped field. As he rode the lift up to his cockpit, Peter reached out to trail a hand against the design painted in bold size over the front of the war machine. It was cold to the touch. The fusion fires at the *Fafnir*'s heart were still banked, the avatar waiting to be summoned to life.

"For today's battle, I left St. Marinus House," Peter whispered to himself as the lift drew even with the cockpit's raised canopy and jerked to a stop. For this fight, he had commandeered part of Victor's campaign to oust their sister, making it his own.

Would Victor believe that Peter was grasping after his own glory again? That he was still self-centered and reckless, as he had been during the Bellerive catastrophe? He remembered that tragic night as if it had happened last week and not ten years before. It was a setup, drawing his lance out there to chase down a terrorist cadre. And the villagers had been killed before his force made it to the scene. It didn't matter. Five hundred and fifty-three people dead, not because of what he did, but because of who he was.

And who was he? That was the question he had hoped to answer when he exiled himself to St. Marinus. An answer he still searched to find.

Climbing into the cockpit, Peter toggled the canopy down and waited while battery-powered motors sealed the command space. Heaters came on at another thrown switch. Kneeling in the cramped space behind the command chair, he slipped out of his thermal gear, his skin puckering in the still-frigid air. When he finally dropped down into the cradling seat, he wore only combat boots, shorts, and cooling vest—all he needed today.

The fusion engine sparked to life with a deep, thrumming pulse as Peter powered up the BattleMech and ran his crosschecks. Gyroscope stabilizer, sensors, weapons—all powered and testing normal. He reached into the overhead and found his neurohelmet resting on the shelf. Tugging it down over his head, he adjusted it for a snug fit and then fastened the chin strap. A small cable fell down from the chin of the full-face helmet, and this Peter locked into a socket built into the side of his command chair. His cooling vest he left unplugged from life support for now, waiting until he'd fully warmed up the cockpit. Which left him ready to go.

Almost.

"Systems report," the computer said, having finished its own series of independent checks and power-up procedures. "All readings normal. Initiate security protocol."

"Peter Steiner-Davion," he said, slowly and carefully as if talking to a small child. "Commanding General, Tharkad Assault Force." He squirmed some at his adopted rank, knowing it to be an honorable award, not an earned one. Not yet, anyway.

"Voiceprint recognized, General Peter Steiner-Davion. Proceed with cross-check," the computer said, asking for his private security key. Voiceprints could be faked. The cross-check was a code phrase Peter had personally entered and that only he would know. He had drawn it from the Unfinished Book, recalled from his studies at St. Marinus.

"Clothe yourself in righteousness," he said, "for that is armor enough." With that, he braced himself for the coming battle.

Now he was ready.

Peter had trained hard in the last few weeks to pilot the captured *Fafnir*. The hundred-ton machine was slow but well armed and very well armored, with over nineteen tons of Durallex Special composite. As it turned out, he needed every gram of that protection as he reacquainted himself with the realities of a live-fire battlefield, and the North Ten Wash was a treacherous learning ground.

Roughly halfway between the Nagelring and Tharkad City, the Wash would become a tangle of sharp, rapid streams come spring when the snow pack began to melt under heavy rains. Now, in the determined grip of Tharkad's long winter, the ten-kilometer stretch of territory was a dangerous composite of frozen ponds, crevices, and flood-piled boulders all hidden beneath a blanket of fresh snow. Add to that the industrious effort made by the loyalists to seed vibrabombs through important stretches of the Wash, and Peter's assault force had their work cut out for them.

Nondi Steiner was personally leading this assault out of Tharkad City, a fact that surprised Peter until he saw the forces arrayed against him. The First Royals spearheaded the drive, with the Twenty-fourth Lyran Guards and the Eleventh Arcturan holding the flanks. ComStar's Sixty-sixth Division had followed as a strategic reserve, with Precentor Dag Kesselring as eager to get into the fighting as Morgan had predicted. Nondi had leveraged nearly her entire army on-planet in this attempt to stop Peter's advance. Those were good Lyran tactics. Commit as much force against your problem as possible, then duck your head and bully forward. Counting the four regiments of armor and mechanized infantry also deployed by his aunt, she certainly held the edge in numbers.

And her strategy almost worked in the first, early hours of battle. She rocked Peter's force back on its heels and stopped dead any further advance toward Tharkad City all right, but Peter recovered from the onslaught through the quality of the troops under his command. That, and the fact that his combined aerospace forces swept the skies clean of loyalist pilots. The brute-force maneuver also cost his aunt a great deal in tactical initiative. Relying on the greater experience of his subordinate commanders, Peter allowed his assault force to break up, pulling apart the loyalist army as they gave pursuit.

The Fourth Skye Rangers, in their trademark style, led the Eleventh Arcturan Guard on such a merry chase that they were six hours from regrouping no matter how that part of the battle went. The others had congregated among the mined expanse of the North Ten Wash. Now the First Kell Hounds shared the center of the allied line with Peter's Twentieth Arcturan. Phelan sulked in the background with his Fourth Wolf Guards, ready to shore up any damaging breach.

"Peter, this is Dan." Colonel Daniel Allard's voice had a forced edge to it, as if he were about to say something neither of them wanted to hear. And he was. "We've held pretty even so far. This may be the time to ask ourselves how bad we want this fight today."

Bad, Peter decided instantly, surprised at his sudden determination but sticking to the gut feeling. Nondi showed no signs of capitulation and certainly no reluctance to throw her army into the teeth of any advance. "If not today, it will be tomorrow," he said, the voice-activated mic picking up his frustration. "We're just too evenly matched for either side to gain a solid upper hand." He knew that every day the civil war dragged out on Tharkad was another day the fighting continued or cropped up fresh on other Alliance worlds. If Peter were going to pay the butcher's price, better to pay it here than across a dozen worlds and with the lives of a thousand good soldiers who simply had the misfortune of being under the command of a determined tyrant.

"Which is a recipe for disaster," Dan reminded him. "The Twenty-fourth is getting more aggressive." On his strategic map, Peter saw this. Allard's Kell Hounds were pinched between the First Royal Guards and the Twenty-fourth Lyran, just as Peter's Twentieth Arcturan Guards fought a pincer between Nondi's Royals and Dag Kesselring's Com Guard division. "Any mistake out here will be a fatal one."

Peter nodded, then broke off from the conversation for a moment as a Com Guard *Viking* suddenly shifted away from its earlier victim and threatened Peter with its broad outline of missile launchers. Alarms rang for Peter's attention as the *Viking* disappeared behind a cloud of gray missile exhaust.

There was no avoiding the pummeling rain of warheads, not in the slow-of-foot *Fafnir*. Peter hunkered down in his seat, stopping to take the missile strike with both of his 'Mech's feet planted and ready. His Guardian ECM suite broke the *Viking*'s improved fire-control lock, which lessened the assault, but nearly half a hundred warheads remained to smash in along his 'Mech's right side. A handful of missiles slammed into the side of the *Fafnir*'s head, pockmarking the armor and cracking one ferroglass shield.

The hard-hammering blows left Peter's ears ringing as he dragged his own crosshairs over the wispy gray cloud and searched for the *Viking*. The reticle changed from red to a flashing gold, and then burned steadily as his targeting system found a solid lock. Peter braced the *Fafnir* forward, leaning into the heavy recoil as each of his gauss rifles spat out a hypersonic mass. Both took the *Viking* in the left leg as the missile exhaust cleared on a light wind. One gauss slug lodged itself in the hip, fouling the joint. The second smashed through the lower leg actuator, gimping the ninety-ton machine and all but rooting it in place.

Peter quickly toggled back over to his main frequency. "Second Company, move west. Pressure the Com Guard." Already he saw two lances of Com Guard heavy armor moving up to the *Viking*'s rescue, but they were quickly caught in a deadly crossfire as his personal company help isolate the wounded assault 'Mech.

Moving in to closer range, Peter tied his two extended-range lasers into his main triggers and fired again. This time, the Viking had more trouble getting off good salvos as Peter pushed past its optimum firing range. Only a dozen missiles peppered the *Fafnir*, hardly enough to shake the monstrous design. Peter's lasers carved angry furrows across the *Viking*'s head and centerline. One of his heavy gauss rifles found the chest wound and carved in over the gyro housing. The *Fafnir* stumbled back under the hard recoils, but Peter held it to its feet.

The *Viking*, though, was finished. Its stabilizer spit out in pieces and chunks through the cracked carapace as the high-velocity gyro tore itself apart against its own damaged housing. The assault machine fell onto its back, and the pilot punched out on his ejection seat rather than risk any further attack under the *Fafnir*'s massive guns. Watching the MechWarrior ride his parafoil toward the enemy's rear lines, Peter hoped he'd find an infantry squad quickly. Shorts and cooling vest were no gear for a Tharkad winter.

"Any ideas?" Dan asked in the following lull. His timing left no doubt that he had monitored Peter's quick battle for any need to rescue him.

At one point in his life, Peter would have taken such concern as an insult to his own skill. Now he welcomed it. It reminded him that he had much bigger obligations out here than just to himself, and he quickly took stock. His *Fafnir* was holding up fine—incredibly well, in fact, considering that every nearby loyalist grabbed any chance to strike at him. And his company had made short work of the Com Guard armor, with only one lance escaping the crossfire. Peter shook his head at the Com Guard division's repeated attempts to make such a hard stand in the face of a fully supported regiment. If not for the Royal Guards . . .

The thought sparked a new idea. Peter checked the strategic monitor, where his computer labored to paint the shifting lines of battle into some coherent semblance of a map. Nondi Steiner still led from the center of the First Royals, but in a decently executed plan, she had committed more forces toward the Kell Hounds than to Peter's Arcturan Guards. Advisable, considering the Kell Hounds were an elite force and well-supported by a crack jump-infantry battalion outfitted in battle armor. But that had placed more pressure on Precentor Kesselring and his Upsilon-grade division, which fielded less than half the strength of a fully supported regiment.

"Dan," Peter called out, switching back over to the all-commanders' frequency, "I need you to commit the Kell Hounds against the Twenty-fourth Lyran Guard. Turn and hammer their flank and get the attention of the First Royals. Pull Nondi east and have Phelan stop-gap any attempt to counter-attack, but do not throw them back. Tie them into place."

Dan grasped the importance of that quickly enough. "And what are you going to be doing while we bog down in a slugging match?"

"I'll lead my Twentieth straight into the teeth of that damned Com Guard division. I'll want aerospace support as well. Make it in five minutes. Precentor Kesselring will try to hold, and we'll shatter them."

"What makes you so certain Kesselring will stand and be broken?" That from Marshal Alden Gray, permanent commander of the Twentieth Arcturan. His tone gave away a trace of concern that Peter might be ready to throw his command away on a hunch.

Peter respected the man for sticking by his men first. "Because I used to be him," he said by way of quick explanation. "He'll stand his ground. He won't believe in disaster, not until it's too late. Once we smash through, the Arcturan Guards will wheel into the rear of the First Royals . . ." He let the thought trail off as two older Burke tanks turned in at him, each with three particle projection cannon trained on him. But one slipped sideways into a hidden crevice, throwing its tread and grounding itself in dangerous territory. The other kept on coming.

As if Peter needed a better example of Com Guard stubbornness. He donated one of his heavy gauss rifles to the advancing Burke, smashing in its forward armor so much that a determined infantryman might work through and shoot the tank crew personally. The tank turned and fled, leaving its companion at the mercy of whatever Arcturan MechWarrior or crew wanted to brave its three PPCs and claim the kill.

"And then?" Dan asked. His Kell Hounds were already moving on a flanking maneuver in compliance with Peter's request.

"And then we put my aunt Nondi out of a job," Peter said. He breathed heavily, feeling the new weight he was adding to his history of regrets. "We destroy the First Royal Guard."

As certain as he had been about Dag Kesselring, Peter's plans hinged on a dangerous assumption. He expected the Com Guard troops to be as determined and inflexible as their commanding officer. They weren't. The Sixty-sixth didn't break, they bent, forming more by accident than design the perfect response to Peter's hard-hitting assault. Back to back with Nondi's regiment, the Com Guard held off Peter's advance while the Royals hammered into Phelan's Fourth Wolf.

Not that the Com Guard troops could hold out long against the Arcturan Guard, who massed twice their numbers and were more at home in cold-weather operations than most other units on the field. Already their line was being pierced by Peter's lighter, faster armor, and what was left remained in severe danger of being chopped into small units and decimated piecemeal. Peter added to their misery as he took a solid stance and fired his heavy gauss rifles in alternating cycles, careful of the hard recoil. Every two salvos, he switched over to his lasers, wary of expending too much of his ammunition. His frugal approach missed out on possible kills, but it made the *Fafnir* a continuous danger that finally bled away the resolve of some nearby Com Guards. Two *Tessen*s, lacking their comrades to make a devastating C^3 lance, turned and fled for the backfield.

And right into the first strafing runs of allied air cover.

Two Wolf Guard *Jagati* Omnifighters speared down below the gray clouds, hitting a deck of less than two hundred meters. Their first salvos caught the *Tessen*s with PPCs and pulse lasers, tossing one to the ground with no legs and sending the second into a more panicked flight. The *Jagatai*s raced past to also chip into the rear of the Royal Guards, spreading more destruction as a pair of Arcturan Guard *Stingray*s chased down behind them on the second strafing run.

It was Peter's final trump card, calling down the aerospace umbrella he had guarded so carefully. If the loyalists sent their own aircraft back at the right time, it could cause a new shift in air superiority. Worth the risk, though. The Royal Guard was Nondi's linchpin. Pull it, and the entire framework of the loyalists' strategy fell apart.

"Press them hard," Peter urged his warriors over general frequencies. "Break their line before it breaks us."

Other reports bled over him as subordinate officers called for supporting fire or warned of a new minefield they had stumbled into. Through the ferroglass panes of his forward shield, Peter saw one of his *Stiletto*s lose a leg to a vibrabomb, sprawling forward into the snow and at least two more mines. One took off the *Stiletto*'s head, shearing away the forward-thrust cockpit and mangling most of the upper torso. Peter cursed under his breath. There was little to do except hope that the fallen warrior had prevented other lives lost.

"No," Peter said out loud. There *was* more he could do. Slamming his throttle against its forward stop, he ran the hundred-ton *Fafnir* up toward its maximum speed of fifty-plus kilometers per hour.

Dan Allard was onto the maneuver before Peter took a dozen steps. Two kilometers away and involved in an entirely different battle between his Kell Hounds and the Twenty-fourth Arcturan Guard, he was still keeping an eye on the man who might become Archon. "Peter, you're too far forward. Fall back! What do you think you're doing?"

"Exercising my right to personal responsibility," Peter called out, not bothering to select his communications for private conversation. "I'm making an adjustment to the battle lines. Right now." He cut two lasers over a distant Royal Guard Manticore heavy tank, exploiting earlier damage done by the strafing aerospace fighters, freezing the turret in its track. "Twentieth Arcturan, press the Royal Guards," he ordered. Then he dialed up the Arcturan Guards' supporting regiment of mixed armor and battlesuit infantry. "Colonel Amzel, clean up the Sixty-sixth division behind us."

The charge worked about the way he expected—hoped—it would. His personal company followed immediately, pulled along in his wake, weapons reaching out to their maximum range as they hurried to overtake Peter. The risk lay in what the rest of the Twentieth Arcturan Guard would do. Marshal Gray might have been in the middle of a weapons exchange, or perhaps he actually hesitated for a scant handful of heartbeats. Not that it really mattered. In the next moment, he was haranguing the troops to follow their general and had committed himself to a forward charge despite the proximity of a Com Guard lance. From their backfield came the Guards' support regiment, swarming what few Com Guard positions were left.

A new pair of strafing fighters finished the Manticore for Peter and flushed a squad of *Fenrir* battle armor from their hiding place behind it. These were Nondi's flankers, bent on keeping the Twentieth Arcturan from slamming into the back of the Royal Guard line. One of the four-legged battlesuits fell to the emerald stings of Peter's pulse laser, the trooper inside sealed into a melted cast of armor composite. Then his extended-range lasers sliced an arm and a leg from a second. The remaining pair bounded at him with leaping strides. One misjudged the distance, gathering itself in a crouch right in front of him. Peter simply walked over it, the *Fafnir*'s blocking feet pulping the infantryman. The last one had worked around to his side, using its trio of machine guns to peck at his armor. A *Bushwacker* from Peter's company answered back with an autocannon that all but tore the *Fenrir* in half.

With a few seconds in which to breathe, Peter checked his tactical screen. Very little remained of the Sixty-sixth Com Guard. Some scattered light armor and fast 'Mechs ran ahead of Peter's support regiment, but not much more. Two or three assault-class BattleMechs had weathered the first storm of swarming attacks. Peter read the tag on one icon as a venerable *Spartan*. A lost treasure from the first Star League, the museum machine could only belong to Precentor Dag Kesselring. It struggled briefly with a full company of Vedette tanks, claiming three of the vehicles before finally falling to the combined might of their light autocannon. Then he was gone as well.

As Peter returned his attention to the forward push, he saw more aerospace fighters pouring down from the clouded skies, chewing up the flankers and leaving him several open paths into the backfield of Nondi's 'Mech line. "We push right through them," he ordered, "and follow their line right up to the back of the First Royals. Colonel Amzel has cleanup duties. We're coming to the aid of the Fourth Wolf Guard, and we're doing it now." And the Unfinished Book help anyone else who stood in their way.

No one did.

With Peter leading the Twentieth Arcturan Guards through the devastated backfield, Dan Allard suddenly wheeled his Kell Hounds away from the Twenty-fourth Lyran and also struck at the Royal Guards. Besieged from three sides, the loyalists didn't know which way to turn, and pressure eased off Phelan's Wolves. The Clan warriors staged a counterassault that belied their lesser numbers, gutting the centerline and breaking the Royal Guards into two pieces. Peter saw Nondi's *Hauptmann* holding the center of one formation, which turned and attempted to fight its way clear of the building disaster. Dan Allard almost cut her off, but was thrown back when the Guards' lightning company threw themselves into the Kell Hounds' path. Their sacrifice bought Nondi enough time to lead out a shattered battalion of mixed 'Mechs and armor. No more.

"Let them go," Peter ordered as the Twenty-fourth Lyran moved against the rear of the Kell Hounds, either in vengeance for the Royal Guards or simply trying to join the retreat. He turned Phelan and Dan into a solid line, containing the Twenty-fourth, while his own Arcturan Guard cleaned up what stragglers were left. His aunt would make it back to Tharkad City, he knew, but right now it was more important to claim a solid victory than gamble on overextending his forces. He stormed through a halfhearted barrage of laserfire, silencing a Guard *Falconer* with his gauss rifles while his command company overran a double-lance of hovercraft.

A few moments later, Dan Allard called over the general frequency. "Peter, General Riskind of the Twenty-fourth is asking for terms of surrender." That was for the benefit of the allied task force, who broke out in cheers. Then he switched over to a private channel. "Apparently your aunt ordered him to charge forward and damn the losses. Anything to bring you down."

So much Katherine's creature. Peter remembered his aunt as a reasonable woman and a compassionate commander—once. Whisper enough poison in someone's ear, and eventually the mind sickens.

"Unconditional," Peter ordered. "The only assurances Riskind will get from me is that I won't throw away lives."

"I think he'll take that."

So would Peter. With the Sixty-sixth Com Guard destroyed and the Twenty-fourth Lyran folding, his aunt had very little left besides the Eleventh Arcturan and remnants of her two Royal Guard regiments. That wasn't enough. Peter would pull his forces back to the Nagelring for refit, and there might be another skirmish or two ahead of him, but nothing short of disaster would stop the allied task force now. The way had been opened, and Tharkad City lay before them.

The end was in sight.

If there had been another way, I would have taken it.
But by the time we had proof of the full extent of
Katherine's tyranny, its uses were very limited.
However, that did not stop us from seizing every
advantage.

—*Cause and Effect,* Avalon Press, 3067

ComStar Satellite Facility Alpha-Five
Portland, New Avalon
Crucis March
Federated Suns
28 March 3067

The sign on the door read UNDER NEW MANAGEMENT, a joke that
tempted a smile from Victor even though the last few months of
fighting had drained most humor from him. Besides, he was actually a guest here, and an uncomfortable one at that. Com-
Star's Alpha-Five facility was a small fortress located just
outside Portland, set on short bluffs overlooking New Avalon's
largest ocean. Waves crashed incessantly against the base of the
bluffs, rolling a barrage of deep, booming echoes up the cliff
face. After so many months of hard fighting, the sound reminded Victor too much of artillery, and as he walked about the
compound, his hands clenched involuntarily into fists.

But then he hadn't come here for relaxation or for ComStar's
messaging services. Station Alpha-Five didn't even have a
hyperpulse generator uplink, an honor reserved for the main

compound located on Avalon Island. It serviced all satellite facilities via a highly secure network currently made suspect by
Katherine's rumored involvement with Martial Gavin Dow.
What the satellite compound did have was a large barracks that
Victor's people had quickly converted into a makeshift hospital
and hangar space for a company of 'Mechs. Although the facilities technically belonged to the Com Guard's 299th Division,
they now stood abandoned. Katherine had called up the 299th
months before, first for the fighting on Brunswick and then
bringing them back to Albion, though garrisoned closer to
Avalon Island than Portland. Rudolf Shakov got in touch with
the local precentor, Eban Farouq, who invited Victor to take
over the facilities. From his time as precentor martial, Victor
knew something about the capabilities of ComStar's computer
systems. Something even more potentially useful than bed space
and maintenance bays.

He pushed through the door and into the compound's main
computer room. His surge of good feelings lasted through a
quick reunion with Rudolf Shakov and less than a minute into
the report handed him by Kai Allard-Liao. His friend had
cleared the room of all personnel below command level before
stoically delivering the bomb. With Ardan Sortek and General
Sanchez also standing by, he handed Victor a message reader
that allowed him to scroll through the same reports the others
had already vetted.

"This can't be," Victor said as if denial would make it so.

Kai nodded to Shakov, who pulled himself to attention before encapsulating the reports. "The Valexa CMM and your
Revenant infantry were overrun by forces claiming allegiance to
the Free Tikonov Movement," he said. "House Dai Da Chi
counterattacked, but recovered only a few prisoners. That much
I confirmed before the Prince's Men ever left Marlette." His
shoulders slumped as some of his discipline flagged. "The
Twenty-third Arcturan Guard battalion was better prepared and
held out at Asano Bay for four days. But when the warrior house
moved in to help secure the site, apparently the Arcturan Guards
decided to hold it against them as well. The firefight was short

and bloody, and House Dai Da Chi has since claimed that we broke the truce. They now hold Tikonov for House Liao and the Capellan Confederation."

Victor swallowed dryly. A Capellan warrior house regiment, and he had left them in garrison of Tikonov at his back. Now, through misfortune or betrayal, they had seized the world behind him. "Sun-Tzu planned this from the beginning," he muttered and smacked his right fist into his left palm in frustration. "He knew I wouldn't bring Dai Da Chi along. If he thinks I won't go back after this civil war is over and pull Tikonov loose again—"

"You won't," Kai said evenly, trying to calm his friend.

"Give me one good reason why not."

Kai gave Victor a sad smile. "I can give you three. First, because Sun-Tzu has *magnanimously* consented to continue offering his support to you in retaking New Avalon. Second, if you attack Tikonov, you might be pulled into a full-blown war with the Confederation, and given the state of the AFFS, I don't think that's wise. And *regardless of that*"—Kai stalled Victor's outburst by slightly raising his voice—"then, third, I shall have to fight against you."

"You will . . ." Victor couldn't complete the idea out loud.

"Victor, how do you think I got permission to leave the Confederation and come to Thorin? Because I wanted to? Sun-Tzu holds too many daggers at my family's back right now to vex him without good cause. So I made a deal, and a public announcement in front of the St. Ives Lancers, that we would submit to Sun-Tzu's directives and Talon Zahn's military command should you ever invade the Confederation."

"Kai, why in blazes would you promise that?"

"Because you needed me on Thorin, Victor. Morgan and Jerry—I mean, Galen—both asked for me, so I came."

As simple as that. Victor nodded, the ashen taste of defeat in his mouth. "Was Sun-Tzu thinking *that* far ahead about retaking Tikonov? Maybe." He shook his head, accepting his friend's sacrifice. "You're right, Kai. I needed you on Thorin. And I need you here."

Victor tried to force the news about Tikonov from his mind. How many men had been lost to Sun-Tzu's ploy? How had he ever won the loyalty from such men, or from Kai Allard-Liao himself? Victor wanted to believe that, first and foremost, they were all as committed to removing Katherine from power as he was. But that was a half-truth. Kai, and most of the others, were here because they believed in him. He glanced around the room, nodding an apology to the other three officers present as he drew them back toward the business at hand. "We'll need everyone by the time this is over."

He moved them all to the room's large holographic display table, a system that ComStar normally used for displaying the chain of HPGs necessary to move a message from one planet to another. It could also call up strategic maps of New Avalon from computer files, and with the proper feeds, displayed battleroom footage as well. That was what Victor had truly wanted from Precentor Farouq's hospitality. A strategic command center. Leave it to ComStar to seed every world with its own personal war rooms.

He called up a map he'd been working on. It showed the eastern coast of Albion, with Portland on the far southeast tip and Avalon Island only three hundred kilometers to the north. Force lines drawn in red light showed the movement of Katherine's units while gold lines indicated Victor's. The lines followed the steady shrinkage of Katherine's forces back toward the northeastern territory of Albion, a dwindling arc that allowed the loyalists to concentrate their forces while pulling units back in pieces to move them over the channel to Avalon Island.

"They have controlled the continent's interior for long enough, it seems. With the destruction of the First Crucis Lancers and the Assault Guard's final stand, apparently they're ready to fall back and stand out a siege of the capital city."

"They'll wait to see if Katherine can rally new troops from other battles." Ardan said. He had helped Victor with the projections, so they were familiar to him.

Victor pointed out the floating numbers, which estimated that Katherine had two regiments on the island and two more ready to gain that safety in the next few weeks. "We'll whittle them down some more by then," he promised. "But if we wait much longer, we can expect to see units straggle in off Marlette or Wernke. We can't allow that to happen. No matter what, I want this battle contained to forces currently on New Avalon. We cannot wait to see what *might* happen later."

General Jonathan Sanchez rubbed one hand against the side of his face. "Moving fast hurt us last time," he reminded them. "We let the Davion Assault Guards expose themselves and get cut off, and the First Crucis threw themselves away in the rescue attempt." He frowned at the numbers. "We can harass them just fine for now, but we'll need a month to be ready for Avalon Island."

"Katherine is no tactician," Sortek said, "but we can't forget that she does have good people working for her."

"I have better," Victor said adamantly, calling up a detailed map of Avalon Island. "One month . . . It will take a coordinated assault to force our beachhead onto Avalon Island, and once we start, we keep driving forward until we surround Avalon City and take the capital itself. Assuming that all commands are still functional, Kai will lead the Outland Legion and Ardan the Second Ceti Hussars in a diversionary push just opposite the mainland. Your landing on Avalon Island is meant to distract the Twenty-second Avalon Hussars and put the Remagan CMM on alert, pinning them in place. Then we hit the north end of the island, which I'm guessing will be the Tenth Deneb's patrol area, and we roll them up with my Revenants and the Sixth Crucis."

"And if the Com Guard 299th shows itself?" Sanchez asked the hard question, alluding to Victor's ties back to ComStar.

The war had already cost Victor almost everything he held dear. His former position as precentor martial would not stop him from doing what needed to be done now. "If they show themselves, they belong to the Davion Heavy Guards and Tancred's Second Robinson Rangers. We send them back to Katherine, and Gavin Dow, in small pieces."

He looked around to make certain everyone knew what was expected of them, what they had to start planing for. "The

Prince's Men I'm holding in reserve, for now. We'll commit them as needed. The same for the NAIS cadre."

"We meet in the middle?" Shakov asked, waving his hand over Avalon City and, nearby, the Davion Palace.

Victor shrugged. "That will depend a lot on how Simon Gallagher and the rest of Katherine's generals plan their defense. We still haven't accounted for the Nineteenth Arcturan Guard or what's left of the Seventeenth Avalon, though I'm guessing they'll be pulled back in toward Mount Davion. Simon will want to protect the palace."

It was Ardan Sortek's turn to frown. "That's assuming they don't go on the offensive," he said. "Jackson Davion is just the kind of man to plan that kind of counterassault." He caught Victor's casual nod. "You aren't worried about Jackson?"

"No," Victor said. "I'm not." And he told them all why.

Katrina found Jackson Davion waiting in the palace courtyard upon her return from the Royal Court. She'd spent a full day calming the concerns and fears of New Avalon's nobles, reinforcing her ties with those she trusted and testing the waters for treason with those she didn't. Katrina had little patience left for another military report.

"Tomorrow, Jackson." She waved off his approach. "I've already heard about Tancred Sandoval's recent push over the Ronde Tableau. We'll talk tomorrow."

He shook his head, but did not attempt to break past her perimeter of security detail. "This will not wait, Katherine."

Agents in her security detail snapped to attention as if someone had yelled "gun," all of them looking for the threat. Katrina stared at her marshal, not sure she'd heard him right. *Katherine?* The name sounded foreign to her, especially coming from Jackson's mouth. He was nothing if not respectful of her position and his own as Marshal of the Armies.

He carried no sidearm that she could see. Nor the sword that his rank and position entitled him to wear even in her presence. There was something else out of place about his uniform, and it took Katrina a moment to spot it. He had removed his epaulets, and with them, his rank insignia.

"Let him approach," she said quietly, then waved her detail into a larger perimeter to guarantee her some privacy. Her security agents did not care for the idea, but no one was willing to make the delicate call of refusing their Archon-Princess.

Jackson Davion approached slowly through their perimeter. "I appreciate the audience."

"Highness," she finished for him, as if he had forgotten her title by mistake. "Or Archon-Princess. Either will do nicely, Jackson." If his lackluster approach indicated what she thought, she wanted to push him to it quickly. Better to evaluate how much of a threat her marshal had become.

Jackson did not disappoint, coming to strict attention in front of her. "Of course, Highness," he said stiffly, formally. "I am here to resign as Marshal of the Armies. I think you know that."

"Be very careful, Jackson." Katrina caught his blue eyes with her own icy gaze. He had no power here, in the shadow of the Davion Palace. This was still her domain. "How I dispose of you may depend greatly on your continued courtesy. I would rather not charge you as a traitor."

He kept his own voice pitched low, away from the careful ears of Katrina's security people. "Which is why I have come to you privately, without speaking to anyone else. You have no reason to charge me with dissention in the ranks or have me questioned in a public forum." He said this last with a touch of threat. "Simply put, Katherine, I have seen the evidence your brother has collected against you. It was delivered to me this morning— I will not tell you how or by whom—and I have since verified as much as I need."

Damn Victor and his constant intrusions. "And this was enough to convince you? Even without my answer or explanation?"

"It is enough to convince a tribunal of nobles, I promise you."

"Thank you for that insight, General," Katrina snapped. "And for that courtesy, do you expect me to simply release you to seek out Victor's camp, taking with you the core of the Watchtower's officers?"

"I don't expect to command again," Jackson said simply, "no matter who sits on the throne." He looked to the nearby guards, summoned quietly by Katrina's security agents. "I believe a quiet transition is best. I do have apartments in the Davion Palace. I can retire to those, under guard, of course."

"Of course," Katrina said with false sweetness, wondering what other surprises Victor had in store for her. None so large as the rude awakening he would eventually receive from her, she vowed. Raising her voice, she called in her guards while keeping up the pretense of civility. "You are most welcome in the palace, Jackson. I've always preferred to keep you close by my side, after all." Until she no longer needed him as a figurehead marshal, at any rate. Then, Katrina told herself, Jackson could share the fate of others who had crossed her.

Once this affair with her brother was settled, there would be no further need to worry about civilities.

29

Tharkad is the home I remember. Despite Katherine's successful campaign to divorce me from House Steiner, she cannot take away those memories. I was Avalon-born but Lyran-raised. I wanted nothing but the best for citizens of either realm.

—*Cause and Effect*, Avalon Press, 3067

Tharkad City, Tharkad
Donegal Province
Lyran Alliance
2 April 3067

Snow fell in small, dusty flakes over Tharkad City, the kind so easily kicked back up into the air on a gust of wind or the brush of a hovercraft's passing. A stiff breeze swept the streets clean and piled the snowfall in light drifts against curbs and into the alleyways. Peter guessed visibility at half a kilometer, roughly two city blocks, but at that range a 'Mech was little more than a dark shadow and ground vehicles were easily missed. His warriors, what was left of them, relied heavily on their sensors to make contact with the remaining 'Mechs of the Second Royals and Eleventh Arcturan Guard. Struggling to tell friend from foe, they had to try and put down the diehard loyalist fanatics with as little damage to the city as possible. By all tallies, there were perhaps a lance or two of defenders left, determined to fight to the last warrior.

Including Nondi Steiner.

Moving his hundred-ton *Fahnir* into the next intersection, Peter weathered the twin lightning blasts of his aunt's particle projection cannon. They snaked along the ice-slick streets with serpentine grace from the distant shadow that was her *Hauptmann* OmniMech. One carved into his left side, burning away armor composite and splashing molten globules onto the street. The second slid past on his right, missed the *Cestus* that trailed along behind him, and caved in the glass entryway of an office building. Long shards of glass smashed down over sidewalk and street like thin icicles.

Wary of inflicting any more damage than necessary on Tharkad City, Peter selected only one of his heavy gauss rifles, wanting to be certain of the shot. The rail-accelerated mass pulled an impressive wake of snow behind it as it sped along the short path to smash into the *Hauptmann*'s shoulder. The sensor image faded in the next heartbeat as Nondi's OmniMech either moved father along or caught a cross street, its thermal image masked by the snowfall and magnetic resonance fouled by the steel supports of nearby buildings.

Peter detailed two BattleMechs from the end of his short line to hold the intersection and paired up two more details to spread out into parallel streets while he continued straight ahead. It was the same pattern his troops had already gone through to take Asgard and The Triad, herding loyalists ahead of them and coming back together as they made a stand. Success had varied so far.

His planning staff had thought that Asgard, in its lonely position on the crest of Mount Wotan, would be the harder target, but the military compound had fallen with a bare minimum of fighting. It had offered mostly static defenses and artillery, with only a few missile-laden 'Mechs and vehicles standing as defenders. That was because Nondi Steiner had ordered the First Royal Guard to hold The Triad at all costs and the Second Royal Guard and Eleventh Arcturan to defend Tharkad City. Peter's Twentieth Arcturan had suffered another thirty percent loss in and around The Triad, and that might have been worse if the Blue Star Irregulars hadn't pushed through with a battalion of heavy machines to bolster his sagging assault. His aunt had broken through that line as well, however, leading a final two companies of defenders on a quick march to Tharkad City, where she had hoped to take personal charge of its defense.

Her reception, by all accounts, had been colder than a Tharkad blizzard. Some fresh general had refused her authority, this Linda McDonald broadcasting on open transmissions that she'd had enough "inconsistent leadership" to make her question "why the hell she was still fighting against her own people when Victor Davion wasn't even on-planet." Dan Allard relayed that cryptic message to Peter, who had seized on it to talk truce with General McDonald. As his people found members of the Eleventh Arcturan Guard, they accepted the Eleventh's surrender and escorted them out of the city. Marshal Gray took charge of that operation, glad to spare the Twentieth's sister regiment and wanting no flare up of hostilities that would lead more death and destruction. With that procedure in good hands, Peter was left to hunt down his aunt.

He found her again—or she him—two blocks up. Peter had already walked past the ruins of two buildings, marking them for rescue crews to check for wounded. They were what was left of one office building and one department store, both hopefully deserted before some loyalist MechWarrior had used them as a shortcut to evade the encroaching allied forces. Nondi had apparently found or created another such hole in the cityscape in which to hide her sensor image, waiting for Peter to walk into her trap. She stepped her *Hauptmann* out quickly, her targeting system active and acquiring him even as the first warning wailed for Peter's attention. Her heavy autocannon blazed with the long fire of an ultra-class weapon, pounding hot metal across the *Fafnir*'s chest and arms. The arcs of twin PPCs scoured his legs, crisping more of his protection into impotent slag.

"*You* brought this on us, Peter *Davion*." Nondi's voice bled over several reports currently coming in, and Peter moved quickly to dial in the emergency command channel his aunt was using for private communications. "You and *Victor*."

She might as well have said Peter and the *Great Devil* for all the loathing she managed to force into his brother's name. Peter squeezed out another gauss rifle shot, more from reflex than deliberation. The mass struck Nondi's OmniMech in the left leg this time, smashing through enough armor to build a small tank.

The *Hauptmann* stood its ground easily and lit back into him with everything it had. Peter was shaken against his restraining straps, holding the *Fafnir* to its feet with careful balance levered through the control sticks. His aunt had chosen a good configuration for city fighting, as the ultra-class weapon was deadly at such close range. "As treacherous as your father," she screamed at him, "the both of you."

A mistake, talking in the heat of a firefight. Somewhere in his mind, Peter knew this. He also knew that his aunt was stepping dangerously close to the very questions he had wrestled with since Morgan Kell had pulled him from seclusion.

"I am not my father, and I'm certainly not my brother," he whispered, never certain if his mic picked it up. He tied both lasers and gauss rifles into his main trigger and hit Nondi's *Hauptmann* with his full complement. The hard recoils of the heavy gauss rifles slammed him forward in his seat, and his *Fafnir* stumbled back to crush a lamppost. Peter might have ridden the hundred-ton machine to the street if he hadn't smashed up against a nearby building. The crunch of broken ferrocrete and brick echoed through his cockpit. "And I'm just as much a *Steiner* as Katherine."

Was he, though? If actions defined one's role or rights, what had he actually done before joining his brother's civil war? Admittedly, he'd been trying to avoid doing more harm, but the fact remained that he had once turned his back on the Alliance.

Then again, what did that say about Katherine's actions, which had finally brought them all here?

Having betrayed her position again, Nondi was forced to deal with his savage counterassault as well as an eager *Cestus* that circled back from Peter's western patrol. The *Cestus* pilot was a bit too eager perhaps. It lost its footing just after the corner and half stumbled, half slid down the street. Eventually the *Cestus* gave itself up to gravity and momentum, sprawling out full-length over the ferrocrete. Standing over the fallen 'Mech,

Nondi Steiner rained lethal firepower over its prone form. Her twelve-centimeter autocannon blasted through the thin back armor of the *Cestus*, tearing at the 'Mech's internals and forcing it to shut down or risk catastrophic reactor failure.

Peter's gauss rifles spoke again and again. He cycled them as fast as he could, determined to distract his aunt from the distraught *Cestus* and any more of his warriors who might arrive. One hypersonic slug missed wide, punching through a building behind the *Hauptmann* and leaving an impressive wound behind. His others all slammed home, cratering Nondi's armor and wrenching her 'Mech's right arm so far back in its shoulder socket that it froze.

"You're nothing like *Katrina*," his aunt said in a furious voice. "Victor's pawn or Morgan Kell's, it doesn't matter, Peter." Her OmniMech dealt out several hundred kilograms of munitions in a storm of razored metal. Her PPCs drew azure lines between the two assault machines, arcing and splitting harsh light against the delicate snowfall. Peter shook in his command couch, wondering how long he or his 'Mech could stand up under this kind of assault. He answered back with another set of gauss slugs as Nondi yelled at him, "You brought war to Tharkad!"

It was her parting shot, and no less damaging despite that it smashed aside no armor. It still found something critical at the back of Peter's thoughts, worrying at his nerves and confidence. Had his aunt followed up with a hard assault just then, he might have fallen back. She didn't. She wouldn't be following with anything.

The *Hauptmann* toppled back against another building, then slid gracelessly to the ground, scraping a large swath off the building's façade. It ended in a sitting position, leaning over drunkenly against its twisted right arm. A martial marionette with its string finally cut. The *Hauptmann*'s head had caved in under one of Peter's heavy gauss rifles, tearing away the left side of its molded "face" and turning the cockpit into a twisted ruin of metal, ferroglass . . . and flesh.

Peter had lasted as long as necessary. Long enough to kill his own aunt.

"Which makes me more like Katrina than I ever wanted to be," he told himself, muting his open-mic transmissions. He stood over her, knowing that this quick, uneventful end would have upset Nondi Steiner. Likely, she had wanted to go out in a fierce blaze, never considering the destruction a failing fusion reactor would cause against the city. But that was the difference.

"I brought war to Tharkad," he admitted to his empty cockpit. "But hopefully I can bring peace to the people of the Alliance."

30

No one "wins" a war. They survive it, at one level of success or another.

— *Cause and Effect*, Avalon Press, 3067

Avalon Island, New Avalon
Crucis March
Federated Suns
20 April 3067

With Prometheus running at the leading edge of the Tenth Lyran Guards, Victor dodged his command company around a stand of golden oak, then led the charge up and over a small rise. Spread before him down a long, grassy slope, a combat command from the Second Ceti Hussars barely held against a new push by strong elements from the Nineteenth Arcturan Guards and scattered remnants of other loyalist units. His HUD a cluttered mess of icons and tactical information, Victor quickly eyeballed the battle to see how it fared. 'Mech corpses littered the valley, sprawled over torn ground in ungainly repose. He counted at least a dozen crashed VTOLs burning into blackened skeletons nearby with no way to tell who they had belonged to, and he estimated four times that number in armored vehicles.

In the lives of infantry, Victor couldn't begin to guess. Hundreds lost, no doubt, in this battle alone. Fortunately, the Sixth Crucis and the newly arrived Second Davion Guards had safeguarded the bulk of allied infantry into Avalon City, allowing them to scatter with greater safety among the parks and build-ings. That left the public spaceport, the military field, the NAIS, and Davion Palace still to be secured.

Skirting the main battle, Victor led his people in a line along the flank, trading fire with the Arcturan MechWarriors. His lasers ate up his heat-sink capacity in a matter of seconds, the temperature in his cockpit climbing dangerously fast through the yellow band and edging into the red. An Arcturan Guard *Dragon Fire* led the charge of a full company toward Victor's position, gauss rifle slamming out silver death as fast as its ca-pacitors could recharge. Its autocannon fired flechette muni-tions, sweeping a gray haze over any nearby enemy. Victor overrode his first shutdown cautionary and switched out two lasers for his cool-firing autocannon, clipping the *Dragon Fire* across the knee joint, severing the leg.

"We pushed the Remagan straight into the Ceti's backfield," Reinhart Steiner broadcast as he led First Battalion over the same rise and joined the fight at Victor's back. "Two o'clock low, by the trees."

Victor had noticed that as well. Only a few hours before, his Revenants had shattered the Remagan militia, depriving Kather-ine of another coherent force. Unfortunately, survivors from that battle were retreating along a path that ran into the lower valley. At the farther reaches, where Reinhart described, he saw their blue-and-red-painted BattleMechs bleeding in by 'Mech lances and the occasional mixed company to worry the rear lines of the Second Ceti Hussars.

Victor throttled down into a slower walk, trading his auto-cannon for lasers, fighting to regain some control over his tem-perature spike. Sweat glistened on his arms and trickled down his neck. His breath came shallow and quick in the heat-scorched air. "Shakov should just about be in position to stop-gap those reinforcements. Keep them moving, Ren. Add some firepower where you can."

A *Banshee* finished off the *Dragon Fire* for Victor as the rest of his company also lit into the Arcturan unit with unbridled fury. They missed a fast lance of *Scarabus* designs that bolted in for the backside at better than one hundred kilometers per hour, hatchets raised. Only two survived to take a swing at Victor's *Daishi*. One missed. The other carved away half a ton of armor from Prometheus's arm. Victor's autocannon took the hatchet-wielding arm and one leg from the *Scarabus*, while his lasers worked through the light 'Mech's chest to slag the gyro into a ruined mass. The remaining *Scarabus* and a MASC-equipped *Stealth* tried to escape over the shoulder of the same rise Victor's Revenants had come down, only to find another battalion of the Tenth Lyran still moving up on the backside. They never made it back.

"Leave Second Batt up top to support the Hussars," Victor ordered as he stepped into the lower valley and cleared the worst of the fighting. "The Second Davion is only twenty minutes out. Have them swing in to help mop up."

Reinhart's reply came in right behind Victor's order. "The Second is still helping safeguard our infantry push into the capital. They're not all in yet."

"I know that, Ren. But the Hussars are spread to hell and gone along the valley, and no telling what kind of pressure the Arcturan Guards are putting on them in other battles." In fact, Victor didn't see Ardan Sortek anywhere, and assumed he had split off to make a stab at the NAIS. "They need reinforcements over here. General Killson is a good officer. She can oversee the infantry push solo."

As if to lend weight to Victor's decision, a reconstituted battalion of the Remagan CMM surged from the treeline. Mixed armor and BattleMechs—perhaps a reinforced company of each—they would have bolstered the Arcturan Guard position with enough strength to tear the Second Ceti Hussars apart. Now they threw themselves at Victor's command company instead, trying to sell themselves dearly for their Archon-Princess.

Victor swung his company out wide in a thinning arc, pulling the inexperienced militia into several subunits clumped together by speed and specialty. Fast armor led the new charge. Assault 'Mechs and slow heavies moved up last. A trio of old Condor heavy hovercraft angled in at Victor's *Daishi*, spraying out furious streams of autocannon fire. Sharp, ringing blows pounded his front armor, striking harder and deeper than regular munitions. A warning telltale brightened on the damage schematic for Prometheus, and Victor saw that the Condors had managed to destroy his right-chest missile launcher. The militia was using the newer armor-piercing rounds!

Slamming his throttle back, he immediately began a backpedaling maneuver that took him into and through a stand of trees. His lasers managed to cut through the skirting of one Condor, spilling its air cushion and sending it in an end-over tumble, before trees blocked his line of sight. The hovercraft couldn't follow him directly, but they could swing around through one of many clearings. It bought Victor a moment to dump his missile-storage bins out of the rear ejection ports. No sense carrying around a full ton of useless warheads, waiting for another salvo of armor-piercing rounds to set them off in a gut-ripping explosion.

The Condors came for him, just as he thought they would. Before they could swing around to target their weapons, Victor had smashed through the side armor of one with his own assault-class autocannon, cutting straight through into the crew compartment. That hovercraft swerved sharply along an erratic path, then barreled straight into a large oak, where it exploded in a mushrooming fireball that quickly burned into a sooty black cloud.

The second Condor had fixed Victor in his sights by then, chewing through more armor as it sped up to ramming speeds. A heat sink mounted in Victor's left arm exploded outward in a grayish mist of wasted coolant. Two of Victor's pulse lasers hammered emerald nails into the front of the Condor, but not enough to shake it off from its ramming attempt. Then, at the last second, the Condor rocked sideways, lifting up on its skirting and nearly spilling over. Victor caught the silvery flash that struck the vehicle in its left side, but it wasn't until the Condor had slid past him to begin a run for the far side of the valley that he thought to look for his guardian. A *Centurion* ran along just inside the treeline about half a kilometer downrange. An impressive shot, considering range and relative speeds.

Then again, it was an impressive MechWarrior.

Victor bypassed the hands-free ComStar system normally at work in Prometheus, toggling for a direct channel to his friend. "Kai! You were supposed to be securing the spaceport."

"Done," Kai told him, slowing to a walk as he moved Yen-lo-wang up on Victor's left. "The Davion Heavy Guards detoured through our operations area and lent a hand. The Outland Legion is down to a single battalion, but that should be enough to cordon off the landing field and prevent any retreat from the palace grounds. Katherine's going nowhere, provided you have someone sitting on the military field." The *Centurion* came to attention only five meters in front of Victor, executing a mechanical salute with the gauss rifle that was its right arm. "Besides, I thought you might need some looking after. Now you owe me."

"So it seems," Victor said sharply, his friend's comment striking closer to the quick than he even knew. But any further comment was spoiled by new threat alarms as his battle computer painted a flashing red icon onto the heads-up display. Victor saw dark movement through his ferroglass shield, back behind Kai's Yen-lo-wang, and didn't think of anything else but bringing up both of his *Daishi*'s arms and shoving Kai to the side.

The ex-champion of Solaris was not about to stumble over his own feet, not in a 'Mech he piloted as if born to it. He walked quickly out of the perilous, leaning position, moving back several meters. Enough that the blue-and-red militia *Falconer* had a clean shot at Prometheus, able to slam home the gauss slug no doubt meant for Kai's back into Victor's midriff.

Kai spun Yen-lo-wang and hurled an identical hypersonic mass back at the *Falconer*, still faster on the trigger—even in an awkward cross-body shot—than Victor would ever be. Prometheus was not to be forgotten, however. Its trio of pulse lasers chewed emerald teeth into the *Falconer*'s side, sending armor streaming down to the ground in fiery runnels. Victor also pulled into an extra-long burst form his twelve-centimeter auto-cannon, digging slugs tipped with depleted uranium in behind the laserfire damage. The pounding assault blew through the *Falconer*'s chest and out the back, completely coring out the left side of its chest. It tumbled back into the trees and out of sight, golden fire spilling from the reactor breach. A moment later, a blossom of fire tore over the wooded stand and shook the ground beneath them.

"Victor, I'm reading elevated heat levels on Prometheus."

The reactor's power spike had dumped several degrees of waste heat into Victor's lap, and he fought for breath as he answered Kai. "That slug knocked a crack through my engine shielding, it seems. I'll be all right."

"That was mine, Victor. You should have let me take that."

Victor struggled to keep his voice light. "There's plenty to go around, Kai. Besides," he said, his humor fading into something slightly darker, "I *hate* owing people."

"So I've noticed." Kai's voice was dry and serious for a moment, but then he bowed Yen-lo-wang at the waist and gestured for Victor to take the lead. "Very well, Victor. My thanks. Now, how about we continue and stamp 'paid' to a few more accounts?"

Tancred Sandoval's mixed companies ran a gauntlet of auto-cannon fire as they charged the infantry line. The towed field guns were parked along a low rise, backing several squads of Cavalier armored infantry and a single heavy lance of Battle-Mechs. The guns rained a hard curtain of razored metal over the killing grounds, picking away at his *Templar*'s armor with needle-sharp teeth. With his druthers, Tancred would have turned aside for an easier path. The demands of the assault argued against it.

Separated from the bulk of his Second Robinson Rangers by a big push from the Com Guard Sixty-sixth, he had led them on a circuitous route that bled time from the operation but saved his people from being overwhelmed in battle. Skirting the Wallace River, he traded a lance of Pegasus hovertanks for a *Watchman* and an *Enforcer* belonging to the Remagan CMM. Then, working their way back toward Mount Davion, Tancred's small force attracted several stragglers from other allied units and added them to his command.

Meanwhile, the Rangers pushed onward toward the Davion Palace, still trying to reach their goal, which was the military field on the backside of Mount Davion. The breaking of any loyalist logistics line was secondary to their real purpose, preventing Katherine's retreat to a waiting DropShip. She could not be allowed to escape justice. Not now. And Tancred would be there.

But first he had to push through this defense line set by the Twenty-second Avalon Hussars.

"Armor against the ridgeline," Tancred ordered, flinging his hovercraft forward and following them up with a lance of heavy Alacorn heavy tanks. "Irregulars, concentrate on those battlesuit infantry. Keep them off our backs." Which left two lances of his Rangers to pile up on the Hussar 'Mech forces. Or so he had hoped, until a *Nightstar* came around one side of the rise and the *Devastator* around the other. The assault machines were easily the equivalent of his second lance, unless he tied one up himself.

"I'll delay the *Nightstar*," he said, peeling his OmniMech out from formation as the first gauss slug took him high in the left arm.

Tancred knew the *Nightstar* and the kind of hurt it was capable of dishing out among other 'Mechs. He swallowed dryly, facing his old ride, then toggled in his large laser with his rotary autocannons. His crosshairs burned a deep gold as the *Templar*'s targeting computer grabbed a hard lock, and Tancred drilled a good measure of scarlet energy and hot metal into the *Nightstar*'s chest. Shoving his throttle forward, he worked to close the distance before the *Nightstar*'s two gauss rifles tore him apart.

They tried. New masses, hurled at hypersonic speeds by the *Nightstar*'s twin rail guns, hammered hard at the *Templar*'s legs and chest. An alarm strobed red in the cockpit as one gut-pounding punch cracked his engine shielding, bleeding waste heat through the armored carapace, and another tore a medium laser from his right arm. The *Nightstar*'s PPC scarred the *Tem-*

plar's left side with molten cuts, switching to the short-stabbing damage of pulse lasers as Tancred forced his Omni straight into the *Nightstar*'s embrace.

Worried for his targeting computer, he had held his rotary autocannon to cautious fire patterns until the *Nightstar* filled his canopy and there was no chance to miss. Dropping his targeting reticle over its centerline, he half depressed his triggering studs to lock in his target. The computer did the rest, making small variations in actuators and myomer tension to hold steady aim through Tancred's extra-long bursts. He grabbed onto the triggers, held them, listened as the autocannon roared through several kilograms of munitions. In the kind of fury no other weapon Tancred had ever fired could produce, the rotary weapons chewed straight through the *Nightstar*'s center armor. Shards and dust from the pulverized composite exploded outward, laying bare the 'Mech's fusion reactor. His lasers finished the job, cutting through shielding to skewer the magnetic chamber.

Golden fire belched out in a furious stream from the *Nightstar*'s ruined chest. With no chance for his dampening fields to shut his 'Mech down, the Hussar MechWarrior punched out on his ejection seat to escape the growing inferno. Tancred never slowed, racing his *Templar* up the rise, glancing at his rear monitor as the ground-shaking explosion tore the *Nightstar* to pieces.

After such a ferocious display, the field guns under his feet worried Tancred not at all. His medium lasers carved into the side of one, melting the barrel, and he kicked aside a second as he continued to work his way up the rise. From the head of the ridge, he looked down on the field to see his motley force tearing through the Twenty-second Hussars. His armored vehicles were through the line in three places, swinging back to stitch new damage into the field guns. Infantry worked in desperation to swing around a number of the large weapons but never fast enough against the Rangers. The loyalists' heavy lance had held out with two 'Mechs during several minutes of hard-pitched fighting, but even these were beginning to fail under concentrated fire.

A few minutes more, Tancred decided, adding his own weapons to the struggle below. Then they had to be on the move. Turning to scorch more laserfire among the field guns, Tancred glanced out his side canopy to see their destination only five kilometers off. Mount Davion, crowned by the palace like some fabled castle fortress of Terran myth. The balance of his Rangers would be climbing up from its shadow by now. If he were going to join them, it would have to be soon.

"Finish up and move on," Tancred ordered, selecting his all-hands' frequency. He soft-fired his rotaries back down into the melee, clipping the arm from a Hussar *Caesar*. "We still have ground to cover."

And a much bigger battle to win.

The New Avalon Institute of Science main campus bordered up against the Davion Peace Gardens to the north and against open, wild woodlands to the east. It was here that Victor found Ardan Sortek and General Jonathan Sanchez besieged by elements of the Com Guard Sixty-sixth, both men trying hard not to fall back through Peace Park. With safety only a few dozen paces behind them, their battered commands slugged it out, throwing back every push sent at them.

Sending ruby lances from his extended-range lasers into the backs of the Sixty-sixth, Victor led his Revenants' first battalion in, with the Second Davion backing them. They rolled over the Com Guard with no reservations. The fighting turned personal and hard-pitched for several moments as the Com Guard struck back, leaping into point-blank combat with the prince's command company. Lasers crisscrossed overhead as wild shots flew wide, and armor crunched under metal-shod fists and feet when nothing else worked. The Sixty-sixth sold themselves dearly against odds turned so suddenly against them. Then they were simply gone.

A *Shootist* lay sprawled over the ground at the feet of Prometheus, its canopy pierced with a half-dozen holes burned through by Victor's pulse lasers. Gray smoke bled from scorched myomer, leaking past seams and rents in the downed

BattleMech's armor. Victor stepped back from the corpse. He found both of his senior officers still on their feet, though Sortek's Hussars claimed only a damaged lance and two Goblin infantry carriers to their name.

Jonathan Sanchez quickly salvaged two solid companies from his First NAIS cadre. "My thanks for the assistance, Highness," he said, strength coming back into his voice. "First Cadre, re-form on a southwest march. We're ten minutes outside of the campus, and it's still ours to take."

Victor wasn't about to argue the point. VTOL reconnaissance had spotted infantry running through the NAIS, but no 'Mech assets. Jonathan Sanchez had asked for the university grounds, wanting to bring his cadets home. There was no reason to deny him that now.

In hindsight, Victor would wish he had. Sanchez worked his cadets out of the battlefield, stepping around shattered 'Mech corpses and burning vehicles. He brought up the rear, pausing as a med unit checked cockpits and vehicle crew quarters for survivors. With every negative report, the general appeared to move a little slower. Once he was certain that no one would be left behind, he walked his *JagerMech* past Victor's location. From the small knoll, they could both look down into the shallow valley that finally dumped out into the NAIS campus. His cadets marched in a long column, wary of minefields and never stringing themselves out so far that they could be easily shattered by ambush. They were a solid 'Mech corps, slowing down only to wait for their commander.

Then the first artillery barrage struck.

The ground erupted as if it had been layered with vibra-bombs, throwing geysers of scorched earth and burning grasses into the air. The NAIS cadre disappeared completely from sight through the dirty curtain. No hastily planned strike had that kind of accuracy or complete saturation—the valley had been planned from the start as a trap. Victor tried to imagine how many artillery pieces would be required for such a display, and couldn't. He sat, stunned, the more so a few seconds later when he saw that half the cadets were down and the other half still reeling from the shocking attack. As some late-arriving artillery continued to pock and blast the valley, Victor finally found his voice and toggled directly for the NAIS command frequency.

"Get out of there. On your feet, cadets! Fall back—retreat!—now, damn it, now!"

Some of those on the ground did stir. The MechWarriors who had managed to stay upright moved, but slowly. Even if they had reacted instantly, it would not have made a difference. The second barrage was more scattered than the first as the hidden artillery teams paced themselves to individual speeds, but it still blanketed the valley end to end and pounded the shattered command with lethal intent.

It was enough to get Sanchez moving. He throttled up into a forward run, heading into the valley after them. "Stop that man," Victor ordered. "General Sanchez, stand fast!" No answer as two faster heavies stormed at the general, slamming their shoulders into his *JagerMech*, knocking him back to the ground.

Sanchez rolled the *JagerMech* onto its front and climbed quickly back to his feet. His mad rush stalled and blocked by the Tenth Lyran, he swung about to face Victor's *Daishi*. "My cadets—my kids! Victor—"

"Your cadets are gone, General." Victor looked past him to where the artillery continued to rain down hard. The cadre had been finished with the second barrage, yet the infantry continued their prearranged assault. He could imagine how the order had gone out to begin their saturation assault, sent by a spy hidden somewhere in the nearby trees or some other spotting blind. Right now, they were likely recalculating to shift the strike into his own grouped regiments.

"They're gone," he whispered, "and you have my condolences." He hardened his voice. "But not my leave to go running into an artillery barrage after them." It hurt to come down on Sanchez like this, but in the heat of anger, a good commander could become a dangerous liability to himself and those around him faster than it took a PPC to cycle.

And Sanchez wasn't the only one obliged to rein in his emotions damn quick. Watching the continual-fire barrage soaking the valley, battering down the NAIS cadre in sight of their alma mater, a cold spike of pain lodged itself in Victor's gut. Sanchez was right. His cadre may have been veterans by now, but they were still kids. They should have had a long life ahead of them. Something more, at least, than the impersonal death Katherine's commanders had given them.

"You've been forcibly transferred, General, and I'm sorry," Victor said. "Take command of the Second Davion Guards and work your way around the NAIS and come at them through the city. If Katherine turns artillery on her own capital, you'll see regiments defecting to us as fast as they can transmit a surrender." He waited to see if Sanchez would hold up, betting on the steel spine of the career general.

Sanchez did not disappoint. "Yes," he said quietly. Then, stronger, "Yes, Highness." He walked his *JagerMech* into the allies' backfield, duty driving him on, but his spirit obviously wounded. Perhaps beyond repair.

Ardan Sortek stalked his *Templar* OmniMech up to Victor's side, transferring himself into Victor's command company without so much as a by your leave, though not exactly needing one at this late stage in the game. "And where are we going, Highness?"

Victor maneuvered the *Daishi* in a tight circle, swinging around to face Mount Davion. It was eight kilometers away, by his estimate. By cutting through the middle of Davion Peace Park, it wouldn't take more than half an hour. Victor couldn't see the Royal Court clustered around the mountain's base, not with the tall park trees in the way, but it was there. As real as the castle that crowned the hill, looking down on the ruined countryside.

"We're pushing on for the palace," Victor said, biting down hard until his jaw muscles ached. "We're pulling Katherine out of there if I have to take it apart stone by bloody stone.

"This ends now."

31

Despite all the things she took from me, I have never felt hatred for Katherine. Anger, yes. Sorrow, certainly. But never hate. I remember who Katherine was before, and can only grieve for the loss of the sister I once knew.

—*Cause and Effect*, Avalon Press, 3067

Davion Palace
Avalon City, New Avalon
Crucis March
Federated Suns
20 April 3067

Katrina Morgan Steiner-Davion entered the emptied Grand Court of Davion Palace alone, ordering her guards away. The doors stood almost five meters tall, carved from solid Avalon redwood and faced with a sculpted gold relief of a kneeling warrior raising a giant broadsword overhead. The warrior's cloak was tattered and burned, his head bowed and shoulders slumped under some unseen weight, but with the rising sun in the background, Katrina had always thought it a magnificent, triumphant piece of art. Not anymore. Now she would remember the slump of defeat she was trying so hard to lift from her own shoulders.

At her lightest shove, the doors swung inward, smooth and noiseless, the sword and warrior splitting cleanly down the middle, with half falling away to either side. She had never asked how such massive doors—they must have weighed half a ton each—opened to such a light touch. Like many things in her years on New Avalon, she simply accepted it. Was that her ultimate failing, never caring enough to delve into such trivial matters? Her brother had always found a great deal to interest him in the minute details. Then again, Victor had also managed to lose two realms by not focusing on the more important issues, while Katrina, in ten short years, had risen to such heights that she had several times been within grasping reach of the entire Inner Sphere.

But it had been taken from her every time. Her dreams of the First Lordship. Her Lyran Alliance. And now her father's realm as well. All gone.

For now.

The marble floor of the Davion throne hall rapped back with sharp-edged echoes under her heels. Red and blue swirled within the golden stone, each tile a perfect square, fit so seamlessly against one another that the entire floor appeared as one titanic carving of cold marble stretching fifty meters wide by two hundred meters long. She lifted her eyes to the grand balcony that surrounded three sides of the mammoth court. During formal receptions, Hanse Davion had always opened the balcony to the common citizens of New Avalon. Two thousand could be seated up there. In formal, respectful rows, the main floor could hold five thousand more. The Davions never thought small. Neither had she.

Her walk to the dais at the court's far end left her with several minutes of bitter thoughts toward everyone who had abandoned her. Her aunt Nondi, killed in the battle for Tharkad City. Richard Dehaver, vanished. The loss of her most important March lords, James Sandoval and George Hasek. Then Jackson Davion. And Vlad, his betrayal coming when she needed him most. The failures of Simon Gallagher . . . well, he would be brought along shortly by her royal guard.

"But they are not my only supporters," Katrina said aloud. "Victor still has several lessons left to learn."

The dais was a circular platform raised one uncomfortable

step above the main floor. Careful of her tight, silver-threaded gown, Katrina stepped up onto it and stood before the trio of thrones. Behind them was a great circular window. Ten meters in diameter and facing north, it allowed the sun to fill this end of the hall with light from morning to eve. At an afternoon court, the heavy ferroglass caught and held the light in a brilliant display that wreathed the ruling family in a halo of gold. Like divine rulers, resting in their mortal cradles. There was one high-backed seat for the First Prince of the Federated Suns, another for a spouse, and that last, smaller seat, for the heir apparent. Katrina trembled, imagining for a moment that Hanse Davion and Melissa had returned to their places, with her brother Victor taking the heir's throne as they all sat in judgment over her life.

Victor, in the seat that should have been hers. The idea was enough to burst the illusion, and Katrina walked forward at a sharp, brisk pace to seize the arm of the magnificent throne her father had once graced and that had been hers now for seven years. She had ordered it draped in a large blanket of brushed white fox upon her own ascension, always warm and soft and comforting. She stepped back slowly, pulling on the fox-fur blanket as she did. It slid away noiselessly, revealing the hammered gold and tooled leather underneath. Katrina draped the fur over her shoulders, wrapping herself in its luxury.

"This will be mine again. One way or another, I will return for what I'm owed."

She moved past the throne, stepping down from the back of the dais and walking over to the window. It looked out on the rear of the palace, where Mount Davion spread out to a plateau shared with the military as a staging ground and auxiliary spaceport. During evening receptions, the launch of a DropShip from that field would fill the window with a rising star. Like a box seat at one of Solaris VII's 'Mech games, the spot offered Katrina the best view of the battle taking place below—only her ticket wagered so much more than mere kroner, and already her champions had all but lost.

Her Twenty-second Avalon Hussars held the military field,

but only by dint of being first on the scene after Simon Gallagher's call to retreat. Katrina might have escaped then, taking the one remaining DropShip and fleeing to the *supposedly* neutral justice of Thomas Marik. She contemplated it too long, however. When the ragged battalions remaining to the Davion Heavy Guards struck at the field, it made any attempt at flight a risky proposition. Even when the Nineteenth Arcturan Guards trickled in to bolster her loyal defenders, slowly squeezing the Heavy Guards to death, she hesitated. The Heavy Guards were no regiment to underestimate, and might have spent themselves to bring down the launching vessel.

Now, of course, it was far too late for any thoughts of escape. Tancred Sandoval's Second Robinson Rangers had chased a few small units belonging to the Com Guard 299th up onto the plateau. Then Victor's Tenth Lyran Guard rolled in, throwing the balance of strength firmly behind his allies. Stragglers from Katrina's broken commands continued to gain the plateau even as she watched—more Com Guard, a company from the Remagan CMM, two lances from her Fifth Donegal—but invariably following them was a mixed company from the Second Davion or the Ceti Hussars. Now Victor's allies formed a steadily shrinking perimeter that turned the military field into a shooting gallery, with her loyalists as the clay targets.

When the royal guards found her ten minutes later, Katrina had found Victor's *Daishi* on the field below and watched as it led one probing charge after another. She waited for some of her loyalists to clip off his attack and render the *Daishi* into scrap, but always he pulled back safely. Only one trap looked promising as a full company of the Twenty-second Avalon threw themselves into a suicide run, but at the last second, a *Templar* shoved into the fight and gave itself in place of Victor. Katrina hoped that it was Tancred Sandoval. She watched Victor's OmniMech stagger back for the safety of his Revenants.

"Prometheus," she said then to the waiting corporal. "Victor named his BattleMech Prometheus. The Light-Bringer. Such a noble name for a machine that brings with it death, destruction, and misery." She turned to the uniformed guard with an accusing glare. "You, you've probably named your rifle, haven't you?"

"Alexis," the guard admitted, nodding reluctantly.

Katrina awarded him a sardonic grin. "How quaint." Only then did she look past the soldier to see that the guards came back empty-handed. "Where is Gallagher?"

The corporal chewed on his lower lip, averted his eyes. "We found him in the Fox's Den, Highness. He cleared the room and locked himself in before he . . . he . . ."

"Shot himself," Katrina finished for him with a conviction that bordered on premonition. The guard nodded. "Simon always was a coward at heart. And incompetent to the end. He couldn't even lose a war with decent dignity." She drew the warm fur closer to herself, returned her gaze to the fighting, and waited out another long, haunted moment. On the field, more of Katrina's loyalists fought and fell while she delayed.

"Get me Jackson Davion," she said finally. "He's under house arrest in his palace apartments. Tell him to take my commands to the army. Tell him to end this."

"H-how?" the corporal asked. "Do you have orders for him, Archon?"

"He'll know them," Katrina said, gazing down on the battle. Then again, she did not need Jackson taking credit for "misinterpreting orders." If this was to end, it would end by *her* direct command. She found Victor again and set her face into a frozen mask to prevent the rage and frustration from boiling past her calm facade. Not that it helped in the end. When she spoke, her voice was frosted with cold fury.

"Tell him," she said, "tell him . . . we surrender."

═══ 32 ═══

Milton once wrote that it is "better to reign in hell than serve in heaven." Such incredible hubris, yet still I wonder if the author didn't strike a chord with most tyrants who have ever read *Paradise Lost.* A shame that Lucifer could not suffer the simple ignominy of being forgotten.

—*Cause and Effect,* Avalon Press, 3067

Davion Palace
Avalon City, New Avalon
Crucis March
Federated Suns
24 April 3067

Victor and Yvonne hosted the intimate gathering in a small anteroom just off the Grand Court of Davion Palace. Neither wanted all the pomp and ceremony or the full regalia everyone would have to don for the throne hall. What Victor wanted was a quick address made against a backdrop of friends and relations, and then to make all final arrangements regarding Katherine's future. Such as it was.

A spot had been left at the front of the room for him and Yvonne, spaced between Tancred Sandoval and Kai Allard-Liao. Isis Marik and Kai also stood together, the two people who had helped him through the wall of grief surrounding Omi's death. Then there was Rudolf Shakov, General Jonathan Sanchez, and Reinhart Steiner, three of Victor's strongest supporters, without whom he could never have made it to New Avalon, much less Avalon City.

Next to Tancred was Jackson Davion, who Yvonne had reinstated not only as Marshal of the Armies but, deservedly, as the Prince's Champion. Of all Katherine's supporters, he was the one man they knew who had followed her out of personal honor, not personal ambition. After him came the on-planet ambassador from Duke George Hasek, a Lyran duchess on behalf of the Alliance, and finally, Agent Curaitis, who had come only under direct orders.

"So many people who should be up there, and aren't," Victor whispered to Yvonne as the two waited off-camera for the signal to begin.

Yvonne glanced around at the small knots of nobles and high-ranking officers, all of them avoiding any look or gesture toward Katherine, who was their captive audience for the short ceremony. "I assume you are not talking about present company."

He shook his head lightly. "Galen Cox. Morgan Kell. Arthur . . ." Victor faltered at mention of his brother, who he considered the first true fatality of the civil war. As Ardan Sortek had been the last. During the final moments of fighting, Ardan had sacrificed himself for Victor by placing his *Templar* in the way of a last, loyalist push. It seemed prophetic, now, that his father's champion had fallen in front of the palace, the final casualty before Katherine's surrender.

"Colonel Vineman and Captain Harsch," Yvonne said, naming some of the later casualties among Victor's command staff. "Precentor Irelon, Francesca Jenkins." She paused. "Omi?" The warmth in her eyes helped offset the small stab of pain that Omi's name still brought with it. "Where would the list end, Victor?"

He swallowed hard. "With the last technician's assistant who lost a limb or a loved one to this damned civil war. They all deserve to be up there."

"They are," Yvonne said, taking his hand and giving it a supportive squeeze. "They are." She moved her hand to his arm and turned him toward the assembly as the holocam crew signaled readiness. "Ready?" she asked, voice tight.

He nodded. "Are you? I get the easy job, remember?"

"We'll see about that."

Victor led Yvonne to the line, dropping her in next to Tancred and trading brief handshakes with the Draconis March duke. Then he took his place between Yvonne and Kai, not speaking until the entire room fell silent.

"Five years," he said, looking into the camera, his voice barely a whisper. He let the words sit for a moment, then continued in full voice. "For five years, the Federated Suns and the Lyran Alliance have been plagued by civil war. Even now, scattered fighting continues on a dozen worlds. Let me be one of the first to ask that, wherever you are, for whatever reason you are still taking up arms against your brothers and sisters, that you now lay down your weapons and help rebuild these shattered nations. This war," he stated with finality, "is over."

Victor never took his gaze from the camera. "Reason and justice must and will replace the blind fury that has too long clouded our vision. Too many citizens and soldiers have closed their eyes knowing little else in their final years but struggle and violence at the hands of their neighbors. Too many children have grown up knowing nothing but this civil war. We must never forget the awful price we have paid to finally win this peace. The Commonwealth my parents once forged from both nations is lost forever, so I ask this of the Lyran Alliance and the reborn Federated Suns. May we never turn down this path again.

"For me," Victor continued, "what I have set out to do, I have done. Katherine's tyranny has ended with her unconditional surrender on behalf of all loyalist forces. The injuries she forced upon our family and on our people can now begin to heal. This is what I need more than anything. And I am not so vain as to think that my presence on New Avalon *or* Tharkad would not be a disruption and a constant reminder of the war I started—was forced to start—and how it was prosecuted to its fullest extent."

Victor looked at Yvonne, and she took his hand. "It was never my intention to reclaim a throne for myself," he said.

"That I could have done seven years ago, after Katherine first usurped the Federated Suns from my regent, and sister, Yvonne. Now, with peace again taking a firm grip on our nations, I hope to leave . . . retire . . ."—he paused between each word, setting them off—"and surrender forevermore my claim to the rule of either the Lyran Alliance of the Federated Suns. These I abrogate with fullest confidence into the care of my brother, Peter Steiner-Davion, and my sister Yvonne Steiner-Davion. May they rule as wisely, and with the greatest love for our people, as our parents would have desired."

Victor saw the shocked looks on many of the noble and military faces at the back of the room, none of whom had been informed of his decision before the broadcast. Even Katherine showed her shock in a sudden stiffening of her spine, bearing up under the news that her rival for power was actually abdicating it all to their siblings. Victor smiled. Only those under the camera's eye had known. Some had argued, but in the end all stood behind him. Victor had never felt so right in any decision he had made in all his time ruling the two nations as he did just then.

"Good night," he said to his people, and his former nations. "God bless and good luck."

"We're clear," a cameraman said, and the team began to gather up their gear as security moved in to hustle them along. The rest of the evening was not for them to journal, but for Yvonne to begin the arduous and necessary task of rebuilding the infrastructure Katherine had so selfishly ruined in her grasping for greater power.

Victor looked at his sister. "As I said, now you have the harder task. But you also have a good team to help you accomplish it."

Yvonne nodded. "I do." She reached back for Tancred and drew him up to her side.

Victor raised his eyebrows. "You know, I kind of like the sound of that. Maybe you two should try it again . . . under more formal circumstances."

Tancred's mouth fell open at Victor's boldness. Yvonne, fortunately, held on to her composure. "Was that an order, Victor?"

She smiled at Tancred. "From the former First Prince, or as the new Precentor Martial of ComStar?"

"A suggestion only," he said. "From your brother. I've watched the two of you chase around after each other for too long now. If you don't want this, it's time you both moved on." He glanced away. "Life too often comes between our duties and our happiness. If you can have both, I suggest you seize it."

Tancred flushed a light pink all the way up his newly shaven topknot, but he couldn't help the look of hope and desire that chased around in his amber eyes. The young duke had certainly held out hope for such a match for several years, but now that Victor was the one placing it on the table, he looked at a loss for words. "And I thought this would be hard *before*," he said.

Yvonne held his hand all the tighter. "Being First Princess, fortunately, comes with a few prerogatives." Her gray eyes danced playfully, warmly, between Victor and her intended. "I can make it an *order*. If you are going to ask, Tancred Sandoval, ask now."

He swallowed, grinned. "Marry me?"

"Of course," Yvonne said, drawing him into an immediate embrace to the applause of a dozen nearby men and women with large ears and expressions of honest hopefulness. A warm feeling that was ruined almost as soon as it had begun.

"How very touching," Katherine said, moving up with her two guards in tow. "I assume you have more entertainments planned for this evening, but I trust I will not be subjected to them as well?" She glanced pointedly at her jailers.

Each of the security men wore the dress uniform of the Davion Heavy Guards. The best choice, by Victor's way of thinking. After everything the Davion Guards had endured, including the crippling or death of five of the eight regiments, they weren't about to let their guard down and dishonor the sacrifices made by their brothers and sisters. Victor wanted to point out that fact to Katherine, who made his skin crawl even in defeat, but in truth it was Yvonne's prerogative to answer.

"You were brought here as a courtesy," Yvonne said coolly,

summoning enough frost to chill a Lyran. "Which is more than you ever gave me or anyone else, *Katherine*."

Their sister shrugged, then shook her golden hair back behind her shoulders. "It doesn't matter what you want to believe, Yvonne. My charities and accomplishments will be made evident at whatever kind of trial you arrange. And I'll be certain to show that Victor's important *evidence* is nothing more than a twisted fabrication constructed to justify his armed aggression. You both have much to learn if you think I'm finished with you yet."

"Except that there will be no trial. No public outcry. No martyred pleas." Yvonne nodded to Victor. "At Victor's suggestion, I am simply invoking my authority to banish you from the Federated Suns for the duration of my life or yours. You are hereby remanded into Victor's custody, at his disposal. And that may be the literal truth." Her sentence declared, Yvonne and Tancred turned their backs on Katherine, as did most of those within hearing.

Katherine wasted no time mounting a new offensive. "So, what is it to be, dear brother? Will you wait until we are out of Avalon City before you order up your firing squad, or are they waiting in the Grand Court?" Her voice was just loud enough to reach a few of the looser ears in the room, making certain that she didn't simply vanish without *any* trace.

Victor shook his head as Kai and Curaitis drew nearer, followed by Precentor Shakov and Reinhart Steiner. With her two guards behind her, Katherine was effectively isolated from the rest of the room. "I don't need to have you shot, Katherine. You're finished, regardless, and I've had my fill of death. You are going to disappear from the public eye. It's as easy as that."

"Nothing is that easy, Victor. And if you think the idea of banishment worries me, you're wrong. I never wanted a trial, I simply expected one. This changes nothing."

"No," Victor said with a touch of anger to his voice, "it changed everything the day your man killed Francesca Jenkins. Not that I expect that name to mean anything to you. Just one more in a long body count. But it gave us what we needed to validate the evidence gathered from Sven Newmark. And Dehaver, of course, handed us even more to use against you."

Was that a flicker of fire in her ice-blue eyes? "It could be argued that you tortured that information from him. No wonder you do not want a trial. He would not make a very good witness."

"Worse than you think," Curaitis said. "He's dead." He let that sit with her a moment. "Apparently, someone smuggled him some poison."

Katherine smiled at him, though her mouth faltered a bit at the end. "You were too kind. Dehaver deserved much worse, I promise you."

"Doesn't matter," Victor told her. "His confession only supports the rest of the evidence we gathered, and it's enough to be shown around, quietly and discreetly, to convince any of your remaining supporters that they really are better off forgetting you. If you were hoping for some kind of outcry to be raised on your behalf"—Victor shrugged—"well, I wouldn't."

"Nice," Katherine commented, nodding once. "You do learn quickly, just as you always threatened. You aren't quite *there* yet, Victor, but you are much closer than I'd ever dreamed you'd be." She drew in a steadying breath, let it out in one long, exaggerated sigh. "What a shame you have no one to share your victory with."

Victor had expected some kind of violent stab, and it surprised him that, coming from Katherine, the allusion to Omi Kurita was far less painful than the kind reference Yvonne had made earlier. He needed no mask to hide his feelings from her, and his open expression was the first thing that seemed to truly frighten his sister. "That's the problem when you've inflicted such a wound on someone, Katherine. Nothing you say can ever really touch them as hard again. Now it's my job to make certain that you can't *ever* hurt anyone else in that same way.

"You'll spend the rest of your life comfortably," he promised her, "but right where I can keep an eye on you."

Mate

A triumphant general, upon returning to ancient Rome, arrived in a chariot drawn by magnificent horses. He led a parade through the streets, followed by wagons laden with the treasures he had plundered and lines of slaves he had taken prisoner. Crowds cheered, and the emperor was sure to reward the general. Yet, by tradition, an aide rode in the chariot with the general to whisper in his ear along the entire way, a reminder that all glory is fleeting.

In the same way, the Clan invasion burned any such illusions from my head. The civil war, I believe, did the same for most people of the Federated Suns and the Lyran Alliance. As for Katherine . . . even in defeat, this was a concept she never understood.

—From the journal of Prince Victor Ian Steiner-Davion, reprinted in *Cause and Effect*, Avalon Press, 3067

Epilogue

Every ending brings with it a new beginning.
——*Cause and Effect*, Avalon Press, 3067

Solitude, Arc-Royal
Arc-Royal Defense Cordon
Lyran Alliance
26 August 3067

Morgan Kell was not on hand to greet Victor as he disembarked on Arc-Royal, sending in his place a video message for Victor to join him in Solitude as soon as possible. Morgan's tone was terse, his face carefully set into a politician's mask, which seemed strange as only Victor would be receiving the message. Unless there were others in the room as he recorded it, Victor finally decided, people to whom Morgan did not want to divulge any feelings.

That in itself was a warning.

Still, the transfer of his sister across Federated Suns space and then into and through the Lyran Alliance had not happened without several tense moments as the occasional noble or eager commander stirred up public sentiment. Then it was out with years of collected evidence and the signed declarations from both Yvonne and Peter that remanded Katherine wholly and without prejudice to Victor's authority. Most of the loyalists retreated with some final bluster or bravado, eventually to fade away quietly. Only at the Blue Diamond recharge station was there anything resembling armed confrontation, and that had been from a fighter pilot on a suicide run attempting to exact his own, final vengeance against Victor.

As Victor's sedan descended the DropShip ramp, he first checked that the armored transport carrying Katherine followed at a close interval. Then he looked to the four short-ranged shuttles grounded on the field nearby. One was clearly marked with the starburst insignia of ComStar. Another showed the triangular head of the Kell Hounds. The last two were both marked by Clan Wolf, so there were no big surprises yet.

Phelan Kell's people had done good work in a hurry. Four months was all Victor had been able to give them, and here it was: a new facility built in the middle of Arc-Royal's Grungurtel Jungle. Though ostensibly a scientific research station, it also possessed a large tower outfitted with all the comforts Katherine might conceivably want, not counting her freedom. She would have a jeweled bracelet that also worked as a location finder, allowing her limited access to the surrounding area. Just to make certain that she stayed close and that no one tried to come in for her, the exiled Wolves would station a solid military force here, complete with 'Mech support. And Victor couldn't imagine anyone of the Clans agreeing to aid her, no matter how much time Katherine had to work on them.

Pulling through the gate, Victor's driver followed directions to an underground parking facility. Victor then left Katherine in the care of Phelan's Wolves, knowing that his interference would only insult them. Besides, Tiaret was with her.

Gavin Dow was waiting for Victor as he stepped off the elevator in Solitude's administrative level. The man's yellow-green eyes were alight with interest, fading just slightly when he saw that Victor had come up alone. The precentor wore his new robes, trimmed heavily in gold and red to denote his new position.

"Good afternoon," Victor said formally, stiffly, "First Precentor."

"It may take some getting used to, Victor, but I think you'll manage." Dow smiled fully, making no secret of his pleasure of his new rank as foremost among all precentors of the First Circuit. "You always do."

"And I hear you play one hell of a game of brinksmanship," Victor said, but only to Dow's continued delight.

Victor still did not have all the information on that political maneuver, except that Primus Mori had acquiesced to the new title and Dow's responsibilities in order to prevent a loss-of-confidence vote and possibly even a second schism. The man had apparently used his tenure as precentor martial *pro tem* to build a strong enough power base for just such a purpose. He remained Victor's overseer, in fact, having balked at letting Victor resume his former post as an autonomous precentor martial. He had, in fact, blocked any return by Victor and the few survivors of the 244th Division at first. He only yielded after Victor took a public oath to ComStar that he would never again—under threat of immediate censure—put any personal interest in the affairs of a Successor State ahead of ComStar's business.

"ComStar needs strong leaders, Victor Davion. You may become one of those, someday, once I'm certain that you have indeed left behind your nationalistic ties."

Victor nodded curtly, then turned for the short walk to the administrative center. Large windows lined one side of the hall, looking out at the distant greenery that stopped only at the ferrocrete landing site. "Does *Primus* Mori have orders for me?"

"Just that you are to accompany me to Tharkad for November's Star League conference. With the civil war over, Martial Davion, we felt it important that you be seen with a guiding member of ComStar's First Circuit. We will share the ComStar table."

Translation: that Gavin Dow wanted to be seen as a political leader and as ComStar's true guiding force. Victor almost said as much, but was distracted as the elevator doors opened again, and Katherine was escorted into the hall by Tiaret and a Clan Wolf MechWarrior. The two men waited for their prisoner to catch up, and Dow traded overly polite nods with Katherine. Her tone, however, was anything but cordial.

"It would seem that our relationship wasn't so beneficial after all," she said, her voice matching the coldness of her eyes.

"Really?" Dow raised an eyebrow, his eyes sparkling with dark humor. "I gained everything I desired out of it."

"I thought the same way once," she said. "See what that has brought me." She stepped past the two ComStar men, not bothering to check on her guards, who followed easily behind her. They might have been a simple entourage for all the care she paid them.

Victor had to give his sister credit. She bore up under the continued humiliation of being a prisoner far better than he would have expected. Of course, in her own mind, she was no prisoner. She still thought of herself as simply removed from power, but always with vestigial tendrils reaching back for it. Victor's job today was to lock that door and throw away the key.

Some of his feelings must have shown on his face. "You won't rest quite as easily as you think," Dow said, staring after Katherine's retreating back. When Victor looked a question at him, the First Precentor simply shook his head. "You have people waiting for you, Martial Davion. I will see you on Tharkad." Bowing over steepled hands, Gavin Dow smiled thinly, then turned for the elevator and, eventually, his own shuttle.

Frowning, Victor accepted this second caution and followed Katherine into the admin center, a round chamber that looked more like a conference room than any kind of functional space. Metal tables were arranged in a half-circle, facing the door, and behind them were gallery seats for spectators. It looked more like a lecture hall or an interview room. Among Clan scientists, perhaps that was an important administrative necessity.

Morgan Kell waited just inside the door, his one good hand reaching for Victor's as soon as he entered the room. "We have a new problem," Morgan said quietly, sotto voce, though Victor could have guessed that by the dour look on Phelan's face.

The khan of the Wolves-in-exile leaned back against a table, arms crossed defiantly as he stared angrily at another Clan warrior who stood nearby in formal attire, including the full-face helmet molded into the totem representation of a large wolf's head. Galen Cox stood with Isis Marik off to one side. Galen looked preoccupied with his own thoughts, though Isis was clearly worried about something. Tiaret, Victor noticed, moved protectively in front of Katherine, spotting something he had apparently missed. Victor returned his attention to the masked warrior.

"Do you have some business here?" he asked.

"I should think so," the man said in a hard, dry voice, and Victor stiffened in recognition. The warrior removed his helm, tucking it under one arm with formal dignity. Though Victor had thought himself prepared for whatever surprise awaited him, he could only stand in complete amazement as Vladmir Ward, khan of the other Clan Wolf, faced him here on Arc-Royal.

Too late, Victor realized he had not paid close enough attention to the khan rankings on the crest of the Wolf shuttles grounded on the landing field. They must have shown the same insignia that were painted into the furred epaulets of Vlad's formal dress.

"Khan Ward," Victor said evenly, trying to recover his mental footing. "I was not told that you had been granted safe passage to Arc-Royal." He glanced at Phelan, who shook his head.

"I neither asked for, nor received, a guarantee of safecon. If it is required that I fight my way free, then I shall do so." Vlad shifted his gaze only briefly toward Phelan, and the animosity that leapt between the two men would have had Victor reaching for a weapon had he worn one. Phelan did, in a holster tied down on his right leg, but he kept his hands well away from it. Vlad looked back at Victor. "That has nothing to do with our business, Victor Davion."

"I wasn't aware that we had business to discuss," Victor said, catching Vlad's smirk of superiority at Victor's use of a contraction. By Clan thinking, such was the sign of a lazy mind.

"There is no need for much discussion. I am here to take possession of your prisoner."

"You are challenging me for Katherine?" Victor's mind spun, trying to sort out why a Clan khan would ever care about his sister's fall from power.

"Challenging? *Aff.*" Vlad seemed quite ready for such an idea. "If that is your preference." His dark eyes moved from Victor back to Katherine.

Victor sensed the unspoken conjunction, and voiced it himself. "Or?"

"War," Vlad promised. "I warned you once before that my Wolves were not bound by the Great Refusal, but that we would honor the Truce of Tukayyid. That truce expired in May of this year. Are you ready to speak for your former nations, to send them back to battle so quickly?" he asked. "I am."

Victor glanced quickly at the others in the room. Phelan looked ready to fight, but then he always did. Morgan waited with stoic neutrality. Victor turned back to Vlad. "You're promising that, in exchange for Katherine, we buy peace?"

"I promise nothing but to attack if you do not give me what I came to acquire. Do you believe this, Victor Davion, or not?"

Victor did. He did not need Phelan's none-too-subtle nod to believe that Vlad would do just as he said. It was also not lost on him that he had given his word to the First Circuit that he would not meddle outside of ComStar business, and Katherine's incarceration on Arc-Royal definitely fell in that domain. Even if it could be construed as a ComStar affair because of Vlad's reference to the Tukayyid truce, Victor could not push Yvonne and Peter into a new war when there was any possible recourse. Without knowing it, Vlad had him backed against a very tricky wall.

"*Aff,* I believe you," Victor said with a shrug. "Take her, then." He discreetly watched Katherine's face as he acquiesced, saw the flicker of triumph that brightened her eyes. What *had* she been up to that Vlad would come for her? He might never know. "If she's your prize, Vlad, take her and welcome to it. You made a good *deal* today."

The barb stuck as Victor all but accused the Wolf khan of acting like a merchant, a subtlety not lost on Vlad, who flushed with dark anger. But the Clan warrior had this day's goal, and so he forced a challenging smile to let Victor know that the comment was ignored, for now, but not forgotten.

As precentor martial, Victor would not have it any other way.

* * *

"Are you crazy?" It was Phelan's first question after Vlad Ward left with Katherine, the door barely closed behind them.

"Perhaps," Victor said. "But if you saw a better solution to all our problems, I didn't hear it."

Morgan Kell didn't miss the implication Victor had hung out there for everyone. "Solution?" He looked questioningly at Victor. "How do you see that?"

"Captive or not, Katherine's presence would always be a concern for us on Arc-Royal, right?" He waited for answering nods all around. "So now she has been *accepted* by the Clans," he stressed the word carefully. "Phelan, what has that done for your credibility in the Inner Sphere?"

"Makes it damn hard to do anything but fight for every last concession." A look of dawning realization brightened his brown eyes. "Not bad, Victor. That might be worse on Katherine than simply locking her away." He rubbed at the back of his neck with one gloved hand. "Still, it burns to let Vlad just walk away with her after everything we went through to bring her down."

"It does," Victor agreed. "And I considered refusing him, until I thought about the penance Katherine will actually have to pay now for her crimes. I don't know what he sees in her or what game those two have been playing together, but I see only one way Vlad will get any real use out of Katherine."

Morgan was faster than his son this time. "He will have to turn her into a warrior."

Victor nodded. "I think it will do her some good, getting to know something of martial honor. We know that Phelan's rise was swift, but even among the Clans, you must first learn to obey before you can lead. Maybe there is some hope for Katherine's eventual rehabilitation."

"And maybe not," Morgan warned him, not sharing in his son's obvious pleasure at the idea of Katherine suffering in a Clan training program. "Still, I think you made the right decision."

So did Victor. And he was glad to finally be rid of official business, trading it for a quiet moment among friends. Isis accepted a light hug, having traveled ahead to Arc-Royal to help design Katherine's gilded cage. Galen Cox looked all too somber for someone seeing a friend again for the first time in two years.

"Not quite the reunion I had hoped for, Jerr—sorry—Galen." Victor smiled sheepishly. "That will take some getting used to again."

"For both of us, Victor, although Hohiro has been helping me with it. He's been using 'Galen' ever since Katherine let it out at the last Star League conference." He came forward and held out his hand. "I'll get to know my name again."

Victor accepted a brief handshake. "It's only right. Of all Katherine's victims, Galen Cox is the only one we can resurrect." That brought on a new sadness, of course, but Victor was learning to live with the melancholy. At least it no longer overshadowed all the good times he had shared with Omi Kurita.

"I read the preliminary report you sent ahead," he said, voice a touch softer. Isis moved up to lay a hand on his arm, offering some comfort, for which Victor was grateful. "He's dead? There's no doubt?"

Galen nodded, confirming the assassin's end. "Minoru showed me his head."

"Then it's finally over," Victor whispered to himself.

"No, Victor," Galen said, sounding about as sorrowful as Victor had ever heard him, even after Omi's death. "It's all getting a lot more complicated." He didn't offer anything more for a moment, then dug a small electronic reader out of his pocket and balanced it on the palm of his hand. Quietly, he passed it over.

Victor lit up the display, which showed a centered piece of highlighted text. It looked like an entry in some kind of medical report, and the reference was lost on him for about three confusing seconds. Then a cold hand grasped at his heart, and squeezed, while he paged up to the top of the report and read the name on it.

OMI KURITA.

Her autopsy.

When Victor found his voice, it was hardly more than a croak. "How certain is this information?" It was all he could think to ask as he paged back down, much more slowly, scanning the report for the previous highlighted entry.

Galen looked at the floor. "Victor, I found it myself. More than that, though . . . Theodore Kurita gave me an open door to help the investigation, but he could have buried that report. Or altered it. He wanted me to find it, Victor. He wanted you to have it, so that you would know without him having to make some kind of official declaration."

Silence reigned for several moments as everyone waited for the news to be shared or for their presence to be waved off. Isis Marik finally squeezed lightly on his arm. "Victor?"

"Did you know about this?" He looked at Isis and found only concern in her doe-brown eyes. He handed her the reader. "Isis, did you *know* about this?" His breath came in short gasps as he waited for her answer, his chest so tight it felt like he couldn't breathe properly. He tried to take a step and found that he couldn't control his legs. He swerved over to lean up against a table.

"N-no," Isis said, after a similar scan of the data. Her voice was quiet and scared, almost childlike. "No, Victor, I swear I didn't."

She started to hand it back, but he waved the reader on to Morgan and Phelan. Victor didn't need it. The phosphorous words were printed on the back of his eyes now, where his brain could think of little else. It had been there, captured in the report where notable entries on family health history and special conditions were entered. "Noted signs," it had termed it, "of past pregnancy. Episiotomy scar indicating natural childbirth."

Childbirth.

It could only have been while he was away fighting in the Clan homeworlds, since Isis had no knowledge of Omi being pregnant. It all fit together. Including a promise Omi had made five years before.

"There are some matters to discuss," she had said on Mogyorod, "you and I. Important matters. Personal. Perhaps . . ." Omi had hugged herself tightly, arms clasped around her middle. Thinking of their *baby*. "Victor, I would never try to take the memory of your brother away from you, but perhaps I can ease your difficulties." He remembered her hesitant, secret smile. "Though I do not promise not to complicate your life immensely."

Victor had thought then that she might be proposing the idea of formal matrimony. Now it was clear that she was ready to offer him some hope for their future in whatever way she was able. And then the assassination attempt drove them apart, and Omi kept her secret.

She took it with her to her grave.

"Victor," Galen said softly, drawing him out of his long silence. "Victor, are you all right?"

Everyone was staring at him. Galen with sorrow. Isis with a certain amount of nervous energy. Morgan and Phelan looking torn between wanting to offer support and varying amounts of moral indignation. Tiaret . . . looked satisfied. Well, of course she did. In the Clans, warriors were immortalized through the right for their genes to produce children. Tiaret no doubt found it fitting that Victor finally had offspring. Not for the first time, Victor found himself taking to the Elemental and mentally thanking her for her outlook.

"I feel . . ." he said, pausing to think about it a moment longer. "I feel fine. Really. I think I like the fact that something of my life with Omi continues on out there. This is supposed to be a time for looking forward, after all." He smiled weakly and stood, his legs still a bit rubbery but holding him up. "I have my own life to put back together right now, but at least there is something to look forward to. This means that part of us, Omi and I, has survived. And that's what we all are, after all." He nodded to the Kells, Galen, Isis.

"Survivors."

About the Author

LOREN L. COLEMAN first began writing fiction in high school, but it was during his enlistment in the U.S. Navy that he began to work seriously at the craft. For eight years now, he has built up a personal bibliography that includes (around the time of this printing) twelve published novels, a great deal of shorter fiction work, and involvement on several computer games. *Endgame* is his ninth BattleTech® novel. He is also the author of *Into the Maelstrom*, the first novel of the Vor series, and *Rogue Flyer* in the fascinating universe of Crimson Skies.

Having lived in many parts of the country, Loren currently resides in Washington State with the obligatory writer's cats: Chaos, Ranger, and Rumor. His family includes his wife, Heather Joy, two sons, Talon LaRon and Conner Rhys Monroe, and a young daughter, Alexia Joy.

(0451)

See what's coming in October...

SHADOWS AND LIGHT
by Anne Bishop   45899-0

An encroaching evil threatens the lives of every witch,
woman, and Fae in the realm. And only the Bard, the Muse,
and the Gatherer of Souls possess the power to stop the
bloodshed.

NIGHTMARE: *A NOVEL OF THE SILENT EMPIRE*
by Steven Harper   45898-2

Before Kendi learned to use his talent of navigating the plane
of mental existence known as the Dream, he had to escape
his physical existence as a slave.

VAMPIRE
by John Steakley   45153-8

This is bestselling author John Steakley's vampire classic:
reissued and *resurrected*. Vampires infest the modern world
and a group of brave people—professional vampire killers—
devote their lives to hunting them down.

To order call: 1-800-788-6262